REVELATIONS

IV
DESTINY SERIES

CJ COOKE

Revelations

By
CJ Cooke

Version 1.0: October 2020
Published by CJ Cooke
Copyright © 2020 by CJ Cooke

Discover other titles by CJ Cooke at www.catejcooke.com

Book Cover Art designed by MiblArt

Formatted by: © 2024 Incognito Scribe Productions LLC

❀ Created with Vellum

Also by CJ Cooke

Refer to my website for all book updates: www.catejcooke.com

Destiny Series

Destiny Awakened

Destiny Rising

Destiny Realised

Revelations

Retaliation

Revenge

Stoneridge Pack Series

Wolf Hunts

Shadow Wars

Blood Feud

Hidden Moon

Stoneridge Shadows

Cursed in Shadows

Freedom in Darkness

THE ARCANE

For all of the people who were told that they couldn't,
Fuck Them!
Prove to them that you can.

PROLOGUE

LYRA

NINE YEARS AGO

S ometimes I wondered if I could gauge my life by the drops of water as they slowly fell to the stone floor of my cell.

I don't know how long I've been here. Probably years. More drops than you could ever count.

At least they don't keep me shackled in this one. Not that there was any need to. They drained me of blood so frequently now that I don't think I can get up off the floor anymore. That's apparently the trick: frequent drains and infrequent feeding. I couldn't remember the last time I ate. My stomach has shrunk in, and my abdomen pulls in angrily showcasing my ribs in all their glory.

The beatings were frequent to start with. Until they realised that having to continually heal myself reduced the amount of light in my blood. Light. What a stupid name. The vampires craved my blood for exactly that. It gave them the ability to walk in the light. The angels who had given our magic that name felt that it made it sound more superior to the other forms of magic. That was always the problem in our world. Everyone wanted to be better than everyone else. It was why we had so nearly lost the demon wars. No one wanted to fight beside those that they felt were inferior to them. Did it even matter? Dead was dead no matter how good you thought you were.

My mind turned back to the day, not long after I had turned sixteen, when my own curiosity landed me in this situation. I had flown down into the realm because I was bored. Of course, that would be what got me stuck in this situation, my own stupidity, I mean boredom. What's that saying about curiosity and cats? Apparently, it applies to angels as well.

I saw him running through the woods in his wolf form and I was curious. Shifters were always fascinating to me. I couldn't imagine what it would be like to have two forms. To be able to feel the mind of another inside your own. Their whole way of life was fascinating. The way that they lived in packs was something I had always been jealous of. What must it be like to know that you would always have someone to support you? Angels were relatively solitary creatures. Whilst it's true that we live within our flight, we only really did that in case we are called to fight. Our flight is our fighting unit, and whilst we trained and fought together seamlessly, after all was said and done, we generally just flew off in our own direction.

Procreation was by allotment only. When a particular type of angel was required, a male and a female angel who are genetically compatible were selected to procreate. Once the child was born, it was sent to the Education Centres where they were trained until they were old enough to be allocated to a flight. I hadn't yet been selected for a procreation assignment. It was only a matter of time though. I didn't know how I would feel about it. It didn't seem right to birth a child and then give it away. That was an opinion that I kept to myself though. You didn't disagree with your superiors if you wanted to live. Insubordination was dealt with by death, it was the only way to stop a flight from being desecrated.

When the wolf stopped to drink from a stream, I landed in a nearby tree, curious to see what would happen next. As soon as I was settled, he turned to look at the trees, cocking his head to the side. It was adorable. This wolf is the largest I'd ever seen, but then I hadn't seen that many. His fur had a sort of shaggy quality that made you want to pet him, although I'm certain that wouldn't go down very well. He's like a mixture of browns and golds. It's pretty. Handsome? He is definitely a he so maybe handsome is the right word?

While I'm pondering the right word to call him, the wolf stepped away from the stream and shifted into his human form. I nearly fell out of the tree when I saw him. He was the most beautiful man I had ever seen. Angels always brag that they are the most beautiful race in all of the realms but looking at him, I knew that wasn't anywhere close to the truth.

He had hair similar to his wolf, brown shot through with gold highlights. It fell to just about his shoulders, and it looked so soft that I wondered what it would feel like to run my fingers through it. He had a neatly trimmed beard and a pair of glistening green eyes. Thankfully he appeared to be shirtless, and really if there was a God who had much of any say about the matter, this man would never wear a shirt again. His muscles looked positively lickable, and I greedily ran my eyes across his torso. Unfortunately, he was wearing a pair of jeans that spoilt the view any further down, but I supposed it was for the best. This man naked might be more than my poor little angel heart could take.

I watched as he lifted his face and scented the air. I knew that the wind was blowing my scent directly to him. It went against all of my training, but part of me wanted him to be able to scent me. To have this small part of me, so that there was someone out there that would remember me. He looked around frantic, trying to catch a glimpse of me and the broken look on his face almost destroyed me. I opened my wings and silently took to the air, heading back to my flight. I couldn't take the confusion that I was feeling. I didn't understand why this male was affecting me the way that he was.

The next night I'm sat in the same treetop, and I didn't even know why I was there. My thoughts have been of him all day. I felt like if I didn't see him again, my heart would stop beating. He came to the stream earlier tonight. He raced into the clearing at top speed and changed from wolf to human mid-stride.

"Why did you leave yesterday?" he asked, looking around the clearing trying to find me. "I won't hurt you, I could never."

I didn't answer him. I couldn't. The punishment for doing so was too great to risk. I'd already risked too much just by coming back here. But my heart cried out and plead with me to do it anyway.

"My name is Wyatt." He told me.

A single tear rolled down my cheek as I took to the air again. I couldn't come back here. I could never see him again. The risk was far too great. It was for his safety more than mine.

The next night I landed in the treetop wanting to kick my own ass. I didn't know why I was doing this to myself, but I couldn't seem to stop. He was already sat in the clearing by the stream. He wore different clothes, so he must have left at some point and returned. I felt my soul lighten as soon as I see him, the peaceful smile of my face soothed into being just by his presence. He came here for me. Even though he didn't know who or what I was.

"You came back," he said brightly after scenting the air. "I was worried that you wouldn't. Why won't you show yourself to me?" he asked, waiting for my response.

I couldn't give it to him. I shouldn't be encouraging him

like this. He started to talk, telling me about his pack, his friends and his life. I listened to him talk for hours. His words wrapped around me and lulled me into a sense of peace that I rarely felt anymore. Not outside of this place, not away from him.

Two hours before dawn, I had to tear myself away from the treetop and return to my flight. They couldn't know that I had been missing for so long, they couldn't know that I came down here to see him. They would punish him as well as me. I shouldn't come back here.

But I knew that I would, I didn't think I could stay away now even if I tried.

When I returned the next night, he was there again. He scented the air as soon as I arrived, and upon catching my scent, he took up his story where he left off last night. After an hour, he started to tell me the story of his family. Of his mother and father and how they were taken from him. The tears brimmed his eyes and his voice hitched as he described the bloody fight as the other wolf killed his father. He described the brutal assault of his mother, while he was forced to watch, wondering why none of his pack would come to help her. He described the way that he watched the life leave her eyes as they left her bloody and broken on the ground.

As the first of his tears start to fall, I didn't even realise that I was moving until I felt my arms wrap around him. I pulled him into the protective embrace of my wings and we sat in the quiet cocoon until his tears ran dry and he trembled in my arms. All the while, I ran my fingers through his hair and whispered reassuring words to soothe him.

I had never felt as complete as I did when he was in my arms and I knew that now I had felt it, I could never leave him. He was mine and I was his. We were meant to be like this, together, for an eternity. And that's when I realised the one thing that I never thought I would ever even consider. *I would fall for this man.* I would give up the light inside me just to be with him. And I wouldn't be losing anything because I had everything to gain.

He sat up and swiped at his eyes, looking at me in awe. "You're an angel," he whispered, leaning his head down to place his forehead against mine. He took a deep breath and as he breathed out, he whispered on a sigh, "Mate." As the whispered word struck at my very soul, I felt it resonate deep within me and I knew it to be true.

CHAPTER 1

WYATT

PRESENT

Sitting in the armchair with my elbows braced on my knees, I felt like the weight of the world was pressing down on me as my head hung down, my hands clasped behind my neck. I almost felt like I physically needed to hold myself together. I couldn't go on for much longer like this.

The Blood Moon battle had been bloody and it had almost raised more questions than answers. It was a bittersweet victory. Yes, the Valkyrie had fought back the demon hoard and the realm would be safe. But to know that the witches' plot had been successful and they had gotten what they wanted anyway; it was hard to accept. They had sacrificed so many, but in the end, they had done it for the right reasons. Only with the gates opened and all of us uniting as one people could the magic flow freely again. Even knowing that, it was a bitter pill to swallow. They had sacrificed so many of my people. I didn't even know if it should be considered a sacrifice. It just felt like murder. How had we let our own petty grievances get this far? We hadn't even known that we were slowly killing ourselves—the inevitable outcome of allowing our magic to fade.

I looked around the library at the other weary faces as we sat in silence. It had only been just over a week since we faced the demon hoard and most are still recovering. Aria spent most of her time sleeping, but given how much she gave in that fight, I couldn't say I blamed her. Kyle was only up and about because of the need to look over the pack. Liam and Sykes were never far from him and Virion and Braedon had taken up guard over Aria while she slept. Watching them made my heart feel like it was going to shatter. I should have that. I did have that. But then it was taken from me.

"The other packs are going to be moving on in the next day or two. I've spoken with the Alphas and we're going to start talks next month to begin forming the Council and then making arrangements for the transfer of everything over. Everyone needs time to heal and recover before we start, but I would be grateful for any help that you can give going forward," Kyle said, leaning back in the chair he had before the fireplace.

One of the first things he had done when he got rid of his father was to burn the big fucking desk that Marcus used to sit at when he was lording it over all of us. I wasn't sorry to see it go. For some reason, that thing brought up way too many memories and we had all stood and watched it burn in silence. The library looked very much like a library now. Small seating arrangements have been set up around the room. Kyle had pretty much taken up residence in the one in front of the fireplace. I think it reminded him of Aria. There was so much to do now that Kyle had abolished the Prime Alpha position and it killed me that I was going to do this to him.

"I'll be leaving in the next few days as well," I said, staring into the flames. I couldn't even look him in the face when I said it.

I knew he was looking at me now, deciding what he was going to do, but I couldn't bring myself to meet his eye. I was such a coward.

"If you can hold off for a while, we will all come with you," he said, making me snap my head towards him. That was not what I had been expecting. "I want to be able to help you with this," he added quietly.

I had helped raise Kyle, his father was a bastard and all but useless as a father. At times he felt like he was my own pup, even though there weren't really that many years between us. I was so proud of the man that he had become, but this, this was too much for me to ask from him.

"Your mother would have been proud to see the man that you have become," I told him sadly. "But you have a lot to do here. A whole society to change. Plus, a brand new mate and a growing pack to look after. This is something I need to do and I've waited far too long as it is. I can only hope that she will forgive me if I ever manage to find her again."

Kyle was only twenty with the weight of the shifter world currently sitting on his shoulders. I didn't envy him. I wouldn't want to be in his shoes for anything in the world. Well, maybe for Lyra. I'd do anything for Lyra. I was not exactly old at twenty-eight, but I felt like I'd seen too much shit in my life already.

Liam and Sykes quietly got up and left us to talk. I appreciated that more than I could express at that moment. They're all good men and I'd known them since they were small, but it was hard enough just talking to Kyle about this, let alone everyone else.

"Will you come back once you find her?" he asked.

"If she wants to come back here, then yes. I'll send word if we settle somewhere else." I wanted to add, *presuming she even wants to stay with me*, but I couldn't voice my own fears.

"I have something for you," Kyle said, standing up and

moving to the roll-top bureau that had been placed in the corner of the library.

Kyle pulled a key out of his pocket and unlocked the roll top, opening up the desk. He rummaged around in one of the drawers and pulled out two small notebooks. One was old, but the second looked relatively new. He passed them across to me before he sat down again and I opened them up in confusion.

"I started decoding it for you, but I haven't got very far," he told me.

I realised that I had in my hand the journal we had found in his father's room. We had all tried to decode it while we waited for them to return before the Blood Moon, but none of us had been successful.

"How did you even manage to do this?" I asked in shock as I started to flick through the pages that he had already transcribed.

"It was actually Aria," he laughed. "Dom gave her that phone that lets her reach the human realm and she called in a few favours from some old contacts. We emailed them a couple of pages and they were able to crack the code and sent us a decoder. I've been working through it since to see what I can find out. I've not got far and it's not pretty. It seems to be a log of favours given and owed. There's some dark shit in there." Kyle stared off into the fire and I could see that what was contained in this seemingly inconspicuous book had deeply affected him.

"You're not him," I told him seriously. "You were never like him. I think that's one of the reasons why he hated you so much."

Kyle flinched at my words. He knew the truth of how Marcus had felt about him, but I supposed it was still hard to hear it from someone else. How a monster like that had spawned a man as true and good as Kyle had always baffled me. Not only that, but Kyle's packmates had basically lived here as well. They had found each other when they were so young and gelled immediately. It was obvious, to those of us who were old enough to know, that they would share a mate bond, but they were too young to care. They could have easily turned into one of the lesser groups of packmates that we had so many problems with. Recently there had been a clash with a pack lead by Isaac that had resulted in Kyle killing him. Isaac was just fucking evil. He had lied to Kyle's father, saying that one of the females in the pack was his fated mate and Marcus had given her to his pack despite her protests. Marcus could have so easily turned Kyle into another Isaac, but thankfully Kyle had a mind of his own and found his own path. His packmates coming to him so early in life probably helped, they were able to be more of an influencing force on him before Marcus could get his hooks into him.

"I hate him so much. Even though he's dead and I know that he's no longer in my life anymore. I can't stop myself from hating him." He clenched his fist and I could see that he was truly struggling with this.

It probably didn't help that Aria was still recovering from the magic drain. I think he needed her more than he realised. She loved to be brutally to the point and she didn't pull her punches, but she had the kindest heart. She loved her mates and was deadly protective over them. As they were her. The Blood Moon battle had been just over a week ago. She slept a lot, trying to recover from the magic drain. When she was awake, she struggled to be around anyone other than her mates. I knew that she was struggling with the loss of life and the feeling that we had somehow lost in the end.

I knew I should stay here. The pack needed me. The problem was that I couldn't prioritise them over my mate any longer. She had been gone for nearly a decade; I didn't even dare think about what she must have endured during that time. Lyra. I couldn't let myself hope that she would ever forgive me. I just needed to find her, help her and she could live her life somewhere that she was safe, even if that was without me. I would endure an eternity of loneliness if it meant that she was somewhere out there, happy and free.

Kyle stood up from his chair and excused himself to go and check on Aria. As soon as he closed the door to the library, I flipped open the book in front of me. A folded piece of paper slipped inside the cover had the decoding information on it. Flipping through the pages, I was blown away by the amount of writing inside. I was privy to some of Marcus' dealings. He used me as his muscle often because he knew I would never risk speaking out against him. It was easier for him to send me rather than risk bringing in another party who could potentially betray him. Even so. There had to be ten times more here than I was ever aware of, and I knew of a lot. It would take days to decode all of the information inside. I realised that once I reached the entry for Lyra, I was going to want to leave chasing down whatever lead it gave me, but I needed to make sure I finished decoding the entire book before I did that. What if she was in here more than once? I quickly shut down the runaway thoughts racing through my mind of everything that Marcus could have put her through over all this time. She was so beautiful and so rare. The only angel seen in this realm for nearly a century. The things that someone as evil as Marcus could have put her through was unthinkable. My wolf raged out of control in the back of my mind as I tried to shut down the thoughts again. I couldn't afford to lose control now. I needed to get this done, then I needed to plan out my next steps. I needed this done quickly but efficiently. I couldn't afford to fuck this up again. Picking up a pen from Kyle's table, I settled back into the seat and started decoding all of the deplorable secrets that Marcus had, secrets that would sully our pack history forever.

Five hours later, when I'm still slumped in the chair, making slow progress with the book, Dom and Caleb found me. Caleb was carrying a plate and a bottle of water and it's only the aching emptiness in my stomach that tells me just how long I've been sitting here. He quietly passed me the plate and they both took a seat opposite to me.

"We spoke with Kyle," Dom said, after we'd all sat in excruciating silence for several minutes.

I just nodded. I didn't know what they wanted from me, but I was in no position to give it to them. Caleb leant forward, bracing his elbows on his knees and steepling his hands in front of him.

"Look, let's just stop fucking about, shall we? I'm getting tired of walking over all the broken glass that you constantly keep yourself surrounded by. We know you have the journal. We know that you are decoding it. We know that once you've done it, you intend to set out to rescue her. We're coming with you." He sat back in his chair with an annoyed grunt and I wasn't quite sure what to say.

Caleb had always been a puzzle to me. I still remembered him as the kid that was a year younger than me and used to follow me everywhere. He was a scrawny thing with scraggly long brown hair, but then something happened when he came into his wolf. He went off to the academy and he came back a man. He filled out more than was usual for a shifter coming into their wolf. He must have spent every free hour in the gym there. Even though he was only a year behind me in the academy, I never really saw him. I heard the rumours though, of the young wolf pushing past everyone else in training. He had cut his scraggly hair short and grew a close-cropped beard that was so short it was almost stubble. But it was more than that. He went off to the academy this clingy kid and he came back completely different. He didn't gel well with the pack again. He was openly aggressive with most, withdrawn with the rest.

Anyone who knew him before he left, knew that he was having problems finding his place in the pack. When Dom approached Marcus about the changes to the academy and the need to start training our young, I wasn't surprised when Caleb went with him. He'd given up on the pack long before then. Looking back now, I knew it was because his wolf just couldn't recognise Marcus as his alpha, even though he didn't know what he was truly like, it was almost like Caleb's wolf recognised it in Marcus.

"Wyatt, you still with us, mate?" Caleb asked, peering at me in concern.

"Why?" Was the most my brain could manage at the moment.

"Because you are pack," Caleb said with a shrug like that was all the explanation that was needed.

"Then what's his excuse?" I scoffed, jutting my chin at the quiet mage in the seat next to him.

"He is pack as well," Caleb said slowly, almost like he is trying to explain something to a child.

They did a lot for me once we managed to get Marcus in chains, and I owed them for figuring out what was going on. In fact, I owed them for a lot. When I gave up and tried to drown myself in whiskey, they kept pulling me out, even though I kept throwing myself right back in. At the time, I thought it was just because they needed me to hold the pack together for Kyle. I sobered up and I stepped up because if there was anyone I owed, apart from my Lyra, it was Kyle.

"Dom was never invited to be a member of this pack unless Kyle has been inviting in new members over the last few days," I said, feeling confused.

"You seriously don't feel it?" Caleb asked me, his face scrunching up in confusion. "Perhaps your own grief is drowning it out," he added quietly, almost to himself.

I did feel it. I just didn't want to admit it. I couldn't bring myself to acknowledge the fact that these two men, sitting in front of me, were my packmates, my brothers. That they were Lyra's other mates. That I had not only failed her, but I had failed them as well. I was swimming too deep in self-pity right now.

Dom is silently sat, taking in what is happening, not pushing me. It's something that I could appreciate. He's five years older than me, but I suppose in the grand scheme of things, that's nothing. We lived for hundreds of years. He had that dark and mysterious look about him that drove all of the women wild. His long dark hair, brown eyes and tanned skin seemed to make them fall all over him. I'd never seen him entertain any women though and I'll admit I always assumed he was gay. He's far more muscular than any of the other mages that I'd met, but in typical mage fashion, he's always impeccably dressed. He's one of those guys I always felt like I should hate, but I just couldn't bring myself to do it. He was a good man and he always fought for what he believed in.

I couldn't bring myself to look at them anymore and I turned my head to gaze into the fire again.

"How can you even bear to look at me?" I croaked out, the weight of my shame slammed into me like a physical blow, and I let myself feel it. Because I deserve it.

I'm surprised when it's Dom that I hear speak first.

"You are my brother." He goes quiet for a while, like he was trying to arrange his thoughts into some kind of order. "*We* failed *you*," he said, his voice breaking.

My head whips up as I go to look at him. How can he say such a thing? Dom looked into the fire, almost as if he couldn't bring himself to meet my gaze and now I'm confused.

"How many years have we known you? How many years were we blind to your pain and what you were going through? How many years was she right here and we were totally oblivious to her pain?" His voice cracked at the end and I could see the sheen of tears shimmering in his eyes even if he was managing to hold them at bay.

I looked across at Caleb to see a mirror look on his face. How could they even think that? They had no way to know. I had no way to tell them. There was only one person to blame and now that he was dead, I couldn't rip him apart like my wolf and I truly wanted to.

I cleared my throat and looked at the two men in front of me. My brothers, even though I had never claimed them as such. Lyra was still out there somewhere and she needed us. We couldn't afford the luxury of feeling sorry for ourselves right now. This wasn't about us. It never was. It was always about her. My Lyra. Our Lyra. Our angel.

"Enough of this. This gets us nowhere. We need a solid plan and we can't make that until we have this fucking thing decoded," I said with newfound determination.

Caleb looked between us both and I could see his resolve settle in as well. We could do this. We could pull together and get this done. "You've been at this for hours, show me what to do and I'll keep going while you get some rest. We can work in shifts and get it done quicker."

"Or better yet," Dom said, standing up and striding to the computer sat in the corner of the library. "Pass it here. I'll scan it in, then we can split it into three and work through it together."

"If you split it into six, it will go even quicker," came a voice from the doorway.

I turned around and saw Aria stood in the door, together with Sykes and Virion. She gave me a soft smile and I couldn't help the relief of seeing them there. I didn't know why I hadn't just asked for all of their help to start with.

Sykes, ever the ray of positivity, slung his arm around Aria's shoulder with a grin. "The others are on their way, you can split that down into nine," he cocked his head to the side and I knew that he was listening to one of them speaking directly into his mind. It was still a bit freaky when they did that. "And Liam is bringing the food," he added.

Aria pulled a blade out of thin air, that girl seemed to love any excuse to have a blade in her hand. "Let's cut the binding and then we can scan the pages once we have them decoded. That way, we get the information we need quickly and we can deal with scanning it later," she suggested.

"Sweetheart," Sykes said, pulling her back against him. "I don't think I've ever seen you make it twenty-four hours without pulling a blade into your hand. Now, while I find that stabby look in your eye all kinds of sexy, I think you might have a problem." He at least had the common sense to dance away from her laughing as she swung for him.

She wouldn't ever really hurt him, but it was nice to see her coming back round to her old self again. I knew that Aria was hurting and that none of us could understand what she was going through. She had ties to so many realms and she felt like she needed to be there to help everyone. I was truly surprised when she stepped back from going to Asgard to help them with their fight there. All I knew was that Frannie had told her something and she was content to stay here and help us. It might be selfish, but I was glad that she hadn't gone. We needed her here. But more than that. I think she needed some time to decompress. I was worried about her. We all were.

Braedon, Kyle and Liam turned up a short while later after Aria had successfully slit the binding on the journal with her blade, and we divided the pages up between us. Dom had made copies of the decoder sheet and we all moved into the dining room where we sat and ate while we worked on the pages that we had left to decode. Now that we only had roughly ten pages each to do, it was quick work and by the end of the night, we were just about done. Everyone looked

exhausted, in more than one way. Kyle's face was ashen and I
knew that he carried the burden of what he had read heavily.

"How did we not know that any of this was going on?"
Liam said quietly as he pushed the last of his decoded pages to
the middle of the table.

I had the entry referring to Lyra clutched in my hand. He
had sold her. He fucking sold her for a favour. But even worse
than that was that he had sold her to the Vampires eight
fucking years ago.

"I didn't even know about most of this. I don't understand how he even carried it off. He had to have had someone
helping him. He wasn't clever enough to carry all of this off on
his own." I frowned. Marcus might have been the evilest man I
had ever known, but he wasn't a diabolical genius. He had to
have been having help. Even if it wasn't for the planning.
Logistically there was no way that he could have done all of
this alone.

"It can't have been anyone in the pack," Kyle reasoned. I
looked at him sceptically at that. That seemed like wishful
thinking at best.

"No, hear me out," Kyle said. "When the demon's
attacked the packhouse, my father placed himself in the panic
room. He sent all of the men out to die. He wouldn't have
relied on a female. There were ten pack guards that survived.
None of them showed any kind of support or disdain above
anyone else. I don't think that they are involved. It has to be
someone outside of the pack," he reasoned.

I couldn't say that I agreed with his logic, but if he was
right, then it was fucking terrifying that we could have some
kind of unknown enemy out there that we weren't even aware
of. Let alone the reason why they would move against us. All
we had was the evidence to show what lengths they would be
willing to go to. The things in the journal were horrifying: kill
squads; sex trafficking; people being sold to be used as food;

children being sold for god only knew what. That didn't even mention the number of secrets that he had recorded in there. Who was having an affair with whom? Who had a proclivity for young boys? Who had embezzled money from covens? There were details of hits people had put out against rival political opponents. There was frequent mention of 'The Farm' which someone would need to look into. I shuddered to think of what that was. Selfishly maybe, I couldn't see it as my problem for now. I only had one priority.

"For now. This waits for tomorrow," Aria said with certainty. "I assume you will be leaving in the morning?"

I nodded and she looked surprised when Caleb and Dom also agreed.

"Come with me," she said, standing up from the table and striding away.

Frowning in confusion, I got up and followed her as she headed into the kitchens and then down into the basement. I tried to avoid this area of the house at all costs normally. All that was down here were some storage cellars, the morgue and the panic room, which had been Lyra's prison for her time here. Aria walked up to the panic room and input a code into the door, which unlocked and swung open on its own. That was new. Someone had changed the time lock. Usually, the door couldn't be opened. When it swung open, I didn't know if it was the anxiety of going back in there or the surprise at what I saw that took my breath away.

"Unfortunately for you, you are the first to have come to us and we haven't had much time to add to the stockpile," Aria said, flicking on the lights and walking to the large table which now sat in the middle. She looked around at the room before starting to speak quietly. "After the Blood Moon, I didn't know what to do or where to go next. My father pointed out to me that not every battle was my own and Frannie let me in on something that she had seen.

She told me that my turn was done, that there would be others that would follow me. A line of heroes to step up and right the wrongs. It helped to know that I could stay here without the guilt that was weighing so heavily on me. But that didn't mean that I wasn't going to help. So I started this, Liam and Virion have been helping me put it together, but there are a lot more things that we need to add. Take anything that you need, if there is anything that you can't see, let us know and we will see if we can source it for you. Just update the inventory list so we can make sure to restock everything," she said, pushing a clipboard across the table to me.

I was still stood, trying to take in everything that was in front of me. I knew that she had been doing something to keep herself busy. She had the garden that she had thrown herself into, but she also disappeared for extended lengths of time as well. I always thought that she just flew off to be alone but clearly not. Dom and Caleb stood on either side of me with the same dazed expression on their faces. Aria walked past me, clapping her hand on my shoulder as she went, and leaving us to prepare alone.

"I'll leave you to it. Don't leave in the morning without saying goodbye," she called over her shoulder, leaving us alone in the old panic room, which I'm pretty sure we were going to need to rename the war room now. Trust the Valkyrie amongst us to have installed a war room. There was no way that I could ever thank her enough for this.

I looked around to take in where to start. The wall in front of us held a massive display of weapons, they were all lovingly organised and situated in proper display holders on the wall. There were cabinets underneath, which I knew would hold more of the same. On the left and right walls were racking, which had been filled with camping and survival equipment. When I turned behind me, I saw packs leant up against the wall, empty and waiting to be filled. Framed on the wall above them was an enormous map of the realm.

"This is incredible," Dom finally said, stepping forward.

"This is so Aria," Caleb laughed, going to examine the wall of weapons. "Did I ever tell you about the time she made me reorganise the weapons closet at the academy? I swear I thought she was going to stab me when she saw it."

Dom strode over to the map and stared at it for a moment. "We know that she was sold to Cassius, who heads up a clan of vampires on the Moon Side." He ran his finger over the map as he spoke. "It would make sense to start the search there."

"And what are we going to do, stride into the Moon Side and start asking if anyone knows where they store the female shifter they bought eight years ago?" Caleb scoffed.

"Shifter?" I asked, confused.

They both turned to look at me in confusion and I realised that I had been so lost in myself, drowning in my own pain, that I hadn't even told them about her.

"Lyra isn't a shifter," I told them. I saw Caleb mouth her name as he smiled softly, finally knowing the name of his mate. "She's an angel."

Dom's mouth dropped open in shock and Caleb looked like his brain had just shut down as a blank look crossed his face.

"Our mate is an angel," Dom murmured with a look of shock on his face.

"But no one has seen an angel since the last war," Caleb said, confused.

"I don't know what to tell you. We barely got any time together. I was out running one day. It was four years after Marcus had taken over the pack. I'd had a shit day. The pack guard was really getting in on me and Marcus was pushing me to train to be an enforcer. They changed me into my wolf form for some bullshit drill and I just took off. I got as far as the stream down on the West side of the property and I just smelt her. I knew immediately that I was smelling my mate, but I couldn't see her anywhere. I knew she was there and I looked for her, but then the scent was gone. I skipped out after training again and went back the next day and she was there again, so I changed into my human form, sat down by the stream and just talked to her. She stayed for hours listening to me, but she didn't show herself. Just before dawn, she left again. But she came back. And then finally, I'm sat there telling her about my family and everything that happened and suddenly there she was, in my arms, holding me tight and telling me that she would protect me." I laughed as I remembered that day and the shock that ran through me.

I was raw from telling her about the loss of my parents, about what had happened to my mother. I never told anyone, not even these two, what Marcus and his men had done to her. What they had made me watch them do. But then suddenly, I had this beautiful angel in my arms, holding me tight and telling me that she was going to protect me. She smelt like sunshine. I knew that sounded crazy, but it was the only way I could think to describe her scent: she smelt like sunshine and mine.

"We met down by that stream every day for weeks. She told me that she could only come to me in secret. If she was going to be with me, she would have to fall, which meant that she would lose her wings. I told her that she didn't have to do that, that we would find a way. She had such beautiful wings. They were bright, shining gold. One day I went to the stream and she wasn't there. I waited all night for her, but she didn't show up. I was frantic by the time that I had to return to the packhouse because I knew that something wasn't right. That next day I made up some excuse at the start of training and slipped out early. I ran as fast as I could down to the stream. I smelt the blood long before I reached it. I knew that it was hers, it still smelt like sunshine. I found her by the side of the stream, barely conscious. Her beautiful wings were gone and her back was torn open. When I pulled her into my arms, she just opened her eyes and smiled at me. Told me that everything was going to be okay, that she didn't have to go back anymore, that she was going to stay with me," my voice broke and the tears fell down my cheeks as I remembered that day. The worst fucking day of my life.

"I must not have been careful enough when I left. I was just so worried about her. I should have waited until the usual time to go to her. Marcus realised that I was up to something and he followed me with four of his men. I didn't even scent them approaching before they ripped her out of my arms. She was too weak to fight them off. Marcus just held her back as the four of them beat me unconscious. When I came too, I was here. In this room. I fucking hate this room. Poor Lyra was curled up in a ball in the corner. The four-pack guards were dead on the ground and Marcus was just fucking laughing. He said that he couldn't afford for anyone else to know about the treasure that he had found. He chained her up and used her against me from that day on. Once I got stronger, he got that fucking witch to curse me. You know the rest," I ended.

I was still so ashamed. So ashamed that I hadn't been able to protect my mate. That she had suffered for all this time because I had failed her. I failed her and I failed them. They were my packmates, they should have been able to trust me to keep our mate safe.

Caleb wrapped his arms around me and pulled me against him. It was strange, but I still found myself sinking against him as the tears finally came. I'd never been held by a man before. I had been thirteen when my father died and he had never held me. He was an old school alpha, but he was a fair man. My mother had been the one to fill my life with hugs. He had this habit of slapping me on the back while he did this booming laugh.

"Wyatt, if this happened six years after you lost your father, then you were only nineteen. You couldn't even shift into your wolf on your own then," Caleb said calmly as he held me tight. "You can't blame yourself for this. There is only one man who is to blame here and unfortunately, he's dead, because I would love to beat the ever-loving shit out of him right now."

"I can't believe that you found our mate when you were nineteen, do you know how rare that is?" Dom said.

I pulled out of Caleb's arms and took a step back so that I could look at them both. Why weren't they angry with me? She had been in chains for nine years because of me. One year down here in this fucking room and then eight more with the vampires, who were doing who the hell knew what to her. I should have known that he would have moved her. There was no way that Marcus could have put in the effort to keep someone down here for nine years, no matter what it would gain him.

"Why are you not losing your shit right now?" I asked them in shock.

"I know that you think that you failed her. But you were nineteen, Wyatt. You were a shifter that couldn't shift into your animal yet. You wouldn't even have come into your full strength. In that exact same situation, neither of us would have been able to do anything more. What matters is what we do now. It matters that we now have the knowledge and the means to find her and bring her home," Caleb said to me sternly. It didn't escape me that he was still holding on to me tightly as he said it. I'm also fully aware of the fact that I didn't want him to let me go just yet either.

I didn't know what it was that tipped me over the edge. If it was the knowledge that my packmates didn't hate me. If it's the realisation that maybe a small amount of the guilt I felt might be misplaced. Or if it's just the relief that finally, after all of these years, I was going to find Lyra and have her in my arms again. But once the tears started, I felt like I was never going to be able to stop them. It seemed fitting that of all the places where I was going to break down, where I felt like my very soul was stripped to pieces, that it would be here, in this fucking room that I hated so much.

CHAPTER 2

LYRA

They'd never been gentle when they threw me back in my cage and today wasn't any exception to that. I felt the bone-deep bruising as I slammed into the opposite side of the cage and listened to them laugh as they closed the door and walked away.

I'm not sure how long I've been in this place. It's been a long time. Years. It wasn't so bad when Marcus had me locked in that room in the packhouse. I might have been shut in the dark. I may have only been given food and water every couple of days. But I could feel him nearby. I could feel Wyatt, my impossible mate, whenever he moved across the room above me. It was comforting, in the darkness, to be able to feel him near. I had survived the angelic warrior training before I joined my flight. That little darkroom was nothing. A year locked in there was nothing. I was only sixteen years old when I met Wyatt. Young for an angel, I was the product of one of the most recent breeding drives and I had only just finished my training. Maybe that's why I used to fly off to be by myself. They hadn't had time to truly break me yet, I had no idea how old I was now. I didn't know how much time had passed.

Angels are immortal and when you know you've got forever, a year isn't that much time. A year was nothing to me.

But here. In this place. Time moves slowly. I had no way to tell how much time has passed. I just floated from one torment to another. Their cruelty knew no bounds and I didn't even have the relief of feeling him nearby anymore. He was lost to me, that hurt more than anything I could endure. Sometimes when I am at my weakest, they torment me with whispers of what had happened to him. My poor sweet mate. They thought they have broken me. They thought that their whispers and torture had broken the poor fallen angel they had at their mercy. They couldn't be more wrong. As soon as the opportunity was in front of me, I would seize it. I would escape and no one would keep me from my mate again.

"Ly," I heard whispered from the shadows.

I took a deep breath and gauged the injuries in my body. Apart from the usual bite wounds from this bloodletting, I was fairly injury-free. I didn't break anything when they threw me in here this time. I was pretty sure that my ribs were just bruised and not broken. I was just weak from the loss of blood. From the repeated loss of blood over the last however many years it's been.

"Ly," whispered again across the darkness.

"Damon?" I croaked back, my voice breaking from the pain of my earlier screams.

"Shhhh. I've left you some bread and water in the corner of your cage, but you need to eat it before anyone finds it. If they find out I keep trying to help you, I'll be punished," Damon whispered to me through the cage door.

Damon was probably the only reason why I was still alive. I had been here a long time before he was allocated as my guard. He was so quiet at first but eventually, watching me go through all that broke something in him. He's too sweet and kind to be a vampire. He was nothing like the others. He did what he could to help me, but there wasn't much that he could do. I appreciated his kindness more than the food and water that he smuggled to me. Not that I would ever say that, I'm pretty sure I would die if he stopped.

"Thank you," I whispered as I felt around in the dark and finally found the bowl and the bread on the ground.

"This is the last harvesting party that is going out for a while. You should get a break from the bloodletting for a while. Just try not to antagonise them. If you can avoid a beating for a few days, you'll have more time to heal. I have to go, but I'm back on shift tomorrow and I'll try and bring you something better," he said before I heard his footsteps fade away.

I drank half of the cool water down before I made myself stop and eat the bread as quickly as I could. I learnt quickly to try and save some of the water for when I'm eating. If I didn't have it to help wash the food down, I only ended up making myself sick and then I felt worse than when I started.

Once I'd finished the bread, I shuffled into the corner of the cage and settled down. There's nothing in here with me. I didn't even have a bucket. I had a corner I sleep in and a corner I did my business in. Once every couple of weeks, they came and hosed the thing down, usually with me still inside. The simple shift that I was wearing was nothing but rags now. It did nothing to protect me against the cold, if it wasn't for my angelic nature, I would have definitely died by now. I may have fallen, but that didn't make me any less of an angel. Well maybe. I did give up my wings—my beautiful wings. Sometimes I woke up in the night feeling the pain of that night all over again. Feeling the members of my flight ripping the wings from my body. That's the only way to leave. It was the only way I could ever be with Wyatt. No fallen angel was allowed to keep their wings. I'd do it again if I had the choice, this was just a part of my story. I would get back to Wyatt. I would be with him again. The first thing that I needed to do is get out of here. I refused to die here. I refused to have finally had something as pure as Wyatt put in front of me and then give up.

Frequent blood lettings made me weak. If I could go a few days without them, I knew I could build up my strength. The problem was that when I got a break from them, they found any excuse that they could to beat me. They broke my bones and beat me bloody to keep me weak. Damon was right. I needed to find a way to avoid them. If I could build up a bit of strength, I could try to escape. I used to try to escape back when they first brought me here. It always resulted in a beating that took me months to heal from. I think it was when I stopped that they first thought they had broken me. I'm just biding my time. Over the years of my quiet compliance, they had become complacent. They didn't watch me all of the time like they used to. I'm fairly certain that I could convince Damon to let me out of the cage. He'd suggested it before and I knew that he wanted to help me. The problem was the clan. Cassius had the whole clan living in the clan house and my cage was in the basement, underneath them. I would have to get past a whole clan of vampires to get out of here. I needed a distraction. I just had no idea what that could be.

Cassius was the head of this clan. My presence here over the last however many years had made his clan the most powerful in the realm. When they drank my blood, it gave them immunity to sunlight for enough time to enter the human realm and harvest fresh humans. Some of them were used for food. Some of them they try to turn. It's hard to turn a human into a vampire, but because vampires couldn't be born, it was the only way to expand the clan. Apparently, most of the humans died. It was virtually impossible to turn any of the species in this realm, so if a clan wanted to get stronger, they had to find a way into the human realm and they had to have the means to harvest enough humans for more than just food. The lesser clans only manage to snatch or lure a few humans at a time, they always end up as food. They didn't have the resources to even try to turn them. If they found a particularly beautiful human, they might try, but generally, their bodies are just used for more than food. They had it worse than any of us.

There was something in my blood that gives them the resistance to sunlight. Unfortunately for me, but fortunately for the humans, it was not a permanent resistance, which meant every time Cassius sent out a harvesting party, they drained me virtually dry. It's almost become a ritual to them. I get dragged out of my cage and hosed me down—no one wants to bite into filthy skin apparently. They strapped me down to a table in front of the whole clan. Cassius gives some bullshit speech about who had earnt the right to take part in the harvest. Then he let them feed from me. Because my blood only gives them limited resistance, it turned into a mass frenzied feeding. Not only did I end up weak from the loss of blood, but I had bite wounds all over my body. Thankfully this time, Edwin wasn't picked for the harvest. There's something about him that's just wrong. He always made sure that he took the blood from my femoral artery. He liked to slide his hand up the inside of my thigh. I'm sure he can smell my fear that he wouldn't stop and he would take too much. I'm also sure that it got him off. He's never touched me inappropriately if you don't count the way that he takes my blood. Cassius never allowed them to touch me in any way that was sexual. I used to think that it was because he was saving me for himself. In the beginning, I think that was what he had planned. But now that he had found a use for my blood, he'd changed his plans for me. He still couldn't stand the thought of any other man having me though. A thought that I am immensely grateful for, as long as it kept them away from me. Edwin still got his pound of flesh. He bites into me viciously, he never releases any of his venom to save me from the pain, none of them do. They enjoy listening to my screams too much. He's like a rabid dog when he starts. He doesn't just bite me once, he constantly releases and resets his teeth into me. I could always tell when he's reaching his fill because he rips his teeth from my flesh without bothering to release his bite. I hated him. I think I might even hate him more than I hated Cassius and he was the one who denied me my freedom. One thing was for definite, when I did find a way to escape, I needed to make sure that Edwin was in the other realm on a harvest because there was no way he wouldn't take the opportunity to hunt me down, and if he found me out there alone, I didn't know what he would do to me.

I sat in the bottom of my cage, looking out into the darkness as I contemplated what had become my life. Damon was the closest thing that I had to an ally at the moment, but I didn't know now how far he would go to help me. I couldn't get out of the cage by myself and I had nothing in here to use as a weapon. The only way out was going to be if someone let me out. That meant that I either had to persuade Damon to release me, or I would need to overpower the guards when they were taking me from my cage. The only time that I got taken out of the cage was for a bloodletting. There were too many vampires around at those times for me to be able to get away and I doubted that I would ever be able to get strong enough to overpower one of them anyway. That meant that Damon was my only hope.

Curling up in my usual corner, I folded into myself to try and conserve some body heat. My whole body burnt from the bite wounds and my ribs throbbed in time with my heartbeat. Every breath was like a gentle reminder that I needed to escape. I'd given Damon enough time to get comfortable with me, I needed to start feeling him out about helping me escape. I'd lingered here long enough. I wanted to get back to my life. I wanted to get back to my mate. As my eyes closed from the exhaustion that always took hold of me when I'd lost too much blood, my mind turned to Wyatt. My impossible mate. It shouldn't be possible for an angel to take a mate. That's what they taught us. Procreation is by allocation alone. But there he was sitting by that stream, telling me about all of his hopes and dreams. My mind took me back to that stream and even though the pain flared through my body from the bite wounds, I felt the small smile form on my lips, as I sunk into dreams filled with his smiling face.

CHAPTER 3

WYATT

We spent three hours down in the war room preparing all of the equipment that we might need. The packs were filled and we had a general plan for our next steps. It was a terrible plan, but it was the best that we had with the limited information that we had.

We knew that Lyra was sold to Cassius, who was the head of one of the largest vampire clans in the realm. All of the vampires lived on the Moon Side of the realm. It was perpetually dark over there. During the day, dark clouds blotted out the sky, only clearing when night fell to show the moon filled sky.

The plan, if you could even really call it that, was to head over to the Moon Side towards Cassius' clan house. We're hoping that we might meet up with someone while we were there to gather some kind of intel on the state of the clan because we needed to come up with a way to break in and get Lyra out. I wasn't going to leave that place unless Lyra was in my arms. I didn't care how many vampires I had to kill to get to her.

By the time we emerged from the war room, it was late at

night, somewhere around midnight, if I was right.

"Right, so sleep and meet back here at 9:00?" Caleb suggested.

I could see him eying me warily. I knew he was worried that I would just take off and take matters into my own hands, but even I knew that I couldn't do this on my own.

"Make it 8:30, I promised Aria that we would check in with her before we left," I told them, hopefully assuaging their fears that I was about to skip out on them. Caleb nodded and they both headed up the stairs to bed.

I saw the light on in the library and knew it could only be one person so I headed inside. Kyle was sat watching the fire and drinking a glass of what looked like Scotch. I hadn't touched a drop since I completely lost it about Lyra, so I sank into a chair opposite him without helping myself to one.

"What's got you sitting in here late at night instead of being tucked up in bed in the arms of your mate?" I asked him quietly. I wasn't really that much older than Kyle, but he still felt like a son to me.

"I just got out of a meeting with the other Alphas. We need to try and get the Council up and running as soon as possible," he said, frowning into the flames and not turning his face to look at me. "They want to abolish the satellite packs. Have all of the shifters gathering together under the main packs," he said, finally turning to look at me.

I could see why that would be troubling him, but I could also see why it would make sense as well.

"What are your thoughts on the issue?" I asked him.

"I'm worried about what issues it will cause. All we will be doing is collecting a larger group of males together and I worry about the safety of the females. I don't want to see any of them pushed into something like Britt was," he finished on a murmur. "But on the other hand, I think it would be good to bring them back into pack life. They are too on the edges now.

Too rogue. We need to be able to regulate them better if we are going to be able to foster better relationships between the other races."

"You don't have to make these decisions alone, you know," I told him. "Just because traditionally the packs have been run one way doesn't mean that you have to continue doing the same," I told him.

Kyle frowned at me, not following where I was going.

"Ask them," I suggested. "Speak with the women and ask their thoughts. You have a lot of pack lands. The satellite packs don't need to move into the packhouse or even the cabins, you could separate them off if that is what they want. I think you might be surprised how many want to come home though. Some already stayed after the battle and there have been no problems with them. Speak to them. Ask their reasons for separating off. I think you will find that a lot of it had to do with Marcus more than anything else."

Kyle cocked his head to the side in thought. "You're right," he conceded. "Thank you. I hear you're leaving in the morning."

"Yeah, but don't worry, we're all going to check in with Aria and the guys before we head out," I said, getting to my feet.

It was late, and I needed to get some rest so that I was ready for tomorrow. We couldn't portal through to the Moon Side. Something about whatever spell they used to cover the sun interfering with the portal magic. It was well known that the vampires portaled over to the human realm for their harvests, but it was such a closely guarded secret that no one had figured out how they did it just yet. Whoever found out first would be able to ask any price they wanted for the information.

I barely remembered the walk up to my room as I fell into bed with a weary sigh and let the exhaustion take me.

CHAPTER 4

WYATT

I found Aria in the kitchen the next morning talking to Liam while he cooked up a breakfast feast. Dom was already there, drinking coffee at the table. Even when he was dressed for an expedition like this, he still looked like he had walked off the pages of a magazine. I was going more for comfort than anything else with jeans, a thermal shirt, fleece and the jacket that was waiting with my pack. Caleb had obviously had a similar thought to me.

We all sat down and Kyle and Aria's other mates all joined us as soon as the platters of food were placed on the table. I was glad that Aria had insisted that we come to see her before we left. I would have run off at first light if not and this was definitely a better idea. Who knew how long it would be before we ate like this again? We had some provisions in our pack, but we would undoubtedly have to rely on hunting while we were travelling to get by. I loaded up my plate with bacon, sausages, eggs, toast and home fries. Caleb and Dom were both doing the same and the others just watched us in amusement.

"I feel like I should be going with you," Aria said after we had been eating quietly for some time.

"If you want to go, sweetheart, some of us can go with you. I have to stay here to deal with the pack; otherwise I would be going as well," Kyle admitted. I knew that it would be hard for him to let her go off with us to do this, but he would find a way to deal with it for her. If that's what she wanted.

"No, you're all needed here," Dom told them. "But, I will admit that I'm fully prepared to send a message for you if we land in some kind of trouble that we can't find a way out of."

Aria frowned but then reluctantly agreed. Whilst Aria's help would no doubt be invaluable, she wasn't well enough to help us. She might not want to admit it, but she was still recovering from the Blood Moon battle. She needed time to heal her mind and her soul before she set off on her next big adventure.

"The plan is to portal as close to the Moon Side as we can get. We should have about a day's hike before we enter. Cassius' clan house is said to be in the centre of the Moon Side. If we can find someone from another clan to speak with, they may give us information. The clans are notoriously always at war with each other. They won't miss an opportunity to deal a blow to another clan," Dom explained.

"What if you can't find anyone? Vampires aren't exactly common. You could wander the Moon Side for days and not come across anyone," Sykes said with a frown.

"If we don't find anyone, then we have to put the clan house under surveillance and find a way inside," I answered with a shrug.

There was no way that I was leaving without Lyra. Even if I had to sit in the shadows and watch that house for the next decade, I would find an opportunity to get inside.

"You're assuming that they still have her. They could have

moved her on or be holding her in a different location," Braedon said thoughtfully.

"Regardless, if you are going to storm the clan house without any intel, then you will call us to assist," Aria ordered us. "You're not going in there blind and alone."

I sat back and looked around the table at the people gathered there. We'd been through some shit the last couple of months, but all of them were sitting there willing to do anything to get Lyra back to us.

"I don't know how I got so lucky to have all of you on my side, but I am really fucking grateful for it," I finally said.

Aria smiled gently at me and Liam wrapped an arm around her and pulled her against his side. I wanted that. I needed that.

I'd already finished my food and Aria had packed away the leftovers to take with us. We all got up from the table without saying anything and Caleb, Dom and I grabbed our packs that were left in the kitchen last night.

"Go kick some ass and know that we are here for you if you need us," she told me, pulling me in for a hug. It's the only one that I'd ever had from her and it should be awkward, but it's not. She's family now.

We all piled out of the packhouse. There's no need to say anything else. Dom quickly pulled enough energy and opened up a portal in front of us. Caleb and Dom stepped through first. Taking one last deep breath of the calming air around the pack, I stepped through the portal. It was time to get our girl back.

CHAPTER 5

LYRA

Damon's hurried whispers woke me from my dreamless sleep. I wished I was someone who could make themselves dream of whatever they wanted. I could spend every night in Wyatt's arms if I could just learn that trick.

"Ly ... Ly ... wake the fuck up, Ly!" he finished harshly.

"I'm awake," I mumbled.

My words were still slurring. I must not have slept for long enough to start recovering from the blood loss. When I moved my arms and legs to sit up, the pain from the bite wounds let me know that I definitely hadn't slept for long enough.

"Shit, you haven't healed enough," Damon murmured.

I could see him pacing along the side of my cage, his hands dug through his hair and he was pulling on it in desperation. I crawled over to the side of the cage that he was pacing on and wrapped my hands around the bars. Using all my strength, I pulled myself to my feet and gritted my teeth against the pain.

"What are you talking about?" I whispered to him, trying to keep my voice steady. "What's going on, Damon?"

"I ... I think I can get you out tonight." Damon stopped

pacing and dropped to his knees in front of me. "I can't keep doing this, Ly. I can't just stand here and watch what they keep doing to you. But we're only going to get one chance. If you aren't strong enough to get away, they will never give you a second opportunity."

"I can do it. You said tonight, right. How long do we have?" I tried not to get excited. If Damon decided that it was too much of a risk and wouldn't help me, I didn't think that I would survive the crushing disappointment.

"There's going to be a party tonight. Something is going on in the clan, but I don't know what yet. I think that once the party is going, I can slip away and let you out. The harvesting party still won't be back and everyone else will be distracted. You should have enough time to get as far away from here to get a decent head start." Damon looked up at me and shook his head. "But if you aren't strong enough to run, you won't get far enough."

I clenched my teeth as I thought through what he had said. This could be my only chance. They never held parties or celebrations. This was the first one since I had got here. And if the harvesting party was still away, there would hardly be any guards. Maybe. But Damon was right, I was still weak.

"How long would I have until you could get me out?" I asked, hating what the answer was going to be but needing to know anyway. It wouldn't be long enough. I needed days, not hours, to properly recover.

"I think you would have maybe ten to twelve hours," he said quietly, looking nervously over his shoulder.

Fuck! Fuck, fuck, fuck!

"Can you get me some food?" I asked him.

"I've brought you some more bread, water, some roast chicken and an apple," he said, pulling out a parcel of food from behind him that I hadn't seen before.

Damon had never brought me this much at once before.

He had to steal the scraps to bring to me, which was why it was usually just bread or whatever else was lying around the kitchen. This was basically a full meal and I suspected that he was giving me his own food. I didn't even feel guilty as he pushed the food through the bars and I quickly opened up the package. He could survive missing one meal.

"How did you get all this?" I asked him as I drank some of the water and then tore into the roast chicken with my fingers.

"They told us to take our food up to our rooms so that they could prepare the hall for tonight. It's how I found out about the party. It's the first time they've let us take food away to eat alone," Damon told me quietly.

Cassius kept his vampires on a short leash. They were constantly watched. Damon was right, something pretty big must be going on if they were deviating from their normal routine like this.

"I'll be healed enough in ten hours," I told him more confidently than I actually felt. "With the extra food, if I sleep, my body will repair quicker."

This was more food than I had eaten at any one time since before I was captured. I tried to eat it slowly, but it was so good. The bread was still soft and not stale like I was used to. The chicken was the best thing that I had ever tasted until I bit into the apple. I felt my eyes roll back in ecstasy as the juice exploded into my mouth.

"Okay," Damon ran his hands through his hair with a desperate gleam in his eye. He looked even less convinced than I did. "Sleep as much as you can, I'll be back when it's safe and show the way out."

Damon gave me one last lingering look and then quietly left the room where my cage was housed. Was this really happening? I was trying not to get my hopes up, but they were already up there. The food was long gone and it sat uncomfortably in my stomach. It was the most I had eaten in years. That, together with the nerves and I was breathing deeply, trying not to be sick. My body needed this. I hadn't lied to Damon, if I could sleep, this should help. There was a reason why they kept me on the brink of starvation. But even with my angelic healing abilities, I didn't know if ten hours would be enough. Fuck, ten days probably wouldn't be enough, but it was all that I had. I crawled over to my usual corner and curled up into a ball. I was worried at first that my mind was running too quickly to let me fall asleep, but my body was so exhausted and the sensation of a full stomach for the first time in years, was enough to lull me back into a dreamless sleep.

It only felt like moments later when a hand touched my shoulder and I scrambled away from them. Touch was never a good thing in what had become my world. My sudden awakening had left me confused and I didn't hear Damon at first over the sound of my rapid breathing and the blood rushing through my ears as my heart raced. Once the panic cleared from my vision and I could concentrate on what was in front of me, I saw Damon crouched in the corner where I had been sleeping, holding both hands up in front of him. He looked like he was trying to calm a wild animal. In some respects, I suppose that he was.

"I'm sorry, I'm sorry, I'm not used to people touching me and not hurting me," I mumbled quietly. Hoping that he wouldn't hear what I was saying.

The look of pity on Damon's face showed that he definitely did.

"We have to go now," he said, reaching one hand out towards me as he stood.

I looked at it. I knew that I should take it, that was what normal people did, right? Damon had been nothing but kind to me and I had no reason to distrust him. The thing is that distrust had been beaten into me and I had been locked in a cage for so long that I wasn't sure I even knew what the appropriate reaction was to everyday situations anymore.

Damon waited patiently for me as all the thoughts ran through my head. Eventually, I reached one hand out and slipped it into his. He gently pulled me to my feet and then held my hand for a moment, as if he was waiting to see if I was going to collapse. It was only then that I realised that I did actually feel a bit stronger than normal. I was nowhere near fully healed, but I was starting to and that was all that mattered right now.

Once he was satisfied, Damon dropped my hand and pulled a pack off his shoulder, he pulled out some clothes and some boots and passed them over to me.

"Put these on. I had to guess your size, but this was the best that I could do," he told me, rummaging around in the pack still.

I pulled on the trousers first, I hadn't worn something like this in years and they felt almost foreign to me. They were made of a thick material that I wasn't familiar with, but I could already feel the skin of my legs warming underneath them. Next, I pulled on thick socks and shoved my feet into the boots. They were a little big, but the socks helped to pad them out a bit for me. While I put the t-shirt on, Damon crouched down and started to lace the boots tightly around my ankles. Finally, he passed me a sweatshirt, which from the size of it I was guessing was his own, and I pulled it on gratefully. This was the warmest I had been in such a long time. I looked down at myself in awe. Clothes shouldn't be this amazing to me, but after spending so long in the rags that had once been a small shift dress, these ill-fitting clothes felt like a luxury to me.

Damon chuckled at the look on my face and rolled the sleeves of the sweatshirt up so that my hands could poke out of the bottom.

"Ready?" He asked me as he stepped towards the door of the cage.

I nodded numbly, losing the ability to speak. This was so surreal. It was like a dream, one which I was so sure was about to come crashing down around me. I almost didn't dare to hope.

Stepping out of the open door of the cage, I looked around me. I had, of course, been out of the cage before but not for anything pleasant, and never walking on my own two feet. I tended to be dragged everywhere like I was less than a person.

Damon reached back and took my hand with a soft smile.

"We have to move quickly. Come on," he said, pulling me gently behind him as he walked out into the corridor.

There was no one out in the corridor, but then there never did seem to be any of the other times that I had been out here. I knew that this room was underneath the house. There were a few cells on the other side of the corridor, but I had never seen anyone inside them in all the years that I had been here.

Damon walked the opposite way down the corridor to where I was typically dragged. That was probably a good thing because I knew that the stairs down that end came out very close to the hall, where they always did the ritual bloodletting before a harvest. That was the last place that I wanted to be right now. The corridor was dark and quiet, the only sounds were our footsteps as we slowly made our way along.

Damon held my hand tightly in his own. I could tell that he was as nervous as I was right now. He was risking every-thing by helping me. I did not doubt that they would kill him if they discovered us.

When we reached some steps, Damon turned around and leant closer to me, whispering in my ear. "It's important that you don't make a sound until we get out of the door. This is the corridor that runs along the far end of the kitchen and there will be other vampires and slaves there. We cannot let them hear us under any circumstances, do you understand?"

He leant back so that he could look me in the eye and I quietly nodded my agreement. I was so scared that I was certain my heart was about to explode out of my chest. It was racing so fast I was sure everyone around would be able to hear it.

Damon quietly led me up the stairs. The door at the top was already propped open and we both squeezed through before he silently pressed it closed behind us. Damon reached behind him again without looking and I slipped my hand back into his. He didn't take his eyes off the corridor to the side of us where I could see a large door standing open. I could hear people moving around and talking inside. That must be the kitchen. If someone stepped out of that door, we would be found and it would all be over. I clutched onto Damon's hand even tighter and he slowly started to walk down the corridor in front of us. This one seemed to run down the side of the room that I was assuming was the kitchen. There was only one other door on this corridor, at the very far end, and it seemed to be our destination.

We moved carefully and quietly as we crept down the corridor. I couldn't stop myself from holding my breath, I was so nervous. One good thing about being absolutely scared out of my wits was that my adrenaline seemed to be running on full and I couldn't feel any of the aches and pains in my body. When I came down from this, it was going to hurt, a lot.

It felt like we had walked for miles when we finally reached the door at the end of the corridor. I couldn't help but keep looking over my shoulder at the way we had come. Every time I did, I thought someone would be there, laughing at my desperate attempt to get away. But every time I looked, the corridor stayed empty and my heart just raced even faster.

The door was propped open again, similar to how the

other had been. Damon pushed it open a small amount and then we both squeezed through before he quietly and slowly pushed it closed behind us. It didn't make a single sound as he did. He must have practised or something. How long had he been planning how to get me out of here? I felt the tears start to form in my eyes before I willed them away. I knew just how much Damon was risking trying to help me and I could only think of one reason why he would. He was too good to be here with these vampires. He needed to escape just as much as I did.

Once the door was closed and I turned around, I realised that we were outside. Before I could even stop myself, I gasped. Damon's hand quickly whipped up over my mouth, and I silently tried to apologise to him with my eyes. He gave me a gentle smile before taking his hand away and holding one finger up to his lips. I nodded my head to show him that I understood.

The cool wind gently blew across my face and I couldn't believe that I was outside again. It had been so long. A smile spread across my face as my eyes gently closed to appreciate something as simple as the wind blowing across my skin.

I felt a tug on my hand and saw that Damon had started moving through the shadows away from the house. I quietly followed after him making sure to carefully look where I was placing my feet.

We walked for a few minutes, skirting around the edge of a grassed area where some larger bushes were growing. We finally reached a fence which ran as far as I could see in the dark in each direction. It was about six feet high and I couldn't see any way around it. I looked up at the top. It seemed like we were going to have to go over. It wasn't topped with spikes or anything, it was just a standard wire fence. I suppose they must rely on the threat of a house full of vampires to keep people out. As it was, I didn't really see what the purpose of the fence was.

Damon crouched down beside me and cupped his hands together. It seemed like we were going over the fence. I had a moment of indecision where I wasn't sure that I would make it, but then I stepped one foot into Damon's hands anyway. I couldn't believe that a six-foot fence was causing me this much anxiety. When I had my wings, something like this wouldn't have even caused me a moment's pause. So much had changed over the last however many years it had been.

Unfortunately for me, I was lost in my thoughts about the new significance of fencing in my life when Damon decided to launch me up over the top of it.

I managed to hold the screech in that was trying to force its way out of my mouth, but Damon shot me straight over the top and I landed in a crumpled mess on the other side. Seconds later, Damon landed in a silent crouch next to me.

"I'm so sorry, I didn't realise that you weighed so little. I think I put a bit too much into that," he said picking me up off the ground and dusting me down.

Damon took the pack off his shoulders and fastened it to my own before he turned me towards the darkness and away from the clan house. "Keep heading away from the house for as long as you can. You need to get as much distance between yourself and here before you stop to rest. Try and find somewhere safe to rest for a few hours and then push on. You have to get out of the Moon Side before you properly stop to rest. Normally it's a few days walk but it's probably going to take you longer in your condition. I've packed as much food in here as I could get for you. There are also a few other supplies you might need," he told me quietly.

I turned towards Damon in confusion. "Why are you telling me this? You're coming with me. You can't stay here," I said firmly.

"I can't," he whispered. When he looked me in the eye, I could see the tears swimming in his eyes. "Cassius can track me because I am part of his clan. It isn't safe for you to stay with me. I'm so sorry, Ly. I'm so sorry that I couldn't get you out of there sooner. That you've been suffering through that for all of these years. Can you ever forgive me?" The tears finally broke free and silently streamed down his cheeks.

"Damon, you are the only reason why I'm still alive. There is nothing to forgive you for. But you can't stay here. It isn't safe for you. There must be a way. There has to be a way that you can break the connection to Cassius." I didn't want to leave him here. He needed saving just as much as I did.

"There is and I'm working on it. Once it's done, I'll come and find you." I wasn't sure if he was lying for me or for himself.

"I don't know if I can leave you here," I told him honestly. It wasn't too late; we could go back. No one would know that I was missing yet.

"You have to go, Ly. You deserve to be free, to be happy. This is your chance for that. You have to take it, for both of us. Something good has to have come from me being brought to this place, to me becoming this monster," he said bitterly as he stared down at his hands, almost as if he was looking at the metaphorical blood that covered them.

"They will kill you," I said quietly.

"I died the night that they dragged me through that portal into this hell." Damon reached one hand up and laid it against my cheek. "Now go, run. Go and live a happy life for both of us."

"I will come back for you. I will find a way and I will come back for you. You just have to survive, Damon. Survive for me. If I can do it, I know that you can too," I said fiercely and I meant it. I would leave this place and find Wyatt and we would find a way together to free Damon, even if it meant killing Cassius.

Damon just nodded sadly before kissing me on the cheek.

We both knew that it was a goodbye kiss. It wasn't that he didn't believe I would come back for him. It was that he didn't want me to. Well, he was shit out of luck because he was my friend. The first real friend that I had ever had. I wouldn't abandon him to this place. I would save him.

I reluctantly turned away from Damon and I felt him lightly push my shoulder in the direction that he had told me to go. I stumbled forward a few steps and when I glanced over my shoulder, I saw that Damon was already on the other side of the fence. My heart broke as I started moving more quickly, my feet breaking out into a run. I couldn't believe that I was going to leave him here. This wasn't right. This wasn't how this was supposed to be. We were both supposed to be free. I didn't let myself look back again. I couldn't. Maybe that made me a coward, but my poor battered heart couldn't accept that looking at Damon now could be the very last time that I would see his face. With determination gripping me, I ran. I would escape this place. I had to. Not just for me. I had to do it for Damon.

CHAPTER 6

We came out of the portal about a day's walk from the edge of the Moon Side. At first, we just walked in silence. We all knew which way we were headed and everything had suddenly become weirdly awkward between us.

It was Caleb who broke the silence first.

"What is she like?" he quietly asked.

I thought about it for a moment, I had spent so little time with her, but when I thought back to those evenings by the stream, even now knowing the inevitable conclusion, I couldn't help but smile.

"She is fiercely protective, strong, so fucking beautiful. She was so sure of herself, of what was right and what needed to be done. When she first talked about falling, about losing her wings so that she could stay with me, she wasn't even afraid. She has this smile that just lights up her face. When she was truly happy it was almost like she shone. She's so small and she looks so fragile, but she must be the strongest person I've ever met. I suppose she will need to be if she is going to come out of this anything like she was before." I started off smiling but as I got further in, I could feel the emotion drifting away from me. Would she still be the same person? After all of this time in captivity, what if they had broken her? What if she had given up?

The guilt slammed into me harder than I had ever felt it before. It had been so long since I had allowed myself to think of her like that. It felt like my chest was going to cave in. My wolf roared in distress. I could feel him spinning out of control in my mind. He was half-mad, having been kept from his mate for so long. Thinking about her only made it worse. My inevitable guilt whenever I did think about her made me feel like I was going to lose control.

I felt Dom move up beside me. He had a calming presence about him. I think it probably had something to do with the strength that just projected from him. He was very like Lyra. He always stood firm beside those that he cared about. He seemed to have some kind of inbuilt sense of what was right and wrong. I didn't think I had ever seen Dom have any sort of moral conflict in his life, he was just inherently a good person.

"What does she look like?" he asked me quietly. It was the most unsure I had ever heard him.

"She's small, probably a little over five feet and petite, you know. Although, I suppose she could have changed. She was still young back then and it's been so long." I drifted off as I brought an image of Lyra into my mind. I almost didn't want to think about how she had been back then. She was bound to have changed having been in captivity for this long, it would be hard enough to look at what they had done to her. But I knew that they needed this, I needed to do this for Dom and Caleb. "She's got long silky blonde hair. Her eyes are such a dark brown that they almost look black, but they're too warm to be black. She's got this cute little nose and perfect pink lips. She's so soft and when I held her, she just fit against me. That sounds weird. I don't know how to explain it so that you'll be able to understand just how perfect she is. There aren't enough words to describe just how beautiful she is," I sighed like a lovesick fool and when I looked at the others, I could see that I had their full attention. "She has the most amazing scent. It's like sunshine. Like when you first step outside in the summer and the warm morning sun beats down on you. When you can still smell the faint scent of dew in the air and the start of the summer flowers starting to open. She smells just like that, like a summer morning."

Dom and Caleb both fell quiet. Even my wolf seemed to have calmed while the image of Lyra floated at the forefront of my mind. We all needed her. I didn't think I had ever realised that Caleb and Dom were both missing something out of their lives. Like they needed something else to be able to be happy. I wondered if we all seemed that way before we meet our mates. Before we meet that one person that was made for us. That made us feel complete. When I had first held Lyra in my arms, it had felt so right. She fit so perfectly against me and I felt an overwhelming calm settle deep inside me. I hadn't even realised that my soul was raging against a void that was inside of me until she had filled it. Maybe that was for the best. The last nine years had been torture. I wasn't sure if my wolf was ever going to be able to fully recover his sanity. If you spent your entire life feeling like that, you just wouldn't be able to survive.

We walked for several hours, we didn't bother to stop for lunch, we just ate the leftover breakfast food that Aria had wrapped up for us while we walked. The land leading up to the Moon Side was strange. It was almost like nothing lived here, like the animals knew that they would be too close to something deadly and had fled the area. Even the plant life was twisted and gnarled and looked like it was dying of thirst. Night was just beginning to fall when we finally reached the area where the Moon Side barrier lay. Because of the encroaching night, it was difficult to tell where the edge was. But then it was like all life just died, even the grass had dried up and died.

"Maybe we should camp for the night on our side of the barrier, set off into the Moon Side in the day," Dom said, shifting his feet across the dead grass and looking around.

There wasn't that much difference between the day and the night on the other side of the barrier and being a few steps away wouldn't make us any safer while we slept. But I knew what he meant.

"Or we could just keep going for a couple of hours, wait until we find somewhere further in where we can camp," Caleb said.

I looked between the two of them. It was rare to see them having a difference of opinion. Sometimes it felt like Dom and Caleb were the same person, they were that well in tune with each other. I could see that something about the Moon Side was making Dom uneasy but Caleb seemed to be riding hard the need to find our mate. I could understand the feeling, I had lived with it for nearly a decade now.

"Well, looks like you get the deciding vote," Caleb laughed, it was stilted and a shadow of an attempt at good-natured, but I appreciated the effort. Maybe the Moon Side was freaking him out as well.

"Okay, I think we should make camp here and Caleb and I should shift and scout ahead for an hour or so and see if we can get any kind of read on what lies ahead," I suggested.

Dom nodded as he thought about my idea. "I'll set up camp and get some food going. Both of you back here in an hour, or I'll assume that something is wrong and come after you." He looked uneasily between the two of us and I could tell that he wasn't completely sold on the idea of us splitting up. It wasn't after all the best of ideas, but we didn't know what we were going into, the maps we had were rudimentary at best. We needed to scout ahead and try and get the lay of the land.

Caleb shifted and then glanced back at me cocking his head waiting for instructions. "We'll head out in separate directions and see if we can get a read of anyone, vampire, specifically. We still need to find an information source and I'd rather we did that sooner than later."

Caleb gave me one nod and then took off. I glanced back at Dom uneasily. I knew that he wasn't without his own protections but I still felt uneasy leaving him. I was just about to say something about him calling for help when he pulled a pot and what looked like ingredients for a stew out of his bag. Yeah, he had this, I wasn't going to insult him by pretending that he didn't.

"We'll call out if we hit any trouble," I told him instead and he gave me a sly smile, knowing that wasn't what I had originally planned on saying.

I gave myself to the shift and set out, angling away from the direction that Caleb had run and opening up my senses. What were the chances of us finding anyone with useful information on the first night? My gut told me none, but my heart couldn't help but hope for a different outcome.

CHAPTER 7

DAMON

After leaving Lyra at the gate, I'd returned to my room to wait. It was only a matter of time before they came for me. My scent would be all over the room where they kept Lyra's cage and there was no way to mask it. My only hope was that Lyra would be able to get far enough away before they discovered that she was missing. She had seemed so weak when I reached her, I had nearly turned back and left her in her cage. She was only ever going to get one shot at this. If they caught her again, no one would be able to get anywhere near her and they would keep her in a hole so deep, she would never be able to climb out. The only reason why I went ahead with the plan was that I couldn't live with the guilt of her being here any longer. I knew it was selfish and in a way, I did have Lyra's best interests at heart. But sitting here in the dark of my room, waiting for my fate to finally catch up with me, I could at least admit, even if only to myself, that I helped her escape just as much for myself as I did for her. Watching her lie in that filthy cage every day, suffering through the harvest celebration was torture. When I slept at night, it was always to the sounds of her screams as they replayed over and over in my head. I was not made for this life and I was glad that it would be coming to an end soon. I was glad that I had done one good thing with it before it ended. I just had to hope that Lyra would be able to get away on her own.

It was mid-morning when they finally came for me. As every hour ticked by, I had started to grow more confident that Lyra might be able to escape. As long as they came for me and didn't set out to recover her first, then she had a good ten hours head start and her scent trail would have already started to fade.

The door burst open and two of the other guards stormed into the room and dragged me from the chair where I was sitting. I didn't struggle. There was no point. They each took an arm and dragged me to the hall where Cassius was pacing in front of his fucking throne like the pompous twat that he was. That's right he had a throne, it was a huge gold monstrosity of a thing. He loved sitting in it and lording it over the rest of us. We all knew what his plans were, to grow the clan large enough that he could take over or take down all of the other clans residing in the Moon Side. Cassius fancied himself as the vampire king and Lyra was his only way of achieving that.

The guards dropped me on the floor in front of the throne and Cassius looked down at me before calmly taking a seat. I could see the top-ranking members of the clan waiting around the room in anticipation of what was to come. The bloodlust was so thick in the air I could almost taste it. Edwin stood closest to the throne and he was practically vibrating with excitement.

Cassius huffed out a deep breath. "What an errant little pet you've become," he said in a disappointed tone.

I said nothing, he was clearly waiting for me to beg for my life, but I wasn't going to. I hated what I had become, what he had turned me into and I was looking forward to it finally being over.

Cassius cocked his head to one side when he realised that I wasn't going to beg. A smile slowly slid across his face and his eyes lit up with excitement. "Did you actually fall in love with her?" he laughed.

I heard the laughter ripple around the room, but I didn't break eye contact with Cassius. I wouldn't take my eye off the greatest threat in the room. I may have come here intending to die, but I also intended to look death in the face when it came for me.

"Hmmm, what to do, what to do. I think I won't kill you yet." He smiled down at me like he was doing me a favour. He even paused as if he was waiting for me to thank him. "Throw him into the cell opposite the cage, I want him to have front row seats for when we drag the angel back. Edwin, take whoever you want and hunt her down. Try not to harm her too much, we need her in one piece for the show when we get back. I think that I will chain you to my throne and make you watch while the clan takes what they want from her. I've been too easy on her all this time. Edwin, I'm sure there are plenty of things you've wanted to do to all that creamy flesh. As your reward for bringing her back, you can have her first and Damon here will watch while you do whatever you want to the woman he loves. And he will continue to watch until he dies of starvation. I've heard it takes about a hundred years or so. I've never seen it happen, but apparently, the first ten years are excruciating."

Cassius cackled in glee and waved at my guards to take me away, Edwin was practically salivating from what had been promised to him. They dragged me through the clan house and then threw me into the cell that faced the room where Lyra's empty cage sat. With nothing else to do, I walked to the back of the cell and slid down the wall to sit on the floor. I had not anticipated a slow death like this. I had assumed Cassius would just kill me in a fit of rage. Closing my eyes, I leant my head back against the wall. I'd done all I could, it was up to Lyra now.

CHAPTER 8

LYRA

I did exactly as Damon told me. I ran. And I ran for hours. I ran until the adrenaline abandoned me and my legs gave way from underneath. I had run blindly in the direction which Damon had pointed me with blind eyes. All that I could concentrate on was to keep moving. One foot in front of the other, as fast as I could move.

As I laid crumpled on the ground, I took a moment to take stock of my body. I hadn't moved this much in years and I was paying for it now. My chest heaved as I tried to suck in enough air to fill my lungs. It felt like razor blades sliced into my every breath. My heart was pounding so hard it physically ached in my chest. All of the muscles in my legs had cramped painfully and I was being racked with full-body pains from the sudden period of intense activity. I hurt, possibly even more than I had in a very long time. But I had never felt so alive. The air that I desperately tried to take into my body was fresh and cold and it tasted like freedom.

Looking around me, I saw that I had come to a stop next to a small grove of trees. The landscape here was so unlike what I was familiar with. Everything seemed to be dying. This was not a place where nature thrived, it lived by clawing through each day fuelled by a determination to survive. I crawled across the dead or dying grass and into the undergrowth. Once I was safely nestled in between the trees, I let myself sag to the ground completely. Drawing my knees up to my chest, I stretched the oversized sweatshirt down over my legs and curled up for a moment's rest.

Damon was right. I couldn't afford to stop yet. I had been running for about three hours. I had no idea how I had managed to keep moving for so long. Three hours was not long enough, though. I needed to put more distance between me and the clan house before I could truly afford to rest.

I waited until I was able to catch my breath and then I dug around in the bag which Damon had given me. I found several packages of food and bottles of water. I didn't know how long I was going to be out here or when I would be able to replenish the supplies that I had. I was keenly aware that I needed to ration myself with what I had. That thought didn't stop me from opening one of the bottles of water and draining it completely. It also didn't stop me from devouring two thick slices of bread, which were already thickly spread with butter and jam. I figured this was the food that wasn't going to keep for long and I needed the energy to get moving again. Once I had got far enough away from the clan house, I would take stock of what I had left and ration from there. For now, I needed to keep my quickly waning strength up.

I finished my food and reluctantly crawled out from between the trees. It would be nice to just close my eyes and sleep now, but I knew that I had a lot further to go before I could afford to do so. Besides, when I finally closed my eyes to sleep, I was pretty sure that I'd sleep for at least twelve hours and I couldn't afford to rest for that long just now.

Climbing to my feet, I started to walk. There was no way that I could run any further, but I figured as long as I kept moving, that was all that mattered. One foot in front of the other, just keep walking. My mind shut off and all I could concentrate on was moving. I should probably have stayed more aware of my surroundings, but I just kept myself heading in the right direction and walked. I didn't pay much attention to what was happening around me, I didn't keep an eye out for a safe place to rest, I was still too close to the clan house to feel safe enough to stop anyway.

I didn't know how long I had walked for. I just kept moving, all I could think was, *just keep moving*. Every time I wanted to stop, every time I felt like I was going to collapse, I turned my mind to Wyatt. His beautiful smile and the way that when he laughed, his whole face would light up. I knew that I would do everything that I could to get back to him, but I needed a plan for when I did. It was the perfect distraction to keep me going through my walk. The issue with getting to Wyatt would be getting past his alpha. He had caused all of this. It was he who had captured me in the beginning, held me in that cell, sold me to the vampires and was basically the reason why I was now running for my life through wherever the hell I currently was.

Looking around myself, I realised that I'd somehow found my way into a wood. It wasn't like the wood where I first met Wyatt. The trees look dead, running my hand across the bark of one close to me, I frowned in confusion. It's almost like it has been burnt or petrified. I didn't understand how there was any life in this place. The grass crunches beneath my feet with a sound like dead leaves. There was nothing green in this place. It's all shades of grey and black, even the dirt on the ground looked more like ash than soil. Had this place always been like this?

I must have been running, or at least moving in what I hoped was the right direction, for most of the day now. There didn't seem to be much difference in terms of light, it seemed to always be on the verge of twilight here, but I had seen the moon rising about an hour ago. I don't know how far I had made it away from the clan house. I'm not sure any distance would feel far enough. They were bound to have noticed that I was missing by now and I had no doubt that Cassius would have sent them out to hunt for me as soon as he realised.

I couldn't go any further, though. I was so tired that I barely felt like I had the energy to lift my feet anymore. My vision was starting to cloud and I knew that I was on the verge of passing out from exhaustion. I needed to find somewhere remotely safe before I did that. Looking around me, all I could see were the strange, petrified trees. They were fairly close together but nowhere near enough to create a refuge for me. The undergrowth was withered away and offered no form of cover. Even if I had the energy, climbing a tree wasn't an option either. Without any leaves and with the branches withered and dying, I wouldn't be any less on display. In fact, I'd just be making myself more visible from further away. It was the same as far as I could see for miles. I didn't have miles left in me, I was ready to drop and I started to conclude that there wasn't going to be a safe place for me to do it.

I spotted three trees standing slightly closer together than most of the others and stumbled over to them. Dropping my pack to the ground, I fought the urge to let my legs give out from under me. If I was going to have any chance, I needed at least some form of cover.

I used the last of my energy to scour the ground a few minutes walk in the distance surrounding the trees I'd picked. Without the weight of my pack, I knew I'd be able to move around a little more, but my last reserves of energy were fast running out. As I walked, I gathered as much broken or dead undergrowth as I could, hopefully without it looking too obvious that I had done so. When my arms were full, I stumbled back to the three trees where I had dropped my pack and fell to the ground. I arranged the broken and dying plants around the base of the trees as best as I could to try and thicken up the ground cover and make it look as natural as I could.

When I got to the point where I could barely keep my eyes open for any longer, I let myself fall to the ground and pulled the pack underneath my head. I made myself drain another bottle of water and quickly ate an apple and some dry bread. When I was done, I let my eyes fall closed and pulled the memory of Wyatt to the front of my mind. I just had to hope that I would wake up before any of Cassius' clan was able to find me. I'd gone as far as I could for now, but I knew in the back of my mind that it would never be far enough.

CHAPTER 9

DOMINIC

After spending an uneasy night camped at the edge of the Moon Side, we spent the next day walking in silence in the direction we knew Cassius' clan house to be. We only had a general idea of where we were heading. No one had ever really ventured into the Moon Side to map it out and its occupants preferred it that way.

Wyatt and Caleb were taking it in turns to change into their wolf forms and scout ahead before returning to the group. So far, they had found absolutely nothing. I couldn't decide if that was a good thing or not. Then again, everything about this place seemed dead, so I doubted there was all that much life left out here anyway.

Wyatt and I were currently walking side by side in silence. It wasn't uncomfortable though. There was something about these men that just felt so right to be with. Not that I felt the same way about Wyatt as I did about Caleb. Those feelings were too confusing to even consider right now. But the three of us together, I could feel it. It was so tangible that at times I thought I could almost see the bond that was forming between the three of us. Mage's didn't have this. It wasn't something that we did, share a mate. In fact, it was rare that a mage would take a mate at all. We bred for the need to continue a line, not to share a life with someone. But what we had here, it felt so much more than a mate bond, it felt like a brotherhood—a promise. We would stand together forever and tear apart the world if we needed to. These men felt like they shared a part of me and I suppose, in a way, they did. Lyra. Our mate. Our angel. Even thinking that seemed ridiculous. An angel. My mate was a fucking angel. I wanted to know more about her. I was desperate to learn more about what she was like, but I didn't want to ask Wyatt. I hated to see the look of guilt and self-loathing that took over his face whenever he thought about her. How he had lasted this long, carrying it all alone, I had no idea. I meant what I told him back at the Pack House though. None of this was his fault, there's nothing that he would have been able to do to prevent it. Maybe once we have Lyra back, he would listen to reason.

The night was drawing in when Caleb returned to us, switching back to his wolf form.

"There's an old abandoned house to the East of us. I had a look around it, but it's completely deserted. Doesn't look like anyone has been there in years. Might be a place to consider camping," he said, digging into his pack and pulling out his water flask.

"I don't need to stop yet unless any of you do," Wyatt said, looking off towards some woods in the distance. Every time he looked that way, it was almost like he couldn't tear himself away from the sight and he kept turning back to it.

"What is it?" I asked him, stepping closer.

"I'm just not tired yet, I've got a few more hours in me if you two are still okay to keep moving," he explained.

"No, I mean, what is it about the woods that keeps drawing your attention back to them," I asked him.

There was something about Wyatt which seemed different suddenly, but I couldn't put my finger on what it was.

"I don't know, I just feel like we need to keep moving that way," he said.

"Is it coming from your wolf?" Caleb asked, cocking his head to the side.

I could see why he would ask such a question. Their wolf half would always feel more comfortable and secure within natural surroundings. This place must be making their wolves uneasy. It was the least natural place I had ever been to. It was almost like someone had taken the natural landscape and sucked all of the life out of it. It was creepy as fuck.

"No," Wyatt simply said, frowning in confusion.

"Well, we have two options: we follow this feeling and trust in it, we don't know what the type of bond is that you have formed with Lyra. An angel mating bond is something we simply have no knowledge of. It could be something to do with that," I summarised, trailing off as I started to think it through. Being a mage, the quest for knowledge was always forefront in my mind, it was how we were raised, what most mages lived for. I was somewhat of an anomaly in our society, a mage who left the fold to do something different. It was only because I had become linked to the academy that the Council had left me alone. I was still gathering and now also sharing information. I was surprised that I hadn't received a summons back now that the academy had fallen. If I was honest, it was only a matter of time. I had no idea how I was going to deal with that when it happened.

"Dom?!" Caleb shouted, drawing my attention back to him. "I said, what was our other option?"

"Oh right, sorry, brain ran away with me for a minute. Well, we follow it and discover that it is some kind of lure from one of the natural inhabitants of this place," I shrugged.

"Oh brilliant, that sounds like fun. Did I mention that the

house I'd found looked like it had been torn apart by wild animals at some point in the past?" Caleb snarked.

"Actually, no, you didn't," Wyatt shrugged.

I already knew what he was going to decide. It was the same conclusion that we would all come to because what other option did we have? If there was any chance that it was Wyatt's bond with Lyra that was calling to him, then we would follow it. Even if it did lead to inevitable danger. It's not like Lyra was just hanging out at a spa anyway. Whenever we did reach her, we were going to have an entire clan of vampires to face. Not only that but an entire clan of vampires who had no doubt been sampling angel blood for the past eight years. There was no way to know what effect that could possibly have had on them.

"Right, well off we go then," Caleb chirped, heading off towards the woods. He was in a surprisingly good mood and something about it made me suspicious for some reason.

We all turned towards the woods, which was really just another collection of dead trees we had encountered along the way. The plan when we had first set off was that we would stretch out our food supplies in our packs by hunting as we travelled. That, as it turned out, was somewhat naïve of us. There was nothing alive in this place. I suppose it kind of made sense why the vampires had gravitated here. The constant state of twilight meant they could move about freely and they didn't need access to anything living here. They had created their own dead zone and ruled over it.

As the trees grew closer, Wyatt cocked his head to the side. "Do you hear that?" he asked.

Caleb nodded. "Three … no four, moving through the trees."

We were out in the open and there was absolutely nothing for us to use as cover.

"Are they moving towards us?" I asked, my ears letting me

down, not being able to pick up on what their wolf senses could.

Wyatt listened for a few more seconds. "No, they're searching through the trees."

"So, do we go around, or do we go find out what is happening?" Caleb asked, still walking towards the treeline. Clearly, he had already made his mind where he wanted to go.

Neither Wyatt nor I answered and just kept following Caleb towards the treeline. Sometimes I wondered if something had changed in us in the lead up to the Blood Moon battle. It was almost like we were addicted to the thrill of the fight. The adrenaline rush of holding your life in your hands and fighting for it.

As we drew closer to the treeline, I strained my ears to try and pinpoint where our potential attackers were lying in wait. I got absolutely nothing, so not wanting to be at a disadvantage from the others, I mumbled a spell under my breath and my eyesight slower flickered and then changed. The scenery around me transformed into shades of grey, which was not all that different to how it looks normally, but white lights radiated from the heat sources of the people moving through the trees in front of us. It just confirmed my earlier thoughts that there was nothing out here alive, as I watched the four figures move silently through the trees. They were still a way off in front of us, but I could already tell that they had fanned out and seemed to be searching for something.

"I have eyes on all four of them. They seem fairly evenly spaced, almost like they are searching," I told Caleb and Wyatt quietly.

Vampires had far better hearing than I did and I had no doubt that we didn't want to draw their attention just yet.

As we reached the treeline, two things happened at once. I noticed that the four heat sources I knew to be vampires seem to be closing in on another, which was huddled close to the ground, just as the wind changed direction and started to blow towards us.

"Lyra." Wyatt breathed out, before changing into his wolf and taking off in the direction of the four searching vampires ahead of us.

Chapter 10

Lyra

The snap of a branch somewhere near me hurled me out of sleep and immediately into consciousness. My eyes flew open, but my vision was obscured by the den that I'd attempted to build around me. It didn't take me long to realise what was happening, though as that familiar, dark chuckle filled the air. They'd found me. He'd found me. Worrying about going back there didn't matter anymore. He would never take me back. All I had left to worry about was just how much pain I'd be in before he granted me the release of death.

A quiet whimper escaped me, even though I tried to hold it back. I didn't want him to know how scared I was.

"Little bird, little bird, you should never have stopped running," he growled from behind me.

That's when it hit me. Fuck him. I may be about to die here, but I'm not going out alone. If I had to finally accept that I'd lost my mate, if everything was going to end here in this fucked up dead place, then I'm not going out quietly. I knew it was inevitable that he would win, but I'd make him hurt before the end. Because I refused to be a weak, cowering animal anymore. I am an angel. I was trained by the best. I took the top spot in my class and I did it through blood and pain. I may have given up my wings, I may have lost my magic, but I refused to be weak anymore. I was awarded the title of Stormchild. I am Lyra fucking Stormchild! I may not have been filled with the same magic anymore, but I was still going to bring down the storm.

My hand slipped out from under me and into the side of the den I'd built. I remembered stacking it in here and a small smirk graced my lips as my fingers wrapped around the end of the thick dead branch that was hidden there. It wasn't a sword, but it would do enough damage.

"Pull her out," I heard Edwin growl.

A vampire stepped in front of me and I saw Edwin standing behind him. He's growling in delight, I could almost see the hate and lust war in his eyes. He knew he was finally going to get what he'd been denied all of this time.

The vampire, whose name I had no idea of, grabbed me around the throat and pulled me up. I let myself go limp, I needed them to think that I'd given up. To continue to believe that I'd lost any will to fight. As he pulled me up towards him, I grasped onto the thick branch as tightly as I could. I couldn't afford to lose it now. In my fake submission, I let my arm fall behind my back to mask the branch as it pulled free from the side of my den and held it tightly behind my back. I knew we weren't alone. I'm not stupid enough to think that Edwin would only bring one vampire with him. I knew that I wouldn't have any time to wait for the right opportunity. The others who were undoubtedly here would be able to see my makeshift weapon that I'm holding behind my back and I needed to move before I lost my element of surprise.

As the unknown vampire pulled me closer to his body, I pulled up the branch at the last second and drove it into his chest. He gurgled in surprise, his eyes opening wide and his mouth dropping open. I had been trained to fight since I was old enough to stand and I knew that the branch was now lodged in his heart. Even if he wasn't a vampire, it's a kill shot. Newsflash, if you stab anyone in the heart, they're going to die!

Edwin frowned at the noise and when his eyes locked with mine, I'm not even sure if he's realised what's happened. As I smiled at him, I must look deranged. Maybe I am. Maybe I hadn't finally got my fight back; maybe I just finally broke.

Edwin dove for me and I knew that I needed to act quickly. He could move faster than me and is much stronger. I may have decided to fight, but I'm still weak and a shadow of my former self. I wouldn't have time to pull out my makeshift weapon from the now dead vampire, let alone swing it hard enough to do any damage to him, so I did the only thing that I could. I let him tackle me, intending to bring me to the ground.

Time seemed to almost crawl to a stop as everything happened in slow motion. His fingers dug painfully into my shoulders and I could feel his claws sinking deep into my skin. His fangs have descended and he roared in my face, spittle flying at me as he pushed me down to the ground. I felt the branch snap in my hand as I'm ripped from the dead vampire and all I can do is grin. A moment of confusion seems to flicker in Edwin's eyes, but we are already falling and he's committed to the move until he at least comes into contact with the ground. For a split second, I knew that I had the upper hand and I used it to my advantage as I ripped one of his hands free, bring up the broken branch shard and drive it into his left eye. Unfortunately, it's not long enough to kill him, but his enraged roar soon turned into a shrill scream of pain as we hit the ground and he pushed me away from him as his hands came up to try and protect his now ruined face.

I heard enraged growls behind me and I expected the rest

of the vampires to tackle me as I tried to shuffle away and put more ground between me and Edwin. I needed to find another weapon before they reached me. What I didn't expect to see however, was two vampires flying across the clearing in front of me, both with wolves tearing at their throats.

Arms came around me from behind and I prepared to fight, but all of the fight drained out of me as someone whispered in my ear. "We need to run, I've got you."

I'm scooped up off the ground by a strong pair of arms and we're moving fast through the trees before I even realise what is happening. I knew that I should be looking at whoever is running with me in their arms, but I can't tear my eyes away from the two wolves battling the two vampires behind us. One of them with a beautiful brown and gold coat. He came for me. Wyatt is here.

My vision started to fade and I felt the exhaustion push past the adrenaline surge of the fight. I tried to fight it, but I couldn't. My body is still trying to heal and I couldn't hold onto consciousness any longer. As the darkness wrapped around me, I willingly let it take me this time, because I knew I was finally safe.

CHAPTER 11

DOMINIC

I didn't even bother to check that the old falling down house was empty before I stormed inside. Caleb checked it out earlier and I'm just hoping that it had stayed empty since then. I couldn't think straight. I couldn't think past the beautiful angel that I was holding in my arms, clutched to my chest, like the most precious cargo that she was.

She was truly the most beautiful thing that I had ever seen and I couldn't stop staring at her now that we'd stopped in relative safety. I had worried that because I was a mage, I wouldn't be able to feel the mate bond like the others. I'll even admit that I was jealous that they would get to have such a strong connection with her and mine would just be a shadow of their own. But now that she was here, now that she was in my arms, I knew that what I was feeling was the mate bond. It was all-consuming and instantaneous. I was made for her and she was made for me. Holding her close gave me a sense of peace that I didn't ever think would be possible for me.

Dragging my eyes away from her, I took stock of our surroundings. We seemed to be in what was once a kitchen. The house was filthy and Caleb was right, it looked like something came in here and tore the place apart. Whatever happened, whoever lived here before never returned after that. Nothing had been set right or cleaned. Everything lay haphazardly in its resting place after whatever took place here.

I needed to get Lyra somewhere I could check her over for injuries. She's clearly weak. She passed out nearly as soon as she was in my arms and it looked like she had collapsed before being found.

Wyatt and Caleb were nowhere to be seen. Hopefully, they would realise this was where I would have taken Lyra. It's the only place that we knew around here after all. They were both fighting vampires when I left them and the one Lyra had fought was still alive as well. It was nothing short of extraordinary seeing her take down that vampire with nothing but a tree branch. When the other one dived for her, I didn't think we would make it to her in time. But then she plunged that shard into his eye with the scream of the avenging angel that she is.

Wandering further into the house, I found a small living room attached to the kitchen, but the old sofa in there is torn to shreds and was more metal than anything else. Heading up the stairs instead, I'm hoping to find somewhere liveable up there.

The upstairs didn't seem to have seen the same level of damage as the rest of the house. One of the bedrooms was trashed, but the final bedroom had only been tossed about a bit. None of the furniture is destroyed, just upturned. I managed to slide the mattress over a bit so that it was lying flat on the floor and settled Lyra on top of it. Now that I'm standing here staring down at her, I'm not entirely certain about what I should do. I needed to check her over for injuries, but I felt uneasy about removing her clothing while she is unconscious. She may be my mate, but she didn't know me yet.

Lyra was lying completely still and I stood and watched her chest move gently up and down. Deciding against removing her clothes, I moved my hands gently over her body. I figured that if she had any open wounds, I should be able to find the blood, save for that, it would be better to let her sleep before checking her over. She's clearly exhausted and half-starved, probably dehydrated too, but I couldn't do anything about that until she woke up.

I made her as comfortable as I could before heading back down the stairs. A crashing noise came from the kitchen and I pulled the knife I had sheathed at my back into my hand. It was extremely possible that we could have been followed here. I just ran, I didn't take the time to cover my tracks. I just needed to get Lyra away from danger. It was stupid, fucking stupid.

Creeping down the last few steps, I heard footsteps approached from the kitchen. Taking a deep breath, I bent my legs slightly and braced ready for whoever is here to turn the corner. I could tell by the noise that it was only one person. I'd taken down demons, I could take one vampire.

"Calm down, Dom, it's only me," I heard Caleb mutter before he rounded the corner to face the stairs.

Fucking wolves and their noses, he could have said something sooner.

With a sigh of relief, I lowered my knife and sagged against the wall beside me.

"Where's Wyatt?" I knew he wasn't here because I only heard one person moving around.

"He's doubling back to grab the packs and then cover our tracks. We took down the two vampires we intercepted, but the injured one got away during the fighting," he flinched as he admitted it. I knew he was going to be beating himself up about it. "They're fucking tough bastards, Dom, they move so fast that they're gone before you even have time to make a move."

My eyes ran over him, checking for injuries. He's got a deep gash that ran from the bottom of his neck, across his shoulders. It must have been pretty bad if it still looked like that, even after he shifted. I fastened my knife back into its sheath because I needed to do something with my hands before I did something stupid like reached out for him. In all the years that we'd known each other, I'd never said anything to him about how I felt. Fuck, I'm not even sure how I felt about him. There had been times when I'd thought I saw some sort of interest in his eyes, but I'd always written it off as an overactive imagination. I didn't even know if I wanted him to have those kinds of feelings for me. I'm such a mess when it came to Caleb. He makes me feel like a confused teenager again and a part of me hated him for that. If there is one thing that I needed in my life, it's to have control over the things around me. But Caleb is like this wild force of nature that burst into my life and made me question everything that I knew to be true about myself.

"I found a relatively undamaged room upstairs that I've put Lyra in, but I could do with some help to put it back together," I told him, desperately needing something else to focus my thoughts on.

Caleb's brow dipped for a second in a frown before he straightened out his face and looked up the stairs. It happened so quickly that I'm starting to doubt that I even saw it in the first place.

It started to grow awkward between us. I'm suddenly not sure what to say. I wanted to reach out for him, check his injuries, make sure that he's okay, but I didn't know if he would welcome it. We ended up just standing there, looking at each other, both of us lost to our own confusion.

Caleb suddenly cleared his throat and took a step closer to

me. "Let's head up and see what we can do. When Wyatt gets here, we can assess what supplies we have and what we might need. Do you think that she is well enough to travel?" he asked and I'm grateful that he's turned the attention back to our mate.

I just shrugged because at this stage, we didn't have any way to know until she woke up. Turning quickly, I headed up the stairs with Caleb trailing after me.

"I couldn't get the bed back together with her in my arms," I explained quietly as we stepped into the room.

I'm suddenly feeling guilty over just leaving her on the mattress on the floor. She should be on the softest bed with silk sheets and her mates at her side, catering to her every whim. She shouldn't have to suffer through laying on a dusty mattress on the floor of this dilapidated old house.

Caleb and I got to work, straightening the furniture as best as we can while working around Lyra, who had yet to move even a fraction of an inch. If I couldn't see her chest rising and falling, I would think she was dead and even though I knew she wasn't, my whole body hurt just from the thought of it. Once we had the old armoire and dresser righted, we've got enough room to get the bed back into position. It must have been a nice place before whatever the fuck happened here. I wondered if the people who lived here were still alive. For some reason, I hoped they were out there somewhere.

We both grabbed hold of the mattress with Lyra still lying on it and carefully lifted it onto the bed. She did look slightly more comfortable where she was. I'm just glad there was at least somewhere in this house that was intact enough for us to make her comfortable.

"I'm going to see if the water is still working," Caleb muttered before leaving the room. He gave Lyra one last longing look before he walked away.

Sitting down on the edge of the bed, I watched her sleep.

It's a bit creepy, but I just couldn't stop myself. I could hear Caleb moving around in the bathroom. I hadn't checked in there yet, but if we have a functioning bathroom, we might be able to hold out here for a day or two while we get Lyra back on her feet. Even if we didn't have a functioning bathroom, we might have to just make do. She didn't look like she was in any condition to move anytime soon.

I gently took off Lyra's boots and started to slip her out of the jacket that she's wearing. I'm at least going to try and make her a bit comfortable. There was an old blanket in the armoire that I laid over her before I started to leave the room. Pausing in the doorway, I took one last look back. It almost felt like it was too easy. How did she come to be out in the trees anyway?

The sound of voices talking downstairs drifted up to me and I headed down to see if Wyatt had any news on the vampire that got away. That's one loose end that we couldn't afford to have right now. Staying on the Moon Side left the vampires at a distinct advantage. We needed to move Lyra out of here as soon as we can.

When I stepped into the room, they both turn towards me, falling silent.

"Did you have any problems?" I asked Wyatt, taking a seat on the rickety stool at the counter where they were sat.

"No. I retrieved our packs and one which looks to have been Lyra's. The missing vamp is nowhere to be seen, but it looked like he took a bad blow. I don't think he will be back any time soon. I've covered over our tracks though, just in case," Wyatt filled me in. You could tell that he had been a beta because of the way he reported off all of the necessary information as succinctly as possible.

"We're going to need to stay here for a day or two until we can move Lyra, where do we stand on provisions?" I asked them.

"We have enough food to last us for probably seven days

and the water pump is still functioning here, so we don't have to worry about that," Caleb filled me in.

"Okay." My brow scrunched up as I tried to think through our next few steps. "I have gently checked Lyra over and I can't see any blood on her. I didn't want to take off her clothes, so I'm not entirely sure if she's injured. She is definitely malnourished and dehydrated. We're going to need to get some fluids into her as soon as possible. Is there any way that we can make some sort of broth or soup for her? I don't think she's going to be able to eat much to start with, but she's going to need to get her energy up if we have any chance of moving her out of here."

"If we go through the MRE's that we have, I'm sure we will be able to put something together. It might not be too appetising though," Caleb said, scrunching his nose up in distaste.

"I checked through her pack and she had some food in there. She might not need it," Wyatt said, looking down at the bag in question.

"How the hell did she get out of there and with a pack of provisions?" I blurted out. It's a question that's been riding the back of my brain since I first laid eyes on her.

There's also a very small terrible part of myself that's, sort of, all kind of fucked up, disappointed. We were supposed to be the ones that rescued her and she went and rescued herself. Not that I'm not proud of her for getting out of there. There's just this, apparently terrible, part of myself that wanted to be able to ride in and rescue my mate. God, I'm such an ass.

Caleb and Wyatt just shrugged. Of course, they have no way of knowing.

We fell into silence for a while, each of us lost in our thoughts.

"Don't you want to go up and see her?" Caleb asked Wyatt quietly.

Wyatt immediately stiffened and I can see his face shutting down. "I'm going to go out and patrol, make sure that they didn't follow us back here. I'll be back in a couple of hours," Wyatt simply told us before he stalked out of the door, shifted and then disappeared.

"That went well." Is apparently the only thing that I could think of saying and I cringed as it slipped out of my mouth unbidden.

"I think we both knew that he was going to find this hard," Caleb said softly, still watching the empty doorway that Wyatt disappeared through.

"Give him time. He's still blaming himself for this."

"She's going to need him when she wakes up," Caleb said sadly.

"She'll have us. And when he's ready, she will have him too."

Caleb just nodded and even though I knew it wasn't going to be that simple, I'm praying that it would be. Wyatt needed to pull his head out of his ass because this was about more than just him. If he hurt Lyra by pushing her away through some sense of his own guilt, I was going to kick his ass.

CHAPTER 12

LYRA

I couldn't help the groan that escaped from my mouth as I slowly clawed my way to consciousness. The first thing that I noticed is that I'm lying on something soft. As sad as it sounds, the sensation almost breaks my brain. I hadn't laid on anything that wasn't a hard floor for years. It's also confusing as hell. My head feels foggy as I try to piece together my memories of what happened. I remembered running and the exhaustion. The overwhelming exhaustion.

Edwin! He came for me. I knew that the bastard would.

A sick sense of satisfaction flooded me as I remembered the shriek he gave as I plunged the broken branch shard into his eye.

It all gets a bit fuzzy after that. I thought I saw Wyatt. Wyatt was here! My eyes snapped open as the memory of the two wolves flooded the front of my mind. Is he here? Was I imagining things? Please don't let me have imagined him. I don't know if I would survive the disappointment.

Looking around, I realised that I'm in a bedroom and the soft surface that I'm lying on is an actual bed. My hands ran across the surface of the slightly grimy mattress that I'm lying on. Before all of this happened I probably would have turned my nose up at lying here, but now, I savoured the luxury that this bed is to me. The room has clearly seen better days. The deep gouges in some of the walls indicated that something terrible once happened here, but judging from the dust lying on every surface, whatever it was, happened a long time ago.

What is this place? I'm almost certain that it isn't the clan house. Even though I only ever saw the cage and the hall where the harvest ceremonies were held, I don't think that Cassius would have a room like this in the clan house. He prefers perfection. Anyway, if I was taken back there, I would definitely be in a cage by now.

I tried to sit up and my head swum in distress. I felt like my tongue was too big for my mouth and I could feel my lips were cracked and dry when I grimaced at the pain in my head. I knew that I was suffering from the effects of dehydration, but I still stared at the water bottle on the table next to me with suspicion. It wasn't one from my pack, so whoever brought me here had left it for me.

The sensible part of my brain knew that I needed to drink it, but I couldn't help but be suspicious if anything had been added to it.

I looked down at myself. I'm still wearing the same clothes that I had on apart from my coat and boots, which are next to the side of the bed. My body hurt, but I knew that I hadn't been injured any further and nothing had been done to me. All evidence suggested that whoever brought me here had tried to take care of me and made me as comfortable as possible.

The fact that I'm alone in this room made me believe that I must have imagined Wyatt. Surely, if he was here, he wouldn't have left me alone. My heart broke at the realisation that I'd lost him again. I knew I was being stupid and he wasn't even here in the first place, but it still felt like a loss none the less.

I gingerly picked up the water bottle and took a deep drink. My body couldn't sustain this amount of dehydration for much longer and even if the water was laced, I really had very little choice but to drink it.

Draining the bottle, I'm just considering my next move when I heard movement outside of the door. My body tensed, ready to fight, but then when a voice spoke to me, nothing but confusion swarmed me.

"Lyra, is it okay if I come in?"

I didn't recognise the voice, but it's definitely male and definitely not Wyatt. That cements it in my mind that he wasn't here. That he was just a figment of my imagination and sorrow swarms over me.

"Okay," I whispered back sadly.

Even though my voice is barely louder than a whisper, whoever is on the other side had clearly heard me anyway and the door slowly opened, revealing a man standing on the other side. He quietly slipped into the room and closed the door behind him.

I took my time to look over him and he stood patiently, letting me do it. He didn't move and stays stood relaxed, no doubt trying to show me that he wasn't a threat. I ran my eyes across his face. He's attractive. His dark hair is cropped short and he has a beard of stubble across his jaw. He's tall and I could see from the strain of his T-shirt that he's well built. Even with that though, he isn't intimidating. He had a soft smile on his face and his blue eyes seemed to sparkle with amusement. He shoved his hands in his pockets and leant back against the door, allowing me all the time I needed for my perusal of him.

He's an attractive man, but there was something about him that I couldn't quite put my finger on.

"Are you a wolf shifter?" I asked him.

Maybe he was the wolf that I mistook as Wyatt in the trees earlier. But even as I think that I know that it's wrong. I would have bet my freedom on the fact that Wyatt had been there.

"Yes," he said softly.

Almost like my words had given him permission, he pushed off from the door and moved to sit on the end of the bed.

"Do I know you?" I asked him.

"In a way," he smiled at me.

His evasiveness is not at all charming and I think that the annoyance on my face just made him smile wider.

Sexy wolf with his sexy smirk, where the hell did he get off having those dimples?

"You must be hungry. I'll get you something to eat. I just heard you moving around and I wanted to see if there was anything else that I can get you."

"Some answers would be nice."

"I promise you will get them. Let me get you something to eat and then we can talk while you eat. This is going to sound strange, but I just need you to eat something first, okay. My wolf is ... let's say unhappy that you look so hungry," he grinned before getting to his feet and striding out of the room.

Well, that was confusing.

I sat on the bed, waiting for him to return. The idea of something to eat wasn't a terrible one and, as usual, I am actually hungry. Part of me wanted to find a bathroom just so that I had something to do, but I'm so dehydrated that needing the bathroom is one thing that I didn't need to worry about right now. I am absolutely filthy though, and I wondered if there was a shower here. I hadn't had the luxury of cleaning myself for years, apart from being hosed down in my cage. Even just standing in the rain would be amazing at this point.

It didn't take long for the man to come back and I realised

that I didn't know his name. Somehow though, he knew mine. I heard him rushing up the stairs, but as soon as he reached the door to my room, he slowed down and slowly approached me with a bowl and another bottle of water.

"We weren't sure what you would be able to eat, so we made a stew. We figured that you could just pick out whatever you want. I've put a couple of the slices of bread that you had with you in there as well," he said almost awkwardly as he passed the bowl across to me.

I stared at the bowl of stew in my hands and didn't know what to do. This was the first proper meal I'd had in years. I almost didn't want to eat it because then it would be gone. Tears sprung to my eyes and I just sat and stared at the bowl as they started to roll down my cheeks.

"I ... erm ... can get you something else if you don't like it," he said, reaching out to take the bowl away from me.

"No!" I said, perhaps a little too forcefully as I cradled the bowl against my chest. "I mean, no, I'm sorry. It's just, I haven't had anything like this for a long time," I muttered, embarrassed at getting overwhelmed by a simple bowl of food.

The man reached past me and pulled a pillow from the top of the bed and placed it in my lap before encouraging me to put the bowl on top of it. It's a thoughtful gesture, to try and protect me from burning myself.

I'm still looking into the bowl like an idiot, trying to memorise the thick gravy with the meat and vegetables and the two thick slices of bread that had been propped against the side of the bowl.

"Just go slow," he said, trying to urge me on. "There's more downstairs if you want it."

I picked up one of the slices of bread and brought it to my mouth. The end sitting in the bowl had soaked up the gravy and flavours burst in my mouth as I bit into it. I couldn't help the groan of delight that accompanied a couple more tears as they slide down my cheeks. It's the best thing I think I had ever tasted in my life.

Almost like that first bite broke the dam of hunger inside me, I practically inhaled the first piece of bread, dunking it back into the gravy as I ate. I must look like a wild animal as I hunch over the bowl, but there was not one single piece of me that cared. As I reached for the second piece of bread, the man took hold of my hand to stop me. I squinted at him in annoyance for getting between me and my food.

"You've got the look of a ravenous wolf about you," he laughed. "Don't worry, I'm not going to take it away from you. Just give your stomach a minute to adjust before you have any more, otherwise you're going to make yourself sick. I'm assuming that you haven't had much to eat for a while if you think that crap is as delicious as you're making it out to be." He passed the bottle of water to me instead and I scowled at him in annoyance for insulting the delicious bowl of heaven that laid in my lap.

Unfortunately, he did have a point and I could feel my stomach starting to cramp painfully already. Even though I didn't want to admit to him that he was right, I took the bottle of water and slowly sipped at its contents.

"You promised me some answers," I reminded him.

"Sure, ask anything you want," he smiled, breaking out the dimples again. Fucking dimples, who invented them? Clearly, they were only made as some kind of way to break women's minds.

"What's your name?" I asked, deciding to start with the easy questions.

"Oh, sorry, I should have told you that first," he blushed in embarrassment and I decided, that coupled with his ability to break out those dimples whenever he wanted, had the potential to make him very dangerous to my sanity. "I'm Caleb."

"You were one of the wolves in the trees that fought the

vampires attacking me?" I don't want to admit that he saved me, even though we both know that he did.

"Yeah, my friend Dom was the one who picked you up and brought you back here," he confirmed. I noticed that he didn't mention the other wolf. I didn't know whether to ask him if it was Wyatt or not. Everything about this man said that he was friendly and my mind and body were both telling me that I could trust him. Just that fact was making me suspicious, though. He was a stranger to me and even though he was an attractive stranger who I had no doubt was extremely charming, I didn't understand why I felt so connected to him. Wyatt was my mate. This felt like it had to be some kind of trick.

"Where is he?" I asked slowly.

"He's downstairs. We didn't want to overwhelm you with too many people when you first woke up."

I nodded, grateful for the thoughtfulness. I desperately wanted to ask about Wyatt, but I still felt a bit like I'm cornered.

"How did you come to be in those trees?" I asked.

"We were looking for you," he smiled.

Even though it's nothing but a friendly smile, I immediately bristle. Had I just inadvertently wandered into another captivity situation? Granted, this cage is much better than the last one, but a cage is a cage, no matter if they put a bed in it for you.

He must see the look of shock on my face and realised how what he said sounded because he immediately drew back a little and held his hands up in surrender.

"Not like that!" he blurted out. "We were coming to save you, Lyra."

This is just even more confusing than before. But the realisation of what he could potentially be saying, who the 'we' in his sentence could be and I felt like I wanted to kick my hope in the ass just in case I'm wrong.

"Wyatt," I whispered, almost as if I'm frightened, saying his name will break the illusion of the dream.

"He's just running a patrol outside. He's been paranoid about us being followed ever since we found you," Caleb explained, but I could see in his eyes that he wasn't happy that Wyatt wasn't here right now. "We didn't know when you were going to wake up. You've been asleep for nearly twenty hours," he said, making the excuse softly.

I didn't know how I was supposed to feel right now. Judging by the awkward shuffle Caleb has going on, I'm guessing that he thought I should be upset. I just couldn't bring myself to be upset. Because he's here. Because he came. I could finally see him again.

Caleb cocked his head to the side as he took in the slow smile that spread across my face.

"You're not angry?" he asked, confused.

"About what?"

"That he wasn't here when you woke up?"

I just shrugged. I understood what he was trying to say, but I'm genuinely not upset, yet I'm not entirely sure why. I felt like I should be, but sitting here and talking to Caleb just kind of felt right.

"I'm looking forward to seeing him," I tried to explain and then scrunched up my face as I tried to think of the words to explain how I felt. "But I like talking to you. That probably doesn't make sense," I added quietly more to myself than him.

Caleb smiled and hit me with those dimples again. "You have no idea how happy that makes me," he said, gently pushing some of my hair away from my face. "Eat," he ordered, nudging the bowl in my lap.

I happily picked up the second slice of bread and ate it at a bit of a less disgusting pace. Keeping my eye on Caleb as I did. He just continued to smile at me while he lounged across the bottom of the bed. I couldn't work him out and that just annoyed me.

"Why would you say that this is crap? It tastes incredible," I said with my mouth full of the stew, which I'm now spooning into my mouth.

It honestly was good, the gravy was so thick and the meat was just melting in my mouth.

"It's just that dried stuff that you add water to. It's the emergency provisions that we brought with us in case we couldn't find anything to hunt around here, which we can't. If you think that is good, I can't wait until you try out Dom's cooking when we get home. Now that stuff is incredible," he looked off into the distance, licking his lips like he's dreaming about food and I snorted out a laugh at his antics.

"Well, it's better than stale bread and dried fruit," I shrugged, scraping my spoon around the bowl to get the last of the stew out the bottom. I wished I had saved some of the bread so that I could have wiped it around the bowl. I'm tempted to lick it clean, but I didn't want to make too big of a fool of myself just yet.

"I can't believe that you've survived this long," he said, sounding astonished.

I supposed it was pretty unbelievable.

I just shrugged again. "I'm an angel."

It's the explanation that we always got to any question when I was in the education centres. I started to think that it was the go-to response instead of 'I don't know'. Any question posed about our nature was always answered with 'because you're an angel'. It just fed into the superiority complex that a lot of angels suffered from. I always thought that it was just an excuse to not give us any real information. Maybe that's one of the reasons why I fell rather than staying in my flight.

"Do you want some more?" Caleb asked me as he watched me stare sadly into my now empty bowl.

My gut response is yes, but I'm painfully aware of my stomach rebelling against the full sensation that I'm so unfamiliar with.

"Maybe later?" I'm not sure why I posed it as a question, but Caleb just smiled and nodded, taking my bowl from me.

"There's a shower in the bathroom if you want to try and clean up a bit. We don't seem to have any power, so unfortunately, it only runs cold water," he almost looked embarrassed as he suggested it.

"I'd love to," I said, jumping to my feet and then taking a minute to try and work through the sensation of my head swimming and hoping that I didn't just fall over.

"It's the room across the hall," he said, pointing to a door in front of him. "Take as long as you want. There's some towels and clothes in there that you can use. They're not the freshest, but it's the best we can do at the moment."

He almost looked like he wanted to say something else and I could see emotions flicker across his face before he seemed to think better of it and turned, leaving me alone upstairs.

I almost dove out of the room and into the small bathroom across the way. The sink had a large chunk taken out of it, but it looked like it would still hold some water. The toilet is in one piece, but it's missing a seat. But the thing that draws my eye, that makes me want to drop to my knees in praise, is the shower in front of me with the cracked screen, which makes the door hang slightly off centre. It's the crappiest, dirtiest and if Caleb is right, probably the coldest shower I'd ever experience. But it's the most beautiful thing I thought I had ever seen.

CHAPTER 13

CALEB

I couldn't help the smile on my face as I walked into the kitchen. Dom is stood glaring out of the window like he had been doing for most of the time that we had been here and Wyatt is nowhere to be seen. I had no idea what was going on with him. No, actually that's a lie, I did. He's beating himself up and I was about ten seconds away from kicking his ass. Lyra seemed to take it well that he wasn't there when she woke up, but I didn't know how she would take it if he continued to avoid her, which was definitely what he's currently doing.

Lyra. Fucking hell, how was she so amazing after everything that she went through?

"How's she doing?" Dom asked me.

Sometimes he freaked me out doing that, asking a question about what I'm thinking about. I couldn't decide if he's really intuitive or if he could actually read my thoughts. Some days it's freaky as all hell. Especially because there are a lot of thoughts that I really didn't want him to know about it. Just thinking that had me blushing like a virgin and I quickly answered him, you know, just in case he could actually get into my head.

"Surprisingly well. Although I'm worried about her judgment, she thought the stew was incredible," I laughed.

Dom smiled. It's nice to see him smile. With everything that we'd all been through, he'd been so distant recently. I felt like I hadn't seen this side of him for a long time.

"I think she should be well enough to move on from here in the next day or two. She's just getting cleaned up. You should go up and say hi," I suggested.

I was worried about how he's going to react to the mate bond and that he wouldn't feel it the same way that we do. I'd never heard of a mage in a mate bond—they kind of pride themselves on being above all of that.

Dom looked up the stairs and I could see the indecision on his face. I wasn't going to let him back out of this, though. Not only would it kill him, but I didn't think I could take losing him either.

"I'll just wait until she gets out of the shower," he said, sitting down on one of the old stools instead.

I'm not going to let him chicken out of this, but he does have a point.

"Wyatt still not back?" Obviously, he isn't because he isn't here, but I just felt like I needed to say something to fill the silence.

"I'm worried he's going to push her away because he doesn't think he deserves her. I don't think Lyra will be able to survive if he does. He is likely the only thing that has kept her going all this time," Dom said, voicing my exact same worries.

I nodded in thought. "Then we don't let him. She's strong, though. I think she could survive anything, she's pretty amazing. But he's only going to hurt her if he does that and I won't sit by and let him."

My wolf growled in agreement in the back of my mind. He had fully accepted that Lyra is our mate, even if she didn't realise it yet. Which I didn't think that she did. It's easy to forget how easy shifters have it when it came to mate bonds though. We had our animals pushing us to a mate, the bonds are impossible for us to miss. But I had heard that some species can find it hard to understand what they are feeling. Especially those who didn't usually have mate bonds or whose cultures didn't embrace them because if there is one thing that we had learnt from Aria being around, I'm pretty sure that it's that all species had mate bonds out there. We'd just been looking for them in the wrong places.

My eyes found Dom who was still sitting on the old stool, looking through the meal ration packs that we picked up. Part of me wanted to be there when he met her the first time. The part that wanted to watch his reaction to his first proper inter-action with her. Running here with her unconscious body in his arms didn't count. But I knew that he wouldn't want that.

I missed the old Dom. The happy Dom that was more concerned about sharing knowledge with those around him rather than hoarding it as the Mage Council preferred. The one who fought to open the academy doors to anyone that needed them. Who wanted it to become a safe place for younger generations to mix and different species to form connections. Then we found out about the threat that was coming for us. It was like a switch flipped in him overnight. He lost that wonder he had whenever he talked about some-thing that fascinated him, whenever he was making plans to make the world a better place. He became serious, hard. It was like he pushed a part of himself aside so that he could do what needed to be done. I wasn't worried about how long it would take him to get that part back. I was worried that it was gone forever. I think we all lost a piece of ourselves the morning that the demons attacked the academy. We lost so many, so many of those we were responsible for. Then we lost even more when the pack was attacked and more lives still were lost at the final battle. I understood why Aria was finding it hard to be around people. Because I felt exactly the same way. It didn't feel like we had won. It felt like a series of defeats and all we had managed to do was survive.

Dom found what he was looking for, pulled out a packet and walked over to the stove. We had managed to get it working because it was one of the wood-fired ones. If there was one thing that there was an abundance of around here, it was deadwood. We were trying to keep its use to a minimum though because we didn't want to draw too much attention to ourselves. Dom quickly got to work heating some water and then making whatever he had obviously decided to take up to Lyra.

I caught the smile on his face while he finished off his offering for her. Maybe I hadn't lost him just yet.

Looking down into the bowl as he passed, I saw what looked like stewed apples and custard. Fucker. I wish I'd have thought of that.

CHAPTER 14

LYRA

The shower hadn't been as bad as I had thought it would be. I'd expected the water to be freezing cold, but it was more lukewarm. It was the first shower that I had, for I don't even know how long. I should probably ask Wyatt how long it's been.

I dried off on the towel that had been left out for me and got dressed in the clothes. They were clearly women's clothes and I couldn't help but wonder who they belonged to. I had been gone a long time and the spiteful voice in the back of my head told me that Wyatt had probably moved on. But he was my mate, so was that even a possibility? Angels were not supposed to have mate bonds, or at least that is what they taught us in the education centres, maybe he hadn't been my mate? What if it had all been a mistake?

My heart was laid heavy with self-doubt as I shuffled quietly back into the bedroom and crawled back into the bed. I pulled the blanket over my head, blocking out the light and hopefully blocking out reality again. I tried to pull back the Lyra I had been. The warrior. The one that I had managed to seize hold of when it came time to fight for my life. But rather than cowering in the back of my mind as I had always assumed she was, it was almost like she flipped me off and then laughed in my face. She was there, she just didn't want me anymore.

It was probably a strange way to describe yourself, but it was the best I could do. I felt fractured. I felt like there was something broken inside of me that had forced all of the pieces inside of me apart and I no longer had any idea of the way they went back together. The exhaustion from the past few years laid heavily against me and I felt like I was staring up at the sky from the bottom of a pit.

A gentle knock came against the doorframe of the bedroom door that I had left open in my haste to dive under the covers. I peered out from the top of the covers, annoyance at my disgusting childish behaviour wracked me, but part of me just didn't care enough to stop it.

I was getting emotional whiplash from myself and I had no idea what was going on with me. Something had changed, something integral inside of me had changed since I had woken up and found that part of me that wanted to fight.

A different man stood in the doorway, holding another bowl. I couldn't help the soft smile that flickered to life on my lips as I took him in. It seemed that these men bringing me food was going to become a thing. I couldn't blame their need to feed me. There hadn't been a mirror in that bathroom, but I had felt the changes in my body while I washed the grime from my skin. I had lost a lot of weight and a lot of that was hard fought for muscle tone.

I couldn't look away from his deep brown eyes. They almost seemed bottomless. When you looked into the eyes of some people, it was almost like you could see into the very bottom of their soul. This man though, he was unfathomable and something about that made me want to look even closer. I could see how easy it would be to get lost within his gaze and there was something about that which sounded so very appealing.

He smiled back at me and approached the bed, offering me the bowl which he held in his hand. The sweet smell of sugar and apples hit me and I wasn't even reluctant to withdraw from my blanket den. I wasn't sure what the yellowy sludge was in the bowl, but it smelt fantastic and for some reason, I knew that I could trust this man.

I lifted the spoon bringing it to my mouth and was just about to cautiously take a bite when he warned me, "Be careful, it might be hot."

I blew gently on the spoon and his eyes immediately locked with my lips. It was almost like I could feel his gaze brush against me. I wasn't sure why I felt this way. It almost felt like I was betraying Wyatt, but then it also felt right to me. Like his hands were made to be on my body. Even though I had never felt them. It was confusing. It also reminded me of how I felt about Wyatt, which just confused me even more.

"You brought me here?" I guessed, desperately trying to change the subject of my train of thoughts and also break the silence.

"Yes. It was the only place I knew of around here where I thought that we would be safe until Caleb and Wyatt could catch up with us," he confirmed. "I'm Dom, by the way."

"Lyra," I told him.

"I know." He smiled and it lit up his face.

In hindsight, it was a fairly stupid thing to say. Of course, he knew my name. He had travelled here with my mate to free me. I was actually kind of proud that I had already got out of the clan house without needing their help. Even if I did need the help of Damon to do it. I wonder what he was doing now. If they knew that he had been the one to help me.

I looked over the man in front of me. He had long brown hair swept back away from his face and stopped just short of his shoulders. He was wearing a black t-shirt and black trousers with heavy-looking boots. I could see his muscles straining against the shirt and part of me was very excited about the prospect of him walking out of the room. With muscles like that, I knew his ass was going to be dreamy and I had absolutely no doubt that I would be staring at it when he left.

I took a bite of the yellowy sludge from the spoon when I realised that I was just holding it in the air in front of my face still. What was with these men being so distracting? Also, why wasn't Wyatt back yet? I was just about to ask that question when the food hit my tongue and the sweet taste of apples and vanilla exploded in my mouth.

I groaned in delight, which seemed to make Dom sit up straighter and a flash of something crossed his eyes. What a strange and exciting side effect! I kind of wanted to do it again.

"What is this?" I asked, staring into the bowl. There wasn't a lot in there. I supposed I should be polite and offer to share with him, but I really, really didn't want to.

"It's just custard and apples," he laughed. "Caleb did mention that you were a fan of that awful stew. I can't wait to get you home and get some real food in you," he smiled.

Okay, so I may be a bit confused and inexperienced in the life of normal people, but he wanted to get me home? Is that something that normal people say to each other? It kind of felt like it had some kind of meaning to it. I was burning to ask what he meant, but I was also embarrassed to point out my naivety.

"Can I ask you a question?" I asked.

He nodded politely at me and gave me an encouraging smile.

"How long was it?" I asked.

The mood in the room immediately changed, but I needed to know. I mean, I didn't even know how old I was!

"One year at the packhouse and then eight years with the vampires," he said seriously.

I much preferred it when he was smiling. He looked almost sad now. I suppose it was pity. Nine years. That meant I was twenty-five years old now. That was a lot longer than I had thought it was.

"Wyatt ..." I started, but then I stopped.

I didn't even know what I was trying to ask. Was he okay? How had he survived this long? Had he changed? Dom probably wouldn't be able to answer any of those questions.

He gave me an understanding look. It was almost like he could follow my train of thoughts.

"He hasn't come back from patrolling yet," he said quietly. He frowned and then, almost like an afterthought, he added. "He's struggling with the guilt."

"Guilt?"

"He blames himself for you being taken, for not being able to reach you sooner," he explained.

It was almost like the floor dropped out from under me as I realised what Wyatt was currently going through. Why he wasn't here by my side. I had stupidly thought that he was just busy. What a crap mate was I? I hadn't even considered that he was hurting. The shame washed over me. All of these years, the thought of Wyatt was what kept me strong. The thought of going back to him and having him in my arms again. I hadn't once thought that he would be suffering too. Don't get me wrong, I know that he would be sad without me. I knew that he was being manipulated to do things that he didn't want to do in that first year, but after I had been sold to the vampires, I suppose I had pushed those thoughts to the back of my mind. I was so consumed with my own suffering that I hadn't even considered his.

"Hey, what happened? Where did you just go?" I heard Dom's voice ask, pulling me from my runaway thoughts. I realised that I was no longer holding the bowl. It had been set on the table next to me and I was currently sitting in Dom's lap. I blinked in confusion at my sudden change of position. I didn't remember how I had gotten here and it was the strangest sensation.

"Erm ..." I really didn't know what to say. Was it weird to be sitting in this man's lap? It felt kind of right, but I wasn't sure if that in itself was weird?

"You suddenly went blank and you weren't answering me," Dom filled me in. "It was like your mind went somewhere else."

"Oh, right. That's a bit embarrassing," I said without even thinking.

Dom laughed and held me tighter. "You were panicking about something," he said quietly.

I could tell that he had no intention of letting me go and I was okay sitting here, for now, so I didn't mind. But what would Wyatt think if he found us like this? I could feel my mind starting towards that spiral again and quickly pulled back.

Life outside of a cage was exhausting and confusing!

"I'm sorry," I said, not really sure what it was that I was supposed to say.

"Do you want to talk about it?" he said, tilting his head to the side in question.

"Erm, no. Maybe. I don't know?" I'm not sure why it came out as a question, but apparently, it was sufficient to break the mood in the room because the smile was back on Dom's face.

He suddenly stood up, still holding me in his arms, turned around and leaned back in the bed, keeping me in his lap. He swung his legs up onto the bed and we stayed like that, me sitting in his lap with his arms wrapped around me. I felt safe.

After a while, I asked, "Will Wyatt be angry if he finds us like this?"

I didn't feel like I was doing anything wrong, but I didn't know how I was supposed to feel in this world that I suddenly found myself in.

"No. He won't be angry." Dom fell silent and I waited for him to speak again. It was almost like I could feel that he had something to say, but he wasn't sure about saying it.

"Do you ..." he went quiet again for a moment before he huffed out a breath and rushed out. "Do you know who you are to us?" he said quickly.

I felt like I was supposed to say yes and it pained me that I didn't know the answer to his question. I didn't want to hurt this strong man who held me so gently in his lap.

"I ... I'm Wyatt's mate," I started and then I paused. He waited patiently for me to say what I was trying to feel. Thankfully I was sitting sideways on his lap, so I took the opportunity to fix my gaze on the wall in front of me and not look him in the face while I asked. "Am I connected to you and Caleb somehow as well?"

That was how it felt, but I lacked the life experience and the knowledge to know what was happening. I'd been raised in an angel education centre. I had been taught all I needed to know about angel life and military tactics. Or rather, I had been taught all they had deemed I needed to know. I knew that I was naïve to this world. It was something that I was going to have to spend a long time trying to rectify.

"Yes, you are," he squeezed me a little tighter, but it felt nothing but calming and comforting. "Wow, this feels really awkward for some reason," he laughed.

He was right. And I was worried it was me making it feel that way.

"Yeah, I know," I smiled, still with my eyes locked on that really interesting piece of cracked plaster in the wall. I hoped that my inability to look him in the face at the moment wouldn't upset him. "Maybe just, you know, say it really quickly and then it will be out there," I suggested.

"I know someone else who says that. You're actually going to love her when you meet her," he smiled before huffing out a breath again. Suddenly Dom sucked in a breath, held it and then rushed out. "We're all your mates."

It was almost like he was holding his breath again as he waited for me to respond. I'm not exactly sure what he was expecting me to do.

"Oh, thank fuck for that!" I sighed.

Dom just laughed, apparently, whatever he had been expecting, it wasn't that.

"I was getting really confused there for a moment." The relief that surged over me felt phenomenal.

Dom was so easy to talk to, even if, at times, I felt like I needed to stare at a wall. But come to think of it, Caleb had been as well. I'd had that with Wyatt once when we were young and unbroken. So much had happened since then, I only hoped that our broken pieces would still be able to fit each other when he finally let me see him again. I could understand his guilt because now it consumed me. I could give him some time if that was what he needed. But I couldn't help but feel that I needed to help them understand a little bit about me. Especially after I had spaced out on Dom earlier. He seemed to have forgotten his earlier concern. I suppose that the whole mate issue had taken over the forefront of his mind.

"Did you know that I was sixteen when I met Wyatt?" I asked Dom.

He relaxed back into the bed and I settled against his body. As I turned, I saw that Caleb was standing in the doorway. I didn't know how long he had been there, but he was smiling at the both of us so seeing me sitting on Dom's lap clearly didn't bother him. I held out my hand to him and he came over and joined us on the bed. Dom shuffled over and Caleb sat next to him, leaning against the headboard and pulling my legs over his lap.

"We didn't," Dom finally said once Caleb was comfortable.

"Angel society is, I think, very different from how you live your lives. We don't have mates or form family units. When a specific angel is required, compatible angels are informed of their requirement to breed. The resulting child is raised in an education centre and when they graduate, they are allocated to a flight which is our fighting unit," I explained. I had explained along similar lines to Wyatt when we had first met.

Dom and Caleb both looked shocked but didn't say anything.

"What I'm trying to say is that it might take some time for me to become familiar with any other way of life," I cringed. Basically, I was trying to say I was going to keep messing-up for the foreseeable future.

Dom opened his mouth to answer just as the distinct sound of a door closing came from downstairs. Both men froze and Caleb cocked his head to the side listening before he slipped out from under me and prowled to the door. He turned back to Dom, gave him a nod and then disappeared out of the room.

I looked at Dom in confusion. Had someone found us? Were we supposed to be running, or fighting?

He must have seen the confusion on my face because he just told me. "It's nothing to worry about."

"We shouldn't stay here for long. We aren't far enough away from Cassius' clan," I told him.

"As soon as you are strong enough, we will leave," he agreed. "I suppose we need to decide where we are going to return to. We had planned on returning to the pack, but we wanted to make sure that you were happy with that first."

I knew that they wouldn't take me anywhere that wasn't safe, but I still needed to know. "Wyatt's alpha?"

"The one you knew, very dead," he told me. There was even a hint of a smile on his face. "The current one is much, much different. His mate, Aria, is who I mentioned earlier that I think you will like. She also had … a difficult childhood."

I wasn't sure what he meant by that, but it would be interesting to meet another woman who was also mated. Maybe she would be a good source of information for the questions I was too embarrassed to ask my men. My men? Was I even allowed to call them that?

I settled into Dom and I could feel my eyelids growing heavy. It was strange that my body was reacting this way, I had been through extensive conditioning through my training and I had never experienced such tiredness before. I suppose I did have my wings then, perhaps that was what was causing this fractured sensation inside of me.

"Sleep Lyra. We will watch over you," Dom whispered to me.

I felt so safe here in his arms that I couldn't have stayed awake even if I wanted to. The weariness washed over me and carried me off into sleep.

CHAPTER 15

DOM

Lyra had fallen asleep almost immediately. I could tell that she was still exhausted. I wasn't surprised, she basically weighed nothing. I had felt just how thin she was when I picked her up and pulled her into my lap. Now that she was here, curled against me, her soft breath blowing against my chest, I didn't want to put her down.

I had worried about the whole mate bond. In fact, I didn't think I fully believed it was real until I set eyes on her. It was a strange sensation to have. To feel so connected to someone, they felt like an integral part of your very being. How Wyatt had lasted this long parted from her, I would never know. It was only that thought that was making me cut him some slack right now. He would hurt her if he didn't suck it up and at least come and see her.

It was Wyatt coming back that had caused Caleb to slip downstairs. I looked down at Lyra's sleeping face and grimaced. I knew I needed to go and talk with him, talk with them both, but I didn't want to leave her.

It felt almost physically painful for me to move her to the bed and slip out from beneath her. She was so sound asleep. I doubt she would ever realise I was gone. That was the only reason I was able to drag myself away from her.

I quietly slipped out of the bedroom and soundlessly closed the door behind me. If things got heated downstairs, I didn't want to risk waking her. She needed the rest and she was right, we needed to leave here soon.

When I made it down to the kitchen, I wasn't surprised at the silence that greeted me. Wyatt was sat on one of the old rickety stools, hunched over a bowl of the stew. He was angrily eating his food if that was even possible. It was clear that he was pissed, no doubt Caleb had something to say to him when he returned.

Caleb was leaning against the kitchen door, almost like he was trying to bar Wyatt from being able to leave again. I could see that out of the three of us, it would be these two that were going to clash the most.

"She's asleep," I told Wyatt even though he didn't look up from his bowl when I entered the room. I didn't miss the slight relaxation of his shoulders, though.

We all knew that Wyatt desperately loved Lyra, she was his mate after all, and you didn't go through what Wyatt had for someone you didn't care about. But this crushing guilt of his that kept him away from her would cause more problems for her than I think he realised. I had been there when she had panicked about him when I had tried to explain to her why he wasn't there. It would seem that they were both dealing with guilt over the same thing. Maybe I was wrong. Maybe it would be Lyra and Wyatt that clashed the most. They did, after all, seem to be very alike. They wouldn't be the first couple who spent a lot of their time fighting and the rest of the time making up.

"Did you run into any trouble out there?" I asked him, deciding to start on the easiest topic.

"No. There are no signs of any other vampires around here. Which I find suspicious in itself," he added.

He was right. All of the clans had to share this small portion of our realm. There should have surely been others in the area, even if they weren't from Cassius' clan. The fact that we hadn't come across any of them was undoubtedly strange.

"We should still try and move on as soon as we can," Caleb said from the doorway.

He was stubborn enough that he would stay there all night. I would know, having had his stubbornness directed at myself more than once.

"Lyra said the same. She thinks we're still too close to the clan. She didn't say how far away they are and even if we knew how long she had been running for it probably wouldn't give us an accurate reading on distance. I doubt she was moving fast. We should think about leaving in the morning," I suggested.

"Will she be strong enough by then?" Wyatt asked, finally looking up from his bowl.

"You'd know if you had been to see her," Caleb snarked.

I expected Wyatt to snap back at him, but he just hunched over his bowl and didn't even meet Caleb's eye. It was a strange reaction for him. Wyatt was the more dominant wolf. He should have seen Caleb's comment as a direct challenge. I saw confusion flicker across Caleb's face as he no doubt noticed the same. Challenging Wyatt or trying to force him to go and see her wasn't the right way to go about this.

I pulled up one of the stools and sat down with him. Caleb remained at his station by the door. This would have been better if he would just sit down with us. Not that I would recommend anyone ever sitting on these stools, it felt like you were taking your life into your hands when you did it. How they were still held together I had no idea.

"She asked about you," I told him.

Wyatt visibly flinched, almost like I had struck him. I didn't know how to help him through this and then I saw what I was doing wrong. Assuming that I should know rather than just asking him.

"How can we help you with this, Wyatt?" I asked him gently.

He still wouldn't meet my eyes, but I was okay with that. If he would speak to me, it didn't matter if he was looking at me. Lyra had adopted the same tactic earlier. Sometimes it was easier to talk if you didn't have to watch the reaction of whoever was listening to you.

"I ... I failed her," he said.

I knew this was how he felt because that was what he always said.

"I know that is how you feel, Wyatt. I can tell you for a fact that Lyra doesn't believe that, but I don't think that you are going to believe me." I wanted to reach out to him, but I didn't know how he would take it. Wyatt and I had never had that kind of relationship. "How can we help you?" I asked him again.

"I ... I just need more time," he said. He gave up all pretence of looking at his bowl and his eyes fell to the floor in shame.

"I don't think that will help you. In fact, I think it will only make it worse. I know that you are struggling with your guilt, Wyatt. I think the only way you are going to be able to get past that is if you speak with her. Even if it is to ask her for her forgiveness, which I can assure you that you don't need."

I could tell that he was wavering, but he still wasn't at the point where he was going to give in. There was one last thing I knew I could say that would push him to go to her, but I felt like a dick that I was going to use it against him. It was going to be the only way though. Hopefully, he wouldn't hate me for it later.

"She needs you, Wyatt, don't fail her again."

Caleb's head snapped towards me and I knew I had surprised him. Wyatt just flinched again, but he got to his feet and he slowly moved out of the kitchen. He was moving in the direction of the stairs, which was a first.

Caleb and I both waited in silence. I think we expected him to just turn around and come back again. To chicken out at the last minute. When we heard him moving up the stairs, Caleb came and sat with me in the stool that Wyatt had vacated.

"That could have backfired so badly," he finally said.

"I know."

And I did. Wyatt needed to pull himself out of his guilt, or this bond we all shared was going to break. Either because of his refusal to forgive himself or because we would push him too far to try and make him.

CHAPTER 16

WYATT

I stood outside of the room I knew she was in for at least ten minutes before I could even work up the courage to put my hand on the door handle. My wolf was practically vibrating in anticipation in my head. He had been furious with me that we hadn't gone straight to our mate's side as soon as we had her back and never left it. I didn't know how to explain to him how I was feeling though. It was the worst part about sharing a soul with an animal. They were so pure. Their emotions and feelings were far less complex than ours. All he could see was that we had retrieved our mate and that we needed her. He didn't understand the concept of guilt. He had felt her absence the same as I had. He had felt the anger at those that had taken her and the desperation to get her back. He just couldn't understand why I was holding back. As a consequence, I had the worst fucking headache brewing.

Taking a deep breath to gain some form of courage, my lungs filled with her scent. The light flowery sunshine scent that was Lyra. That was what finally broke me. What made my feet move as I pushed through the door.

She was curled up on her side, sleeping peacefully. She

truly did look like an angel. She was so perfect. Her long blonde hair spilled across her pillow and her pink lips were slightly parted as she breathed softly. I could tell just by looking at her face that she had lost a lot of weight since I had seen her last. Just the fact that she was here, that she had survived what she had been through, was a miracle.

I dropped to my knees at the side of the bed. Even though I desperately wanted to climb in with her, I couldn't. I didn't deserve to. My wolf whined as he took in the changes in our mate. The evidence of her suffering. His sadness was the closest thing that he could feel to my own guilt. My forehead dropped to the mattress and tears welled in my eyes. Dom was right that I needed to find a way to work past this. I just didn't know how. It was crushing. If I let myself feel it, it felt like these emotions were smothering me. I was suffocating in my own guilt and I didn't think that even her forgiveness would be enough to save me.

Fingers ran through my hair and I felt her nails softly scratch against my scalp. My silent tears turned into sobs. I couldn't hold them back any longer. She didn't say anything and I was grateful that she didn't. I wasn't ready to listen to anything, not yet. She silently waited for me. Her very presence supported me.

When I finally felt like my tears had run dry, I gathered all of the fractured pieces of my courage and looked up to meet her eyes. Her soft brown eyes glistened with the tears that were silently falling and that was all that it took. I climbed into the bed beside her and pulled her into my arms. Burying my face into her hair, I whispered the only words that I could speak.

"I'm so sorry, please forgive me."

Lyra pulled away from me and I felt my heart shatter; it exploded into a million pieces. If I had thought that I had felt grief before, it was nothing compared to this. Nothing compared to the rejection of my mate. I scrunched my eyes shut, like the coward I was. I couldn't bear to see the look on her face. I don't know what would have been worse, anger or disgust. I was so confused when I felt her hands gently stroking my cheeks, even more confused when I heard her speak.

"I'm so sorry that I failed you, Wyatt," she whispered.

My eyes opened of their own accord at the confusion from, not only her words, but the guilt in her voice, that mirrored my own.

"I promised that I would protect you and I didn't," she told me.

"No, you didn't fail me. It was me that failed you. I should have protected you, I should never have let Marcus take you. I should have found a way to save you." All of my guilt and the thoughts where I had second-guessed myself gushed out of me as I confessed all of my self conceived failings to her.

When I was done, Lyra sat up in the bed and frowned at me. "Is that truly what you believe?" she asked. She almost looked angry at me.

I leant up on my elbows. It felt strange having her looking down at me like this with anger flashing in her eyes. Normally my wolf would rebel at anyone taking this dominant position over us, but he was almost giddy to have Lyra do it. I'd roll my eyes at him if I wasn't worried that she would think I was doing it at her. My wolf was loving this side of Lyra we had never seen before.

"I am your mate, Wyatt. I don't know what that means to you, but to me, it means that we are two halves. I am not a small piece of you; I am your equal. I didn't need you to save me. If it had been that easy to get away from Marcus or Cassius, I would have done it myself," she huffed in annoyance.

I couldn't help the small smile that came across my face. She was a fierce little thing. She always had been, from the very first moment that I finally laid eyes on her and she promised that she would protect me.

"Is that not how it is supposed to be?" she asked, doubting herself.

"You're right. That is how it is supposed to be. Shifters have always seen their mates as someone that they need to protect. But someone recently showed me how wrong that belief was. I am sorry, you're right, you are my equal. But I still feel like I should have done more. Just because you are my equal doesn't mean that I shouldn't have been there for you, that I shouldn't have tried to save you."

I think we were both struggling to explain our position, but equally, I didn't think that mattered because we also understood each other. I knew that she was trained as a warrior before she met me. I could see how treating her like a damsel that needed to be saved could be insulting. That didn't make me want to do it any less though.

I pulled her back into my arms and she snuggled into the side of me.

"You didn't fail me either," I told her seriously and I felt her relax against me.

"I can't believe that it was nine years. It was hard to gauge time where I was, but I thought it had only been five, maybe six years. But nine!" I felt a twinge of guilt at her admission. Then she added. "How did you cope, Wyatt? How did you last that long if you were feeling this way?"

I couldn't help the laugh that slipped out of me. She was truly perfect.

"How did I cope? How did you cope?" I scoffed. "I'm pretty sure that what happened to you wasn't exactly easy."

"I know it's probably strange to say this, but it was pretty easy. Yes, there were times when it hurt, when the pain was nearly unbearable. But I'm an angel. I was raised in a way that I don't think you understand. I have been conditioned against pain since I was three years old. I have been taught many ways to withstand torture and interrogation. It still hurts, but the pain is something that I am familiar with."

I didn't even know what to say to that, but if there was one thing for sure, I would spend the rest of my life making sure that she never had to know pain like that again.

I held her close in my arms. "I hate that you had to go through that," I whispered through her hair.

Having her here with me was so surreal. It almost felt like it was impossible. We had been apart for so long. It was the quietest I had known my wolf to be since she was taken. There was a time when I was worried that he would go rabid. He was half insane once we lost her and keeping him controlled was exhausting. But now that I held her in my arms, he was finally happy. He was finally quiet, lounging in the back of my mind.

Lyra leant her head back to look up at me and all I could see were her pouty pink lips, hovering just out of reach.

"I missed you," she murmured, a slight flush brightened her cheeks. She was so beautiful, she was mesmerising. I didn't know how I got so lucky to have this woman as my mate, but I would never let her go again.

I couldn't hold back and there wasn't a single part of me that wanted to as I leaned down and softly kissed her lips. She sighed against my lips as she kissed me back. It was soft and gentle. A promise of what was to come.

"You need to rest more so that we can get out of here," I said, reluctantly pulling away from her lips.

"Will you stay with me?" she asked as she settled her head against my chest.

I felt her yawn and her breaths were already evening out.

"Always," I whispered to her. And I meant it. Nothing would make me leave her side again.

I laid there for hours, holding her in my arms, wide awake and watching her sleep. She was so peaceful lying there, her face relaxed in a dreamless sleep. I had wanted to stay awake for the entire time that she slept, but the peace that I found in her arms lulled me into a sleep of quiet contentment. It had been years since I had been able to properly sleep without having to try and stay at least slightly aware of my surroundings for fear of losing control of my wolf.

I didn't even realise I had been asleep until I felt Lyra's soft lips brush across my own. I felt her smile against my lips as I moaned in contentment. This is what we should have been doing all of these years. This is how we should have woken up every morning.

With the feel of his mate so close, my wolf pushed to the front of my mind. There was only one thought that he was pushing through to me and it was the first time in years that we had agreed on anything.

Bringing my arms around her, I gently rolled, pressing Lyra back down onto the bed so that I could hover over her body. She had shed her trousers in the night and her bare thighs now grazed up the sides of my own.

I ran my thumb across her bottom lip, feeling her breaths puffing gently as the arousal flooded her body.

She was so small beneath me and so delicate. There was a small part of me that was saying this was a bad idea, that we could wait, we didn't need to do this right away. Almost as if she could read my mind Lyra interrupted my thoughts.

"I need you, Wyatt," she simply told me.

And that was all that I needed to hear.

I would do anything for her, I would never hold anything back from her. She was the most important thing in the world and I would tear apart anyone that tried to come between us again.

Unable to hold back any longer, I ran one hand from her hip up the length of her bare thigh, her skin pebbling as I traced my fingertips across her.

This time needed to be gentle. She needed to feel how much I would worship her, what the future held for her if she would agree to be my mate.

"You have to understand what this means before we go any further," I told her, trailing the fingers of one hand down her neck and across her collar bone, causing her to arch in need against me. It wasn't fair, she wouldn't be able to think clearly if I continued to tease her, but I couldn't keep my hands off her. "If we do this now, you will be my mate. We will be bonded for the rest of our lives."

"I'm failing to see a downside to that," she murmured, flicking her tongue out to catch the pad of my thumb as it took a second journey across her bottom lip.

"Say it ... say that you'll be mine," I begged her, needing to hear the words more than I would ever care to admit.

"I was always yours, Wyatt. Just as you were always mine."

I couldn't hold back any longer and my lips slam against hers. I should be gentle, but I just couldn't hold myself back and she was returning the kiss with the same urgent force that I felt myself. I slowly lowered my hands to her waist and took hold of the bottom of the shirt that was hiding her from my view. I'm almost reluctant to pull my lips away from hers, but as I moved down her body and laid the first kiss on her stomach, she rewarded me with a moan that set my cock harder than I'd ever felt before.

I took my time, slowly moving the shirt up her body, exposing her skin to me inch by inch. Each strip of skin that is exposed, I take my time exploring with my tongue, teeth and lips. Kissing and nibbling my way up her body.

By the time I pushed the shirt over the peaks of her breasts, I had never been more relieved in my life by the fact that we didn't think to pack a bra for her.

Her dusky pink nipples are already pebbled hard and begging for attention. Wanting to brand this moment into her memory for the rest of her life, I dragged my tongue around the edge of one nipple, ignoring the tip before moving across to repeat the action on her other side.

Lyra whimpered and writhed with need beneath me and every time she moved her hips, she ground her soaking wet core against my cock. I felt like I could burst here and now, but I needed this to last, I needed to make this everything I'd been denied for the last nine years. We may have eternity together, but I wanted to make this one night stand out before any other. This wasn't going to be some quick fuck, this was me taking Lyra as my mate and making her mine forever.

Leaning back, I took in the sight of my mate spread out beneath me. Her eyes are half-closed as she panted in need, her breasts heaved with every breath. In nothing but her panties she was the most glorious thing I had ever seen. All milky white skin and flowing blonde hair. Even though she no longer had her wings, she was still the most magnificent thing I had ever seen. She was made to be worshipped by men and she would be for the rest of her days.

I couldn't hold back any longer and my head dipped down as I took one of her nipples into my mouth and pinched the other between my fingers. Lyra rewarded me with a breathy sigh and it only took me moments to have my lips back on hers as I dragged my tongue against hers. I would never get tired of kissing this woman.

Lyra's hands grasped at my clothes and I leant back enough for her to tear my shirt over my head and I'm wriggling out of my trousers and boxers next. I don't give her the luxury of removing hers, tearing them from her body instead. My need to feel her against me outweighs any common sense that I had right now. She gasped at the sudden violence and I had a second to feel bad before my mouth closed over the wet heat between her thighs and all thoughts of anything but her left my mind. She tasted like heaven and if I died right here, right now, I knew I'd be able to finally say that I had lived my life right.

Running my tongue along the length of her, I had to grab her hips and pin her to the bed as she let out a breathy moan and writhed beneath me. I circled my tongue around her clit and her back arched off the bed. She's so responsive. I couldn't wait until we had her between all three of us.

As I took my time to feast between her legs, she seemed to settle into my rhythm, pulsing her hips to ride my face. Finally, letting go of her hips, I pulled one of her thighs over my shoulder so that I could hold her against me and using the other hand, I slowly sank one finger into her heat. I knew she was close to coming as I felt her pussy quiver around me, so I pushed a second finger into her and renewed my efforts against her clit.

Lyra sucked in a lungful of air and I knew she was on the precipice of an orgasm, just before she fell, I sucked her clit into my mouth and gently bit, causing her to explode beneath me. Pumping my fingers into her and gently lapping at her clit I let her ride the wave of her orgasm until she sagged beneath me.

I crawled back up the length of her body, dropping kisses as I go because I just couldn't seem to stop myself.

"I want to touch you," she told me in a breathy voice that did nothing but make me harder.

"Next time," I told her, "if you touch me now, I'm not going to last and I need to be inside of you."

It's the truth as well. I felt like I was on the verge of coming myself. Nine years is a long time to go without, but as soon as I met her, there was never going to be anyone else for me.

Lyra's legs came around my waist and she pulled me closer, grinding the head of my cock against her wet pussy. I slowly pushed myself inside of her as she whimpered and sighed beneath me. She's so tight that I had to stop halfway and withdraw a little before pushing on.

By the time I'm hilt deep inside of her, I already knew that this wasn't going to last half as long as I wanted it to.

"Fuck, baby, you're so tight," I groaned out.

Lyra started to move beneath me, needing more and I couldn't deny her. I never would be able to. I knew that I should go slow, but I couldn't. The alpha in me needed to dominate and now that I could feel her wet heat wrapped around me, I felt like I was about to go insane. I tried to start out gentle, but pretty soon, I'm pulling out and pounding straight back inside of her. Her back arched and she clung to me as she moans. I could already feel her pussy starting to pulse around me again. There's no way that I'm going to be able to hold back when she comes, but there's also no way I'm going to come without her getting there first.

I dropped one hand back down to her clit and started to circle it with my thumb.

"Come for me again, Lyra. I want to feel your pussy coming around my cock," I groaned as I found myself slamming into her.

It didn't take long before her moans started to get louder and then her pussy clamped down and I couldn't keep my rhythm any longer. Just as I spilt myself inside her, I wrapped her in my arms and bit down into her shoulder, leaving my mark. As I felt her teeth sink into my neck, I came again from the sheer bliss of the bond snapping into place between us.

We stayed like that, wrapped up in each other, as we came down from the high that only sex can bring. My tongue darted out and I lapped against the mark I'd set into her shoulder, it's high near to the point where her neck meets her shoulder and I could feel myself starting to grow hard again at the thought that everyone would be able to see it.

"I can feel you," Lyra whispered, "I can feel the bond."

She's right. It's like I can feel her presence nestled against my heart. It soothed my wolf and for the first time in nine years, he retreated from the forefront of my mind, curling up deep inside me where he could feel his mate. The relief nearly brought tears to my eyes, the constant ache of his ever-present rage finally eased.

Lyra must be able to feel that my mood is changing because she clung to me tighter and started to whisper words of love and forever to me. I held her tighter as we reassured each other that we would never be apart again until she fell asleep in my arms. I meant every word that I said, she was my complete world and nothing would ever hurt her again.

CHAPTER 17

CALEB

W e had slipped upstairs about four hours after Wyatt had left. We hadn't heard anything from up there, so we were taking it as a good sign. It must have gone better than we could have hoped because when we looked into the bedroom, they were both cuddled up asleep on the bed, so we left them in peace.

Dom made another of the disgusting stew meals from the pack for dinner and we saved some on the stove for Wyatt and Lyra when they woke up. I had no idea how she thought that it tasted good. It was foul. Unfortunately, the majority of the meals which we had brought with us were the same because when we were looking through the shelves, we thought that they sounded the least offensive. Now I wished we had grabbed some of the pasta ones instead.

Dom and I were both sitting at the table, pushing our food around and reluctantly eating. I would be glad to get away from here.

We didn't see Wyatt or Lyra all night. We had cleared space in what would have been the living room of the house and laid out beds on the floor in there. It was probably the most destroyed of all of the rooms, but that just meant it was easier to clear out. Plus, with it being on the ground floor, we could keep a better watch on the house.

I ran the patrol in wolf form and there wasn't any sign of anything for miles. It was almost suspicious how empty this part of the realm was. We couldn't rely on that for long, though and we were all conscious that another patrol would probably be sent out for Lyra as soon as that wounded vampire made it back. If we had been able to hunt him down and kill him, we probably could have lingered here longer, but he disappeared after the attack and we couldn't find his trail. Vampires were fucking fast. We needed to leave tomorrow, whether Lyra was strong enough or not. If she was too weak to travel, we were just going to have to carry her. I'd feel much better once we were out of the Moon Side and back with the pack.

"Will you have enough energy to portal us out of here once we clear the Moon Side?" I asked Dom.

It was hard for him to open a portal but to open one for four people to travel through was going to push his endurance. Even though he didn't admit it to us, I knew portaling us here had been difficult for him.

"As long as I don't need to use any of my magic between now and then, I should be fine," he admitted. "If we run into trouble, we may need to rest another night." His face scrunched up in embarrassment as he said it and I knew that he hated having to admit to the limitations in his magic.

Mages had, like the rest of the species, seen a decline in their magic over the years. After the Blood Moon battle, we should hopefully see a change in that, but who knew how long it would take, or if it would even happen in our lifetime. Maybe it wouldn't even affect those of us that were already here but only those born after the battle. Too much was unknown at the moment. The Mage Council was researching what they could, but it was far too soon to know. No one wanted to ask the witches. Kyle and the Shifter Council were going to have a hard job trying to get any shifter to trust a witch again. I don't know how the other races would be with them, they hadn't suffered as heavy losses as we had. I suspected that the trust would be broken no matter what though.

When I got back from patrol, I slipped into the makeshift bed we had made while Dom kept watch from the window. It seemed a bit redundant if I was honest, but the lack of any kind of patrols or life in the area had put us all on edge. It was almost like this part of the realm was on the verge of something happening and everything was holding its breath just waiting. It was making me and my wolf antsy and I didn't feel like there was any chance I was going to get any sleep. Especially not when our mate was asleep upstairs.

"What was it like out there?" Dom asked, his gaze fixed out the window.

"Same, nothing anywhere. I couldn't even pick up any tracks," I told him, voicing my earlier thoughts. "It's starting to creep me out."

"It does seem unusual, but we have never really had much of anything to do with the Moon Side. We have no way of knowing what the vampire population is like."

"They can't be having the same problems as us. They don't breed like we do." It was easy to think that everything fell back on the loss of magic, but it felt like something else was going on around here.

"Perhaps. I suppose the real question is, is it anything that we need to worry about. The vampires have historically kept to themselves. They don't interfere with the business of the rest of the realm," Dom said.

"Unless they're stealing your mate," I scoffed. "Besides, once Aria finds out about them portaling into the human realm to retrieve humans, you know she's going to be on the warpath."

"They need to eat," Dom argued. "The only other option is genocide and I don't think even Aria would go to such lengths."

He was right. As fierce as Aria was, she was one of the best people that I knew. She wouldn't hurt someone if she didn't have to, or at least I didn't think she would. But she was also very protective and she had grown up amongst the humans. Despite her experience with some of them, I knew she still had people in the human realm she considered family.

"Let's just agree that it can be a problem for another day. At the moment, I think all I can cope with is getting Lyra out of here and somewhere safe," Dom said, finally turning from the window to look at me. "I don't think I'm going to get much sleep. I'll take the first watch if you want to sleep for a couple of hours."

"Okay, but wake me up in three hours. You need to sleep if you are going to be able to portal us out of here. I'd rather miss a night of sleep and get Lyra away from here as soon as possible," I told him.

Dom just nodded in agreement and turned back to the window.

I was so geared up, I didn't think I was going to sleep, and it was only when Dom shook me awake a short while later that I realised I even had. I must have been more tired than I realised.

"Caleb, wake up. I think I saw something in the tree line behind the house," Dom whispered.

I was immediately awake and on my feet.

"Stay here, I'll go and check it out," I told him, already moving and not waiting for his answer.

"I'm going to wake Wyatt," Dom told me as I slipped out of the room.

I immediately shifted into my wolf and stalked into the trees to the side of the house so that I could circle around to where Dom had seen something under the cover of the trees, or at least under what cover the dead, leafless trees could provide.

I caught the scent straight away, but it was unfamiliar. One thing I was grateful for was that it wasn't the injured vampire from before.

I laid down on my belly in the dead undergrowth and surveyed the ground around me. I could see the tracks which lead to the edge of the treeline behind the house, but then they seemed to back away. It looked like someone had come to investigate the house but then left rather than attack. It was making me uneasy. They could easily be going to gather rein-forcements for an attack, or they could have realised that Dom had seen them and were now trying to lure one of us into a trap.

My first instinct was to follow the tracks and take down whatever had made them and was posing a threat to my mate. My wolf was wholly on board with that idea and was straining to go. But I needed to be sensible. Our first priority was to get Lyra out of the Moon Side and then have Dom portal us home. If we ended up getting into a fight that meant Dom had to use his magic, he wouldn't have enough magic to be able to get us out of here. I suppose we could have him go through the portal with Lyra alone and Wyatt and I could follow over ground, but I had a feeling that we would have hell to pay with Lyra if we did that.

A slight breeze was blowing towards me in the direction that whoever had been watching us had left. I couldn't scent them close by, so I shifted back into my human form and decided to wait for Wyatt to see what he wanted to do. We hadn't established a hierarchy in our little pack, but I sure as fuck didn't want to be the one that was in charge. Anyway, if we were going to follow the tracks, I needed to do it with backup.

I didn't have to wait long until Wyatt's brown and gold wolf bounded up to join me, shifting back to his human form as soon as he saw me.

"What have you found?" he asked, crouching down beside me.

"Someone has been watching us. They didn't stay here long and then they went back the way they came. It isn't the vampire we injured in the attack. I didn't want to follow the tracks alone in case it was a trap. What do you want to do?" I asked him.

I saw Wyatt cock his head to the side in thought. He ran his fingers over the tracks in the dirt and brought them to his face to get a read on the scent.

"It's not a scent that I am familiar with," he said, squinting into the trees where whoever had been watching us disappeared. "Let's follow it for a while, make sure that they don't double back towards the house. Dom is going to stand watch over Lyra. If they keep leading away, I think we should head back to the house, pack up and leave," he suggested.

We were all on edge, having Lyra in this unfamiliar territory. It was especially hard for Wyatt and I because of our wolves. I wasn't so sure that leaving straight away was a good idea, though.

"Is she strong enough to leave now?" I asked.

"She will have to be," he said sternly.

And that was exactly why I didn't want to be the one that was in charge.

CHAPTER 18

DOM

Wyatt and Caleb had been gone for nearly an hour and to say I was on edge was an understatement of epic proportions. I had packed up what little we had and the packs were ready to go. Lyra was still asleep, but I wanted her to get as much as possible. Before he left, Wyatt had said we were leaving as soon as they got back. I wasn't sure that she was ready for that yet, but Wyatt was right. We had been here for too long and if someone had found us, we couldn't afford for word to spread about where we were. Plus, the sooner we got Lyra back to the packhouse, the better she could recover. We could actually get her in a proper bed and get some proper food into her.

I stood to the side of the bedroom window, watching out the back of the house. I could hear Lyra sleeping peacefully. Normally, that would be a sound which would put me at ease, but right now, it did nothing but make me more anxious. I hadn't anticipated how strong the mate bond would be for me. I stupidly thought that because I was a mage it would be muted. Apparent but weak. I had been wrong. So very wrong.

I caught movement in the trees and I swear my heart stuttered to a stop for a second. When Wyatt and Caleb emerged, gently jogging towards the house, I breathed a sigh of relief.

"Dom? What's wrong?" Lyra sleepily whispered from the bed.

I turned around and saw her sitting up in the bed, rubbing her eyes. Her long blonde hair was knotted around her head, but she still looked fucking beautiful.

"Someone was in the trees behind the house. We need to leave," I told her, trying not to sound worried.

"Where's Wyatt and Caleb?" She asked, her voice hitching in anxiety.

"They're just coming now," I told her, not wanting to admit that they had been to investigate. I had a feeling that she would be pissed and I didn't want to stress her out anymore. "Do you think that you are strong enough to walk?" I asked.

"Of course," she laughed, swinging her legs over the side of the bed.

I grabbed her boots from beside the bed and knelt beside her, intent on putting them on her feet. Thankfully she was already dressed.

"What are you doing?" She asked in confusion.

"Erm, I was going to help you put your boots on," I said, my face flushing in embarrassment. It had been an automatic reaction. I suppose it was a bit weird considering I had met her for the first time only yesterday.

Lyra just laughed softly and pushed her feet into the boots that I had placed at her feet, saying nothing as I tied the laces securely in place. Once they were on, I felt her fingers run through my hair and I couldn't stop myself from leaning into her touch.

"Thank you," she murmured.

I was just helping her to her feet when Wyatt and Caleb came up the stairs and into the bedroom.

"The tracks head away from the house and then disappear," Wyatt told me without me even having to ask. "Are we ready to move out?"

He was all business and back to his gruff self. If that was what it was going to take to get us all out of here, then I knew for a fact none of us was going to mind. Once this place was behind us, I would finally be able to relax a bit.

"We're all packed up and ready to go," I told him.

Wyatt's eyes flicked to Lyra and I knew that he was anxious about her travelling so far. We had a day's hike to the edge of the Moon Side. As soon as we were clear, I would be able to portal us back to the packhouse. That day's hike would feel like an eternity, though. Having Lyra weakened and out in the open was a nightmare. A necessary nightmare but a nightmare nonetheless.

"Okay, then we head out now. We need to hike hard for a couple of hours and get some distance between us and the house before we stop for breakfast. I'll carry Lyra," he said, stepping towards her.

Lyra immediately stepped back and crossed her arms over her chest. "You absolutely will not be carrying me," she huffed.

And so it began!

I couldn't help the smirk that came to my face and when I looked up, Caleb had an identical one on his own. At least we weren't laughing though. I got the impression that if we did one, or perhaps both of them, would turn that annoyance to us.

"Lyra, you're still weak, we need to move fast. It doesn't matter if one of us carries you, it doesn't make you any less than the strong woman that you are," Wyatt said, trying to placate her.

She just shook her head at him, stubbornness setting in. "No, I can walk just fine."

Sensing that they were about to set into an argument and

needing to save the time, I decided, against my better judgment, to step in.

"How about Lyra starts out walking with us but promises that if she starts to feel too tired or like she needs to slow down, then she tells us and lets one of us carry her for a short while," I said, stressing the short just in case my mate turned the anger brewing in her eyes towards me.

"Fine," they both huffed at the same time, stretching the smirk on Caleb's face even bigger.

These two really were far too alike and it was going to cause us no end of problems, I could already see it.

CHAPTER 19

LYRA

He wanted to carry me! Like some kind of child or invalid. If I still had my wings, I knew that my feathers would be ruffled around me in frustration. Bloody overbearing ass of a wolf! I huffed in annoyance again. I think that the guys could tell that I was still brewing in anger because they had been walking in silence for the first hour of our hike and left me fairly alone. It was only once we had broken into the second hour that Caleb drifted a bit closer to me. I must have looked like I was calming down.

Dom was leading the way and Wyatt was walking a few steps behind me, almost as if he expected that I was going to collapse any minute and he would have to step in and swoop me up into his arms. Not that I didn't enjoy being in his arms. Sleeping cuddled up with him last night had been like all of my dreams come true. I had thought about it for so many cold and lonely nights, but the reality was even better.

I had Wyatt back. And two other mates as well. Talk about mind-blowing.

My calf muscles were starting to feel like they were on fire and my feet were aching, but I would be damned if I was going to ask one of them to carry me. Besides, they had said, we would be stopping after a few hours for something to eat, which would be soon. Maybe if we could rest a little every couple of hours, I would be able to walk myself out of here. Even that thought set me on edge. Admitting that I was weak like that was hard for me. I hadn't been lying when I told Wyatt that I had been through conditioning as a child. I had been starved to the brink of death and beaten regularly and I had recovered quickly. This slow process of healing was frustrating. I knew I had given up my wings when I decided to fall, but I should have still had access to the inherent abilities of being an angel. I had assumed I would still have access to my magic as well, but I hadn't felt any sign of it since I first woke up in the cell at Wyatt's pack.

"Let's stop here for something to eat," Dom suggested.

We weren't quite out in the open, there was a scattering of trees along the route that we were taking and we settled down against a small grouping which provided us with some cover. One good thing was that we had clear sightlines for anything that could be approaching us. The bad side though, was that we were fairly on display no matter where we stopped.

I sunk to the ground and tried not to groan from the tiredness that I was starting to feel. Wyatt gave me the side-eye as he and Dom started to rummage through the packs, pulling out some food and bottles of water. He was watching me so closely that I knew he would be able to tell that I was starting to hurt. It was endearing and also incredibly annoying.

I leant my back against one of the trees and stretched my legs out in front of me. The last thing that I needed was for my leg muscles to start to cramp. Caleb must have had a similar thought because he sat down next to me, pulled one of my legs across his lap and begun to massage my calf muscles. The aching pain flared each time he dug his fingers into my muscle, but it felt like bliss. A groan slipped out of my mouth as I sank back against the tree. I realised that I was all but admitting that I wasn't faring too well, but I was just going to ignore it and hope that they did as well. Caleb chuckled in amusement but kept going. This one was definitely a keeper.

Dom and Wyatt passed out granola bars and I got a bowl of the cold stew that was leftover from last night. Dom offered to start a fire and warm it up, but I didn't see the point. It wasn't the worst thing I had ever eaten, in fact, it was still a lot better than what I had, or rather hadn't, been eating over the last nine years.

I caught the way that Caleb cringed when I took my first mouthful and I almost burst out laughing. Could it be possible that my guys were food snobs? They would not survive in an education centre if that was the case.

We set off walking again after resting for about half an hour. Wyatt was confident that if we carried on the way we were, we should be able to get to the border in about ten hours. He had factored in the stops along the way without my even having to ask. That meant by the time I was ready to take the fifth stop, we should be at the border. As long as we could keep the pace up. I didn't have high hopes for myself, but I was going to try my best. Getting one of them to carry me would be my last resort unless I was slowing us down. Then I would just have to suck up my pride and ask.

It didn't take long for me to get bored. This whole place was just more dead trees after more dead trees. There was nothing to look at here. Whenever we made it out of the trees into the dead grass, there were just more dead trees in the distance. There was something so wrong about this place. It suited Cassius though. He deserved a place like this.

After the second stop, I decided that I needed to break up the silence a bit. The guys were still on the lookout, but we hadn't seen anything since whoever had been watching back at the house. Talking probably wasn't the smartest thing to do, but I had been alone in a cage for nine years and now that I had the opportunity to actually talk to someone, I didn't want to just walk in silence.

"What's it like at the pack?" I asked, deciding that if we were going to speak, the best course of action would be to find out some more information about where we were going.

"Better than it has been for a long time," Wyatt said.

Caleb huffed out a breath when he realised that was all Wyatt was going to say and then he explained what had happened in the recent months.

"Dom and I didn't live in the pack up until recently. Dom was the headmaster at an academy for our young. We train them when they reach their peak at twenty and come into their magic. We had received word from one of our seers that there was an impending attack on the realm by an army of demons and we decided to use the academy to try and prepare them for a fight. Then Aria happened." They all laughed at that. Aria was the friend that they had all mentioned before. "She had been living in the human realm and she got sent here by the human government because they believed that people possessing magic had been responsible for a series of attacks in the human realm. We had no idea what magic she had, but she had been living life in the human realm as a sort of cat burglar that helped out women in trouble. That's a story you'll have to get her to tell you. Anyway, she came storming into the academy kicking ass and found three of her mates there."

"Caleb was our combat teacher and she completely kicked his ass," Dom laughed.

"Actually, she never kicked my ass!" Caleb said, clearly upset at the insinuation. "Because I knew that she could and I wasn't that stupid."

All three of them laughed and I couldn't help but join in. This Aria did sound like someone that I would want to meet.

"Anyway, she took a group of the women under her wing

and she started an Elite training program. In just over two months, they outshone nearly every student at the academy. It turned out that it was part of her inherent magic, but we didn't know that at the time. Then the demons attacked the academy."

All three of them fell quiet and I could feel their pain like it filled the air around us.

"We lost nearly everyone, the academy was destroyed. Aria fought like the warrior that she is and she got a handful of us out. She stayed behind at the academy and fought back the hoard so that we could try and escape back to the pack. She met up with us again before we got there and she protected us all of the way back. I still don't know how she did that. How she managed to fight for so long. We'd all be dead if it wasn't for her. We made it back to the pack and then we were attacked again as four of them had followed us, but we didn't suffer any losses that time. She cut them down before they even reached us." Caleb cleared his throat and I knew that he was trying to clear the emotion from his voice.

"We knew that it was just the beginning and Aria and her mates went off to try and find us an army to help. She even picked up a couple more mates along the way. While they were gone, the pack was attacked again and we lost a lot. Marcus, who was the alpha who captured you, just hid while everyone else died. We ended up imprisoning him after and that was when we found out about you from Wyatt. He'd put a curse on Wyatt so that he couldn't speak about you or what had happened. When Kyle, his son, came back, he challenged Marcus and killed him. He's alpha now and the pack is much better under his care. Everyone is still trying to rebuild and heal, but we're getting there," he said sadly.

"What about the demons? Did she find an army?" I asked, suddenly worried about what I was taking my mates back to.

"Yeah. She brought back the Valkyrie army and on the day

of the Blood Moon, we faced them. The Valkyrie army defeated them," Caleb said, reaching across and taking my hand in his.

"Why did they attack?"

"It was all part of some plot to force everyone's hand. All of the realm gates were closed. All of the races had segregated themselves. By doing it, we had unknowingly cut off the natural flow of magic. The God Realm, Asgard, which was the first to close, was on the verge of dying. Some fucking bitch Goddess manipulated the witches into opening the portals for the demon hoard to force us all to come together by slaughtering all of us."

I tried to wrap my brain around what he was saying, but it was hard going. How did you even get someone to do that for you? To attack a school? A school filled with innocent people?

"So as you can imagine, the realm is quite a mess," Dom filled in. "The pack, even though it is rebuilding and trying to work past its loss, almost seems to be in a better position than before. Marcus hurt so many, I think even though we lost so many to the demon attack, it's the first time that the pack has had any hope for a long time. Kyle is a good Alpha and there is no way that Aria would let him step a foot out of line."

They all laughed at that and I found myself even more excited to meet this Aria character.

By the time we made our fourth and final stop before the border, I knew that I wasn't going to be able to get back up again as I dropped to the ground. It wasn't just the pain wracking my entire body, I was exhausted and I felt like I could barely keep my eyes open. We were ahead of schedule because we had managed to keep up our pace, but I think Wyatt had realised that I wasn't going any further. We decided to light a fire this time and make some food. We hadn't eaten anything but granola bars all day and we were all hungry. I think the guys were even looking forward to the idea of the stew even if they all thought it was disgusting.

As much as this trek through the Moon Side was exhausting me, it was also nice in a strange kind of way. Once we got started talking, it gave me the opportunity to ask questions of the guys and get to know them better. Especially Dom and Caleb. Wyatt and I had spent those first few weeks sitting by our stream getting to know each other, but there was a lot that we still needed to catch up on. I could tell that was a conversation for us to have alone though and not with the others.

Wyatt had changed since I first met him. When I met him, he was still just a boy. He hadn't had his first solo shift yet. The past nine years had clearly been difficult and the man that he had grown into was far more withdrawn than the boy I used to know. It was sad in a way but also not. He had grown up and become a man and he had done that through hard times, feeling more alone than most people will ever experience. But he had survived and he had come out the other side of it stronger. We were not only together again, but we had others in our bond. I had to believe that would help make it stronger. We were a family and we would always have each other. He didn't have to be alone ever again. Once he realised that, I knew he would be able to work through any problems he was facing.

We had finished our food and Wyatt scooped me up off the ground and started walking. Part of me wanted to complain, but there was no way I was going to be able to walk the rest of the way and I was just glad he had saved me the humiliation of having to ask.

I leant my head against Wyatt's chest and listened to the steady beat of his heart as it lulled me to sleep. I had never felt safer than I did when he was holding me. We were nearly out of the Moon Side. Almost away from Cassius' influence. I'm not naïve enough to think that he would never be able to get to me in the rest of the realm. But I did know that it would be a lot more difficult and I would at least have allies at my side to help me.

I only slept for about an hour before I heard Caleb's soft voice.

"Lyra, open your eyes baby, you need to see this," he whispered to me.

When I opened my eyes, I could see all three of them smiling down at me and it truly warmed my heart. Wyatt turned so that I could see what lay ahead of us and it was so beautiful that it took my breath away, tears forming in my eyes. There was a part of me that didn't think I would see this again.

There in the distance, the sun is rising above the lush green trees. The sky is lighting up in orange and yellow waves. The start of a new day. The start of a new life.

The border for the Moon Side loomed just in front of us. A strange line where the shadows stop and the light began. The further away from the border you got, the more life seemed to return until a lush green forest stands before us.

"Little bird, little bird, you didn't think it was going to be that easy, did you?" a voice laughed from behind us.

The guys all spun as one to face the oncoming threat as Edwin and five others emerged from the dead treeline behind us. Dom and Caleb came to stand in front of Wyatt, who still had me in his arms. Wyatt clutched me tighter against his chest and I knew that we had little to no chance of us all getting out of here while we were outnumbered like this.

We were standing in exactly the middle between the vampires and the border and we all seemed to come to the same decision simultaneously.

"Run!" Wyatt shouted to the other, turning on his heel and sprinting towards the border.

Dom and Caleb took off and keep pace by Wyatt's side as they sprinted for the border. I knew that they must be able to move quicker than Wyatt because they didn't have the added load of carrying me, but neither looked like they would move ahead and save themselves, even though I was desperate for them to do it.

"Can you open the portal from here?" Wyatt asked Dom.

He just nodded his head and started murmuring under his breath. I had no idea what he was saying, but I knew an incantation when I heard one.

I could see the vampires closing the distance between us. Edwin was cackling in glee. He clearly didn't think that we were going to make it. His one empty eye socket stood stark and still bloody against his face. He hadn't made any attempt to cover it over. If I knew Edwin as well as I thought I did, I doubted he ever would. He probably enjoyed how uneasy it made everyone when they saw him. He caught me staring at him and he just grinned and licked his lips.

I looked towards the border, which was rapidly getting closer, but I didn't think we were going to make it. I didn't think we would be able to cross before they reached us. A portal was starting to flicker to life a few metres from the border and I watched in fascination as it started to grow. I didn't realise how much energy it would take out of Dom to create it, until I noticed that his steps were starting to slow as he continued to mutter the incantation.

Glancing back over Wyatt's shoulder, I realised that the vampires had gained closer still. I desperately searched inside myself for any scrap of my magic to try and help but came up blank. It's like there was a gaping hole inside of me instead of the well of magic that there was supposed to be. I growled out my frustration and just as I opened my mouth to scream my outrage, it turned into a scream of pure terror as Dom's feet stumbled beneath him and he started to fall. His exhausted face turned to me, his lips still mumbling his incantation and I could see the look of goodbye in his eyes.

In the space of time between one step and the next, I felt Wyatt's muscles bunch beneath me as he threw me to Caleb and transformed into his wolf. Caleb caught me out of the air, hugging me tightly to his chest as Wyatt's wolf caught Dom across his back before he could fall to the ground. His feet stumbled at the sudden weight, but he kept moving forward, barely slowing at all.

I sighed in relief as Dom clutched desperately to Wyatt's fur and he kept mumbling the same incantation.

Turning back to the portal I could see that it looked to be about fully-sized now. It glittered an incandescent blue, urging us all to run faster. It was almost like it was the last incentive that we needed, a final goal, a promise of freedom and Caleb and Wyatt seemed to put on an inexplicable burst of speed.

The vampires were mere steps behind us as we passed through the barrier and I could feel the tension fill Caleb's shoulders as they just charged straight through after us, the daylight seeming to have no effect on them whatsoever. But it was too late. The portal was just there and even though I felt Edwin's hand reach out for my hair, and his fingers grazed over the length, Caleb had already leapt and the cold sensation of the portal covered me before Edwin could grasp hold.

CHAPTER 20

WYATT

We landed on the other side of the portal in a crash, all heaped on the ground. Dom was out for the count and crushing me, his full weight laid across my back. He's not exactly a small man and I could now say from experience that he weighed an absolute tonne.

Caleb came through the portal just after us and must have somehow managed to turn himself as he fell through because he's currently lying on his back with Lyra sprawled across his chest.

The portal spluttered and then flickered to a close, thankfully, without any of our pursuers following us through.

I shifted back into my human form and we all groaned at the various bumps and bruises we got from the landing. Lyra seemed a bit dazed and Caleb was still holding her, concerned.

Watching her push herself through our hike out of the Moon Side was one of the hardest things I had ever done in my life, and I'm including the nine years that I was separated from her in that. Saying that though, I was so fucking proud of her. But also, a bit infuriated. The bloody woman wouldn't ask for help, even when it was obvious just how exhausted and how much she was hurting. She just kept going. I knew for a fact that she would have walked all the way to the end if I hadn't just taken the choice out of her hands. The weird thing was that I was expecting a fight from her, or at least some form of reluctance, but she just sank back into my arms with a soft sigh. I wished I'd have just picked her up hours earlier and I was almost kicking myself for not just doing it. I could see that this was going to be how it was with Lyra, a constant back and forth for the rest of our lives, and I couldn't fucking wait for it.

"How the fuck did they break through the border like it was nothing?" Caleb muttered angrily, finally breaking the silence as we all just continued to sit on the floor.

"They'd probably drunk some of my blood," Lyra murmured.

Her eyes were still closed and she was still laid across Caleb, not looking like she had any intention of moving any time soon. In fact, she sounded like she was on the verge of passing out again. Because Lyra had her eyes closed, she didn't see the way that Caleb and I both froze and were looking at her in horror. Dom didn't move a muscle because he was still out cold and I suspected that he would be for some time. Obviously, we knew that after eight years being held by vampires, they would have drunk her blood. But what she had said was something completely more than we had expected.

"What do you mean?" Caleb asked her carefully.

"When they drink my blood, it gives them the ability to temporarily walk in the sunlight," she murmured again, half asleep.

Caleb and I looked at each other in alarm. This was bad, this was really fucking bad. I struggled to my feet and looked around to see where we were, sighing in relief when I saw the packhouse behind us. I grabbed Dom and hauled him up, slinging his arm around my shoulders as I wrapped mine around his waist. He was completely out for the count and I was going to have to drag him as far as I could, hoping that someone would see us and come and help. Caleb had the easy job and had Lyra cradled in his arms again.

"We need to get into the house and tell Kyle," I told him urgently.

He just nodded grimly at me and we started our shuffle towards the house. Lyra had already passed out again.

From an outside perspective, we must have looked a sight with two of our party unconscious. At least we weren't bleeding. In fact, considering what we went prepared to walk into, we had come out of this relatively unscathed. As long as you didn't count the danger which we had now inadvertently put the pack in.

Thankfully we didn't have to make it very far before two of the Elites came rushing out of the packhouse. Echo scooped up Dom's other arm and took some of his weight from my shoulders, which were already screaming from the strain. Nix was just about to help Caleb with Lyra when I asked her to find Kyle instead.

"We'll be in the sitting room," I shouted to her retreating back as she ran back up the steps, waving over her shoulder to indicate that she had heard me.

We managed to get Dom up the steps to the packhouse, he didn't stir even once as we dragged him up between us. Echo was huffing from exhaustion by the time that we got him to the sitting room. He was really fucking heavy.

We dropped Dom perhaps a little too heavily onto a sofa and then shoved his feet onto it to make him a bit more comfortable. He was just going to have to sleep it off there because there was no way I had the energy to carry him up the stairs.

Caleb placed Lyra down onto one of the other sofas a lot

more delicately. He gently smoothed her hair out of her face and she curled onto her side with a sigh.

Echo just stood looking between us all and her mouth hanging open, her eyes kept flickering back to the sleeping form of Lyra. I could tell that she had a million questions running around her head, but she didn't ask a single one of them. I kind of respected her a bit more for that.

Kyle came rushing through the door with Aria, Liam and Nix trailing after him.

"You found her!" Aria breathed out quietly when she took in the sleeping forms of Lyra and Dom in the room.

Everyone just stood around, looking shocked. Fuck, I was shocked! It wasn't until this moment that it actually felt like we had got her back. Back in the Moon Side, I think there was still a part of me that expected her to be ripped out of my arms any second.

"We might have fucked up?" Caleb said with a visible wince.

Kyle looked confused and ushered us to the other side of the room so that we could try and disturb Lyra and Dom as least as possible.

"Explain," was all he said as he sat down at a grouping of chairs, pulling Aria into his lap.

Aria raised an eyebrow at his possessive move but then sank back against him. The rest of us all fell into the remaining seats, Echo and Nix leant against the doorframe to the room, keeping watch. Aria had trained them well. Even when they weren't on duty, they were always on the lookout. Training as Elites had changed everything about them. They had all grown into exceptional women.

"We found Lyra being chased through the Moon Side by some vampires. She'd got herself out already." I couldn't help but smile at that. "We took shelter at an old abandoned house and rested for a couple of days so that she could regain some strength. But one morning we realised that we were being watched, so we moved out quickly. We had nearly made it back to the border when one of the vampires who got away from us before caught up with a squad of vamps. Dom managed to get a portal opened just past the border and we ran for it, there were too many of them for us to fight. When we passed through the border, they followed us straight across. They didn't come through the portal, though. Lyra managed to tell us when we got here that when they drink her blood, it gives them a temporary immunity to sunlight," I filled him in.

Kyle's face scrunched up in thought and I couldn't help but feel bad. We shouldn't have come back here.

"I don't see the problem," Echo said from the doorway.

"Nothing is stopping them from following her here and attacking the pack to get her back. If her blood has that type of properties, then it would give them a distinct advantage. She would be too great an asset to lose," Kyle explained. "They will be coming for her."

"Let them come," Aria said icily. "Then they can learn what we do if they try to take one of ours. They will withdraw once we kill most of them. If needs be, we wipe out their clan." She sounded so cold and detached. This was not the Aria that we had all come to know.

Kyle nodded in agreement, but I could see the wheels still turning in his head. We could be bringing so much trouble to the pack. We could be bringing a whole other fight to them and they had barely recovered from the last one. Worse, this was my fight. Could I really expect them all to take it up with me?

"I can see what you are thinking," Liam said and I looked over to where he was lounging against the wall next to the fireplace. From his position, he could see all of the room but, apparently, he had been spending his time keeping an eye on me.

"You are pack," he said forcefully.

Aria cocked her head to the side in confusion. "What were you thinking?" she asked, genuinely confused. This was one of the things that I loved about Aria, there wasn't a single part of her that would think we shouldn't be here or that would hesitate to protect us.

"That they shouldn't have come here. That they were bringing too much trouble to the pack," Liam answered for me before I could even open my mouth.

It was exactly what I had been thinking, whether I would have worded it that way to Aria though, was a different thing. I knew what she was like and she was fierce when it came to protecting the people she cared about.

"That's just ridiculous," she said, standing up so that she could stand over me. "You are family. You belong here with us. All of you do. Now, if I hear one more word about that, vampires will be the least of your problems. I won't hesitate to kick your ass if I need to," she said, crossing her arm and glaring at me. Now that was the Aria that we all knew and loved.

I knew she meant it as well. This was Aria, she didn't waste time saying things that she didn't mean.

"Okay, first things first, you've all been through a lot and you need to rest. Aria and the Elites will arrange for the pack to be on watch. We will discuss more when you've all had a chance to recover. Our priority now is to get your mate somewhere comfortable and starting to heal," Kyle said. "I wish I had come with you, old friend. I should have been by your side in this from the beginning. We won't abandon you now just because things might get difficult. Aria is right, Wyatt, *you* are family."

I could feel the tears well in my eyes and I didn't dare move in case they fell. I did not want to cry in front of these people. Kyle gave me a knowing look and I tried to subtly clear my throat. All of these years, I felt like I was on the outside. Like I was existing but never truly living. I had lost an integral part of myself—my mate. My wolf mourned, slowly turning rabid as he longed for her. It took everything I had to just survive. To survive Marcus and the things that he would make me do. And now, to sit here and have the people around me declare me family, I don't think they could ever understand just how much that truly meant to me.

Kyle clapped me on the shoulder and smiled. "Stay in the packhouse for now. There aren't any cabins free at the moment that are ready, but I would prefer to have you here where it is safer. Your old rooms are of course still available, your things are still in them. If you want to move to a suite, only Marcus' old suite is ready for anyone to stay in at the moment."

A shudder ran through me at the thought of staying in Marcus' old rooms.

"It's fine. Our rooms are all together anyway. We will be fine in them and Dom will be able to find us easier when he wakes up."

"I keep telling you no one is going to want to stay in there. You should let me change it into a gym," Aria chastised Kyle.

"We already have a gym," Kyle laughed, rolling his eyes.

"Okay, so I'll accept that what I really want you to do is change it into a gym for me." Aria grinned. "One where I can hang that portrait of Marcus and throw knives at it."

"Always with the knives!" Sykes laughed, joining us in the living room. "Someone called for help with a removal," he laughed, clapping his hands together and looking across at Dom.

"Is it wrong that I kind of want to draw on his face and take a picture?" Aria laughed.

I looked around at us all now creepily watching Dom sleep

and felt the need to protect him from his past students and the amok they would probably run if left to their own devices.

"Let's just get him up to bed and everyone can get some sleep. Tomorrow we can go through what we know and make a plan for moving forward," Kyle suggested, tugging Aria into his side while she muttered about needing somewhere to throw knives.

Sykes and Liam managed to pick Dom up off the sofa and started the slow process of moving him to his room. I was so tired that I felt dead on my feet, but that didn't stop me from gently cradling Lyra in my arms and carrying her up the stairs to my room. When I got to the door, Caleb opened it wide for us to pass through before hesitating in the doorway.

"I think I'm going to stay with Dom tonight and keep an eye on him. Give you and Lyra some time alone," he said nervously.

Caleb backed out of the room and closed the door quietly behind him before I even had any time to say anything. Whilst I appreciated having the opportunity to be alone with Lyra, I knew there was more going on with Caleb than he was telling me. He'd always been close with Dom, ever since they went off to the academy together. I'd caught the confused looks that they both gave each other. I didn't think either of them really understood their feelings for each other. Part of me thought it was none of my business and I should let them figure it out on their own, but when I looked down at the beautiful sleeping woman in my arms, I couldn't help but wonder how she would feel about it all. The last thing in the world I was going to let happen was for her to get hurt. She had been through so much in such a short life already, she deserved to be happy now.

CHAPTER 21

LYRA

I woke to the most confusing set of sensations that I almost felt like my brain was going to explode from sensory overload.

I blinked my eyes to try and clear my vision of sleep and focus on my surroundings. I was in a beautiful bedroom. The walls were painted a soft cream colour, it was simply furnished with just a bed, a bedside table and a desk in the far corner. There were a couple of doors in the walls that I'd need to investigate soon, in the hopes that one led to a bathroom, and an enormous bay window which was currently letting the sunlight stream into the room. I was never going to get tired of seeing the sun.

The bed dipped behind me and the arm which was banded across my waist tightened, pulling me further into the body, which was wrapped around my back. Wyatt was so warm and toasty, coupled with the fact that this bed was so soft that I was starting to think it had been made of actual clouds and I was in heaven right now.

"How are you feeling?" Wyatt's voice rumbled from behind me.

I took a moment to actually think about that before answering. I ached all the fuck over, I felt bone tired exhausted and I still had that fractured empty feeling inside of me.

"Hungry," I replied, giving him the safest answer that I could.

Wyatt chuckled and I felt him kiss the back of my neck, causing me to sigh softly. Actually, being able to be here, in bed, in his arms, was more than I had ever let myself hope for. It was perfect.

"Why don't you go and have a hot shower to see if it helps those aching muscles I know you must have, while I go and get us some lunch? We've already missed breakfast."

A cold draft ran down my back as Wyatt sat up in the bed and when I rolled over to face him, I couldn't help the grin that lit up my face to find him in just a pair of boxer briefs. Now that was a good sight to wake up to in the morning. Screw the sun!

"How long have I been asleep?" I asked him when his words suddenly registered.

"About a day and a half," he smiled at what was no doubt the shocked look on my face. "Don't worry, Dom is still out of it and Caleb is keeping an eye on him. He thinks it will be another day or two before he comes round properly. He pretty much drained himself getting a portal open that quick that was big enough for all of us."

Worry for Dom flashed through me and Wyatt came and sat back on the bed beside me, pulling me back into his arms.

"Don't worry sweetheart, it's nothing he hasn't done before and I know for a fact he would do it all over again if it meant that we could get you home safely." Wyatt gently kissed the top of my head before he stood back up and pulled on some jeans and a shirt.

My stomach took that opportunity to scream at us and Wyatt broke out into a massive grin. I felt the heat rush through my face as I flushed in embarrassment. Now that he's mentioned it, I was absolutely starving.

"I won't be long," he laughed, slipping out of the door and closing it behind him.

As soon as the door closed, I stumbled out of bed. I felt so uncoordinated. It was like my muscles were refusing to work. I shook it off, it was probably just because I had spent the last eight years sitting in a cage. Once I got my strength back up and started training, it would come back to me, I was sure of it.

Someone had thankfully stocked up the shower with everything that I needed and it felt good to finally be able to wash and condition my hair. The cold shower I'd had at the abandoned house had been good, but I hadn't been able to properly wash my hair. This steam-filled slice of heaven was exactly what I needed, but I didn't linger under the spray for too long because I was also starving.

As soon as I was wrapped up in a towel, I ventured back out into the bedroom, realising that I had no clothes at all. Caleb was sitting on the bed with a book in his lap, reading. He looked up with a smile as soon as I entered and I came to a sudden stop. How had I ended up going from locked in a cage to having these three doting men around me?

"Aria sent some clothes up for you," he told me after I just stood there and stared at him like a weirdo. Thankfully he just smiled, cocking his head to the side. He at least didn't look like he wanted to run away from me.

"Oh, thanks. I was just thinking that I didn't have anything to wear." Something felt a bit awkward between us and I wasn't really sure why. "How is Dom?" I suddenly asked, needing to fill the silence.

"He's fine. He's at that stage where he periodically wakes up, says something really strange and then passes out again. The last one was something about him not wanting to be a tree. I almost feel like I should start writing them down just so that I can remind him about them later," he grinned.

"Have you known him for a long time?"

"Sometimes it feels like it but no, not really. It's only been three years. But he came into my life when I was going through a difficult time at the pack and it almost felt like he saved me in a way. He understood what I was going through, having been through similar back where he grew up. We just seemed to bond over it," he shrugged and looked away.

You know when you have that feeling that you're poking at something that you probably shouldn't be, but you just can't seem to stop yourself from doing it? Yeah, I was totally feeling that right now.

I sat down next to him on the edge of the bed, still wrapped in my towel and probably showing off far too much skin.

"Do you want to talk about it?" I asked him quietly. "I have basically zero life experience and I've spent the last nine years imprisoned in solitude, but I'm pretty sure that I'm a good listener. We can find out together if you like."

Caleb glanced up at me and gave me a reluctant smile. "How can you even joke about that?" he said, shaking his head.

"I don't know. I feel like if I sit here and cry about it, that I'm letting them win. And apparently, I'm a bit of a spiteful person because there's no fucking way that I'm going to let them win."

"It's kind of hot when you curse," Caleb laughed in shock.

I cocked my head to the side in thought. Surely I'd cursed in front of them all before. I tried to think back through my memories, but to be honest, most of them were hazy at best and I was used to having conversations with myself in my head, so I couldn't even remember if I'd been saying things out loud. In the end, I just shrugged.

"When I was growing up in the education centre, saying it was strict would be an understatement. But they couldn't police my thoughts. I probably use the word fuck in my thoughts more than any normal person."

"You're a normal person," he pointed out, sounding a little offended by my implication that maybe I wasn't.

I shrugged again. "I'm not so sure that I am. I think I might be a bit fucked up."

I tried to laugh it up, but I was a little worried about it. I was guessing that we had made it back to the packhouse, given how lovely this room was and how Wyatt and Caleb seemed so much more relaxed. I wasn't sure how I was going to do being around people for the first time, though. It was different when we were at the abandoned house. It was just me and my mates and even though it was a little awkward at times, it was just easy being with them. I wasn't so sure how I would do when I was suddenly faced with a room full of strangers. I really hoped that I wouldn't freak out, but I was also a bit scared that I probably would.

"You've been through more than most people do in a lifetime, I think you're allowed to be a bit fucked up," he said, giving me a wry smile.

I nodded, saying nothing. I didn't know how to explain that I didn't want that. That I wanted to just live my life and not let Marcus or Cassius have any hold over me. It felt like if I spent the rest of my life hiding from what had happened to me, then it was all for nothing. I'd never truly be free. I might as well still be sat in that cage.

"Here's the clothes Aria brought for you," Caleb said, passing me a small pile.

The atmosphere between us was so awkward and I just didn't know what to say. In some respects, it had been easier in the abandoned house because it was like we were in our own little world. But here, in the real world, I didn't know what was expected of me.

"This is like massively awkward, isn't it?" Caleb suddenly said.

I looked at him and took in the look on his face before we both burst out laughing.

"I'm so glad that you said that," I managed to get out between laughter.

That was how Wyatt found us a few minutes later, just laughing at each other while we sat on the bed.

"What did I miss?" Wyatt asked, smiling at us both.

We quieted down for a second and both looked at him, but the laughter just burst back out again. Wyatt seemed really confused but shook his head and brought a tray over to put on the desk. It was absolutely filled with food and my mouth watered just looking at it.

When I was finally able to get myself under control, I jumped off the bed and quickly threw on the clothes in the bathroom. When I came back out, Wyatt and Caleb had their heads together whispering. It took them a moment to realise that I was there, but when they did, they suddenly jumped apart and started putting sandwiches on plates and passing out drinks.

"Yeah, that wasn't suspicious at all, you covered that up really well," I smiled as Wyatt passed me a plate with a massive sandwich on it.

Wyatt sighed and his shoulders sank. I was starting to kind of worry that I had said something I wasn't supposed to. See, this was my problem, I think I'd forgotten how to act around people.

"We were just discussing what to do with the rest of today," Wyatt explained.

"Okay, I'm not so sure why you needed to do that in secret, though," I frowned, confused.

"Wyatt doesn't want to introduce you to everyone," Caleb said.

My heart sank, had I been reading all this wrong. Did they not actually want me here? I had assumed that they had come to get me because they wanted to start a life for me. Maybe all they really wanted was to set me free so that I could move on to have my own life somewhere else.

"Oh right," I murmured, not sure where to go from there.

Should I be offering to leave? I was positive that I wasn't strong enough to be going anywhere at the moment, not that I even really had anywhere to go. I suppose I could maybe see about returning home, but when I had given up my wings so that I could fall, I was warned that by doing so, I would never be allowed to return again. Wow, if I had thought that it was awkward before, it had definitely ratcheted up a notch now.

"I just think that she should be resting and regaining her strength. We can do introductions tomorrow or maybe in a few days when she feels up to it more," Wyatt said with a shrug.

Caleb looked over at me and I could see the uncertainty in his eyes. Unfortunately, I had no idea what it meant.

"Okay, here's what I think we should do," I suggested. "I am out of practice with the whole people thing, so I'm going to need you to explain to me how you are feeling because I'm having problems reading your expressions."

I was a little embarrassed admitting it, but it seemed like it was going to save us a lot of heartache in the long run.

Wyatt pulled the chair out from the desk and swung it around to face us before sitting down with his plate of food. Caleb came back over to join me on the bed.

"I think you should get out and meet people. Even if it's only for a short amount of time each day. I don't think hiding up here is going to achieve anything but make you more nervous about seeing everyone," Caleb rushed out and then shoved an enormous bite of sandwich into his mouth, almost in an attempt to prevent himself from having to speak against any time soon.

Wyatt rubbed the back of his neck uneasily before turning his gaze away from us and becoming overly interested with the corner of the room. "I'm worried about your safety and I only just got you back. And maybe, I just don't want to have to share you with everyone just yet," he said quietly with a shrug.

I felt my cheeks pinch from the massive grin that took over my face. How cute was he?

"How about a compromise?" I proposed. "Let's go down for just a little bit, show our faces and say hi and then come back up here. If we stay inside the house, then you can be happy that we're still safe," I suggested.

I didn't want to admit that saying hi was probably the most I knew about social interaction, so what I was suggesting was probably the extent of what I was capable of when it came to socialisation. I had a terrible feeling that I was just going to say the wrong thing and insult the new alpha. Maybe I could request a view with my next cage?

"I think I would be okay with that," Wyatt reluctantly agreed.

I could tell that he wasn't, but I was grateful that he was at least going to try for me. Caleb didn't say anything, so I tried to surreptitiously glance his way without him knowing. Unfortunately, he caught my eye immediately, but he gave me a big grin and then rolled his eyes. I was nearly certain that Caleb was expecting me to stick around. Maybe I should just come out and ask them. The problem was I don't think I was prepared for them to tell me no. For now, I was happy just soaking up what I could get. All of that can be tomorrow Lyra's problem.

We ate in relative silence, but it didn't feel as awkward as it did when it was just Caleb and me. Maybe it was because I was more comfortable with Wyatt. After all, I'd had that time to get to know him when we were meeting up down by the stream. Once he got over his concern for my safety, I think I'd really like to go back down and see if it's changed.

It didn't take long before we had eaten everything that Wyatt had brought up and he couldn't put off us going downstairs for any longer. My hair had just about dried from the shower and I was dressed in the stretchy trousers and tank top that Caleb had said Aria brought for me. I was comfortable, but I didn't really feel like I was appropriately dressed to be meeting the new alpha. Wouldn't he expect me to dress up a bit or something?

"Do you maybe have a hairbrush that I could use?" I asked Wyatt while self-consciously running my hands through my still knotty hair. It felt a lot better than before now that I had coated it in about half a bottle of conditioner.

Wyatt disappeared and came back with a hairbrush which I gratefully accepted and I spent the next half an hour working all the knots out of my hair. I think he was just happy that it was delaying us leaving the room, to be honest. About ten minutes in I was ready to just hack the whole lot off, but my vanity had me persevering and I was glad that I did.

Standing in front of the bathroom mirror now and looking at myself, I could see the old Lyra starting to shine through. The glaring difference was my lack of wings and I allowed myself a brief moment of sadness when I thought about them. I didn't think I would ever get used to the fact that they were gone. That I had to give up a part of myself just so that I could be with the man that I loved, well men now I suppose. As always, when I thought of them, a shadow of the pain I felt in losing them, surged through my back and shoulders. It was like the pain of losing them would forever be tied with any thoughts of them. It was more pain than I had ever experienced and after growing up in the education centres, I had experienced my fair share.

I stared at my reflection for a moment and took in the differences. My cheeks were more hollowed and my arms were basically skin and bone. I'd lost a lot of weight and a lot of muscle as well. I doubted I would be able to swing a sword now, let alone stand my ground in a fight. I could feel my ribs and my legs weren't in any better condition than my arms were. Urgh, I definitely wasn't looking my best. It was as good as it was going to get though and I reluctantly left the bathroom.

When I stepped back into the bedroom Wyatt and Caleb's eyes immediately snapped to me. Wyatt smiled broadly and Caleb's mouth dropped open. I shuffled back and forth on my feet, uncertain about what was happening .

"Wow," Caleb breathed out.

He must have seen the uncertain look on my face because he quickly clarified.

"You look so different now that your hair is … well like that," he added awkwardly.

I knew what he meant. Now that it wasn't a matted mess around my head. I'd be annoyed if it wasn't true, so I just smiled to let him know that I wasn't upset. He visibly deflated when I did, which was actually pretty funny.

"It's going to take me some time to gain some weight back," I said, running a hand and a disapproving glare over my arms.

If I was honest, my appearance made me a bit uncomfortable. I started to wish that it was really cold so that I could cover up with a massive jumper, but unfortunately, it was actually quite warm. It was probably because I wasn't used to having the sun shining down on me. I would love to go and lie outside in the sun, but I could wait another day or two if it would make Wyatt a bit happier.

When we finally made it downstairs, Wyatt led us into a library where four people were sitting seemingly deep in discussion. As soon as we walked through the door, they all fell quiet and I got that horrible feeling that you get when you think you've just interrupted something important.

"You're awake," a bubbly brunette squealed jumping up off the sofa and coming over to us.

She immediately hugged Caleb and gave Wyatt one of those shoulder slap things in greeting and then she was stood in front of me with a huge grin on her face.

"I've never met an angel before," she said, looking me up and down. "Virion tells me that you are all skilled warriors. We're going to have to fatten you up so you can show me some moves," she grinned.

"Babe, stop crowding the angel like a crazy person. Trust you to introduce yourself by asking about fighting, next thing you know you're going to be whipping out your knives to show her," a man behind her laughed, pulling her back a few steps.

She playfully punched him in the stomach and then stepped into his waiting arms with a smile.

"She'd probably love to see my knives," I heard her grumble quietly.

One of the other men that she was with approached us with a kind smile on his face and held out his hand for me to shake. He was young, in fact, he looked younger than me. He had sandy blonde hair and gleaming green eyes. He was built fairly similarly to Wyatt and Caleb, so I was guessing that he must be a shifter too.

"Lyra, it's a pleasure to meet you. Welcome to the pack, we are all very glad to finally have you here. My name is Kyle, this is my lovely mate Aria. The other two are Sykes and Liam. Unfortunately, the other two in our mate bond are currently in the Fae lands. We had not expected you to return quite so quickly or I am sure that they would have delayed their journey," he explained.

I racked my brain for why his name seemed so familiar. Caleb and Wyatt had both mentioned Aria to me before, so I knew that she was the friend that they had spoken about, but Kyle's name was ringing a bell for me as well, but I was drawing a complete blank.

"It is a pleasure to meet you all too," I told them, feeling quite proud of my social skills. "To be honest I'm relieved to meet some friendly faces, I'm a bit nervous about meeting your alpha," I told them.

Sykes, the one who was currently holding Aria, grinned at me and said, "Why are you nervous?"

Aria elbowed him in the stomach, causing him to 'oof' out a breath. That was a pretty solid hit. She obviously had put some force behind that elbow and I would be interested to see how her fighting style differed from my own when I was back in shape.

"I suppose I'm not sure what I'm supposed to say or do. I don't really have a good track record with pack alphas," I told them nervously wringing my hands together.

The cheerful mood in the room suddenly dropped and Kyle stepped forward again, his head hanging in shame.

"I can never make amends for what my father did to you Lyra, for what he apparently did to so many other people. He is my greatest shame and I will spend the rest of my life trying to right the wrongs that he made." As he spoke, he looked me dead in the eye and I could see his sorrow and shame sitting in the tears that made his eyes glisten.

I sighed, which I think Kyle initially took as a bad sign. "That's why your name sounded familiar," I said, rolling my eyes.

I took a step forward and put a hand on Kyle's shoulder,

silently praying that I wasn't committing some kind of shifter crime that I wasn't aware of.

"You have nothing to apologise or make amends for. Your father's actions were his own. I will help you right his wrongs if you need," I told him and I meant it. "Although, give me a week or two, as I need to get back a bit of strength first," I tried for a joke, but it seemed to fall flat.

"You would really help me," Kyle asked, frowning in confusion.

"Of course. Unless that's inappropriate or something," I mumbled, looking at Wyatt for some kind of indication if I was doing something wrong. I hoped he would at least warn me if I started to wander into cage territory.

Wyatt just grinned at me and looked pretty proud, so I was going to guess that I was on somewhat of the right track.

Sykes barked out what I was coming to think was his signature laugh. "Inappropriate. You're hilarious!"

Aria elbowed him in the stomach again before striding forward and grabbing my arm, spinning me on the spot and marching me over to the door. My first reaction was, here comes the cage, but then she slung her arm over my shoulder and shouted back to the guys.

"You guys suck, she's coming with me to meet the girls," before she said to me, "We can grab you some supplies as well, clothes and stuff. You're going to need more than one change of clothes."

Aria had me marched out of the library before any of the guys could say anything and before I knew it, we were headed towards the main doors and what looked like outside.

"Oh, I'm not supposed to be going outside today," I told her nervously as she dragged me closer to the door.

"What! Why?" she asked, thankfully coming to a sudden stop at the same time that the others emerged from the library.

"Wyatt explain yourself! Why does Lyra think that she isn't allowed to go outside?"

For some reason, this seemed to have made her spitting angry and unfortunately for Wyatt she was directing it all his way.

All of the guys took one large step away from him, leaving him to weather the storm of her anger alone. Wyatt rolled his eyes muttering at the guys about abandonment before speaking up.

"Because we haven't discussed the potential threat of an entire clan of vampires storming the pack and stealing her back to place her in a cage and torture her for another decade," he said snarkily.

Aria seemed to immediately deflate. I was certain that there was a story behind her reaction and I really wanted to know it, but I wasn't sure if it was polite to ask or not. She seemed like she wanted to be my friend, but she was also the alpha's mate, so maybe this could be a pack thing. This new life needed to come with a manual or something!

Wyatt's words suddenly registered with me through my train of thought.

"It's daylight," I pointed out.

"They walked in the sun when they crossed the barrier," Wyatt replied with his hand on his hips.

"Yes, because they had recently drunk my blood," I said, confused.

"How long does the effect of your blood last for them?" Kyle asked me.

"Four days and it is now five days since the last ritual. They only ever drink from the vein, they have never taken any of my blood to store. I suppose they assumed that I would never be free of them and saw no need."

"We only need to worry about an incursion at night then,"

Aria said with a smile, taking hold of my arm and preparing to pull me out of the building again.

Now that we had stopped for a minute, I was actually starting to feel a bit tired again and a wave of nausea flowed over me, causing me to stumble forward. Wyatt immediately swooped in and caught me, scooping me up into his arms.

"Sorry, just felt a bit weird for a second," I said, trying to just shrug it off.

This was ridiculous, I should be able to be up and about for this short amount of time. We had just spent a whole day hiking out of the Moon Side. Although thinking along those lines, we had just spent an entire day hiking out of the Moon Side, maybe it had taken more out of me than I thought.

"I think you need more rest, sweetheart," Wyatt said quietly to me almost like he was giving me an opportunity to disagree if I wanted to.

I knew just how much he wanted to keep me by his side and safe and I understood how much it was costing him to even give me the option of leaving with Aria, even if it was just outside.

"I think you might be right," I told him, even I could hear my words slurring that time.

Wyatt frowned down at me in concern and started taking me back to our room. I glanced over his shoulder at the others, worried that I might have offended or upset them but all I saw were concerned faces.

I dropped my head down onto Wyatt's shoulders and closed my eyes and that was the last thing that I remembered.

Chapter 22

Caleb

Lyra was asleep before we even got back up to the room and Wyatt and I had tucked her into bed before moving back out to the corridor where Kyle and Aria waited for us.

"Did I push her too far?" Aria asked, looking concerned.

"No, I think she is just exhausted but fighting it," I said, trying not to make her feel too bad. I knew that she was just excited to have Lyra back with the pack where she belonged.

Kyle was frowning looking through the door to where Lyra was sleeping. "Who do we know that can come and check her over? I'm concerned that this isn't normal, but what do we really know about angels?"

He was a good alpha. He genuinely cared about everyone that he considered part of his pack, even though we hadn't formally asked Lyra to join, she was still one of us.

"Dom will know who we can trust to ask," I suggested.

We couldn't forget that Lyra was the first angel which anyone would have seen for nearly a century. She was clearly priceless to the vampires and I dreaded to think what others would think of her. The witches and mages would be fascinated by the properties of her blood. We were going to need to protect her, especially while she was in this weakened state.

Kyle nodded thoughtfully. "Let's see how she is tomorrow and then discuss it with him. Hopefully, he will be awake by then. In the meantime, I'll see what we can get put together in the kitchen to start trying to build her strength back up."

Kyle and Aria retreated downstairs on a mission to see what they could do to help Lyra and it warmed my heart to watch them go. I had spent too many confusing years in this pack feeling alone and unconnected. My wolf would not recognise Marcus as his alpha and it had meant a lonely life for me. But now, I had a place in this pack, I felt like I was at home and, most importantly, I had my beautiful mate by my side. I had been worried about how she would feel being here. It wasn't exactly a happy place for her. If she wanted to leave, of course, I would support her in that, but there was a small part of me that really hoped she would be happy enough to stay here. I think we could have something special with these people in our lives. I was certain that together we were going to make changes to our world and those changes were going to be for the good of everyone, not just the ruling alphas.

Turning back to the bedroom, I saw Wyatt tucking Lyra gently into bed. She was completely out cold. It would do her good to rest. Hopefully, she could get a few more hours in and then we could maybe try and tempt her with some more food. So far, she didn't seem to have any issues eating, she just needed to keep it up.

"I'm going to check on Dom," I whispered to Wyatt.

He didn't look up at me, but he nodded in acknowledgement. I knew he wouldn't leave Lyra's side while she was asleep. We were going to need to persuade him to get some sleep soon though because I also knew that there was no way he would sleep through the night and leave her unprotected.

I quietly closed the door behind me and left them to it,

slipping next door into Dom's room. He was still passed out in his bed. He must have woken up at some point though because the food I had left next to his bed was gone and the bottle of water was empty.

I was worried about him, not that I would tell anyone else. He'd experienced magical drain before and he wasn't doing anything unusual now, but it made me feel anxious seeing him like this. He was normally so solid and strong. But seeing him like this made me realise how vulnerable he really could be. I understood now why he rarely used magic whenever we had to fight. If this happened in the middle of a battle, he would be killed for certain. I wouldn't be able to cope if I lost him. Maybe when Lyra is feeling better, we should all spend some time training with Aria. We could all do with updating our skills and I knew the others would do anything if it meant that we could protect Lyra better.

I sat on the edge of Dom's bed. I knew that I shouldn't wake him, but I needed to talk to someone and in the past that someone for me had always been Dom.

"You're thinking so hard that I can hear it from here," Dom mumbled, his face smushed into the pillow as he laid face down on the bed.

"I just came to check on you, see if you need anything," I said, trying to play off the weird way that I was sitting here watching him sleep.

"No, you're not. You're freaking out about something and you need to talk," I could hear the smile in his voice as he immediately knew why I was there.

I sighed in defeat, but I was still reluctant to talk about it. It was easier when he was unconscious and I could pretend to myself that I wanted to talk through my problems. Now that the situation was staring me in the face, I didn't know if I had the balls to talk about it.

"Start with something easy," Dom said gently as he turned over and pulled himself up to sit against the headboard.

I started to wrack my mind for something easy. The problem was none of it felt easy.

"What if they come for her?" I said, my voice cracking with worry.

"Let them come. They won't get anywhere near her. It might even be for the best, it would give us an excuse to take out the clan and remove the threat entirely."

I hadn't heard Dom speak so violently about anything before. The Blood Moon battle and its lead up had changed him, but then again, it had changed all of us.

"But that's not what's really bothering you, is it?" he asked knowingly.

You see this was the problem with letting people get to know you. You gave them the ability to call you out on all your shit and read you like the unwilling book that you were.

"Is it Lyra?" he urged.

"Part of it, I suppose." Okay so apparently this was going to happen. I sighed almost like it was going to somehow miraculously fill me with courage. "She's my mate and I have all of these feelings for her, but I don't know. I don't know how to act around her. I don't know how I'm supposed to be and I feel a bit like I'm failing at this already."

"Caleb, you're right, she is your mate but you also only just met her. It's okay to not know how to act because you don't know each other yet. She probably feels exactly the same. Just get to know each other, everything else will come in time," he said and he was making sense. "Talk to her about it," he suggested.

I nodded, still trying to buy myself time. It was something that needed to be said, that needed to be put out there but it had the potential to ruin everything and now that I had suddenly got so much in my life, I was all too aware of exactly how much I had to lose.

"But ... what if I didn't have those feelings just for her?" I asked quietly, my eyes fixed on the floor. I couldn't bring myself to look at him. I couldn't risk seeing the disgust or disappointment in his eyes. "She's my mate, I'm not supposed to feel like this about anyone else," I said, feeling utterly ashamed of myself.

I felt Dom's hand grasp my shoulder as he sat up and moved closer to me. "There isn't a right or a wrong way to love someone," he whispered, his voice cracking as he spoke.

I looked at him in confusion and I could see the emotions rolling through his gaze, but I didn't let myself hope what they could possibly mean.

"I feel like I'm doing something wrong," I told him, my voice breaking embarrassingly.

"Caleb, I promise you that you aren't doing anything wrong. This person that you have feelings for though, I need you to tell me who it is. I need there not to be any confusion between us about this," he said. I could hear the desperation in his voice and in that moment, I allowed myself to hope.

I opened my mouth to tell him. I wanted to tell him. I was so fucking scared that I had read this situation wrong, but I didn't know how much longer I could take this.

Dom's eyes were locked with mine and I would swear that I could see hope lingering there.

"I ..." I started, but then a knocking on the door startled us apart.

Wyatt opened the door and leant in.

"Hey Dom, it's good to see you awake. Kyle wants to talk about the vampire clan and security for tonight. You two coming down?" he asked.

"Yeah, yes, sure," I mumbled standing up and wiping my

now sweaty hands on the tops of my jeans. "I want to actually talk to Aria about a training schedule as well."

"You and your training schedules, I thought we would have seen an end to those by now," Wyatt laughed.

Dom and I both walked over to Wyatt by the door and almost achieved the pretence that nothing had been about to happen. Wyatt turned to leave just as we reached the door and I heard Dom quicken his pace behind me.

"Fuck this," he muttered before his hand came over my shoulder and pushed the door closed in front of me.

As I turned to look behind me to see what he was doing, his hands came to my shoulders and he pushed me back against the door. I didn't have the chance to ask what he was doing before his lips met mine with a longing desperation that matched my own.

I could have sworn that I heard Wyatt's voice on the other side of the door mumbling "about fucking time."

But I was so lost in Dom that I didn't care if I did. One of his hands stayed on my shoulder and the other cupped the back of my head, holding me in place. His lips moved confidently across mine as he kissed my upper then lower lip, before drawing my lower lip into his mouth and biting it gently.

That was all I needed for the dam inside of me to burst and my hands came to his hips, pulling him tight against my front.

I had never been with a man before. I had never had feelings for any man before Dom and I had absolutely no idea what I was doing or what I wanted to do. All I could think at that moment was that I needed to feel his body pressed against mine. I needed the reassurance that this was real.

Dom broke away from the kiss and leant his forehead against mine. "I really hope I wasn't misreading the situation and you were going somewhere else with that earlier," he whispered.

I couldn't help but laugh. "No, not at all. But I can't believe you let me sit there and squirm, you fucker!"

"Hey, I was just as unsure as you were. This isn't exactly something I've done before," he said, stepping back from me but keeping a smile on his face.

"This is a bit crazy, isn't it," I said softly. "What's Lyra going to say though?"

"I honestly don't know. All we can do is talk to her about it. I think if we are all open and upfront about everything we can work through this. Or at least that's what I'm hoping. I don't know what we have between us Caleb, but I'd really like to find out."

"Yeah me too."

It felt like an enormous weight had lifted off my chest. I knew what Dom was saying though. I didn't know what I wanted from him, but I knew that the feelings were there and I wanted to see where it was going to take us. Fuck, I was nervous as fuck about telling Lyra though.

"Come on, let's go and see what's happening downstairs. We don't need to deal with all this right now," Dom reassured me.

I gave him a nod and we headed downstairs to the library, which seemed to be the only room in this house that anyone used. It was ironic given that we had all hated it so much during Marcus' reign as Prime Alpha.

Wyatt gave us a small smile as we entered the room and I realised that I hadn't imagined his voice outside of the door as Dom had closed it. How obvious had it been to everyone else that Dom and I were beginning to develop feelings for each other? Fuck, were they all laughing at us behind our backs? I knew that this was an unusual situation, humans had taken huge strides forward in same-sex relationships, but it was still virtually unheard of in our realm. But, what the fuck did it have to do with anyone else anyway? As long as

Lyra, Dom and I were happy everyone else could just fuck off.

But Lyra! What was she going to think?

I looked around the room in panic as I realised that everyone was looking at me, waiting for me to answer a question which no doubt had to do with the conversation they had all just been having while I was spiralling in my own mind.

"Kyle is concerned about how Lyra is doing mentally after everything she's been through. He was wondering if it would benefit her to speak with someone about what happened to her?" Wyatt updated me, obviously registering the confused and slightly panicked look on my face.

"Right. I've spoken with her a little, she has some worries which I won't go into in case she doesn't want me talking about it. I think for now she is dealing with it. She seems pretty resilient. I haven't spoken with her at length, but it seems like her childhood was pretty fucked up at that education centre she's mentioned. I'd say that we keep an eye on her, help her build up her strength again and just support her if she needs it. We can always address it with her later if she seems like she needs any additional help," I suggested.

Everyone nodded seemingly in agreement with me and I caught the smirk on Dom's face as he no doubt knew exactly what had distracted me.

"She mentioned something to me about being conditioned against withstanding torture since she was three years old," Wyatt mumbled, his eyes locked onto something outside of the window.

We were all shocked into silence. What kind of fucked up stuff did angels do to their children? Aria had a look of tortured pain on her face. Out of all of us, she would probably understand the most, having gone through an abusive childhood herself at the hands of the humans. Maybe it would do Lyra some good to speak with her? It might help to be able to talk to someone who understood. The problem was that I wasn't entirely sure that Lyra understood that there was something wrong with the way that she had been raised.

After a few moments of silence, everyone started to get an awkward shuffle on. I was relieved when Kyle decided to move on and started talking.

"Aria and the Elites have got a security patrol organised from sunset to sunrise. I have suggested that you three stay out of the rotation because I think it would be good to have a second line of defence at the packhouse. In other words, I want you to stay with Lyra. Dom, don't take this the wrong way, but I get the impression you're not really ready to jump into a fight," Kyle grinned. "How do you feel about that?"

Wyatt bristled a bit at the suggestion that we not be included, but I could see that he was starting to be persuaded when Kyle mentioned us as a second line of defence.

"Wait, do we know how big this clan is?" I asked.

"No, we won't be able to get any information until Lyra wakes up and can speak with us more," Kyle conceded. "But if the properties in her blood have allowed them to walk the human realm in daylight hours all these years then we can assume that they have plenty of opportunities to expand their numbers."

"But I think it is unlikely that they would bring the full clan here for any kind of confrontation," Dom pointed out, making us all look at him in question. "The only solid information which we have ever known about the vampires is that they require human blood for sustenance and that they cannot survive without a constant supply of it. It would be logistically unfeasible to bring a large fighting force into the realm where they have no food supply. It seems unlikely that they would be able to transport and store the amount of blood that would be required for such an expedition," he pointed out.

"Unless they just bring it in convenient human-shaped packages," Aria pointed out.

I could tell that this knowledge was hard for her. She had grown up in the human realm and still had people she considered family there. Knowing that the vampires could hunt so freely there wasn't going to sit well with her. It was no wonder she was so on board with the vampires bringing the fight to us. I was under no illusion that she would take whatever opportunity she had to take out as many as she could.

"Agreed, but the human blood slaves which they have are now a rare commodity without Lyra's blood to allow them easy access to resupply. It would be ill-advised to risk their safety when they have no guarantee of being able to replace them if they don't retrieve Lyra immediately," Dom argued.

He had a point.

"That's, of course, assuming that he isn't insane and just throws everything he has at us because he doesn't have a sane thought in his head," I pointed out.

"Yes, that would be the assumption," Dom agreed with a grin.

"Regardless, apart from the Elites, our fighting force at the pack is relatively small," Liam pointed out.

Unfortunately, he was right. Some of the pack guards remained and there were also Aria's other mates and us. But apart from that, the pack numbers had drastically reduced.

"We will need to increase our numbers soon, but that is a problem for another time," Kyle agreed. "For now, I'm happy with Aria's plan unless anyone has any problems."

We all shook our heads and mumbled that it was okay. Deep down, I think we all felt like we wanted to do more, but while Lyra was so weak, it was hard to stray far from her side.

"Thank god," Aria huffed. "Because I don't want to share with anyone else, I've never had the opportunity to fight a vampire before," she said, giving us a slightly evil smile.

"You're welcome, sweetheart," Kyle laughed.

"You give the best gifts," she sighed.

"Hey, you can't take credit for the vampire gift, that's not fair," Sykes huffed, who had stayed quiet up until then.

"You snooze, you lose," Kyle grinned sitting back in his chair with his arms crossed.

"Fine," Sykes sulked. "I get angels!" he suddenly shouted. "If angels come too, I call dibs on them," he looked pretty pleased with himself for the idea.

"I am glad that the danger my mate currently faces is causing you so much entertainment," Wyatt gruffed out, looking pissed.

"Yeah, sorry about that," Sykes said, sinking down in his chair and turning on the kicked puppy look that he seemed to be able to pull out whenever needed.

Wyatt smirked at him. "I'm only playing with ya kid."

"Kid, what are you, like twenty minutes older than us?" Sykes laughed.

"Longest twenty minutes of my life if I am," he grumbled back.

"Exactly how much older are you though?" Aria asked, cocking her head to the side. "I know it's super rude to ask but I just really want to know, so I'm asking anyway."

Wyatt laughed. Trust Aria to say it out loud, that was always her philosophy, just get to the point.

"I'm eight years older than them," he said with a sad smile. "I was thirteen when Marcus took over the pack. Kyle was this precocious little five year old who was left to his own devices because Marcus was a shit. For some reason, he latched on to me and we survived through it together. Then these other two came along a year or so later and I got lumbered with them as well."

We all knew that wasn't how he really felt. He loved the guys like his own. I think them coming along gave him a purpose that he desperately needed during a very dark time in his life. Even if he was still just a child at the time.

"He makes it out like he didn't do anything, but even though he was barely a teenager himself, he basically brought us up. Wyatt made sure that we had proper meals at the right time, that we had clean clothes. He kept us out of trouble and he helped us with our school work. He taught us how to fight when we got older and he kept us out of Marcus' way when he was on a rampage. No one in the pack knew what was going on inside the packhouse. Marcus had everyone seeing him as the perfect father and the perfect alpha. They all thought that he was so generous taking Wyatt into his home after what happened. They had no idea what it was really like," Kyle told Aria.

We all owed Wyatt a lot, but I don't think he would ever believe that we did. He just wasn't that kind of person.

CHAPTER 23

LYRA

Waking up in bed again was definitely disorientating, especially because I had no idea how I got here. The sun was still shining brightly outside and I had no idea how long I had been asleep for, it could have been hours, or it could have been days.

I sat up in bed with an involuntary groan. My body still felt like hell. Despite having such a soft bed to sleep on, for the first time in a decade, all of my muscles ached. I also had a throbbing pain starting behind my eyes. All that time, sat in that damp, dark cage and yet now I was apparently getting sick. Or at least I assumed that was what was happening to me. Angels don't really get sick, but since I had given up my wings, I wasn't entirely certain just how much of an angel I was still. I should have tried to do some more research into it before I took the leap. Unfortunately, it was out of my hands. One of the other angels had seen me sneaking off and had followed me. They reported me for visiting the realm below. Thankfully they didn't see me meeting with Wyatt, or it would have been much worse. As it was, I was given the chance to either stop or fall. I chose to fall. There was no way that I could have stopped

and if I continued, I was risking my entire flight being termi-
nated on grounds of desecration. I may not have wanted to
spend my life with them, but I didn't want them all to die
because of me. Instead, I chose to fall and those same angels
that I was giving up my wings to save, ripped them from my
body. It wasn't their fault. I could see that several of them
didn't want to, but that was our way. Those were our orders
and no one went against the orders of the Archangel Council.

I swung my legs over the edge of the bed and sat up,
considering my next steps. I was alone and I felt strange about
wandering around this house on my own. It wasn't like I lived
here, or at least I didn't think that I did. We probably needed
to discuss this at some point, you know, before things started
to get a bit weird.

Deciding that this was the perfect opportunity to snoop, I
started to move around the room, which was clearly Wyatt's. It
almost felt like he didn't live here, it was so tidy. The desktop
was empty and there was one shelf above it that held a few
books, a couple of crime books and interestingly a few text-
books of agriculture and land management. The rest of the
room was bare. One of the doors led into a closet which held a
handful of clothing items, mostly just jeans and shirts. The
only other door led to the bathroom I had used earlier in the
day, or at least I was almost certain that it was the same day.
Even the bathroom was sparse though. There was a set of
shampoo and shower gel in the shower that smelt like tea tree
and mint and a toothbrush and razor next to the sink. The
products that I had used when I showered had clearly been left
by someone else, if I had to guess, I would say Aria.

There was nothing personal in this room, apart from a
couple of books. No photographs of his parents, no memen-
toes of his childhood, nothing that really spoke of his person-
ality. It spoke of a lonely life; a half existence and it broke my
heart to see. It may not have had the bars, but it seemed like

Wyatt had existed in little more than a cage himself. I couldn't help but wonder if it was self-imposed as a result of his guilt or if this was just what life under Marcus had been like for him. There was nothing here that made me think of the kind and passionate man I knew Wyatt to be.

I didn't get time to snoop any further, not that there was really anything to snoop through, before Caleb came back into the room.

"I didn't expect you to be awake so soon," he said, looking nervous.

"How long was I asleep for?"

"Just a few hours. Dom is awake again. He's just making some soup for you both down in the kitchen. He should be here soon," he shifted nervously on the spot before looking around and deciding to take a seat on the sofa. "I should warn you that Kyle and Aria are going to be on the case about helping you build up your strength so be prepared for the nagging to now commence," he said, giving me a shy smile.

Something had changed with Caleb since we had arrived back at the packhouse. He had seemed easy to talk to when we were at the old abandoned house, but now it was almost as if we weren't quite sure how to act around each other.

"Have I done something to upset you?" I asked him as I slowly sat down on the edge of the bed, leaving as much of a gap between us as I could.

"No, why would you ask that?" he asked, looking confused and also, if I was reading him right, slightly panicked.

"It just feels like ... I'm not sure how to even describe it, almost like we aren't as comfortable around each other now that we are here," I tried explaining.

Caleb thought for a second, but I could tell that it was because he was trying to find the right words to express himself rather than any attempt to try and deceive me. "I think that I'm a little unsure about how to act. It's confusing. I have all of these feelings. You're my mate and I'm obviously very attracted to you. But I also don't really know you yet. It feels like maybe we missed a few steps, the ones where we got the chance to get to know each other."

He looked at me with that slightly panicked look again and I smiled, wanting him to understand that I wasn't upset by what he had said. It's not like he had said anything that wasn't true.

"How about we start on a few of those steps," I suggested.

Caleb relaxed a little and I was so close to laughing at him, but I managed to hold it back. I understood how he felt because I felt exactly the same. It was kind of nice to know that I wasn't the only one who felt this way. It was just funny how panicked he seemed about it all.

"Let's play a game," Caleb suggested, suddenly brightening up. "I ask you a question, you answer and then ask me a question. I then have to answer your question, answer my original question and then ask you another. The only rule is that you have to tell the absolute truth."

"Okay, that sounds easy. Do you want to go first?"

"Sure, okay let's start with an easy one ... what were your parents like?"

"I never met them. Who was your closest friend when you were growing up?" I had no idea if this was the sort of thing that I was supposed to be asking, but it felt right.

"I didn't really have any friends when I was a kid. I was this awkward, gangly kid that the others kind of avoided and made fun of more. Then Dom found me. I've never been closer to anyone than him." I catch a slight blush to his cheek, but I won't prod any further if that is as far as he wants to go. "My parents were good people, they would have loved you. My mother died in childbirth trying to give birth to my little sister who was stillborn. My father loved her so much. They weren't fated mates, but it was almost like he just couldn't go on without her. He disappeared about a year after she died. Before that though, we had a happy life. My Mom loved to cook and she was always in the kitchen trying things out. I can always remember that our house smelt like whatever was baking in the oven. My father doted on her. He worshipped the ground that she walked on. We were truly happy back then." He cleared his throat suddenly and I could tell that this was a painful subject for him. I slipped my hand into his and he gave me a sad smile.

I really didn't want to keep playing this game because now that we'd started it seemed like a terrible idea. It was only going to make us sad.

Caleb didn't ask another question after his answer and I could tell that he was stuck reliving the sad times of his past as his eyes shuttered to me.

"Tell me about when you met Aria at the academy," I blurted out, hoping to turn to a happy subject.

Caleb huffed out a laugh and some of the sadness seemed to drop away from his face. "Oh my god, the day that Aria Graves was quite literally thrown into the academy. The humans had decided that half-blood kids were losing control and responsible for several violent incidents and decided to deport them all back here to the academies. They set up a global testing scheme and Aria got caught up in it. She knew she had magic, but they had her cornered and sent her here. She landed in the academy in a pissy mood, trusting no one and hating everything about us. To be fair, she didn't get the best impression from a lot of people. But she met Kyle, Liam and Sykes on her very first day and I think they helped her a lot." He laughed as he thought back to that time and it was good to see a smile on his face. "She walked into the gym for my class, there was an incident and everyone saw all the scars covering her back, but she didn't hide behind it, if anything it just made her more determined to prove us wrong. We all thought she had little to no magic and then suddenly she's pulling out these swords seemingly from her ass and proving to us all that she was much stronger than we would ever know."

"She seems like the kind of person that would shake things up," I smiled.

"She saved us all so many times," he said, pulling me closer to him. "I'm worried about her now though, she's changed. I think she's struggling with the aftermath of what we went through."

I nod because I can only imagine what they'd all seen and had to do. I knew they'd only told me the highlights of what happened here, but it was horrific nonetheless.

"Things like that change a person. Give her time, she needs to work things through her own head. All you can do is be her friend and stand by her when she needs you to."

"You'd be okay with that?" he asked me slowly and almost reluctantly.

I frowned in confusion and he must see that I didn't understand his question.

"You'd be okay with me being her friend?"

"Why wouldn't I be?" I felt like I was missing something and it was like my worries of not knowing what a normal society was like came crashing into reality.

"Because she's a woman and I'm your mate," he trailed off silently.

"Do you intend to have sex with her?" I asked him bluntly because I could see where this was going and I didn't want him to feel like he had to change his life for me.

"Of course not, no baby, I would never. You are ..." I shushed him with a finger over his lips and a grin on my face so that he knew I wasn't angry.

"Caleb, you can be friends with whoever you want. You don't have to change yourself or your life just because I happen to be a part of it. I want your life to get bigger because I'm in it, not smaller."

Caleb pulled me closer and dipped his head down to kiss me gently. Pulling my bottom lip into his mouth, he gently bit down and it set a fire inside of me. I knew that he wanted to take things slowly, but having him close to me was making it so much harder.

Grabbing me with both hands, Caleb pulled me over him, so I was straddling his lap and ground me down on top of his hard length. We were both fully clothed, but it hit me exactly where I needed it and my head fell back on a sigh.

Taking the opportunity, he started to kiss and nibble his way down my neck and I couldn't stop myself from grinding my hips down against him again. He groaned against my neck as he pulled me harder against him, making me cling to him harder and I can feel the slickness growing between my thighs in response.

Holding hard to the last shreds of my sanity, I forced myself to pull away from him.

"I'm sorry, you said that you wanted to take things slowly," I blushed kind of embarrassed at how hard I'm finding it to control myself around him.

"I have no idea why I thought that was a good idea," he grinned, swinging me around so my back landed on the bed and he nestled between my thighs. "If you want me to stop, just say. If you want to set a limit, that's okay too."

The fact that he would stop if I wanted to, and I can clearly tell from the hardness currently nestled between my thighs just how much he didn't want to, filled me with love and appreciation for this man. There were so many that wouldn't put my needs first, that would take my silence as a yes. My mates were better men than any I had ever met before.

"Don't stop," I panted, "don't ever stop."

My words are all he needs and we both become a blur of

movement as we pulled each other's clothes off until we could finally feel ourselves skin against skin.

"You are the most beautiful woman I have ever seen," Caleb breathed as he gazed down at me lying beneath him.

He trailed his fingers over Wyatt's mating bond and he sets a shiver loose down my body. "If we do this, I won't be able to stop myself from marking you and finalising our bond."

"I want to wear your mark, Caleb. You are mine and I am yours and I want the whole world to know it."

His head dipped down and he sealed his lips to mine again as one of his hands lightly traced a path down my side. The two different sensations of his rough dominating kiss and his light trailing fingers set my senses ablaze. As his tongue slips into my mouth, stroking against my own, his hand finally trailed back up my side until he was cupping my breast and slowly rolling my nipple between his fingers.

He pulled my thigh up around his waist with his other hand and then dipped his fingers into my core as he wrapped his hand around the back of my thigh. The tips of his fingers trailed through the slickness gathering between my thighs and I ground myself against him.

Breaking from the kiss, he grinned down at me. "I can't decide what I want to do to you first."

I could feel my cheeks flushed with heat because there's something that I wanted to do, but for some reason, I'm finding myself embarrassed to ask for it.

"What's with the delicious pink that's flushing across your cheeks?" Caleb asked me as he trailed his lips and kisses across my blushing cheeks. "Tell me what you want," he whispered into my ear.

I'm grateful when he stays there nibbling on my ear lobe because I'm suddenly too embarrassed to ask while he's looking me in the eye.

"Can I ... taste you?" I asked, unsure about how to phrase my question.

I know I'm being ridiculous. I'm laying here completely naked with him and the thing that's got me embarrassed is telling him that I want to feel him in my mouth.

"Never be embarrassed to ask me for anything that you want," he whispered into my ear. "And I'll let you taste me if you let me taste you," he said, pulling back and grinning down at me.

Suddenly Caleb rolled us both so that I was straddling him and he was on the bottom, taking the opportunity to hold onto my ass.

"Now turn around and wrap those sweet thighs of yours around my face," he said with a grin, slapping my ass.

I cocked my head to the side, trying to figure out what it was that he wanted me to do. But Caleb helped me out by guiding my body until I've got one knee either side of his face and his beautiful cock hovering right in front of my face. I can't stop myself from licking away the bead of liquid glistening on the tip and the way that his breath catches when I do fills me with a sense of satisfaction. Taking hold of him in one hand, I take my time to explore his length, enjoying the way that his breath hitched and he groaned when I do something he likes. But I'm down here for a reason and I slowly run my tongue along the length of him before taking just his tip into my mouth and swirling my tongue around him.

"Fuck!" Caleb groans out, but then he buries his head between my legs and it's my turn to be overcome with sensation as his tongue lashes against my clit.

It felt so good that it was almost enough to throw me off what I wanted to try with him, but once I managed to get my brain to function past the sensation of him working my clit, I took as much of him into my mouth as I could. I have to keep one hand wrapped around his base because there was no way that I would be able to get all of him into my mouth. As it is, I can feel him pushing against the back of my throat, but it isn't the most unpleasant of sensations.

Swirling my tongue around his length, I pulled back up. I dived down again, trying to swallow as much as I could and Caleb rewarded me by pushing two fingers inside of me. I groaned in delight, which just made him groan as well. I couldn't help the smile that wanted to form on my face. It's almost like we're in a competition of one upmanship and basically, everyone's a winner.

"Just like that Lyra, that feels amazing baby," Caleb groaned, his head dropped away. "Just relax your throat and you'll be able to go further."

His hips started to rise and fall in time with the movements of my mouth and every time I took him deep, he pushed just a fraction deeper. I could feel the stretch of my throat as he drove himself ever so slightly deeper. Combined with the way that his tongue circled and flicked across my clit, the sensation was intoxicating.

I could feel the orgasm building like a storm brewing inside of me. There would be no holding back from it, and I had absolutely no intention of stopping it. Caleb seemed to hold me on the brink, teetering on the edge, desperate for that last little push before I would fall.

"I can feel your pussy quivering around my fingers. Are you ready my love, do you want to come?" he growled.

"Please," I said on a breathy moan as I licked up and down his length.

Taking him back into my mouth, Caleb waited until I had as much of him in my mouth as I could take before he sucked my clit into his mouth and swiped his tongue back and forth.

As the orgasm tore through me, my moans and screams were muffled by my mate's cock still in my mouth. I pushed further down on him, taking him further down my throat than ever before.

"Oh ... fuck ... shit! You need to stop doing that or I'm going to come," Caleb panted out.

I drew back slightly because even though I was riding that wave of satisfaction right now, there was still a part of me that wanted Caleb deep inside of me. I wanted to feel his cock push his way into my wet pussy and I wanted to see his face when he came. I wanted to see what he looked like at the point of his release and I wanted to feel him come deep inside.

I moved off Caleb and he grabbed my hips, pulling me to straddle his lap as he sat on the edge of the bed. It was perfect, it was absolutely what I needed and as I sank down onto his length, moaning at the feel of his perfect cock stretching me wide, I watched his face as his eyes fluttered close and he dropped his forehead down to mine.

Caleb took a minute to catch his breath as he held on tight to my hips, ensuring that I didn't move yet. Running my fingers through his hair, I took the time to truly look at him, my perfect, beautiful mate.

Once he seemed like he'd got himself back under control, his grip lessened and he started to move me up and down over his cock. This position was perfect, with his arms wrapped tightly around me and my nipples grazing across his chest as I move, I felt like I could feel him all through my body.

One of Caleb's hands ran up my spine before he wrapped his hand around the back of my neck and used it to control my movement. His other hand dropped down to my clit and as soon as he touched me, I knew it won't be long before I was falling into another release.

My speed started to pick up as I chased the orgasm that was on the horizon. Caleb gripped my neck tightly and every time I hauled myself up his hard cock, he used his grip to crash me back down over him.

His thumb worked at my nub ceaselessly and his lips dropped down to my shoulder. I knew he was getting ready to leave his mark on my body and it was the thought of his teeth closing down over me that pushed me over the edge again.

I cried out as the orgasm felt like it slammed into my chest. Caleb bit down hard and the bond flared to life between us as my own teeth bit down into his shoulder. Caleb groaned out his own release with his teeth still set in my shoulder before he pulled back and gave it a lazy swipe with his tongue.

I felt like I'd lost all of the bones in my body as I just slumped forward into him, completely worn out. With one of those delicious masculine chuckles, Caleb picked me up and swung us both around so that we could snuggle up together on the bed.

This whole bond forming business was tiring but definitely the best thing I'd ever done in my life. As my eyes fluttered closed in exhaustion, I briefly remembered that Dom was supposed to be coming up to our room and wondered what could have happened for him to take so long.

CHAPTER 24

LYRA

I t's official, Aria is insane! Training was going to kill me. I'm pretty sure that sitting in that cage didn't cause my muscles to waste away, but rather they disappeared. I didn't have any anymore and it would be impossible to build them up again.

As I flopped down on the grass, wet from the morning dew, Echo backtracked from her run with a laugh. She slumped down onto the grass beside me. She didn't even look winded and I'm panting like a cow in labour. I mean she's not even got the decency to be a bit sweaty.

"Stop being so hard on yourself. You could barely even stay awake for more than a couple of hours a few weeks ago, you've got a long road to walk if you want to get back into condition," she told me patiently.

They'd all been telling me this for the week that I'd spent training with them. Or rather for the week that I had dragged myself through trying to keep up with them. Damn, these girls were like machines. They moved like they had been training their entire lives. I'd even go as far to say that they were better than some of the angels that I had seen, and we took combat very seriously.

"It's humiliating," I huffed out, hauling myself back up into a sitting position.

"We all started in the same place. We know how hard it is."

"But I'm an angel. I have been through training. I left the education centre in the top five of my class. I gave up my wings, I shouldn't have to suffer through this as well," I told her quietly. I hadn't spoken to anyone else about this, not even my mates.

Echo seemed to sense the change in my mood, even if it had been nothing but sullen for the past week. I had definitely not been a good training partner, more like a petulant yet persistent child.

"Suffer through what?" she asked gently.

"I gave up my wings to be with my mate and to save my flight. I don't regret that. I would do it again in a second. But I didn't realise just how much I was going to lose. I don't know what I am anymore. I don't think I can call myself an angel. I don't even feel my magic anymore. I thought it was just because I was weakened, but I feel empty. No ... it's more than that. I don't know how to explain it," I struggled. "I feel like I'm broken."

I knew she could see the unshed tears that collected in my eyes. I couldn't let myself cry right now. Echo was a good person, but this was humiliating enough as it was. I knew that it was just my fucked-up childhood making me think that way, but I couldn't help it any less. Right now, I'm weak. And I hate that. But having to admit it was infinitely worse.

"I didn't know that angels had magic," Echo said, frowning in confusion. "Like active magic?" she questions.

"Yes, of course," I could see the confusion on her face and I'm not surprised. In the time that I'd been here, it was clear that this realm, or at least shifter society, knew very little about angels. I didn't know if that was because it was something they had never known or if it was just knowledge that had been lost over time.

"Angels all have magic in their blood. We call it light. It is what allows us to perform small amounts of magic, things like healing or increased speed or agility. But the strongest of us can also have inherent magical abilities. No one knows how it happens, the Archangel Council has tried to breed more angels with these abilities, but it appears to be gifted at random. My full name was Lyra Stormchild. I was gifted this name because I had the ability to call and command the storm," I explained to her.

There was a time when I would have said this with pride in my voice. Maybe that's why I had lost my magic now. I'm being punished for that misplaced pride. Now speaking about it brings me nothing but pain. They call losing your wings 'falling', but I had no idea just how far I was going to fall.

"But the light as you call it is in your blood?" she asked.

"That is what we were always told," I confirmed to her.

"Then losing your wings shouldn't have affected it. Something else must be disrupting your connection with the light," she reasoned.

It was a reasonable theory now I thought about it. Either that or the vampires just fucking consumed it all. I couldn't even say that out loud though, the thought was too much to even bear.

"We should ask Frannie," she said, suddenly standing up.

I had heard whispers of this Frannie. Some seemed to talk about her with respect, but I had also heard others calling her a crazy old woman.

"In fact, why haven't your guys already taken you?" she asked, bracing her hands on her hips.

I could see that something about this pissed her off. The Elite girls were all fiercely protective over everyone and it seemed like that had extended to me now, as well. Echo reached down for my hand and hauled me up to my feet.

"Well at first it had something to do with Wyatt being afraid she was going to eat his ears or something, it was all quite confusing. But then Kyle told us that she had gone to the Mage Council and he wasn't sure when she was going to be returning," I explained.

I also might not have told them about just how bad I actually felt. I had tried to keep it to myself for now. Even I knew that was stupid, but for some reason, I was doing it anyway. Well, no, it was because I didn't want them to worry. I didn't want them hovering over me every two minutes. I wanted the freedom to be able to come and train with the Elites. I didn't want to feel like I was still in a cage, but how do you explain that to the people who were willing to put their own lives on the line to save you? That sometimes they made you feel like you were right back in the cage and it was their own actions that made you feel that way. No. For now, I was happy to just avoid that nightmare and suffer through this feeling alone. I was still trying to kid myself that once I got my strength back it was all going to magically get better. But on my darkest days, it felt so much worse than that. I wasn't getting my strength back, it didn't matter how much they fed me or attempted to train me. In fact, and I hardly dared admit this even to myself, if anything I was getting weaker. It had been so subtle at first that I hadn't even noticed it. But I can now. Sometimes I felt even worse than I did when they first found me in those woods. It comes and goes, but the lows, the lows sometimes felt like I was a breath away from death.

"I suppose the next option would be to talk to Braedon when he gets back tonight," she said thoughtfully. "He's supposed to have some kind of soul magic. Maybe he will know something."

"Soul magic?"

"Yeah, you know that all of Aria's mates received a magic boost when they mated with her." I nodded in confirmation. "Well, Braedon was the last mate that she took. He didn't think that he had any extra but then in the Blood Moon battle, something happened, no one's really sure what, and Hel called him a Soul Whisperer. Again, no one knew what it was so he and Virion have been in the Fae lands to see if Virion's father could help. I'm not sure what they will have found out, but Aria had word that they are due back tonight," she explained.

"Soul Whisperer, I feel like I've heard something about that, but I can't put my finger on it," I murmured.

I had that annoying feeling of a memory deep in the recesses of my mind that I couldn't quite grasp.

"Well, hopefully, they've already got their answer. Maybe it will be something that can help you."

I shrugged. I suppose it wouldn't hurt to ask. Equally, I also wasn't going to get my hope up.

"Right well, I've got another two laps to get in. Go in and find one of your delicious mates to take your mind off things. I'll let Aria know to tell Braedon to come to find you when he gets back." With that, she gave me a wink and took off on a run around the pack lands.

I staggered off towards the packhouse with the full intention of following her advice, after a shower, of course, because I did not smell good right now. I was just about to head up the stairs when I heard a commotion coming from the library. I didn't know why I did it, well I do, and I'm sure you did too, but I decided to find out what was going on. It probably had absolutely nothing to do with me but seems as everyone was still on alert about the potential for an attack at night which had yet to come, there was also a good chance that it did have something to do with me.

I heard a deep voice inside. "We found tracks on our way back, looks like someone had been watching the packhouse."

"Did you follow them?" I heard Kyle ask. I could tell that he was annoyed by the tone of his voice.

"Of course, we followed them," the other person scoffed. "They led away from the house for about a hundred yards, but then we lost them."

The room went quiet. I wasn't sure what to do. I felt like this involved me and I wanted to go inside so that I could ask some questions, but I was also fully aware that I wasn't a member of this pack and I wasn't sure if I would be welcome.

In the end, I backed away from the door and headed upstairs. If they wanted to involve me, they would. Otherwise, I could always ask Aria about it later.

I rushed through a shower and got dressed in jeans and a t-shirt. I was hungry again already, and I was trying to work up the courage to go down to the kitchens when the door to the room opened and Caleb came inside. The grin on his face was always a welcome sight, but it was the plate in his hand, holding the enormous sandwich that immediately got my attention.

"I think I might have to start trying harder to win your affections if the sandwich is getting a better welcome than me," he said, passing the plate across to me.

I grinned at him, but still took a massive bite before I said anything. Thankfully, my never-ending appetite was starting to put some of the weight back on my body. Unfortunately, it was doing nothing for my low energy levels. Echo was right, I would have to talk to someone about it soon. My mates were going to be angry when they found out that I had been keeping it from them, though.

"Who was in the library with Kyle?" I asked, trying to sound like I was just trying to make idle conversation and failing miserably.

"Why do you ask?"

He started to look nervous, which just made me want to know even more.

"I just heard voices and I didn't recognise them," I shrugged, playing it off as nothing. "So, I think I'm done with training today. What are the others up to? Maybe we could do something?"

"Aria's other mates have returned. It was just them filling in Kyle. Wyatt has gone out with them for a bit, but Dom is around here somewhere." He gave me one of his blinding grins and it was nearly enough to distract me.

Caleb squinted at me suspiciously. "You want to wait on the steps for Wyatt to get back?" he asked knowingly.

I knew that I was blushing, but I was also grateful that he wasn't calling me out on anything. I just nodded and he held out his hand for me. Taking it, he led me downstairs and we sat down on the steps. It was actually pretty nice. The sun had just come around and was shining softly down, Caleb had positioned himself on the step above me, so I was sat between his legs and leant back against his chest. It was nice, just sitting in the sun, feeling my mate's arms around me. We didn't talk, we just sat in comfortable silence, enjoying each other's company.

Dom came and found us about twenty minutes in. The fact that he was carrying a plate of cookies with him made it all so much better. He sat down beside me and passed a cookie back to Caleb, then one to me. It hadn't escaped me that whenever one of my mates showed up, they were always bringing me food.

We ate in quiet companionship. I leant back in Caleb's arms and Dom leant against my side, his arm wrapped around Caleb's leg so that he could hold my hand.

"Get back into the house!" we heard Wyatt's voice roar across the clearing in front of us.

He strode out of the treeline and as soon as he saw us, he started to run towards us.

"Get back inside!" he shouted again.

I could feel the hairs on the back of my neck bristle with annoyance, but then I saw his face, the worry and panic that was written across his features and I quickly got to my feet and retreated the few steps back inside the front door. Dom never let go of my hand and Caleb stayed at my back, scanning the clearing for danger.

Two other men dashed out of the treeline, following Wyatt. No one seemed alarmed by their presence, so I was assuming that these were the two other mates of Aria that I had yet to meet.

Even though I knew that it would be annoying Wyatt, I stayed just inside the door waiting for him. I was happy to go inside when it clearly meant this much to him, but my angelic nature would not allow me to cower away from any threat. I may not have recovered my strength as I had expected, but that didn't mean I would take any fight laying down.

Wyatt rushed through the door, pulling me into his arm and walked a few steps further into the house with me. I could feel in the crush of his arms just how much he was trying to hold it together right now.

"Who was it? Who was watching the house?" I asked, letting any pretence of not knowing what he was originally doing go.

Caleb and Dom were immediately at our side, waiting for the information as well.

Wyatt panted heavily, his eyes darting around as if he was trying to find the threat. His grip on me did not loosen and I realised just how hard this must be for him. He had lost me once, I didn't realise what this continuing threat must be doing to him.

The other two men had caught up with us, one of them

pulled a sword from his back and stayed in the open doorway
while the other ran towards the library, presumably to find
Kyle. He was the alpha, after all.

"Did you recognise the scent?" Kyle asked as he joined us
all standing by the door.

"Yes and no. It's the same one that was outside the abandoned house on the Moon Side, but we don't know who it is.
It isn't the vampire who escaped us," Wyatt filled in.

I didn't have the luxury of being able to pick up scents as
the shifters did. It wasn't a skill that angels possessed. It was
definitely something that I wished I could do, though.

"How fresh was it?" Kyle asked, blowing my mind. I
hadn't realised that they could pull that much information
just from scent alone.

"Fresh enough that we should have seen them." Wyatt
frowned. "Sykes is following the trail, but I'm not going to
hold out any hope of him finding them. Whoever they are,
they seem to just be able to disappear."

Now that got my attention.

"Or fly away," I murmured.

Every head snapped to me as they heard what I had said.
The problem with just having two legs, or four I suppose, was
that it made you think two-dimensionally. When you were
used to having wings, you started to remember that up was
also an escape route.

"Fuck!" Caleb breathed, his hands pulled through his hair
as he paced in front of me. "Don't we have enough to worry
about with an entire clan of vampires?"

"But you fell," Wyatt said, looking panicked. "They cast
you out; they can't come back for you now."

He looked completely broken as he spoke. I could see from
the faces surrounding me that the thought of angels terrified
them. I couldn't blame them, they knew nothing about them,
apart from the fact that they tore the wings off someone and

left them for dead. It probably wouldn't help them if they were more aware of my species. Most were extreme in their belief that the Archangel Council was the ultimate authority. The rules and laws which governed our kind were supposed to be unquestionable.

"It is unlikely that the Archangel Council would send someone down here for me. Like you said they cast me out, as far as they are concerned I'm not one of them anymore." I cringed as I said it. I wasn't going to lie, it really fucking hurt to think about. "But there are some among the flights who are extreme in their beliefs. One of them could have taken it upon themselves to hunt me down to exterminate me. They will believe me to be a corruption. But I don't think that is going to be the case. These angels hold the Archangel Council rulings above anything and they ruled that I was to be cast into the realm. Unless they have changed their minds, I don't think that they would come after me."

I looked at the door, trying to decide what to do.

"No!" Wyatt said, moving in front of me. "I can see what you're thinking and you're not doing it."

He actually looked angry, which just made me angry, but I took a deep breath and reminded myself that I was supposed to be understanding about how this situation made him feel.

"If they are here alone and just watching, they might want to talk," I reasoned.

This was bad. If this was an angel watching us, then I needed to talk with them. If they seemed to be here out of some form of concern, maybe they would know something about my lack of energy. The problem was, I had been hiding it from my mates, and I could already tell that Wyatt was going to be pissed if he found out this way.

Everyone was looking at me like I was crazy and I knew that I was going to have to tell them the truth, even if just thinking about it was making me want to throw up.

"I need to speak to them," I said quietly, looking Wyatt in the eyes.

I saw the pain flicker through his eyes and I realised immediately how it must sound.

"It's not like that," I told him, walking up to him and laying my head on his chest. His arms immediately came around me and I let out a sigh of pure contentment. Working up the courage I finally added, "I think that there might be something wrong with me."

I spoke softly, but I knew that he heard me because his arms tightened around me, almost like he was trying to draw me closer even though it was physically impossible.

"Let's take this into the library," Kyle suggested.

I felt the others move away from us, but Wyatt just held me close, almost like he was afraid to let me go. I was quite content just to stay where I was for the time being. Facing this was not something that I wanted to do. I had been avoiding this for a reason. I didn't want to see the inevitable pain in their faces. Only now I realised that keeping this from them was only going to cause them more pain.

We all crowded into the library. I could see Aria and Echo standing shoulder to shoulder by the doors directly in my eye line. The men had taken up seats around the library and Caleb and Dom had purposefully left a seat empty between them on the sofa for me. I reluctantly sat down between them. It wasn't the fact that I would be sitting between my two mates that was making me reluctant. I was just very aware of the fact that these men gathered here in this room were about to tell me what I was going to do. They may be doing it because they were under the illusion that it would be keeping me safe, but they were taking my choice away from me nonetheless.

Aria caught my eye again as she leant towards Echo and whispered in her ear. I saw the ghost of a smile flicker across Echo's face before she locked eyes with me, giving me a subtle nod. The men in this room may be about to steamroll me with their good intentions, but it seemed that the women were on my side.

"Lyra, you can't go out there and just face down whoever this is until we at least have some more information," Wyatt said calmly, now that he had some time to calm down.

I knew they would be suspicious if I just flat out agreed, but I decided to at least try to come across as being understanding.

"But what if they just want to help? How are we ever going to gather more information about them without being able to confront them?" I asked, trying to at least sound reasonable.

"I'll take watch on the rooftop tonight," Aria offered. "Now that we know that this person is potentially an angel, we have more idea about how they are moving in and out of the area. The Elites will continue to patrol the grounds. I agree with Lyra, I don't think that we need to assume that this person poses an immediate threat; however, we still have the risk of an attack from the vampire clan," she reasoned.

Now I'd admit that I may have forgotten about that part in my eagerness for answers.

Echo caught my eye again and I saw her understanding there as she nodded at me in encouragement. Fuck, time to just get it over with, I suppose.

"There's something that I need to tell you," I said quietly, hoping that no one would hear me over their discussions about guard rotas.

Unfortunately, they all fell quiet and looked at me in expectation. Double fuck.

I looked up and Aria smiled kindly down at me. Clearly, Echo had already filled her in, it was to be expected the Elites only held allegiance to one person, and that person was Aria.

"Since we've got back, I haven't been feeling right." I

stumbled over my words because even I didn't really know how to word it. My hand came up to my chest as I pressed the heel of my hand into my sternum. "I feel like I'm missing something. I can't access my magic. I can feel my body starting to recuperate, but I don't have the strength that I know that I should. If anything, I feel weaker sometimes."

I didn't dare look up. I didn't want to see the look in their eyes. Everyone was quiet and I didn't even want to know what the emotion was that was pushing that down. I kept my eyes fixed to my lap, shame washed over me. Not only because I'd been keeping this from my mates, but also because I was an angel and I shouldn't be admitting to weakness like this. I had been bred to be strong and I felt like I was failing at my very being.

But it was more than that, more than I was admitting, more than I could even really admit to myself. I didn't just feel like it was missing. It felt like it was draining away. That the blackness inside of me was spreading. I was afraid that I might actually be dying. All the courage in the world couldn't make me admit that out loud, though. I couldn't bear the crushing look on Wyatt's face. I didn't want to see him break. I didn't want to have to admit that it was even a possibility.

I saw Dom's hand come down towards me before I felt it gently grasp my thigh. His thumb rubbed reassuringly across my leg. An arm came around my shoulders, that I knew belonged to Caleb. My two mates moved in closer to me, bracketing me with their bodies and reassuring me with just their presence alone.

Wyatt must have gotten fed up waiting for me to look at him because in the next instant, he had dropped to his knees in front of me, each hand gently holding onto my knees. I couldn't not see his face. Even though there was pain there, there was also something else. There was love and understanding.

"You should have told us this earlier, Lyra. We could have been searching for an answer for you," he told me gently.

"I thought that if I regained the strength in my body that it would come back. I thought it was just because I was weakened," I admitted. And it was the truth. Or at least it had been the truth in the beginning. "But then I was too scared to tell you," I admitted quietly.

Wyatt's hands on my knees tightened a fraction as he winced like I'd dealt him a physical blow. Maybe I did. He definitely felt it, that was for sure.

"I just didn't want to hurt you even more than I already have," I told him, finally looking up and meeting his eyes.

I reached out and ran one hand down his cheek. Before I could drop it, he caught my hand and pressed it back against his cheek as he leant into it. I could see the tears shining in his eyes even if he was holding them back from falling.

We hadn't been dealt a fair hand. The cards seemed to have been against us from the start. I was terrified that if something did happen, it would break Wyatt beyond repair. Caleb and Dom might get through it because they had each other. I wasn't blind to the looks that they gave each other, or the companionship they had together. Wyatt didn't have that with anyone else. He was the moon to my sun. He wouldn't survive without me. I already knew that. He already knew that.

"Okay, then we face this together," Dom said, breaking through the silence that had descended through the room. "The four of us together."

I couldn't take my eyes off Wyatt, it almost felt like turning away was tantamount to giving up and I would never be willing to let him go. As that thought settled into me, I realised that I wasn't ready to just roll over and accept what was coming for me. I had three amazing mates who I had barely had a chance to get to know. I wasn't going to just lie down and die, accepting the hand that fate had dealt me. It was time to be strong, it was time to trust those that stood with me. I had found that fire to fight again, the same as I did in the woods when facing down Edwin. I may have let them take my wings, but I wasn't going to let them take anything else.

"Let's head outside," Caleb said, reaching for my free hand.

"We'll stay inside. I'm happy to let you handle this yourself but stick to where we can see you, I want eyes on you all at all times. Any threat to the pack, be it one of us or all of us, will face the same response," Kyle growled standing and turning to Aria and Echo. "Prepare the Elites to be ready to advance on your command but keep inside the buildings. We don't want to scare them off until we have all of the information that we need."

Echo grinned and Aria gave the scariest grin I had ever seen. I was starting to worry about her, but I could see the side of her which the guys had referred to being fiercely protective. The fact that she was turning that towards me and my mates would have me forever grateful. I had a feeling that we were going to need her on our side before the end.

A shimmer of magic glided across Aria and I saw her change before my eyes. Her clothes morphed and changed until she was coated in fighting leathers, blades were strapped to her thighs and waist, and I could see the pommels of two swords strapped to her back. But what caught my eyes the most were the pure white wings that fluttered at her back, almost like they were stretching from finally being freed from confinement. Pure jealousy was the first emotion that shot through me. She had wings and she chose to keep them confined and unused. That was quickly followed by shame and sadness before I could reign any of it in. I knew that she saw it because when I locked eyes with her there was nothing but an echo of sadness shining back at me. There was no pity there. Only the emotions of someone who understood loss because they had experienced far too much of it themselves. I could see it shining in her eyes, I had caught glimpses of it before, but for some reason now she let the armour fall and showed me her true feelings. Aria was drowning in pain and grief, and she didn't seem to be fighting it anymore.

As quickly as she showed me, her eyes shuttered and it was hidden away again. No one else in the room seemed to see what I had seen in that brief moment. It was something that was shared between just the two of us. No one else would be able to understand, anyway. You had to have experienced soul-shattering loss yourself to be able to recognise it in others. What worried me though was that Aria seemed to be holding all of that pain far too close to herself, almost like she bore it in some kind of punishment. She was the first to stand up and help others, but who was helping her?

Kyle's eyes suddenly snapped to her and a flicker of a frown marred his features. Did he feel it? Did he feel the pain that his mate was hiding inside? It was almost like he caught the faintest hint of something but wasn't sure if it was real.

"Echo, with me," Aria said, striding out of the room and walking away from the moment.

Kyle watched her go before turning back to the room and organising everyone else inside.

I had already decided that if Aria was going to hide her pain from everyone but me, then I would be the one to help her through it. Who knew, maybe it would help us both? Was it terrible that I was glad I wasn't alone in this? Regardless, she needed to speak with someone and I would be that someone for her.

CHAPTER 25

DOM

W e had been standing in the clearing in front of the packhouse for five of the longest minutes of my life. Even though I knew that my packmates were here, Aria and the Elites were close by and others from the pack were only a call away; I had never felt so exposed standing here with my mate waiting for some unknown enemy to come to us.

Lyra was unnervingly still. Her eyes were locked on the treeline but at the canopy rather than the ground. It was almost like she knew where they would be coming from. I supposed she would though, if it was an angel. They had likely been through the exact same training. I was sure I had seen something pass between her and Aria in the library before we left. How hard must it have been for her to see Aria's wings when she had lost her own so violently? We would need to check in with our mate after all of this.

Wyatt and Caleb were shifting uneasily where they stood. However difficult this was for me, it was going to be infinitely worse for them. Their wolves would be pushing them to shift so that they could protect their mate. The fact that they were holding back the shift was actually quite impressive.

I caught the slight tension in Lyra's muscles and I knew that she had seen something. My eyes snapped to the canopy where she was staring and I squinted into the distance. I couldn't see anyone, but now that I was concentrating, I could feel it. A foreign source of magic, strong magic, amongst the trees. I couldn't smell lingering scents like the wolves could, but I should have caught a residual layer of this magic if this was whoever had been watching us.

The tension seemed to leave Lyra before she spoke. "No one will harm you here, Aurel."

A burst of light laughter flowed across the clearing before an angel seemed to appear out of midair and landed on the ground a few steps in front of us. He dropped to the ground in a slight crouch before standing tall. His silver wings stretched to their full length at his side. It seemed unnecessary. It seemed like a slap in the face to the wingless angel in front of him and the smirk on his face showed just how much he knew it. was.

We all fell silent. Lyra stood staring at the angel in front of her as he seemed to examine her with his eyes. I didn't like it and the low growl coming from Wyatt showed that he didn't appreciate the way that this angel was looking at our mate, either.

"You're not looking too good, Lyra," he finally said.

Lyra just shrugged. "It's been a strange few years," she said nonchalantly. "How long have you been watching me?"

"About seven years. It took me a while to find you."

They went back to the stare-off. Questions were burning inside me, but I knew not to interrupt. I didn't know anything about angels or their politics. Lyra was the only one who knew how to get the information that we needed.

She stood tall and proud. She looked stronger than she

had in days, but he was right. If you looked closely at her, you could see the drain. She had built up a small amount of the weight that she had lost, but she was still too thin. But it was more than that. It was almost like instead of shining bright she was slowly starting to dull. To fade. Now that she had told us the truth, I was kicking myself that I hadn't noticed it before.

Aurel locked eyes with Lyra and I could see his eyes flicking between hers before he suddenly changed. It was like the cocky angel in front of us dropped the façade. His shoulders slumped and his face showed the pain that he was feeling beneath. It was surprising, his mask had been that convincing.

"Why have you been watching me, Aurel? The Council would not have approved this, you are putting the flight at risk by being here," Lyra told him.

"I am here on Samuel's orders. A lot has changed since you left, Lyra. When they cast you out it was the catalyst for change. You willingly sacrificed your wings to save us and it did not go unnoticed."

"It wasn't just for you," she said quietly. "Samuel is a fool if he thinks that the Council will not exterminate the flight if they catch wind of this insubordination. But you have still not answered my question, why are you watching me?"

"Samuel has a way to bring you back into the fold," he smiled. "It is not just our flight that is unhappy with your exile. There are others. They cannot exterminate all of us. The Council were afraid of the Stormchild and took the first opportunity they could find to get rid of you, they have underestimated the response that it would garner amongst the flights."

"There is no way back, Aurel, and I don't want to come back. It makes no difference, the Stormchild is gone." Lyra looked away and I knew how much it cost her to admit that her magic was out of her reach.

Aurel frowned and opened his mouth, no doubt to ask

what she meant but apparently, Wyatt had heard as much as he could.

"What do you mean that you watched her for seven years? If you knew where she was all of this time, why didn't you help her?" he growled.

"She was safer where she was and I did not have authority to intercede," Aurel shrugged.

"They repeatedly tortured her and drained her of her blood."

I could see that Wyatt was barely holding himself back now. His eyes flashed with the anger of his wolf.

"Better that than dead. Being imprisoned at the clan house kept her out of the reach of the Archangel Council," Aurel snapped at him.

All of the anger seemed to drain out of Wyatt and I could see that he was trying to wrap his head around this.

"What do you mean that the Stormchild is gone? What have you done?" he questioned Lyra.

"Wait," Caleb suddenly interjected and I could see the annoyance flash across Aurel's eyes. "You're talking about civil war, why would you all go to such lengths because Lyra had been exiled?"

It was a good question. From the way that Lyra had told us, it wasn't uncommon for angels to be controlled with the threat of exile or even death. The fact that some chose to die rather than live without their wings spoke volumes of the pain that Lyra must be going through. But if this was an everyday occurrence, or rather, an everyday threat, why would enacting it upon Lyra be enough to spark others talking of a coup?

Aurel cocked his head to the side and smirked at Lyra. "Have you been underselling your importance, dear Lyra?" he laughed.

She rolled her eyes, clearly unamused by him. "Just

because I am the first Stormchild for centuries does not mean that there will never be another."

"Centuries? No dear Lyra, you are the first Stormchild since the Originals."

He paused as if to let the information settle in Lyra before continuing. "Now I will ask you again, what do you mean by the Stormchild is gone?"

Lyra didn't answer immediately, it was almost like she was weighing up the information which he had given to her before she exposed her weakness. There was more to consider here than any of us had expected. What exactly were we about to get drawn into?

"I have lost my magic," she told him.

It was almost like she had slapped him. Aurel reared back as soon as the words had slipped past her lips, shock blazed across his face.

"That is not possible. Your magic is an inherent part of you, you cannot just lose it," he took a step closer to her, but Wyatt's immediate growl caused him to falter. "Unless ..." he looked around Lyra as if registering our presence for the first time.

Lyra stood still, no emotion showing on her face. She allowed his perusal, but I caught the slight clench of her jaw. She did not like standing out here in the open as much as we did. From her accounts, angels were bred to be one thing alone, warriors. It would be against her very nature to stand here, vulnerable and admitting her weaknesses.

"This is even better than Samuel could have hoped for," Aurel suddenly grinned. "I need to update him." He took a step back and I saw him tense as if preparing to take flight.

Before he could even move, Aria was there. Fuck knows where she had even come from. One moment she wasn't there and the next she had Aurel restrained and a sword digging into his wing joint. Echo stood beside her; a knife held at Aurel's throat.

After the briefest moment of shock, Aurel burst into laughter and grinned at all of us surrounding him. "You are constantly surprising me, dear Lyra."

"Now, I don't believe that the party is quite over yet and you haven't told the lady everything that she needs to know," Aria whispered menacingly into his ear. "Answer her questions, or we'll all find out just how easy it is to separate an angel from their wings."

Aurel shuddered at her threat. "Oh Valkyrie, if only I couldn't feel those solidified mating bonds of yours. We could have had so much fun, you and I, with that shiny, shiny set of blades." He licked his lips and we could all see the hard-on he was suddenly sporting.

Fucking hell. The last thing we needed was some crazy, horny angel in the mix. Although it would be amusing to see Aria's mates' reaction to his flirting with her.

Aria dug her sword further into his wing and Aurel bit into his lip, his eyes hooding in lust, freaking the rest of us out even more.

"Fine, fine," he sighed. "I'll tell you so that the Valkyrie can stop flirting with me."

Aria pushed him away from her in disgust which just seemed to amuse Echo, but she dutifully removed her blade from his throat, holding it loosely at her side.

"The only way for an angel to lose connection with their magic is if they deny their mating bonds. Once the first bond has been recognised they must all be completed. Deny them for too long and an angel will start to wane." I saw indecision flicker across his eyes, almost like he wasn't sure if he should tell us everything. When he spoke again, I could see why he wouldn't have wanted to. "Loss of magic comes first, then the angel will start to fade. Without their magic, they essentially become mortal; eventually, they will succumb to death."

Shock blasted through me and I saw the same feeling on both Caleb and Wyatt's faces as well. He was telling us that Lyra was dying. She didn't seem so surprised and that was definitely something that we were going to need to talk about.

"You need to solidify all of your mate bonds, dear Lyra. The two that you have will not be enough to sustain you," he added sadly.

Okay, this wasn't terrible. There was only me left to bond with Lyra. It wasn't that we didn't want to, we just hadn't really had the opportunity to spend any time together yet.

"Once you have your other two bonds in place, your magic should return. Samuel is convinced that there is a way to bestow you with wings. He is trying to gain access to the Archangel library, but the Council has it locked down tighter than usual. We think that they know something is brewing," Aurel continued as if he hadn't just dropped a massive bomb on us.

I looked at Wyatt and Caleb, who were wide-eyed staring back at me. Fuck! Could this get any worse?

"Samuel is going to be ecstatic when he finds out that you have discovered your bonds. This will draw even more angels to our side," Aurel continued.

"Just stop!" Echo sighed. "Read the room dude. Fuck, you're either weird or conceited. I can't decide."

Aurel looked around us in confusion, not understanding what he had said wrong. Then his eyes flicked back and forth between the three of us before he turned back to Lyra.

"Ooooohhhh. Oh, this is awkward," he grinned.

I was fast starting to hate this angel.

"Aurel, I am only going to say this once and you need to listen very carefully because I'm starting to doubt your intelligence." Lyra paused to make sure she had his attention before she continued. "I want no part in your coup, I don't give a shit about the Archangel Council or whatever any of you have planned now. No one spoke up for me, no one stood by me. I was betrayed by one of our own and you left me to rot for nine years. I will not be your puppet and I want no part in that life anymore." Then she turned her back on him and just walked away.

Lyra headed inside the house and we all stood awkwardly looking at Aurel. I was so fucking proud of her for standing up to him. She was right, they just wanted to use her to put themselves in a position of power. I couldn't blame her for not wanting a part in it. She had a life here now. We were her life and she deserved to be happy after everything that had happened to her.

"That's your cue to leave, in case you didn't realise," Echo stage whispered to Aurel.

"I like you, you're feisty," was the last thing he said before he opened his wings and flew away.

The five of us that were left standing outside fell into silence. The relatively short conversation that we had just had threw up more problems than we even knew we were facing.

"I suppose we head back to the library," Echo said, still looking in the direction that Aurel had flown.

"To the bat cave!" Aria cheered walking back towards the house.

We all just followed her having no idea what she was talking about.

I was surprised when we got inside to find Lyra already waiting in the library. Maybe we spent too much time in here. Someone in the pack had laid food out on one of the larger tables and everyone helped themselves and then settled around the room.

Lyra stood beside the fireplace staring at the flames. She made no more toward the food or really gave any indication that she was aware we were all here. She was so lost in thought that she startled when I passed a plate to her. Taking the plate, she gave me a gentle smile and I led her to the sofa where we had been sitting before, settling her between Wyatt and I. As soon as we were in place, Caleb sat at her feet, leaning back against both our legs. It was comforting to feel them both surrounding me and I closed my eyes to allow myself a moment to calm the rage of emotions passing through me before we tried to deal with the situation we had inadvertently ended up in.

"So maybe we should fill everyone in first," Caleb said, breaking the silence first.

"No need, we were able to hear through our connection with Aria," Kyle told us, looking at Lyra in concern.

Everyone fell silent again. Lyra was just slowly eating the food which I had put in front of her. No one really seemed to know what to say.

"Angels have developed a society which revolves around control," she began. "The Archangel Council makes every decision on how we live our lives and everyone follows them blindly. If you speak out against them or make any unsanctioned move, the punishment is usually death. They are brutal and unwavering. The official word is that it is impossible for an angel to have a mate. Breeding is by allocation alone. Relationships are weakness and we are bred for one thing only ... war."

We all flinched at the world she was describing. It was not a life. It was barely an existence.

"If you want to stand by this Samuel and Aurel, you will have our support," Kyle told her as Aria dropped down into his lap.

I could see the confusion on Lyra's face and apparently so did Aria because she just smiled and told her, "You are pack. Trust me, I get how hard that is to grasp in the beginning."

"Is it terrible that I don't know if I want to be part of that fight?" Lyra winced, clearly waiting for some kind of judgment from us which she would never receive.

"Of course not. I say fuck them all," Echo laughed before shoving an enormous sandwich in her mouth. It actually looked pretty good. Why is sandwich envy such a real thing? They always taste better when someone else makes them.

Aria grinned clearly agreeing with Echo as everyone else chuckled at the bad influence she was clearly having on her.

"Who were the Originals?" Kyle asked.

I reran the conversation in my mind until I could remember what he was talking about.

"They were the first seven Archangels. They were executed by the gods when they tried to take over the human realm a couple of thousand years ago. After then the Council was formed. There are seven seats, whoever takes the position takes on the name of their seat, adopting the name of one of the original seven and discarding their previous identity."

"What? When did angels try to take over the human realm?" Aria said, looking confused.

"Two thousand years or so ago. The Originals believed that humans were made to be ruled over and believed that they should be the ones to do so. The gods disagreed and intervened, removed the angels from the realm and executed the Originals for their crimes. In the end, it was the beginning of the end for the old religions anyway and some new religion was formed featuring the seven. I'm not sure, it's not something that's openly endorsed by the Council, so we don't really learn much about it," Lyra shrugged.

Aria's mouth dropped open and I could see that what Lyra was describing must be pretty significant to human history.

"How about we just stick to the main problem that we have and leave all that for later because I don't know about everyone else, but I'm starting to feel like we all need a vacation or something," Sykes suggested.

Everyone nodded, but I'm not sure which part they were agreeing with.

"We need to find your other mate so that you can solidify your bonds," I told Lyra.

I caught her flinch and I hoped that it wasn't aimed at the thought of solidifying her bond with me. Almost like she could read my thoughts, she reached out and took hold of my hand, snuggling against my side at the same time.

"If it were that easy every shifter would be with their fated mates. How are we supposed to even know where to start looking?" Caleb pointed out.

Everyone looked at me for some reason. "As far as I am aware, the Mage Council has not found a way to trace fated mates, and even if they had, I would be reluctant to allow them access to Lyra until she has access to her full magic."

I knew exactly what would happen if we were to take her to the Mage Council. The first angel sighted in a century. They would be all over her. They would want to take her apart and learn whatever they could about her. They would be relentless in their pursuit for the information and it would place Lyra at even greater risk. The last thing we needed at the moment was another player to enter the game.

"What about the witches?" Liam asked with a flinch. They were definitely still a sore subject around here.

Kyle looked reluctant at first but then asked Aria, "Have you had any update from Aeryn?"

Aria shook her head. "Not recently, nothing past the last message."

Wyatt sat up in interest, no doubt because he was not in the picture on what they were talking about either.

Kyle sighed and filled us in. "We may have sent Aeryn back to her coven to keep an ear open for rumblings in the covens."

"You've placed a spy in one of the covens?" Caleb said shocked.

"No! Not exactly. Aeryn was called home because her mother is dying. She's just keeping us updated on anything else that happens which we might need to know about," Kyle said evasively.

"Dude, that's like the definition of a spy," Echo pointed out. "Next you're going to try and say that Nix didn't return with the Felidae Pack so that she could spy for you on Trace."

Aria actually laughed at that.

"You are a bad influence," Kyle huffed at Aria.

"And yes, Nix is keeping an eye on Trace. I don't trust him," Kyle added.

"Well, I agree with you there, something about him just doesn't add up, but that's going to have to be a problem for another time. How are we going to trace Lyra's additional mate?" I asked.

"It's a shame your Soul Whisperer doesn't know how to use his magic," Lyra said sleepily against my side.

Everyone in the room fell quiet. It seemed to be a running theme at the moment. We all stared at Lyra expectantly except she was very nearly asleep, snuggled up against me. I don't think she really had any idea what was going on. She didn't answer and I knew that she was basically already asleep. I didn't have the heart to wake her and I doubted that anyone else would, either.

"Come on, sleepy girl," Wyatt whispered, scooping her up in his arms as he stood up. "Let's get you back to bed."

Caleb helped Wyatt with the door and I was about to follow when Kyle stopped me. "We'll meet back here in the morning to finish this," he told me.

I nodded, I knew that Braedon's magic was a source of contention for them. He had been the last of Aria's mates to gain any magic and no one really knew anything about it. If

Lyra had information, they were going to want it and I was impressed that they were willing to wait until the morning to get it. Especially as it was barely afternoon now. I suppose it's hard to wake up a woman when you've basically just learnt that she is slowly dying. It didn't matter, though. There was no way that we were going to let her fade away like that. We had only just found her, we weren't going to let her go that easily.

Chapter 26

Damon

I didn't know how long I had been sitting in this cell. The only way I could gauge the passage of time was by the increasing amounts of hunger I was feeling. I could hear the blood running through my veins, taunting me. It whispered of what I craved but was out of reach for me. Every so often, one of the other clan members came down to taunt me. Apparently, they had a pool going on how long it took for me to start chewing on myself when the madness of starvation started to set in. I wouldn't give them the satisfaction.

A few days after they threw me in here, Edwin turned up in a rage and beat me until I passed out. I'm not naïve enough to think he stopped right away either. It probably wouldn't have been as bad if I hadn't laughed at the gaping hole where his eye used to be. Thinking about it now still brings a smile to my face. I knew Lyra still had some fight left in her. The fact that her cage has remained empty and Edwin's rage was so thick, just proved that she slipped from his grasp. That she was still free. As long as she was free, all of this would have been worth it. She was too pure to rot away in that cage.

They may have stolen my human life from me and turned

me into a monster, but they never managed to tear the humanity from me. Saving Lyra was my last chance at redemption and I could only hope that when the time came, it was enough to save my soul. The laugh burst out of me, who was I kidding? There was no saving me from what was inevitably coming my way. If hell truly did exist my ass was going to be roasting down there alongside the worst of them. If I did end up down in the pit, at least I'd have the satisfaction that fuck Edwin would be joining me at some point.

I'm still staring down at my arm when the two guards pulled open the door to my cell. Surprisingly we seemed to be foregoing today's daily beating and they each grabbed an arm and dragged me out of the cell. Maybe we're going to have an audience today instead. I'm so far into the madness of my hunger that I didn't really care what they did to me anymore. The scrap of sanity that I had left hoped that they weren't dragging me to see that they had Lyra back in chains, but apart from that I didn't have the energy to care about what was going to happen.

They dragged me through the corridors, my legs dragging behind me. I didn't have the energy to even try to walk any more. I knew the hunger would be bad, but I didn't realise just how quickly it would hit me. The closer we got to the hall, the more my hope began to fade. The only reason why I could think they would bring me here was that they had her again. I'm sorry, Lyra. I tried.

My head dropped down, the last vestiges of energy that I had failed me. I just didn't have it in me to hold it up any more. Why would I want to see how broken she was before I really had to?

When they dropped me suddenly to the ground, I didn't even bother trying to catch myself before I hit the ground. I might have given up hope already. Lyra lasted eight years in that hole that they kept her in. I'd barely even started and I'd given up already. I was such a joke. I could hear the twitters echo around the room as the rest of the clan apparently agreed.

"I'm glad to see that your break in the cells has been relaxing Damon, although it seems like you haven't been having enough visitors to keep you busy. I'll make sure to set up some kind of schedule for you," Cassius crowed from his throne.

No one said anything for a moment. I'm pretty sure that he was waiting for me to beg him for mercy or something. I'm not quite that crazy yet!

"She was very beautiful, our little angel," Cassius said casually. "I can see why you would feel the need to try and help her, how you fell in love with her."

I knew that I shouldn't, I knew that it was stupid but I just couldn't help myself and I looked up to see what was happening in front of me. The sight was shocking, to say the least. Cassius was sat at the head of the hall in his usual throne but beside him sat a smaller throne which Venette was sitting on. If it wasn't shocking enough that Cassius seemed to have relinquished even an ounce of his power to someone else, the swollen belly that she resting her hands on nearly blew me away. What the actual fuck!

"Oh yes, you didn't hear the wonderful news," Cassius said with a smug fucking grin on his face. "The beautiful Venette is expecting the first ever vampire child to be born. Something to celebrate, don't you think?" He cocked his head to the side and smiled down at me.

I'm not sure if he thinks I'm stupid or if he's just hoping that the insanity of hunger has fully taken grip of me. Either way, he clearly has a plan for this so-called celebration and I'm not going to play into it.

"Dear little Lyra has gone to ground," he started with fake

concern shining in his voice. "It's just not safe for her out there without her wings, without any way to protect herself. I know that you thought you were saving her, that you loved her so much that seeing her in that cage hurt you. Foolish men in love always do foolish things. I can't hold that against you. And with all of the good news in the clan at the moment I'm finding myself feeling somewhat sympathetic to your cause. Help me find her Damon, help me save her from the dangerous world out there that would harm a poor helpless angel like the beautiful Lyra. If you tell me where she's gone ... I'll give her to you."

The hunger must be clouding my mind because, for a moment I started to think that he was right. She was out there all alone, with no one to protect her and no way to protect herself.

I knew that Cassius could see the doubt and weakness in me when he added, "When Edwin caught up to her, so did the wolves. And of course, it was the wolves who sold her to us in the first place. I wonder where they will sell her next. A mage tore her away from them, but it's only a matter of time before the pack finds her."

Holding back the smile on my face took every ounce of effort that I had, I feel the corners of my mouth flicker and can only hope that he thinks it's either because she got away or that I'm just that fucking crazy. He didn't know. He didn't know about her mate. The wolf pack would be the safest place for her if he could protect her now. Of course, there was a chance that he was right, that they came for her again for other reasons, but this was the whole reason why she wanted to be free. To return to him.

Cassius must have thought that my quiet is my resolve weakening. "Just think Damon. She would be yours, in your bed every night to do with what you will. All I would need in return, as a small token of thanks, would be access to her blood. We can draw it like the humans do if you don't want any other to touch her, that would be your right to decide."

If he was right and I was in love with Lyra, I might have taken him up on it. Unfortunately for him, the motives behind me freeing her had nothing to do with love and everything to do with the last scrap of humanity that I still retained. They wouldn't understand that because the change did something to them that it didn't seem to be able to complete with me. It stripped them of everything that they previously were and turned them into these monsters. All that they care about is power and blood. I'm surprised he even came up with the theory that I was in love with her if I'm honest.

"Just think Damon, with Lyra at your side we would be the strongest clan on the Moon Side. Who knows what this new generation of vampires will be able to do. Any human we harvest will only be needed for the resources they provide. The clan will grow faster than any in history. First, we will take the Moon Side, then we will take the human realm. It will only be a matter of time before this entire realm falls at its knees before us. This realm has always looked down on us, treating us like vermin, like we're beneath them. They have no idea of the terror that we will rain down on them."

His laughter rippled around the room as the rest of the clan joined in with him. His eyes shone bright with what I was starting to think was true madness. He really did think that he was going to take over the realms. Fuck my life, how did I get tangled up with this shit?

Cassius was on a roll and the clan was just lapping up every word. I couldn't help but zero in on Venette's stomach, what the fuck was even growing in there? This was bad, this was really, really bad. I was so far out of my fucking depth that drowning just sounded like sweet blessed relief right now.

Cassius got up from his throne and came to crouch down in front of me. The gold goblet of blood in his hand hovered just in front of my face. The sweet smell of fresh blood flooded my mouth with saliva and the heavy weight of shame landed on me when I realised just how much I would do to have it.

"Drink, Damon. The hunger is holding too tightly to your mind right now." Cassius pushed the goblet to my lips and I didn't even try to deny him as I gulped down the still warm blood. He gently ran his hands through my hair as he helped me drink, looking like the benevolent leader he wanted us all to believe him to be.

"You will stand beside me, Damon. We will conquer the realms together. You as my second with the beautiful Lyra by your side. All you have to do is bring her back to us," Cassius crooned in what he no doubt believed was a soothing way.

As if to seal the deal, he leant in close and whispered in my ear. "No other vampire here has had her. Your beautiful angel is still pure. You could be the first to breach her walls, to have her begging for your cock. Would you like that, Damon? Would you like to see her pretty lips close around your cock? Would you like to feel her sweet warmth wrap around you as you spill down her throat? I was going to save her for myself, but now I see the truth. She was always meant to be yours, Damon, she was always meant to belong to you."

Cassius strode back to his throne before taking a seat and pulling Venette's hand to his lips for a kiss.

"Take him back to his rooms," he directed the guards. "Feed him until the hunger dissipates so that we can speak properly."

The guards picked me up from the ground and pulled me back to my feet. The small amount of blood that I'd had gave me enough energy to stand, even if I was leaning to the side on one of the guards. It's only Cadell and I knew that he wouldn't mind. As they led me from the hall, I heard Cassius shout out to me.

"You will give me an answer when I see you next Damon and it will be the answer that I want."

Cadell and the other guard that I didn't recognise led me back to my old rooms. Someone had been in and cleaned, the bedding had been swapped out for silk sheets and there was a crystal decanter set out on the table filled with fresh blood. The other guard stayed at the door and Cadell helped me inside, closing the door behind us. He settled me at the table and poured me a glass of blood before passing it to me and sitting in the opposite seat. He didn't take a glass for himself. At first, suspicion hit me as I couldn't help but think that I'm about to down a glass of poison. Then I realised that I didn't really care and it would at least see an end to all of this madness so I throw the blood back and drink it down as fast as I can. Cadell just silently filled the glass again and then sat back in his seat, looking at me.

"The only way you can protect her now is to do what he says. He's never going to stop until he has her again. At least this way you can protect her while she is here," he finally said.

The blood is starting to clear my mind, but I know it will be a while before I'm fully back to myself. Unfortunately, in the current state that I'm in, what he's saying is actually making sense.

CHAPTER 27

LYRA

I woke up tucked up in bed again. I really needed to stop doing this. Although, this time I'd got two men snuggled up against me which was definitely a better way to wake up. At some point, I rolled over to lay my head onto Dom's chest and hooked one leg over him. His hand was resting high on my thigh and judging by the pattern he's tracing across the back of my thigh with his fingers, he's not as asleep as he's making out to be.

Caleb had snuggled up against my back with his arm wrapped around me and his fingers threaded through mine, our joined hands resting on Dom's chest.

A relaxed sigh flowed out of me and a feeling of contentment settled over me. Ever since I completed the mating bonds with Wyatt and then Caleb I'd felt different. Almost like my mind felt less hectic. I didn't think that the waning strength I'd been experiencing had changed at all, but I wasn't really paying that much attention to it to be able to tell. Denial, my name is Lyra.

It was hard yesterday, or this morning, or whenever it was,

hearing Aurel basically confirm that I was in fact dying. I didn't even know how I felt about the possibility of a fourth mate. I thought that the three I had, and I am counting Dom in that even if we hadn't completed our bond, it is only a matter of time, were enough. In fact, if I'm completely honest with myself the thought of three was a bit overwhelming at first. But the fact that the guys all knew each other, and there was definitely something going on between Dom and Caleb, actually helped. What would it even be like to bring in a fourth mate into our group? Would the others even be prepared to accept that? But then, what choice did we really have, it was either that or die? And these men were made for me, they are my missing pieces, would I even want to give one up without even giving them a chance? This was just so confusing. Sometimes, I think my life had been easier just sitting inside my cage.

"You're thinking very loudly," Dom muttered from beneath me. I could feel his voice vibrating through his chest and I'm not too embarrassed to admit that it was doing things for me.

"Surely the definition of thinking is that it is done quietly," I smiled back at him.

Dom's chest rumbled with laughter and I was sure that I could feel Caleb smile against my back.

"Talk to us."

"I was just thinking about whether I wanted a fourth mate or not," I said honestly.

Caleb sat up in the bed and rolled me so that he could see my face.

"You can't be considering not seeking them out," he said quietly.

"I'm not that stupid. I know I'm going to die if I don't. It would just be nice to be able to do this the way that everyone else does, without all the pressure. I can't help but think that it isn't fair on you guys." I looked between Caleb and Dom as I spoke because I wanted them to see the truth in my eyes. I knew that this was going to be just as hard on them as it was on me.

"Lyra," Dom whispered, running his hand down my cheek so that he could cup my chin and turn it towards him. "We would do anything for you. If that means welcoming another mate into our pack then that is what we will do. It just means that you will have one more mate to love you, one more mate to protect you."

"But what if you hate him?"

"Lyra, he's a part of you, he was made for you, how could we ever possibly hate him?" he asked gently.

I hadn't thought of it that way. Would fate be bitch enough to group together a set of mates that hated each other? I mean, she sat me in a cage for nine years, so I'm guessing she's not my biggest fan.

I saw Dom look over my shoulder at Caleb for a moment, but when I turned to see what was happening, all I saw was Caleb smiling down at me. I squinted back in suspicion, which just made him grin even wider. They were definitely up to something!

When I turned back to Dom, before I could even open my mouth to talk to him, his lips crashed against mine and I just melted into his embrace. Caleb's lips pressed against my neck as he dropped kisses over my neck and shoulders while Dom dominated my mouth. His hand came up into my hair and he tipped my head to the angle that he wanted so that he could slip his tongue along mine with ease. There was something so hot about the way that he was just taking control and from the growl of approval that came from him, I think he knew it, too.

His arms tightened and he pulled me closer into his body

until there wasn't a breath of air between us. My leg hooked over his hip and one of his legs slipped between mine, his thigh pressed tight against my already wet pussy. There was something about these men that as soon as they kissed me, I was ready to go.

I heard the door click closed and pulled away from Dom to look around in confusion.

"It was just Caleb leaving," Dom said, dropping kisses along my collar bones. "He's just giving us some privacy."

"Oh, okay," I sighed as his fingers pulled the straps of my cami top down exposing my breasts to his lips.

"We can ask him to come back if you want him too," Dom told me and if I wasn't mistaken, he sounded a little unsure of himself at that moment.

I cradled his face in my hands and tipped it so that he was looking me in the eye. I didn't want there to be any misunderstanding between us here.

"Dom, I want you, if in the future that includes Caleb or anyone else then we can try that, but right here, right now, all I want is you."

The smile he gave me in return was simply beautiful.

Dom rolled onto his back and pulled me with him so that I was straddling his hips. It put his very hard cock exactly where I wanted it and my hips just moved on their own as I ground down onto him. The friction of my panties rubbing between him and my clit wasn't quite enough and I knew that I needed more.

I pulled him up to sitting so that I could pull off his shirt. My hands were roaming over the muscles on his chest, following the dips and valleys. Pushing him back down, I followed the path of my fingers with my mouth, kissing and biting my way down his body.

Once I reach the waistband of his boxers, I hooked my

fingers inside and then looked up to meet his eyes as I slowly started to draw them down.

"Feeling the need to be in control?" he asked, smirking down at me.

With a grin, I just shrugged and then continued unwrapping him like the gift I knew that he is.

His hard cock sprung free of his boxers and I licked my lips in anticipation. He's thick and long and beautiful and I wrapped my lips around the head with a moan of appreciation. I sucked the salty bead of precum leaking from the tip before taking him out of my mouth and running my tongue along the length of him, wetting his length with my saliva.

Taking my eyes off the feast before me I peered up at Dom to see him looking down, watching me, panting in desire. I ran my tongue along him, keeping my eyes locked with his, loving every second of watching the emotions running across his face. Opening my mouth, I sunk down his length, taking in as much as I can. I can feel him pushing against the back of my throat and I tried to take him deeper.

Eventually, Dom threw his head back with a groan and I couldn't help the smirk of satisfaction that I got knowing that I was doing this to him.

I sat back up and pushed him down flat on the bed. He's right, I did feel the need to be in charge right now. I'm not sure why that is, but there is something in me right now that makes me want to dominate him. Pausing for a moment to consider that thought, I worried that I was about to do something wrong.

"What's wrong?" Dom asked. "What changed?"

"I ... it's just you're right, I do feel like ... erm ... I want to be in charge and I was worried ..." I trailed off, not sure what to say.

"Hey," Dom said, cradling my cheek in his hand and

angling my head so that I was looking at him. "There is nothing wrong with that. We are both non-shifters finding ourselves as part of a pack and that's bound to bring some kind of weird side-effects with it. Being dominant, feeling the need to control this, that isn't strange, even if we weren't in this weird pack type thing."

I laughed at his strange explanation but also, I kind of thought that he was right.

"I'm with you 100%, do what you need to do," he said with a grin. "I am very much looking forward to it."

I'm still straddling his waist, so I dipped down and seal my lips to his, my hands on his chest pushing him down into the bed as I take over the kiss, my tongue battling with his. Dom's hands rested on my waist as he let me take complete control.

Reaching down, I took hold of his hard length in my hand and lined him up with my entrance. I'm already wet and ready and I don't want to wait. I wanted to feel him inside me. Locking eyes with him, I made sure to keep him lying where he was while I slowly sank down his length. His hands stayed on my waist and he helped me lower myself down on him. I knew that he wasn't going to stop me, I knew that he wanted this just as much as I did, but there is some part of me that needed him to lie back and just let me do what I wanted with him.

As soon as I had reached his hilt, I took a moment to get used to the feel of the fullness I felt with his cock inside me. There was something perfect about this moment, about having my mate here with me.

As I slowly started to move, Dom's hands on my waist guided me over his length, but something inside of me isn't happy with that. Taking his hands in my own, I pressed them down into the mattress, pinning him there. Rocking my hips up and down his length, I took him in, lying there beneath me. As he watched where his cock pressed into my body, his eyes fluttered closed in ecstasy.

"Yes, baby, just like that," he groaned, his hips coming up to meet mine.

Releasing his hands and leaning back, I felt him slip deeper. His hands coming up to cradle my breasts as he rolled and pulled on my nipples. Working myself over him I couldn't help but feel like this man beneath me was worshipping me and my body and it felt so right.

One of his hands dropped to my clit and his thumb started to work me as I quicken my pace over him. Whatever it was inside of me that needed that sense of control, purred in contentment at the way that this man was worshipping my body.

"Come with me sweetheart," he moaned, "I want to feel your sweet pussy clamp down around me as I come, I want to hear your sweet moans as you come all over my cock."

His words spurred me on, wanting to feel exactly what he was describing. This side of him was so different from what I was used to seeing out where everyone knows him and it was a side of Dom that I very much like!

The feeling of my impending orgasm crept up on me, it felt like it was wrapping around me, taking hold of my entire body. With it came the overriding need to claim my mate. Looking down at him lying beneath me, I knew that he was mine and the bond urged me to complete the link between us.

Darting forward I sank my teeth into his shoulder causing Dom to cry out in ecstasy as he came from the sensation. Snapping his hips up, he slammed his length into me, pushing me over the brink as I came with him. I feel Dom's teeth sink into my shoulder, overlapping with Caleb's mark and I moaned in delight.

The bond hummed to life between us as Dom cuddled me into his chest while we both caught our breath. It was like a missing part of me just clicked back into place and the satisfaction of feeling that while lying here in his arms was enough for my eyes to flutter closed as I dozed sleepily against him. After a short while, Caleb slipped back into the room and curled up with us again, the three of us falling asleep in each other's arms.

CHAPTER 28

LYRA

I had woken early wrapped up in Dom's arms. Wyatt hadn't come back to the room last night and Caleb seemed to have slipped out again. Whilst I liked to think that they were sleeping elsewhere, if I had come to know Wyatt like I thought I had, I was fairly certain he would have spent the night patrolling the pack territory for signs of Cassius.

I quietly slipped out of bed and crept out of the room without disturbing Dom. He didn't even stir when I managed to untangle myself from his arms, so he must need the sleep.

The packhouse was deathly quiet. Everyone else must be asleep or outside on patrol. I'm still feeling pretty sore that they won't let me do any of the patrols, but with my declining state, I suppose I had to admit that they were right. Even if I didn't want to admit it out loud.

Deciding to go and find Wyatt, I stepped outside and took a deep breath of the fresh air. It's so beautiful and peaceful here—nothing like Angelus with its rocky, barren landscape. The sun was just starting to rise and the sky was starting to turn into a wash of pinks and oranges. We should really find somewhere that we could sit and watch the sunrise one morning, I bet it's beautiful.

I had no idea where Wyatt would be patrolling, so I decided to just walk the perimeter of the house and see if he found me. I'd only made it to the first corner of the house, where the trees came closer to the house, when I froze. I could have sworn that I heard something in the trees. Scouting through the dim early morning light, I tried to see what could have caused the noise. When I didn't find anything, I'm suddenly unsure whether I should keep going or return back to the house. I wasn't armed and I knew that I was still weak, but surely I was safe here. I knew that Wyatt and several other of the pack members had been patrolling and I'm barely any distance from the front door.

Unsure of myself now, but not wanting to look stupid if it's a member of the pack out there, I turned back in the direction that I was going and started to walk again. Slower this time and more alert, I made my way around the corner and start walking down the side of the house. I can't escape the feeling that someone is watching me, but now I just felt like I was being stupid. Once I got to the back of the house, I was just going to duck in the back door and pretend that was what I had intended all along.

It's not until I'm halfway down the side of the house that I heard another noise and froze. This time I'm certain that it was a branch snapping and I knew that someone was shadowing me through the trees. The brief second I took to consider whether to run back to the front or make a dash for the back door, was all it took for him to make his move and I suddenly found myself pinned against the wall of the packhouse with Edwin laughing in my face.

"I can't believe that you truly are this stupid to just wander around alone. Did you think that you were going to be safe here, little bird? Did you think that they would be able to keep you from me?"

I couldn't stop looking into the jagged wound that used to be his eye. He hasn't bothered to cover it over, leaving it as just a deep gaping hole where his eye once was. Something about it makes me feel weirdly proud of myself.

"Why are you smiling, little bird? Were you starting to enjoy your stay with us? Cassius is going to be so pleased when I bring you back, I bet he will let me keep you for the night. Would you like that? Me and you, alone, all night long." He leant in and ran his tongue up the length of my neck, groaning.

"You fucking idiot," I wheezed out, catching the look of confusion on his face just before he got snatched away from me.

Wyatt and Caleb both dragged Edwin away from me. He's fighting and screaming, but with two full grown wolves already having hold of both of his arms he didn't really stand a chance. I could tell that Wyatt was already starting to lose control and Caleb didn't seem that far behind him.

"You should have taken a bite while you had the chance Edwin," I taunted. "The sun's coming up and you've got nowhere to go."

He paused in his struggles for a moment while he registered where he's being dragged to, the front of the house and into the clearing, where the sun is already starting to shine brightly down. His struggles picked up in intensity and he managed to throw Caleb off and then kicked him in the ribs, throwing him back towards the treeline. With his free hand, he grabbed Wyatt around the throat and began to squeeze.

Wyatt was too far gone though and the only way he was going to let go now was if Edwin could choke him out first and he's far too close to the front of the house to have time to do it.

"You loved every second of it, I know you did, little bird. I bet as I was biting down on your creamy white thighs you were getting wet for me," he laughed.

Clearly, Edwin had zero sense of self-preservation, most people would be begging for their lives right about now.

Caleb launched himself back at him again and this time got hold of one of Edwin's legs. He's thrashing and trying to kick him off, but it's just making Caleb dig his teeth in further, shredding Edwin's leg in the process.

Aria and her mates had already come out of the house to see what all the commotion was and are standing waiting in the sun for us. None of them move to intercede and I think they realised that this was something that my mates, Wyatt especially, needed to do.

As soon as they reached the very edge where the shadows meet the sun, Wyatt suddenly stopped dragging Edwin. As Wyatt stepped back, Caleb lets go and they both start to circle the now bleeding vampire. Both of his arms are shredded and the leg that Caleb had hold of looks like it wouldn't take his weight even if he did try to run.

Wyatt and Caleb keep darting in and tearing into him. They're just playing with him now, punishing him for the last nine years. I couldn't say he didn't deserve it. By the time that they're finished with him both of his legs look a mangled mess and he's barely even fighting any more. His blood has sprayed across the grass where he laid and I'm pretty sure there's a few leg chunks mixed in there as well.

When Wyatt darted in and snapped his jaws a breath away from Edwin's face he didn't even seem to have the energy to flinch away, but that didn't mean he didn't have enough left in him to keep talking shit.

"He's going to come for you. He's going to drag you back to that cage and bleed you night after night after night. Maybe if you're lucky he'll throw in a couple of wolf pelts to keep you warm," he cackled at his own joke, but it's more of a wet hacking sound than anything else.

I can only hope that he's doing it on purpose to goad Wyatt into ending it for him because if he is, then he's at least getting what he wanted as Wyatt grabbed one of his chewed up arms and dragged him out into the sun.

At first, he didn't seem to be affected but then as Wyatt backed away, his skin started to smoke and then his screaming began.

I don't know how long it took as his skin smoked, then started to just burn away. He didn't pass out for a very long time and no one moved until his body had nearly melted away.

Wyatt and Caleb transformed back into their human forms and Kyle passed them towels to clean off as much of the blood as they could. Dom appeared behind me and wrapped his arms around me as I stood and keep vigil over the suffering of my biggest tormentor. Every scream that came from him reminded me of my own. As he withered away to nothing, I try to send my pain along with him, but the memories of the cage and the harvesting stayed with me. I think as he slipped into whatever hell he deserved that he dragged a part of my soul with him. I'll never be free of him, even as I watched him burn away to nothing, I knew that he would still be the thing that haunted my nightmares.

CHAPTER 29

WYATT

I left Lyra in bed with Caleb and Dom to rest. They needed to talk between the three of them anyway. I didn't think that Lyra would really care, but the other two definitely needed to get things out in the open. They had been dancing around each other for years. It was a relief to see them finally admitting to their feelings.

Surprisingly when I went to investigate, the library was empty for a change. I wandered around the packhouse, trying to find Kyle and Aria. From the brief conversation we had with Lyra earlier, there was definitely something going on. Kyle has two of the Elites embedded as spies and I haven't seen any of the others apart from Echo since we got back. Aria mentioned that they were doing the night watches which would account for why they aren't visible through the day, but I had a feeling that something more was going on. The problem was, I wasn't the beta of this pack anymore. Even though Marcus kept things from me, I still knew a lot of what was going on in the pack. I suppose now I was just an ordinary pack member, but I had valuable knowledge which Kyle should be making use of. Or maybe I was just trying to justify myself there. Either way, I now found myself searching through the packhouse trying to find them. I know that they didn't go upstairs, but I'm still praying I don't find them in a compromising position anywhere else in the house. With five mates, it's only a matter of time.

In the end, I only find Aria with Liam down in the old safe room. Her own personal armoury is definitely starting to take shape. I've been meaning to come down here since we got back anyway. As soon as I step in the room, Aria has a smile to greet me. It doesn't quite meet her eyes, and I wonder just how much everyone else can see behind the cheerful mask she adopts most days.

"Wyatt! I'm surprised that you were able to tear yourself away from that lovely mate of yours," she grins.

The word mate fills me with a warm feeling I would never admit to anyone else. It still doesn't feel real, it doesn't feel real that she's finally here, finally with the three of us.

"She was asleep when I left her, but I'm sure Caleb and Dom will be enough to keep her busy if she wakes up."

Liam slapped me on the shoulder with a bark of a laugher while Aria just rolled her eyes and turned back to what she was doing.

"What brings you down here looking for us anyway?" he asked me.

"I was just wondering where everyone is," I said casually, moving over to the map that's on the wall. Checking it over I can see that the old abandoned house that we found on the Moon Side isn't marked and we should really add it on. It might even be worth thinking about setting it up as a safe house.

"Virion and Braedon went up to sleep when the whole flaming vampire thing went down and Kyle and Sykes went for a run," Aria filled me in, moving over to where I was standing by the map. "Is there anything that you can add?" she asked, indicating to the map.

I point out the rough location of the abandoned house to her and float the idea of setting up a safe house which they both decided to put past Kyle because they agreed it's a good idea.

"And what about everyone else?" I asked as Aria and Liam started to brainstorm what they would need for a safe house.

Aria looked up and scrunches up her face in confusion. Granted, it's been a while since we were on the subject and have moved on to other things.

"Where are the rest of the Elites, Aria?" I asked, getting to the point.

"Well, we can't get much past you, can we old man?" Liam laughed.

"Seriously, I'm only eight years older than you! You need to knock that shit right off!" I huffed. I'm not really annoyed, this was just starting to become a thing between us all now.

Liam and Aria looked between themselves and I know that I'm on to something from just that one look.

"We're trying to gather information on The Farm that was mentioned in Marcus' journal. We believe that someone was working with him, but we don't know who we are up against. There was no reference in the journal to a partner which seems unusual given that he was keeping dirt on everyone else," Aria told me, looking serious.

She's right. There was no way that Marcus wouldn't have some kind of insurance against whoever he was working with.

"Maybe we haven't found everything yet," I suggested.

Liam just shrugged. "At this stage, I don't think we ever will. He had a lot of shit going on, just trying to unravel what we already know about is going to take a lifetime, especially if we are going to set right as much as we can like Kyle wants."

I'm not surprised. Kyle was always a good guy. It was

inevitable that he would want to make amends for what his father had done in the name of the pack. I'd give anything to be able to bring that fuck back to life so I could get my chance at him as well.

"The shit that was in that journal. I'm almost terrified to find out what The Farm even is," Liam shuddered. "There was stuff in there about people eating fucking kids!"

Liam and I had drifted back to the table in the room where we were preparing the list for the potential safehouse. Looking over my shoulder, I realised that Aria was still standing at the map, even if I didn't think she was truly focused on it. When I turned back to Liam, he looked just as worried as I was about her. I gave him a nod and a slap on the shoulder before leaving him to comfort his mate. When we first found Lyra in the Moon Side, I thought that talking to Aria might help her. Now I'm starting to think that maybe it might help Aria to talk with Lyra. Misery loves company and those two had been through lifetimes of shit. I might even have a bottle of whiskey hidden somewhere from my drinking days to help them through it.

I'm at a loss as to what to do next. I don't want to disturb the others because they need some time alone and I'm not quite ready for us to be together like that just yet. I ended up wandering into the empty library and sitting in front of the fire like old times. Staring into the flames I couldn't help but turn my mind to the idea of where Marcus could have hidden his secrets and just how bad the secrets we haven't yet found are going to be.

CHAPTER 30

ARIA

Digging my hands into the dirt, I made room in the raised bed to plant the seedlings that had sprouted in the greenhouse. I once read a book about PTSD that said finding activities to occupy and clear your mind can help when you're trying to deal with the trauma of an event. Back when I was a kid that activity had been training, learning how to fight, and how to defend. That was how I dealt with feeling like a victim, by making myself stronger.

But now, training didn't hold the same calming pull for me as it once did. All I saw when I pulled my blades was blood. I saw the faces of the students from the academy who never made it out. The same distorted versions that we found on the battlefield in their reanimated corpses.

If you had told me all those years ago that gardening would become my new sense of peace, I would have laughed my ass off at you. But there was something about cultivating a life that helped me deal with all of the death that had surrounded me for months. As soon as I set foot in this realm, it felt like it followed me wherever I went. I'd only been able to pull on my Valkyrie form once since, in defence of Lyra, because the thought of entering into a bloodlust again terrified me so much.

I knew I should talk to my mates about this. They were with me through this journey as well, even if they didn't have as much blood on their hands as I did. I saw their lingering looks of concern when they thought my back was turned. The cautious silence that preceded me when I entered a room sometimes. I just wasn't ready yet. Thor had stopped by a few times and I had spoken briefly with him, at least as much as I was ready to. He's a surprisingly good listener. My mother still hadn't been able to come to visit me. She wasn't doing well. She'd refused any visitors, especially any of the Valkyrie. I think Odin may have gotten his wish and finally broke her when he tore her wings from her. I didn't know how Lyra was surviving as well as she was when my own mother, a centuries-old warrior, had suffered the same and yet it had left her a shell of the person she used to be.

As if my thoughts have conjured her into reality, I saw Lyra walk out of the kitchen door of the packhouse. She seemed to hesitate for a moment and then with what looked like an actual physical shake of herself, strode across the small kitchen garden and dropped down to sit on the grass beside me. Like always, she immediately turned her face to the sun, closed her eyes, and leant her head back for a brief moment while she appreciated the feel of it on her face. I'd noticed that she did it every time she came outside. I suppose you learnt to appreciate the little things like the sun on your face when you'd spent nine years sitting in the dark.

"You're gardening," she said, clearly confused.

I couldn't blame her, even I think I'm acting weird.

"Yep." I popped the 'p' as I responded just so that I could feel a bit like my old self even if it did feel forced and foreign now.

"You're a Valkyrie and if the stories I have heard are correct you have always been a fighter, a defender of the women from your realm," she said. I wasn't if it was supposed to be a question or not so I just nodded. "But now you are gardening?"

I looked down at the row of seedlings that I'd just planted in the ground and the dirt that covered my hands. I could see where the confusion was probably coming from.

"It helps," I shrugged.

"It helps you ... become a better fighter?" she frowned.

Her confusion is just adorable and I couldn't help the bark of laughter that poured out of me. My laughter just confused her even more and I couldn't help but wonder if this was the look I had on my face when I first got thrown into this realm.

"No, it helps to calm my mind." I took a deep breath as I wondered just how much I was willing to admit. But when I looked up into Lyra's face, I realised that this broken angel in front of me was the least likely to judge me. She was just as broken as I was and just as much of a fighter.

"I take it that someone filled you in on the fight that we've just been through?" I asked her and she responded with a nod. "I'd never been in a battle before I came here. Yeah, I fought and I put down some people. I may have even taken some lives. Actually, that's a lie, I totally did take some lives, but the limp dicks definitely had it coming and it was done out of necessity. The point is that I had never experienced war—mass loss of life. And I had definitely never been responsible for it. I knew what I was going into. I knew what I was going to do and at the time I wouldn't have made any other choice. I still wouldn't. I did what I needed to make sure that I survived. We all did. But now that it's finished, or at least that part has finished, I ... I feel like I don't know who I am anymore."

My vision blurred with the unshed tears that collected in my eyes and I swiped furiously at them when they dared to fall. I hated feeling weak and admitting this, it was the weakest I'd felt for a long time.

"When I was six years old, I was given a dagger and put in a room with a human man who had murdered nine women. My teacher told me his crimes and that I was not allowed to leave that room until the man had suffered enough to pay for the crimes that he had committed. When she left, a film began playing of the terrible things that he did to those women. They played it on a loop for the three hours that I was in there. I only left once he was dead and there was not a second where the dagger that was put in my hand was not in use," she told me.

What. The. Actual. Fuck!

"When I left that room, I was not the same child that went inside. I attended that room once a week until I graduated from the Education Centre at the age of fourteen. I went in that room 416 times, each time a different person was inside. Sometimes I was told to punish them, and sometimes I was told to extract information from them. More times than not that person was not alive when I left that room. Every single time I was drenched in blood when I left."

I could see that she had grown cold and detached as she told her story. That she packed herself away into a corner of her mind while she recalled the horror of her childhood, the things that they made her do.

"The point I am trying to make is that I was conditioned throughout my childhood to deal with blood, death and all the horror that is associated with it. By having it forced upon me, I learnt how to detach from what I was doing and what I was seeing. But that is not the right way to live, Aria," she explained.

Wait. What? That wasn't where I thought she was going to go with that.

"If there is one thing that I have learnt over the last nine years, it is that life is precious. It is hard to take a life, to deal with the consequences because it has to be. It should never be easy. It should leave a mark with us and even if we were justified in taking those lives, we should have to bear those marks. It teaches us to appreciate the beauty and the chaos that life brings to us. It reminds us of what it means to be alive. But those marks do not mean that you are broken, the very fact that you feel them makes you a better person than I. It's when you don't feel those marks any more that you need to worry, that's when they've finally succeeded in breaking you."

We sat in silence while I considered what she had said. She was right of course, the fact that it affected me just proved that I wasn't the monster I feared the bloodlust had turned me into. I was still just me.

"All of that death though ..." I started.

"Now you're just trying to justify your pain. Death is not an end. It is just another step on our journey—an inevitable step at that. Everything and everyone has to take that step at some point. Some reach it earlier than others, some curled up warm in their beds and others with the help of someone else. But you, Valkyrie, better than any of us, should know that death is not the end of their stories."

She had me there. Britt was proof of that.

"Does heaven exist?" I blurted out, suddenly needing an answer.

"The afterlife from human religions?" she asked. I nodded to let her know that she was correct. "If it does it is not in the Angelus realm," she said coldly.

"What do you think happens when people die?"

"We move on to the next step in our journey, whatever that may be," she said as if it was obvious. When she turned and saw the look of confusion on my face, she continued. "Some will be reborn into different realms, still continuing their same lifetime, Valhalla for instance. Some will start a new life entirely. Restarting somewhere else, in a different time. Everything circles back around at some point, Aria."

"I don't know what to do, I don't know how to get back to myself again. I feel like I'm just pretending to be me," I sighed, everything I'd been holding in finally making its way out of me. Holding it in was so exhausting.

"You're still you. You might be a bit different, but you're still the same person. Experiences make us grow. Why would you want to go backwards?"

I took a moment to think about what she had said. There was something refreshingly different about Lyra. It was almost like she had retained a part of her innocence even after everything she had gone through. She seemed to have a way of looking at the simple side of a situation, disregarding all of the bullshit. Either that or she was a bit of a sociopath.

"It still hurts," I whispered.

Lyra nodded and we sat in the sun, both of us confused by our thoughts but savouring the companionship.

"How are you feeling about the whole fourth thing?" I asked her. "When I realised that I had more mates out there, it was shocking, to say the least."

Lyra cocked her head to the side as she considered her words. I started to realise that Lyra wasn't the type of person who just acted without thinking. Even when she spoke, she only said exactly what she meant.

"I'm worried that it will be difficult for Wyatt, Caleb and Dom," she finally said. It wasn't what I had expected her to say.

"Screw them! How are you feeling?" I smiled at her and was rewarded with a genuine laugh in return.

"I don't know. I only ever thought that I had one mate and that thought got me through all the time I was sat in that cage. Knowing I had Wyatt to come back to was all the motivation I needed to survive. Then suddenly there was Caleb and Dom. Even before I knew they were my mates, they were just so easy to be around. All of us together just feels so right." A blush flushed across Lyra's cheeks and I made a note to circle back around to that later.

"I know what you mean, my guys, always the first to know!" I said, throwing my hands up in the air. "There I am stumbling around like an idiot and then one of them will just go 'but Aria, he's pack'," I growled the last part doing my best imitation of Kyle, personally I thought it was spot on.

Lyra cracked up, laughing at my frankly perfect impression and I was a little insulted.

"Oh that was perfect and you know it!" I scoffed, shoving her shoulder. "Anyway, what I was demonstrating with my amazing impression was that the guys would be fine, they share a bond as well as you, you don't need to worry about them."

"Would it be okay to admit that maybe I'm a bit excited about finding this mystery fourth then?" Lyra turned to me with a grin.

I couldn't help but take a moment to take in the two of us here. In another life, maybe we would have just been two women talking about our love lives, maybe over coffee. God, I'd kill for a caramel latte right now. It seemed unfair that we had so much hanging over us right now, or rather Lyra had so much hanging over her right now. If Frannie was right, I'd had my turn at the gauntlet of death and now it was Lyra's turn. I wondered how many of us there were going to be before we got to the end? Fucking hell, was there ever going to be an end?

With that one soul-destroying thought in mind, I got to my feet and brushed the dirt and grass off my ass. Reaching a hand down to help Lyra up, I told her. "Come on, let me teach you about a human tradition called comfort eating."

CHAPTER 31

DOM

We found Lyra and Aria sat in the kitchen eating ice cream and drinking whiskey. From the giggles alone, it looked like they had been on the whiskey for a while. I didn't know how they were stomaching the combination, but they seemed happy enough. In fact, Aria looked lighter than she had for a long time. It was nice to see a bit of the old Aria shining through.

"Well, now I feel like we're about to spoil all the fun," Sykes said, pulling out a chair at the table and stealing a bite of ice cream straight from Aria's spoon.

She gave him a sloppy grin and leaned into him for a kiss. As she sat back up, I caught the relief on his face. They had all been worried about her.

"Lyra, this is Virion and Braedon, who you haven't properly met yet," I told her, pointing across to the two of them as they took seats at the kitchen table.

Liam stuck his head in the fridge and started to pull out sandwich makings, laying them on the table in between everyone.

"I think we might need to get some real food into you two,

at least real enough until we can get dinner sorted," he laughed as he started to construct a sandwich.

Caleb was already on the job for Lyra, although she seemed decidedly less drunk than Aria was, who was swaying slightly in her seat. When he placed the sandwich in front of her, her eyes lit up like it was Christmas and she dove in. Maybe when you're deprived of food for nine years, you get a better appreciation for what you had when it was in front of you.

The rest of us sat around quietly and a bit awkwardly while the girls ate. Aria seemed to be finding something amusing and every so often would crack up laughing spontaneously until something caught her eye to distract her. She was not going to hear the end of this from her mates, especially because Sykes had got a photograph on the phone they used to contact the human realm of her with her eyes crossed, trying to see some mayonnaise which had somehow got on the end of her nose.

The impatience of waiting for them, or at least Aria, to sober up a bit seemed to be getting to Braedon though, not that I could blame him.

"Lyra, the others got the impression yesterday that you might know something about my magic."

Hope shone in his eyes. Virion had been certain that his father would know something about the magic Braedon had been gifted with but it was a dead end.

"Hel called me a Soul Whisperer," he clarified.

Lyra was still chewing a mouthful of the sandwich as she nodded and Braedon looked like he was going to explode with the anticipation of waiting the ten seconds it took for her to finish chewing.

"Old magic," she said, reaching for her sandwich again only to have Braedon snatch it away from her.

Her eyes filled with sadness at the loss of her food and Wyatt and Caleb both surged from their seats with a growl.

"Sorry, sorry," he said, pushing the food back towards Lyra and then holding his hands up in the air as he moved back into his seat.

Wyatt bristled with anger, but one hand on his arm was all it took for him to slowly sit back down. Caleb followed his lead, but a low rumble was still flowing out of Wyatt. I could see Kyle tense in his seat getting ready to intervene, but Lyra just snuggled into Wyatt's side and he seemed to calm at her touch. I suppose given everything he had been through it would take some time before Wyatt would be able to handle what he would perceive as a threat against Lyra. Given what had happened over the last nine years, taking food from her was going to set his wolf off easily. In fact, maybe that was one of the reasons why Caleb and Wyatt seemed to be trying to feed her all the time. That theory didn't quite explain my own actions though.

Lyra took a small bite of the sandwich again and Wyatt immediately deflated but she made sure to finish it quickly so that she could speak as well.

"You are trying to find out more about what your magic is and what you can do with it?" she asked and Braedon gave her a hopeful nod. "I'm afraid that I do not know much, but perhaps if you tell me what you have already found out, I might be able to tell you more."

"During the Blood Moon battle, Hel tried to rip Aria's soul from her body. We think I was somehow able to hold it inside her. Hel called me a Soul Whisperer and really that's about it," Braedon shrugged.

I could tell he was trying to play it off like he wasn't both-ered he didn't know anything about his magic, but we all knew just how deeply it was affecting him. He had been cast out for not being powerful enough and had grown up in

Asgard where power was everything. To have had this within his grasp and yet so far out of reach was beyond cruel.

"Where have you looked for information?"

"Only here with the pack and with Virion's father in the Fae lands. We haven't really had much chance to go any further afield," he explained.

Lyra nodded thoughtfully and took a moment to arrange her thoughts before she began speaking. "As I said, I don't know much. Soul Whispering is magic that allows you to see and manipulate souls. You should be able to develop it to see a sort of aura for people which will help you determine their moods and motivations. You can also harvest souls and send them on to the next step of their journey. Either the one which is predetermined for them or one of your own choosing. It is very old and very powerful magic."

"Where can I get more information?" Braedon asked eagerly.

"I would think someone who has the same or similar magic," Lyra said, cocking her head to the side as she thought.

My stomach plummeted as I came to the realisation of a potential source of information which I hoped no one else would. It was the worst possible avenue for us to take and one I was not even going to suggest if they didn't realise it themselves.

"Other soul harvesters may be of assistance, the Valkyrie or Wraiths. I suppose some Gods may know more, Hel, of course, but she is unlikely to assist you."

I internally sighed in relief when she didn't say it. Of course I was tempting fate, because then she opened her mouth and said it.

"Or perhaps a necromancer. They practice different magic, but it may be something that they have collected information on."

"Well at least for now Valhalla and Asgard are no go areas

for us," Kyle said, looking over at me and I felt my stomach drop.

This was just not fucking happening.

Everyone turned to look at me expectantly, apart from Aria who just looked a bit confused.

"No. It's too dangerous," is the first thing that comes out of my mouth and as soon as I say it, I know it's a mistake.

Aria looked like someone just gave her a new sword with the way that her eyes light up and the others had looks varying from pissed off to amused. The only two who didn't seem to be weighing in were Caleb and Wyatt, probably because they didn't have anything invested in this.

"This could be your only way to find Lyra's fourth mate," Kyle pointed out. "To have Braedon look at the ties that bind her soul."

I squinted in annoyance at him because he's not wrong. This was the only way we currently knew about. No one in this realm had ever been able to find a way to trace a person's fated mate. If they did, it would give them power over every race and there was no way that they would be keeping that secret. They could ask for any price. Demand any favour in return. People who had the potential to live for hundreds of years would go to any length to find the missing piece of their soul.

It made sense that if there was a way to trace a fated mate bond, it would be through old magic no one had seen or heard of for generations.

"What about Frannie?" Sykes suggested.

Wyatt visibly shuddered and I couldn't help the smile of amusement. He still wasn't over seeing Frannie chewing on Octavia's ear after he killed her. Ever since he had actively avoided her and I think the day that Madame Nines took her to the new Shifter Council headquarters to help with the set up was the most relieved I had ever seen him.

"She's not going to be available for some time. Madame Nines is using all of her energy trying to get everything set up at the new Council Headquarters and Frannie has been helping out with some liaison tasks. We can't afford to distract them from that unless we have no other option," Kyle told us. "If it comes down to it, I will request their return, but I don't think that it would be wise advertising Lyra's presence here to the rest of the packs. Not until we know exactly who we can trust and who we can't. It would be too great a risk that they would retrieve your fourth first and then use him against you."

Fucking hell, I hadn't even thought of that. Aurel was about to go and update the angels on Lyra's condition. What if they went after her mate first? Were we about to enter a race to get to him first or would they help us find him? It seemed like they wanted something from Lyra so the most likely option would be that they would use him as leverage to get her to do what they wanted.

"Shit!" Wyatt swore, surging from his seat as he started to pace around the kitchen. "We've wasted too much time and now they have a head start."

He looked over at me and I could see the panic and question in his eyes. I frantically searched my mind for any possible alternative. Anything.

Fuck!

"I'll go alone," I sighed in defeat. "If I portal in, I should be able to get in and out in a few days."

"Absolutely not!" scoffed Lyra.

I think this was the first time I had ever seen her angry and I'm not sure what it said about me because as she stared me down with fire burning in her eyes, it lit a fire in me and my cock became painfully hard at the sight of her. This was the angel that came out of the nightmare education camp, the angel we would have faced in battle if fate had made different plans for us. This was the fire that she was struggling to find again, the fire that we needed to help to relight in her.

"Why is this place so dangerous?" she asked and boy was she pissed when she said it.

"The Mage Council operates on a system of hierarchy. The most powerful families hold the Council position, weaker families are relegated to less important roles. Power and knowledge is everything there. My father,… holds one of the Council seats. He's possibly the worst of them," I explained cautiously.

"Does he pose a danger to you if you return?"

"Not as much as he would pose to you if you accompanied me," I told her, already seeing where she was going with this.

Lyra glared at me. The rest of the table was silent, not wanting to get involved, even Aria seemed to finally be sober enough to know that she didn't want to step into this.

"We do this as a pack," Lyra said, locking eyes with me. I could see that she wasn't going to waver on this, but I didn't want to either. Taking her to that place was my worst nightmare. Even I didn't want to be subjected to it.

"Why is it so dangerous for you?" Aria asked quietly. I knew that she was trying to diffuse the tension, but it wasn't helping.

"The Mage Council has the authority to order me to stay on site. My father will ensure that I comply with whatever means he deems necessary," I said evasively.

"And if you refuse?" Aria asked through clenched teeth.

"I will be made to comply."

"Meaning?" She wasn't going to let this go and everyone here knew it just as much as I did.

"There are rumours of mages being stripped of their magic, but no one has been able to prove anything," I admitted.

Everyone fell silent. It didn't need to be said that stripping a mage of their magic would kill them, they all knew it just as much as I did.

Lyra's eyes were wide in panic and I could tell that her mind was running a mile a minute trying to find a solution.

"You can't go there alone," she finally said.

She's right, as much as I hated to admit it. I needed someone to watch my back. In the past, I would have asked my brother, but now, I didn't know who I could trust anymore.

"Then we go as a pack," Caleb said firmly.

"It's too dangerous for Lyra, if they found out what she is ..." I drifted off because I didn't really want to say it out loud.

Wyatt was scowling down at the table. He was our alpha whether he wanted to admit it or not. What he did now was going to go a long way towards determining if he was ever going to be ready to step up.

"We go as a pack and Lyra comes with us," he finally said. "You can't go alone, you need us to watch your back. I won't leave her behind. I need to keep her with us. We're stronger when we're together."

And there was the alpha that we all knew he was, even if I didn't particularly agree with what he was saying.

"She would be safer here."

"I know," Wyatt growled.

"*She*," Lyra said lowly, glaring at me, "will not be left behind like an inconvenience."

And, now I was in trouble!

"Lyra, please, you have to understand," I begged. "We've only just got you back ..."

She stood suddenly from the table and it looked like the glare in her eyes only got worse. Like, I was legitimately a bit worried about what she was about to do.

"If anything were to happen to you when we were there, I don't think ..." My voice broke as I spoke and I struggled to hold my emotions at bay.

"And I would feel exactly the same way if anything happened to you and I wasn't there," Lyra told me gently as she moved to my side and slid into my lap. "It is no more dangerous for me than it is for you. Don't make me sit here and worry about you."

I nodded because what else could I really do. Selfishly I wanted her with me. Leaving her behind would have been one of the hardest things I ever would have had to do. Taking her with me, taking all of them with me, would be the stupidest thing I would ever do in my life. That didn't mean that I wasn't going to though. They were right, we were stronger together, even if it did put us at a greater risk. No one had ever jumped into danger for me before I came here and I met these people. I had been smothered by family since I had been born and yet I had never experienced a true family until I came here. Until I found these people. This group of strangers who would become the strongest family I would ever need.

CHAPTER 32

LYRA

I could tell that Dom wasn't happy with me for forcing the issue of going to the Mage Library with him. Deep down, I knew he just wanted to keep me safe, but I needed him to realise that I wasn't some cowering creature he needed to stand over. I needed the freedom to be my own person and whilst I may not have wanted to go back to being the naïve young angel, fresh out of the education centre, I needed to find my way back to a part of that. I needed to fight for what I wanted. I needed to remember what that felt like. But apart from that, I didn't know if I was ready to be separated from any of them, even if it was just for a few days.

"You all packed up and ready for the morning?" Wyatt asked, breaking into my thoughts.

I looked around at the room I was currently sitting in. It was Wyatt's, but it seemed to have become ours. I still felt a bit like I was invading his space though.

"Yeah, I suppose. It's not like I really have all that much stuff to pack," I said, realising just how true that statement is.

"We've not really had the chance to talk about what

happens, have we? What with everything that seems to keep happening," he said, taking a seat next to me on the bed.

"No. I don't want to seem like some needy female, but I'm assuming that we are all going to stay together," I told him, a small voice in my head laughing at how ridiculous I sound right now.

Wyatt just draped an arm around my shoulders and pulled me closer to him. "There is nothing in the world that could keep us apart again," he told me, pressing a kiss to the top of my head. "Do you want to stay here or do you want to move on from the pack once we have this situation settled?"

I hadn't thought about it this far. Should we stay with the pack? I hadn't met much of the pack, only Aria and her mates. I had spent too much time trying to recover from what we now knew was the loss of connection to my magic. I had heard parts of conversations about what was happening with the pack, what Kyle was trying to achieve for the shifters with the formation of a council. It also seemed like something which should become interracial and I couldn't help but wonder if that was something they had considered yet.

"I think I'd like to stay here for now," I told him, not committing to anything.

Wyatt nodded thoughtfully. It was nice sitting here in his arms. Getting to be two people, together, not thinking about where we were going to run to or the next problem that needed to be solved.

"Come with me," he said, suddenly standing up and grabbing my hand to pull me to my feet.

I let him lead me down the stairs and out of the house. We wandered through the trees hand in a hand for a very short distance, but Wyatt took it slowly. I knew he was doing it on purpose so he wouldn't tire me out and it pained me to admit that I needed him to. After a few minutes, the trees thinned out and a house came into view. It was nothing like the massive packhouse we had just come from. To start with, it was only two-storeys high. It was made completely out of wood and it looked like it had been sat here, unloved, for quite some time.

"I know that it doesn't look like much," Wyatt said, suddenly sounding unsure of himself. "No one has lived here for years, but if we put some work into it, I think we could make it nice. It's big enough for all of us and it has room for ... you know ... if we were to expand the number of people that lived here," he trailed off quietly.

The smile crept across my face as I realised Wyatt was suggesting this house would be big enough if we wanted to start a family. I had never thought about the possibility that I could ever have one. It wasn't something that happened where I was from. We didn't have family units. Angels didn't bond with their children. The thought of forming something like that with my mates thrilled me more than I thought it would. Obviously, the scary thoughts of if I was even going to be a good mother started to creep in at the sides of those thoughts, but I pushed them away for now. I was going to just let myself be happy with the situation we had. There were far too many problems to think about now and in the near future to start inviting in even more. For now, we deserved to just be happy in this moment.

"Can we go and look inside?" I asked him, grinning at the thought of being able to make this place a home for us.

"Of course," he laughed, jogging up the steps and swinging the doors open.

As I moved inside, I knew immediately this was going to be the place for us. The downstairs of the house was all open plan and I loved it. I hadn't realised until now, just how much I needed that. It was obviously a side effect of my imprisonment—cage life had apparently left some marks on me.

In one corner of the downstairs, a basic kitchen was set up.

Most of the cupboard doors were missing and a few were hanging off. There weren't any appliances and the dust and grime were thick on every surface. The rest of the downstairs was empty. There wasn't any furniture, the floors were wooden boards and the walls looked like they had once been painted possibly white, but the dirt in here had changed it to a kind of grey-ish brown colour.

"Okay, so inside is pretty terrible, but if you just try and think of what it could be like and just ignore everything you can see now," Wyatt winced, mistaking my silence for being upset.

"I love it," I blurted out, interrupting him before he could talk himself out of this. "But who's house is this? Won't they mind if we take it?"

"It's one of the pack's houses. It's been empty for years. It doesn't really belong to anyone. The pack used to be a lot bigger, smaller pack groups and families used to live in these houses away from the packhouse. Marcus didn't give a shit about the pack and things broke and degraded over time. He refused to pay for the repairs and half the pack ended up living in squalor. Kyle is slowly renovating them, but now that the pack has become so small, a lot of them aren't needed."

Wyatt moved around the downstairs, looking around the empty space. The far wall had a staircase leading upstairs that I wandered over to, while he started to look around what was left in the kitchen.

"Be careful on the stairs," he called over to me, "I'm not sure how stable they're going to be."

It looked fairly dark at the top of the stairs, but I knew Wyatt wouldn't allow me to wander about this place if there was anything to fear about it, except for the apparently rickety stairs. Heading upstairs, apart from the odd squeal of what could be rotten wood, the stairs thankfully held firm. They opened out into a small hallway which had several doors

leading from it. It was different from downstairs and had walls
sectioning it off into different rooms. There were two doors to
my right, two doors in front of me and a set of double doors to
my left. Deciding to leave the double doors to last, hoping
they held something exciting. I started from the furthest on
the right with the intention to move along.

Peering through the first door, I found just an empty
room. Well, empty apart from the same grimy dust that was
downstairs. The next door had a very broken and smashed up
bathroom. Next was another empty room and another next to
it. This wasn't quite as exciting as I thought it was going to be
for some reason. But next, I had the double doors and I stood
outside of them, feeling strangely nervous about what I would
find inside.

The left door opened an inch and then stuck in the frame.
My heart rate spiked as my first thought was that someone was
on the other side, but I quickly realised that it was just the
wood that had warped. Trying the right door, it came free with
a shove, causing me to stumble forward into the room. It was
massive, taking up probably about half of the floor space of
the upstairs. This would be our bedroom I realised, one that
we would all share together. A blush flushed across my cheeks
at the thought of all of us together, in one bed. That seemed to
have been something that the guys had avoided up until now.
Is this something that they would want? Now that the reality
of it was in front of me, I realised that it's something I had
never known I wanted. But all of us together just felt right.

I felt Wyatt walk up behind me before I saw or even heard
him. He was sneaky for a wolf.

"Can we really make this our home?" I asked him quietly.

"I know it doesn't look like much, but once we clear it out
..." he started, misunderstanding what I was saying.

Turning around, I wrapped my arms around his neck and
leaned up on my toes to kiss him gently on the lips. Tears brim

in my eyes, but I didn't want there to be any misunderstanding about why they were there.

"It's amazing, Wyatt. I don't care that it will take some
work to fix up. This is a dream come true. I want this with
you, with all of you. It's just ... I need you to tell me that this is
real," I snuggled into his chest and felt his arms wrap tightly
around me.

"This is real. You deserve something nicer than this, but by
the time that it's finished, we will have made this our home,"
he whispered against my hair as he laid his cheek on top of my
head.

We stood like that for a while, just feeling the reassurance
of having each other nearby. It's strange, but sometimes, in the
quiet, I almost think I can feel Wyatt's wolf straining against
the surface of him. Like he was trying to reach out to be with
me. There was a quiet sense of peace and strength in that
feeling.

CHAPTER 33

DOM

Stepping back into the Mage Library after all of these years was a lot more underwhelming than I had expected. All four of us portaled across from the packhouse to the front steps of the library. It was the usual stepping off point for portal travel.

A few mages were walking about, minding their own business. The entire thing looked the same as it always had. A sense of annoyance and disappointment set over me that it was just life as normal here when so many others in our realm had been fighting for their very existence just a short while ago. It was almost obscene, the way that life here was so unchanged. I would bet they hadn't even stopped for a moment when they realised what was going on, and make no mistake about it, they would have known. I had, after all, told them over a year before about the visions and the prophecy. They just decided it wasn't something that warranted the attention of the Library.

The others had paused on the steps behind me as I stood and took in the familiar sights around me in disgust. I didn't want us to linger here too long though. We couldn't afford to draw attention to Lyra and even without anyone being aware of her heritage at face value, her beauty was enough to draw any mage's attention to her.

"Follow me, we need to go to my apartment and then we can see about trying to find the information we need," I told them, quickly moving up the steps and through the main doors.

I heard Lyra gasp in awe as we moved inside. It was a beautiful building. It had been made to be awe-inspiring, it was nothing but a power move, though. The entrance opened out in a round hallway and had a staircase spiralling around the edge. The bottom three floors of the building were dedicated to the library, but the five floors above that were laid out as apartments for the important mage families. In the centre of the space, a massive chandelier hung, reflecting the light throughout.

I moved straight to the staircase with the others following, jogging up the stairs to the fourth floor. I'd never hated the fact I couldn't just portal straight into my rooms more than I did right now. I needed to get Lyra inside and away from any curious stares before anyone started asking questions. I could already see the interest we were getting from the few mages we passed on the stairs, although that could also have been from the fact that I was sprinting up the stairs and no one ever had any sense of urgency around here.

Luckily, we made it to the door without anyone intercepting us, I was under no illusion that we'd be so lucky the next time though. We should have prepared more before we came here, we should have gone over what our cover story was going to be, who to trust and what information we were prepared to reveal. Better yet I should never have agreed to bring the others with me. Fuck!

Caleb, almost as if he could sense my spiralling emotions, was immediately at my side as soon as I closed the door. With a calming hand on my shoulder and an understanding look on his face, I felt seconds away from just wrapping my arms around him and giving in to the need to let him hold me and tell me everything was going to be okay.

There was a reason why I left this life. A reason why I walked away from my family, the backstabbing and the constant need for one-upmanship. This place was built to not only discover knowledge, but also to share it. That was the purpose of a mage. To share knowledge with the world. To promote betterment through learning and understanding. But this dark and twisted culture that it had created instead was rotten to the core. Knowledge was still coveted, but it was hoarded. Sharing with the other races was never done. The journal we had found in Marcus' possession was not as shocking for me as it was for the others. That was what life as a mage had become. Secrets, bribery and extortion, were the only things they seemed to care about any more. The families were now in a constant battle to try and rule over each other. Kyle's idea of a council was a good one, but the Mage Library was a cautionary tale that he needed to heed because this is what his council could become if they give in to the lure of power. The seductive whisper of power is hard for anyone to ignore.

"Where are we?" Lyra asked, her sweet voice pulling me out of the turmoil running through my mind.

Looking up, a part of me is relieved to see that my rooms are still the same. My family had a large apartment on the top floor of the library, which was where all of the head families lived. I moved out from there as soon as I was able to. My father was more than happy to have his sole focus on my brother, the child of the family that wasn't a disappointment. I didn't know how he put up with my father being in such close quarters with him all the time, but then they were two sides of the same coin. I didn't know who my mother was.

Stone was born a year after I was and she left as soon as she recovered from the birth. Her duty was done. She had borne the two sons she promised to my father and she ran as far away from him as she could. I couldn't blame her. I'd grown up with him, I knew exactly what he was like. It wasn't like he had loved her anyway. All he cared about was power. The Farsight line had strong magic and my father was all about increasing it, anyway that he could.

"These are my rooms. Every important mage family has some sort of apartment within the library. I am lucky enough to have rooms away from my family," I told her as I strode further into the apartment.

It was small, but perfect for what I needed. It was my first safe haven away from my father. It had been fairly easy to get them allocated to me. None of the important families wanted rooms these small and none of the lower families seemed to be willing to enter the cut-throat life of living in the library. My father would never have allowed me to go too far back then though, he still thought I was going to come around. That I would return and take up the legacy of the Farsight name.

The apartment had a small sitting room with a kitchenette over in the corner, a tiny bedroom was attached which had a double bed and a chest of drawers in it—nothing else would fit. Then there was a small shower room attached. It had been like a slice of heaven the first day I sat in the armchair, in front of the fire. The quiet had settled in around me and I was finally able to start planning my way out of this nightmare.

Lyra and the others made themselves comfortable in the little sitting-room and seemed to watch me expectantly. I could tell that Caleb knew I didn't want to be here. He's got that slightly worried scowl on his face he seemed to constantly wear when I first met him. Deep down there's a part of me that's jealous of the fact he didn't have a family pressuring him through life, but then I realised just how heartless that was of me and the shame sets in for even thinking it.

"Sit down Dom and just take a breath," Caleb said, with nothing but understanding on his face.

Lyra takes the seat next to me and I all but haul her onto my lap, immediately feeling soothed by her presence. Mages don't take mates, but I couldn't help but wonder if this mate bond was something we were supposed to have as a people.

"We need a game plan. We need to find information on tracing the mate bond and also on Braedon's soul magic. Do you have any idea how to go about doing it?" Wyatt asked.

"The only thing that I can do is look in the library for answers. There may be some mages researching specialist subjects who have an idea about where to look, but I don't think it would be smart to draw their attention," I told him. Wyatt just nodded in agreement.

"What do you want to do first?" Lyra asked, snuggling against me.

She felt cold to the touch and I pulled the throw off the back of the small sofa and wrapped it around her. Wyatt immediately jumped up and set about starting a fire in the fireplace. We lived for this woman. I wondered if she knew just how tightly she held onto all of our hearts.

"We need to decide what our priority is going to be. Once I start making enquiries and drawing attention to us, we are probably going to have to make a quick exit from here. In any event, it wouldn't be smart for us to linger too long," I sighed.

The pressure of keeping Lyra safe was strong, but I knew if I said anything about it I was only going to piss her off. She was so used to looking after herself she got pissed when any of us suggested otherwise, but I didn't think she truly appreciated her weakening state. She struggled to stay conscious for more than five hours at a time.

"You're suggesting we don't ask about Braedon's soul magic," Caleb said, looking concerned.

"It's not that I don't think we shouldn't make enquiries. I just think we should start out looking into tracing a mate bond. If those enquiries come up empty, then we can look in that direction as an alternative. Drawing the attention of a necromancer is never a good idea. Doing it while Lyra is in a weakened state would be foolish," I winced even as I said it, expecting the backlash to come straight away.

"You're right," Lyra sighed.

The others look just as shocked as I am and as she looks between us, she lets out a soft chuckle which instantly makes me hard. Lyra was the most beautiful creature I had ever been in the presence of, but when she smiled it was like the whole world held its breath just to appreciate the sight of her.

"I can admit that I might not be on top form," she smiled at us and I could see the other two were just as blinded by her as I was.

"I don't know how I would feel about us returning to the pack without at least attempting to find out something for Braedon," Wyatt said, frowning. "Aria and her mates have given so much. I think we should try to help them with this if we can."

He's right, as much as I hated it, he was right. But it had been so long since I was last here and I had no idea what had been happening in my absence.

"I know how you feel because I feel it too. But none of us knows what has been happening in the library since I left here six years ago. We need to tread carefully. If we don't find anything on this trip, I promise you I will return when Lyra has bonded with her final mate and find answers then," I told him.

Wyatt just nodded, but I could see that he was still troubled. It must be hard for him to be torn between us and his feelings for the pack as a whole. Without the academy, I didn't have anything apart from the people in these rooms that I felt any kind of commitment to and I'm including the Mage Library and my own family in that as well. I had no ties here at all. I didn't even know why I kept these rooms, if I was completely honest, I had no intention of ever returning to them.

We were all lost in our thoughts when an abrupt knock on the door startled us in our silence. Climbing to my feet, I warily approached the door. There was no window next to it and no way to see who was on the other side without opening it. Not that in a world of magic, it would be much use. It's not like they wouldn't be able to just come right in, even if I didn't answer the door. It was only social norms and etiquette that was stopping them.

My heart bottomed out into my stomach as I pulled the door open and saw who was standing on the other side. I supposed I shouldn't be surprised. It had taken him a whole ten minutes to get the information we were here—my father must be getting slow in his old age.

"Master Farsight, your father requests the presence of you and your companions for dinner this evening," Carlton, my father's valet informed me.

Carlton had been with my father for as long as I could remember. I had absolutely no idea how old he was because he looked exactly the same as I had always remembered him.

"Of course, Carlton, let him know that we will be there," I told him, gently closing the door when he turned to leave.

"Fuck!" I cursed as soon as I strode back into the little living room.

"Why is having dinner with your father a bad thing?" Lyra asked me as I dropped back down onto the sofa with a melodramatic sigh.

"Because he is an overbearing, manipulative ass and if he

thinks that he can benefit anything from it, he'd sell your soul just as soon as he looked at you. He is a dangerous man. We cannot trust him and we absolutely cannot tell him about what you are."

Wyatt looked about as stressed out about this as I was. "Then why are we going?" he asked.

"Because refusing him will just make him fixate on us when he realises that we are hiding something from him. It's safer to play the game and just hope that we can play it better than him until we leave," I told them seriously. They needed to appreciate just how serious this situation was.

"We need to get our story straight then," Caleb jumped in before Wyatt could say anything else. I knew he would have my back and just accept that if I was saying this place was dangerous, then it was.

"We should just tell everyone that Lyra is a member of the pack. It's the truth, after all. If they assume that she is a shifter then that's their business," Wyatt said thoughtfully, surprising me that he is on board with the situation.

Lyra was quietly frowning where she sat and I turned to her and took her hand.

"I don't want you to think that I'm ashamed or you, or anything like that, this is all for your safety," I told her earnestly.

She nodded slowly, looking me in the eye and I could see the sincerity shining in them. "I'm sorry that I've put you in this position, I should have stayed back with the pack, shouldn't I?"

"No. You were right to come. It might be dangerous here, but until you have formed all of your bonds, it's going to be dangerous for you everywhere. At least this way we are all together."

Lyra just nodded and snuggled back against me. Wyatt was still looking concerned, staring into the fire and Caleb was watching me with Lyra, a smile on his face. I meant what I said to her, all of us here together was the safest that any of us could possibly be. Especially for Lyra, nothing could ever hurt her with the three of us by her side.

"Why don't you get some sleep sweetheart," Caleb suggested as he watched us both sitting together. "It will make it easier for you to be on guard this evening if you get some rest now."

Ordinarily, I would have expected her to argue. She always seemed to force herself to keep going until she literally dropped from exhaustion. I supposed that is to be expected with her background though. But continuing with the surprises, she just nodded and got up.

"You're right. If you don't mind, I'm going to take a nap," she said, looking back at me.

"Of course, I don't mind. The bedroom is just through that door," I told her, pointing to the doorway across from us. "Do you want anything before you sleep, anything to drink or eat?"

"No, I'm fine," she said with a yawn.

Wyatt scooped her up and silently carried her into the bedroom. He'd been quiet since we got here and I knew the thought of having Lyra somewhere that wasn't safe was going to be playing on his mind. In Wyatt's mind, the pack would always be the best place for her. Even when we were not there. But I'm almost certain there was something Kyle was holding back from us. There has to be a reason why he was placing the Elites into other packs and in a coven. I didn't think he would withhold any important information from us, but I did think he would keep it from us until he had proof he was right. Until then, there was no way I would be happy to leave Lyra there without all of us to protect her. Even if that did mean bringing her here within the reach of my father. At least I knew where I stood with him.

"I should get some clothes arranged for us if we are going to be expected to attend dinner tonight," I told Caleb, after the door to the bedroom closed behind Lyra and Wyatt.

I made no move to leave the sofa. I didn't really want to leave. If I could, I'd just stay here. I hated this fucking place and everyone in it.

Caleb slowly got out of the chair and sat down next to me.

"It's going to be alright, you know," he told me quietly. "We won't let him hurt her and we won't let him hurt you."

I didn't know how he always knew what the root of my problems were, but he did. I think he was supposed to be my mate just as much as Lyra was, but I didn't know how to express those thoughts to him. All of these feelings are just new and, at times, overwhelming. Ironically the only person that I think would understand what I was going through was him and yet he was the one person that I was the most scared of talking to about them.

"I hate this place," I told him. Caleb sat and listened, like I knew he always would. "I hate him, I hate what he expects me to be and the things that I end up doing, even though I don't want to. It's like he gets under your skin and manipulates you into what it was that he wanted you to do all along. He's always playing the long game and even when you think you're doing something as a big fuck you to him, you only end up doing the thing that he wanted all along."

We sat in silence for a moment as Caleb mulled over what I'd just said.

"You left here and you left all of this behind you. You created something at the academy that everyone said was impossible. This is not your life and you aren't bound by the expectations of your family any more. We will do what we need to and then we will leave. You never have to come back here ever again, if you don't want to. We don't need them. We can start building our own library, one that would be open to everyone," he said carefully.

"How do you always know the right thing to say?" I asked him in wonder.

"Because I know you better than I know myself. We were supposed to happen. It was always going to be us. We just didn't see it at the start," he told me honestly.

My lips pressed against his of their own accord. I loved this man so completely, even if I had no idea of what, physically, that meant for us just yet. But he held my heart in his hands. As Caleb's hand came up to cradle my cheek, it didn't even take a thought for me to rest my head in his hand. Everything about him was just natural, being with him took no effort. He was right, this was always supposed to happen. There was no me without him, I'd spent my entire life waiting for both he and Lyra to stand by my side. I just never knew that I was waiting for them.

"They could call me back," I finally admitted. Caleb looked confused and I knew that it was time to admit this to him. "The Council could request my return to the library. If they do, our laws require me to obey."

Caleb looked at me, his mouth open like he wanted to ask something, but couldn't get the words out. "And if you don't?" he finally asked.

"No one ever goes against the Council."

"We will deal with it if it comes, as a pack," he told me with a smile.

It's hard not to smile when he does, because he's right, and we will.

"When we get out of this place, we need to sit down and speak with Lyra," I said, suddenly feeling more sure of myself. "I can't give this up, I need her to know how important this is for me, I hope for both of us."

Caleb searched my eyes for a moment and I'm suddenly terrified he's going to change his mind.

"I don't think you need to worry, but I agree we need to talk to her. I think she will be happy for us, Dom," he said quietly. His eyes were flicking to the closed bedroom door. "I think Wyatt already knows. In fact, I think he's known for longer than we have."

I laughed quietly because I heard what Wyatt said through the door when I first kissed Caleb. He's right, apparently, he has known for longer than we have. I wondered if it was obvious to anyone else?

I nodded slowly. Sitting here, I felt like there was so much I wanted to say to Caleb, but it also felt like there was no need for me to say anything at all. I already knew he felt the same way, that he was thinking the exact same thing I was.

"What can I do to make this easier for you?" Caleb asked me.

"Just be here," I said because that was all I could ever need from him.

We took a moment to just sit, to just be, but then I steeled myself ready to drag myself away.

"I'm going to sort out some clothes for us. I should have known this was going to happen and just come prepared," I sighed.

Dinner with father would be a formal affair, we would all need dinner jackets and Lyra was going to need a gown. It's not exactly hard to obtain things like that around here. It was a place of magical learning, after all. We had entire families that specialised in conjuring. The problem was I don't want to be wandering around the library. I wanted to stay here with the family I'd chosen and make sure they're safe.

Caleb offered to come with me, but I made the excuse it would be quicker for me to go alone. It would, but it would also be safer for them to stay as out of sight as possible. The conjuring families had never been appreciated as much as they probably should be and they were all on these lower levels anyway. It wouldn't take me long to get what we needed and then when I came back, we could all make a game plan for how we were going to get out of this place as quickly as possible.

CHAPTER 34

LYRA

Waking up in a strange bed is infinitely better when I'm waking up beside one of my mates. Wyatt must have fallen asleep not long after I did, because the last thing I remembered was snuggling into his arms and now he's peacefully sleeping next to me.

I'd caught him in moments over the past few days where he'd seemed to be worrying about something. I couldn't decide if it was me that he was worried about, or something to do with the pack. Whenever he saw me watching or someone else approached that look wiped from his face and I didn't think he would admit to it ever being there in the first place. Now, he looked nothing but relaxed. He seemed at peace.

I tried to unwrap myself from him to get out of bed without disturbing him, but as soon as I moved his arms wrapped tighter around me. Dom had me worried. I knew that he didn't want to be here and that he was worried about all of our safety, but I thought it was more than that. He truly seemed to hate his father. I knew that there was a story there and I was almost afraid to know what it was.

I ran one finger down the bridge of Wyatt's nose and traced

his lips. I knew he wasn't asleep, but a flicker of a smile crossed his lips just before I leant into him and kissed him softly.

"Mmmm, I want to wake up like this every morning," he murmured, holding me close.

"We can and we will, we just have a few things to do first," I reminded him.

"Don't remind me," he grumbled. "I don't like this. It's unfamiliar and my wolf doesn't know what's a threat and what to guard against."

"Imagine how I feel, everything is new," I laughed.

Wyatt leans back a bit so that he can look at my face. "How are you feeling about all of this?" he asked.

"Urgh, that's a bit serious. Let's get through the terrifying, murderous family bit and then examine all that later," I said, trying to keep my most serious look on my face.

Wyatt just laughed and thankfully dropped the subject. I just didn't feel like doing all the feelings at the moment. We really did have too much going on right now.

"We should probably go and see what the other two have been doing?" he suggested.

Now that's a thought that brought a smile to my face. Caleb and Dom were so cute together. I may have been living my best cage life for nearly a decade, but even I had seen the way that they looked at each other. I'm confused about why they seemed to be holding back though.

"Why do Caleb and Dom pretend they don't have feelings for each other?" I asked Wyatt, realising that we had the perfect moment alone for me to be able to ask my questions.

"You've noticed that too, huh?" he grinned.

I just nodded because I wasn't really sure there was anything else to add and I didn't want to distract him from answering my question.

"I think it's partly because it's new to them and they aren't sure what they want from each other yet," he said slowly, almost reluctantly.

"And the other part?" I asked half worried and half intrigued.

"I think they're worried about what you'll think about it," he told me, watching me carefully for my reaction.

"Why would they be worried?"

Wyatt started to look uncomfortable and I got the feeling that I'm not supposed to be asking questions about this. "That you won't accept them being together," he told me carefully.

"I care about them, I would never deny them something that would make them happy," I told him, taken aback by the idea that I would purposefully make them unhappy by keeping them apart.

"There are some who would not want to share their mate, even with another one of their mates. There are a lot of cultures that do not support same-sex relationships, the mage community is one of them and a lot of shifters would not be accepting either."

I took a moment to truly think about what he was saying. We didn't have the same sort of understanding of relationships in Angelus. Physical intimacy occurred within flights when angels needed the release and we didn't form relationships. Because procreation was done by assignment and relationships didn't really form, I supposed we had a more fluid outlook on the issue of pleasure.

"Should I speak with them about this?" I asked him and Wyatt visibly winced at me continuing the conversation. He clearly didn't want to be part of this, but we were all mates together, he's part of this whether he wanted to be or not.

"Probably, but let's wait until we get back to the pack and we aren't constantly looking over our shoulder. We can't afford to let anyone here find out and think it is a weakness that they can exploit."

I nodded in agreement. He was probably right. There was something here, with Dom's family, that he had left behind him, in the past. They weren't going to be the type of people he was going to want to know about this, especially if these people think what they were doing is wrong.

"Come on," Wyatt said, holding out his hand to me as he climbed off the bed, "let's go see if there is something to eat around here."

Having slept most of the day away, my stomach was definitely protesting at being ignored. It was strange how quickly you could get used to eating regularly. If I went back to the cage life now, I'm not sure I would be able to survive again.

Back in the living room, Caleb was reading a book on the sofa, but Dom is missing.

"How long has he been gone?" Wyatt asked, immediately on guard.

"He's just nipped back out to pick up the clothes he ordered for tonight. There's food in the fridge if you two are hungry," Caleb smiled across at me and added. "Did you sleep well, sweetheart?"

"Yep," I told him, as I climbed into his lap for a cuddle.

Wyatt headed straight to the fridge and pulled out an enormous platter of sandwiches, there's seriously enough there to feed about ten people. It was almost like a challenge and my stomach and I were happy to accept it. Wyatt must see the look in my eye, because he left the platter on the table in front of me with a chuckle. Grabbing a sandwich in each hand, I leant back into Caleb and pulled his book in front of us so that we could read it together while we eat.

CHAPTER 35

CALEB

S tanding outside of the door to Dom's family's apartment, the nerves radiating from Dom were strong. I knew that he didn't want to be here, not at the library and definitely not standing here waiting to go inside and see his father. He was doing this for us and the fact that he would set aside his own past to do this meant a lot, to all of us.

We seemed to have subconsciously formed a triangle of protection around Lyra. Dominic was taking the point standing directly in front of the door and Wyatt and I had flanked her on either side, keeping her safe in the middle of us. This was why we needed a fourth. Her back was too exposed and my wolf was feeling agitated enough just being in this place and also being able to feel the pain coming from Dom. I would give anything to be able to shift and go for a run now, but I knew that wasn't going to be an option until we got away from the library. We couldn't afford for any of us to be going off alone in this place.

Dom had barely finished knocking when the door stood

open and the same man who relayed the invitation to us was standing in the doorway.

"Welcome home, Master Farsight," he told Dom, opening the door wider for us all to move inside.

"This isn't my home," Dom grumbled under his breath.

The man, whom I'm assuming is some kind of servant, made no acknowledgement of the comment and led us further into the apartment. The opulence here was astounding. When Dom first told me that his family had an apartment at the Library, I knew from my basic knowledge of mage culture that this was a big deal. Only the old families lived here. It was a status symbol, but it was one that I never really understood. I always thought that living in a large house, like the packhouse, away from the library would be a bigger display of power and wealth, but now walking into this place I could see just how wrong I was.

The floors were clearly made from marble and heavy velvet fabrics hung in all of the windows. They didn't have light fittings; they had chandeliers and I suspected that they weren't made from crystals. The furniture was clearly expensive and priceless antiques seemed to stand in strategic positions around the room. And this was just the entryway. This place screamed money and it screamed it in a way that reminded you that you'd just stepped outside of your social class and you were very much not welcome here.

Dom strode through the entrance hall and without really knowing what else we were supposed to do, we all just trailed behind him. When he entered a room off to the side, an older mage rose from his chair and approached him. This must be his father and whilst he had invited us to be here, he really didn't look too happy about it.

Dom came to a stop standing in front of him, they didn't embrace, they didn't even shake hands. In fact, they just stared at each other for a moment and there was nothing but arrogance written across his father's face.

"You aren't even going to introduce your companions to us?" he finally asked, turning from Dom and immediately locking his eyes on Lyra.

I couldn't say I blamed him, she was beautiful. But that didn't mean that I liked it. My wolf and I both agreed that he had no business looking at her, but we were also sensible enough to know that he held all of the power in this place and the last thing that we could afford to do was insult him. Unfortunately, Wyatt either hadn't come to the same conclusion or just plain didn't give a shit, because the low rumble of a growl echoed around the room and Dom's father broke his perusal of Lyra to give Wyatt a knowing smirk.

"This is Wyatt, Caleb and Lyra. We have travelled here from the pack for research purposes," Dom told him, keeping things as vague as possible as we had already discussed.

"Lyra, what a beautiful name," he murmured, turning back to her, clearly dismissing Wyatt and I as inconsequential.

Dom's expression contained nothing but rage and disgust as he watched his father take a slow perusal of Lyra's form. On any other man, it would have been sexual but on him, it was nothing but predatory. Dom was right, we should never have brought her here because I could already see him calculating just what he could gain from this moment.

"This my father, Gareth Farsight, and my brother Stone," Dom told us and I realised that someone else was still sitting in an armchair beside the fire.

Stone slowly rose from his seat and strolled across to us like he didn't have a care in the world. He'd dressed in a three-piece suit and the crisp white shirt that he was wearing underneath is unbuttoned down past his chest, showing off a glimpse of his tanned skin beneath every time he moved.

Dominic looked remarkably like his family. They all had

the same tanned skin, dark brown eyes and dark hair, even if his father's was starting to grey at the sides. They all were tall and muscular and power radiated from them, not just from their magic but from the way that they dominated a room with their looks alone. The difference between Stone and their father, though, was that he didn't seem to really care why we were here at all.

He came to a stop in front of Lyra, picked up her hand and dropped a kiss to the back before he wordlessly walked back to his chair and dropped back into it. Picking up the tumbler of whiskey from the small table next to the fire, he took a sip and turned back to stare into the frames, effectively dismissing us.

Lyra just cocked her head to the side as she watched it all, confused about what she was supposed to do now. She's not the only one. This is just awkward.

"I suppose it's nice to meet you," she said, calmly turning back to Dominic's father, who just threw his head back and laughed.

Before the situation could get any more awkward, the servant walked through a set of double doors to our right and informed us that dinner was ready to be served. We all wordlessly followed him into an equally opulent dining room and took our seats around the table. The seating arrangement wasn't lost on me though. Gareth took the head of the table and Stone sat directly opposite him at the other end, only four chairs were remaining, two on either side. No matter how we arranged ourselves, Lyra would have to sit next to one of them. Dom and Wyatt wordlessly took the seats bracing Gareth and I had to say that I agreed with them, Stone was clearly the lesser of two evils here. Hopefully, he would just continue in his attitude and ignore us all for the time that we were here. In the end, I took the seat next to Dom and Lyra sat down next to Wyatt. My wolf liked that we could keep an eye on her this way without having to pretend that we were watching her out of the corner of my eye.

Stone sat back in his chair with a smirk and I had the sudden feeling that we may have completely misread the situation.

The servant from earlier, whose name I really needed to learn, comes out and lays a salad in front of everyone.

"Are you so afraid of your people that you feel the need to only return to the family home if you have friends with you?" Gareth suddenly said, sitting back in his chair and completely ignoring the food in front of him.

Dom picked up his glass of wine and mirrored his father's move.

"Well, I needed at least one person that was worth talking to while I was here," Dom said, an unfamiliar smirk stretched across his face.

"Yes, it must be difficult to find someone of the same intellectual level as you, perhaps you could try amongst the lower classes or the inbreds on the lower levels," Gareth told him.

Lyra's mouth dropped open in shock and it was taking everything that I had to be able to school my expression into something neutral. I knew that Dominic's father hated him, but I didn't realise quite how bad it was.

Stone, on the other hand, wasn't saying a word, he just sat in his chair with his elbows braced on the table still drinking his whiskey and watching it all unfold in front of him.

No one touched the food. Dominic and his father were too locked in their power play to pay any attention to the small issue of food, Stone didn't seem to care and the rest of us were probably wondering if it was poisoned, or at least I was.

"Perhaps you should just tell me what you want to know and then we can cut the embarrassment of your presence here as short as possible," Gareth sneered.

"Oh, where would the fun be in that father? You must be

slipping in your oh so very, very old age if your spies haven't been able to uncover our purpose yet." Dom smiled.

Gareth bristled at the comment and I'm not sure if it was the dig at his age or the incompetence of his spy network. It weirdly felt like it was probably the latter. Of course, there was no way for them to have found out why we were here because we hadn't actually made any enquiries yet. Dom wanted to wait until after we were put through the torture of this dinner and I could see now why that was.

"You're right, maybe I should have them look a bit closer at your companions," Gareth smirked sipping on his wine.

Dom just shrugged and turned to his brother. I had never heard Dom talk about his brother much, I knew he had one, but that was about it. Right now, they didn't seem that friendly, but I saw a flicker of emotion cross Dom's face before he shut it down. It almost looked like it was hurt. What must it have been like for them both to grow up with this man? There must have been a time when the two of them were the only support and comfort that they had, how had they got to this place where Stone didn't seem to even give a shit that his brother was here.

The uneaten plates of salad were taken away and replaced with steaks. My mouth was watering and I was starving, but there was no way that I was going to eat if no one else did. At this point, I was fairly certain that Gareth wouldn't think twice about slipping something into at least one of our plates of food.

"So, I hear that someone finally had the good sense to burn that school of yours down," Gareth commented, finally starting his food.

"They were attacked by a demon horde and hundreds of the students were killed," Wyatt said coldly. "I would have thought you should have at least had some concern about the demons coming to your precious library."

"It was only a matter of time before someone had enough sense to cull you animals. And why would the demons come here, the witches have more sense than to allow their pets to attack us," he laughed.

"Just exactly when did you become aware of the witch's association with the demons?" Dom questioned. I could hear the cold anger in his voice and it was fairly apparent that shit was about to go down.

"When would it have been, Stone?" Gareth asked, looking across at Stone as if he didn't already know. "It must have been about a year ago that they came to us looking for the invocation rituals."

The room fell into a deathly silence. I felt like my wolf was vibrating in anger inside of me. Only Dom had been there with me, none of the others would know what it had been like that day. The day that we fought for our lives and watched the students around us, the students that we should have been protecting, slowly be slaughtered while there was nothing we could do about it.

Wyatt's eyes flashed in anger as his wolf pushed for the shift. I felt like I was barely holding my own shift back. When I locked eyes with Lyra in front of me, I could see the pain swimming in her gaze. She had listened to our story and she knew what had happened. Like any normal person, she felt our pain as well. Dom's family were not, however, normal people.

Dom suddenly stood and we all looked around unsure what to do.

"I will not share a meal with a man who has so much blood on his hands," he looked to the rest of us and we followed suit and stood as well.

We followed Dom out of the apartment listening to his father's laughter, chasing us out of the door. He didn't even bother to close it behind him as he marched away from that place where he had grown up—the place where nightmares were clearly made.

The front door closed with a resounding slam and Dom took off his jacket, throwing it on the sofa next to him. He came to a stop in the middle of the living room with his back to us. He didn't say a word, he just stood tensely in the middle of the small living room with his fists clenched at his sides. If I hadn't known that he wasn't a shifter, I could have mistaken him for one now. He looked like he was trying to hold back the shift. I wanted to comfort him, I wanted to pull him into my arms and tell him that everything was going to be alright. We could leave this place right now and none of us would think any less of him. He never had to come back to this place and these people ever again if that was what he wanted. But my eyes flicked to Lyra instead. We haven't had that conversation with her yet and it seemed like something we should talk about before openly flaunting my feelings for Dom in front of her.

As I met Lyra's gaze, she smiled brightly at me and nodded her head. I know that my face scrunched up in confusion because I had no idea what that nod meant. I knew what I wanted it to mean. I wanted it to be her telling me it was okay and that I should go to him, but there wasn't any possibility that it could be that when we hadn't had the opportunity to speak with her yet.

She rolled her eyes and sighed, reaching across she grabbed my hand and pulled me to Dom before she wrapped him in our arms. I was confused, but I was going to go with it, because at the end of the day, I was doing what I had wanted to anyway. Dom's first reaction was to stiffen, but then almost as if he needed a moment to realise it was just us, he relaxed against us and his head dropped down onto Lyra's shoulder. We ended up with Dom in the middle and both of us holding on to him. The bedroom door clicked shut as Wyatt left the room to give us some privacy and as soon as it did Dom's shoulders shook with silent tears as he wrapped one arm around me behind him and the other around Lyra in front, holding us both against him.

We stood there in silence while Dom worked through his pain and his grief, clinging to us like we were his lifeline. No one said a word, but it wasn't needed. We were here for him, I didn't think he had ever had this in his life before.

When Dom finally raised his head, drying his face on the shoulders of his shirt, he looked Lyra in the eye and simply said, "I love him as well."

My initial thought was that I was going to throw up. I'm not sure this was really the time to get into all of this, we had enough going on without having to work through our own drama.

"I know," she smiled.

Wait, what?

I peered at her over Dom's shoulder and she just rolled her eyes at me again and laughed.

"Wyatt thinks that you were worried about saying something to me," she said with her eyes flickering between the two of us.

"We didn't want to upset you," Dom said. I'm staying quiet, I'm too shocked and worried to be able to interject into this conversation.

"Why would I be upset?" she asked, genuinely looking confused. "Wyatt said that as well and I still don't understand. I thought that it was common for mates to have a bond between them."

"Not like this, I don't think. We don't feel like this towards Wyatt, for example," Dom explained.

"I just assumed that because some of Aria's mates ..."

"What? Who?" I blurted out because this was news to me.

"Erm, is it supposed to be a secret? I don't know if I'm supposed to say anything now," she said, looking worried.

I honestly had no idea who she was talking about and while the thought of finding out was strong, I kind of respected that they may just want their privacy. You know, what with going through the exact same thing myself.

"You're right, don't tell us," I reluctantly told her.

Dom laughed at the disappointment in my voice, which just made me suspicious that he knew more about it than I did.

"But turning back to your earlier question, I don't actually know if it's common or not, Aria is the only fated mate bond we have seen for a long time, in our pack at least. Mages don't ordinarily have mates, although I'm starting to wonder if that is really the case, or if we have just been led to believe it," Dom said, sitting down on the sofa and pulling Lyra into his lap.

It made me laugh to see him like this. I had grown so used to the slightly withdrawn Dom that I had got to know at the academy. Once the pressure of saving the world was lifted from his shoulders, he seemed to change, even if he was still dealing with the loss of so many of our students. Seeing him like this now, with an almost shifter-like need to touch and be held, was very different for him. But it was nice to see him finally being who I think he was always meant to be. He deserved to be happy, especially if his father had always been like that. I don't say this often, but wow, he is a twat!

My arse had barely hit the sofa beside Dom when I sprang back up at the sight of Stone just walking through the living room wall. The sound of my growl drew Wyatt out of the bedroom and in the space of time that it took to blink, he had Stone forced against the wall looking like he was ready to tear his throat out.

"It's alright," Dom said, passing Lyra across to me and getting up to pull Wyatt off his brother.

Stone just stood there smirking at Dom, which wasn't really the most sensible thing to do, because if anything it just seemed to make Wyatt want to hurt him even more. I had never thought about it before, but Wyatt was definitely the Alpha of our little pack. I'd never seen such anger in his eyes as I did right now, while he was defending the people he cared about.

"You can let him go," Dom told Wyatt, gently putting his hand on his shoulder. It was a smart move, if he tried to pull him away, there was every chance that Wyatt was going to lose it.

With one last hard shove against the wall, Wyatt moved a few steps back from Stone. I held Lyra tightly against me as I watched them. I trusted Dom and I knew that if he was saying that Stone wasn't a threat, then he wasn't, but my wolf and I didn't like this, we didn't like this man, whom we hardly knew, being anywhere near our mate.

Stone seemed to have no concept of self-preservation as he smiled across at Dom and just completely dismissed the enraged shifter who was standing in front of him.

"Some fun friends you have here, brother," he laughed.

"Be serious Stone, you have no idea what you're walking into here," Dom sighed.

"Me be serious? Okay, how is this for serious? *What the fuck Dom?*" he ended on a shout. "Why the fuck would you come back here? Are you completely out of your fucking mind?"

Now agitated Stone seemed to come out to play as he threw his arms up in the air and started to pace in the tiny space which Wyatt was allowing him.

Dom stood quietly, watching him. I don't know how he was managing to keep so cool about this situation. But almost as if he knew it was going to happen, Stone continued to talk.

"Father is out of his fucking mind. Something is going on

with him, I can't go into it with you now, but here is not a safe place for you. And you shouldn't have brought your little entourage here with you. Fuck! It's like you've waved a red flag in front of him and now he's going insane, fixating on your beautiful friend here. You can't have gotten this stupid since you've been away," Stone sighed and sadness flashed across his face.

It was like he was a completely different person to the indifferent ass we had met, not even an hour ago. What the fuck was going on in this place?

"I had no choice, the information we need is vitally important to our survival. As soon as I have what I need, we will leave," Dom told him seriously.

I was really starting to think we should have listened to Dom in the first place now. I was struggling to remember why we had thought it was such a good idea to come here with him. He had tried to warn us and we had ignored him.

"You should have come to me, reached out to me. You know I would have helped you. We could have done this quietly," Stone finally stopped his pacing and stood in front of his brother. He looked crushed.

"I couldn't afford to speak so openly about it yet. I need to keep this between as few people as possible," Dom said quietly, looking uncomfortable. "I haven't heard from you for months, Stone. For all I knew, they'd either caught you or turned you."

"Wait. What are you talking about? What are we missing?" Wyatt growled.

He looked all kinds of pissed off right now and I was glad that it wasn't directed at me for once.

Dom and Stone looked between each other uncertainly. Something was going on and for some reason, Dom was keeping it from us. That, for a whole bunch of reasons, was not sitting well with me.

Dom turned and looked at us, his eyes finally resting on me and I can see the worry dancing in them. He should be worried, this is all so new and I can't believe that he is going to taint the way that we were starting out, with secrets and lies. My face must betray my feelings because the worry in his eyes quickly turns to sadness and loss.

Stone, not realising what he is interrupting, jumps in to explain. "Something is happening here at the library that we can't explain. This place has always been a place of secrets and manipulation, but about seven or eight years ago, it started to get worse. Mages in the lower families started to go missing, the ruling families became even more secretive. Our father has always been a controlling bastard, but he started to get worse. Obsessing with how he was going to get stronger, how to increase his magic. All of the ruling families started acting the same. It was like they suddenly started a war between themselves and now they have this race to become the most powerful first. I suspect that whoever gets there first is going to make a move to seize power from the rest of the ruling families," Stone explained uneasily.

"What the fuck?" I sighed. "Why wouldn't you have come to us about this?" I asked Dom.

"This place, it's always like this. It's a constant battle between the ruling families. The lower-class mages used to be blindly unaware of it," Dom admitted. He almost seemed ashamed to admit it.

"So, what's different now that has made you so worried?" Lyra asked. It was a good question, if it was always like this, then why were they getting so worked up about it now?

"Lower-class mages have started to go missing and I think they might be doing it," Stone muttered, starting to pace again.

"Doing what?" Lyra asked kindly.

She went to stand up to go to him, but I tightened my grip

on her. I couldn't bring myself to let her go when I was so uncertain about what it was we had actually walked into. She gently patted the back of my hand and just sat back against me again. Not trying to struggle free.

"He's different. There's something different about him. He's changing," Stone muttered, while he paced. He suddenly came to a stop and turned back to Dom, "I think he's getting stronger. It was barely noticeable at first, if he is, it's happening slowly. So slowly that I just can't be sure."

"This sounds crazy," Wyatt muttered, finally relaxing and coming to sit beside me. He picked up Lyra's feet and pulled them across his lap, keeping hold of her ankles.

"I have to go," Stone said, pulling Dom into a hug. "I can't be gone for too long, or he will notice that I'm missing. Be careful, don't trust anyone while you are here. I'll find you tomorrow so we can talk more."

Stone took two steps back looking uncertain for a moment. "It's good to see you again, brother. You even looked happy here, I'm glad you got to find that for yourself."

Without waiting for Dom's response, Stone backed up through the wall again and just disappeared.

Silence fell across the room as we all seemed to just be frozen where we stood.

"What the fuck have we just wandered into?" Wyatt suddenly exploded.

Dom dropped down into the armchair in front of us with a weary sigh. "I have no fucking idea."

He sat forward, bracing his elbows on his knees and dropped his head into his hands. I wanted to go to him. I wanted to pull him into my arms and tell him that it would all be okay, that we would get through this and everything else together. But something was holding me back. It felt like he'd been lying to me. Like he had kept this from me and I don't know how I truly felt about that yet.

Lyra snuggled into me and I squeezed her against me. It comforted my wolf having her so close by and he was agitating from picking up on my own distress.

"When I left, I wanted Stone to come with me. I wanted him to come to the academy, to get away from this fucking place and everything that it does to you. What it twists inside you and the things it turns people into," Dom spat in disgust. "But father was already starting to change, he was becoming even more secretive and volatile. He was always a bastard, but he was infinitely worse. Stone was adamant that something was happening in the library, something that involved father. He wouldn't come with me. He wanted to stay. He wanted to keep watch and find out what it was he was up to. I shouldn't have let him. I should have made him come with me. He kept me updated over the years while I was at the academy, but about six months before the attack, he stopped. His messages had started to get increasingly desperate. He thought that he was onto something, but he couldn't tell me what and then he just suddenly stopped, all I could get out of him was that he was safe and looking into something. The messages got further and further apart. I thought he'd just given up."

When he finally looked up, there were tears in his eyes. I kind of felt bad for doubting him, but I didn't understand why he hadn't just come to me about this in the first place, especially since we had grown so close recently.

Lyra went to stand up again, but I held on tight. With a laugh, she wiggled out of mine and Wyatt's grip and went over to Dom. At first, she hesitated standing in front of him, but then she sank to her knees and tilted his head so that he had to look at her.

"You don't have to feel bad for being worried about your brother. You also don't have to feel bad for letting him walk his own path when he wanted to."

Dom looked confused for a moment, but she continued on.

"We don't have to be here if you don't want to be. We can leave now and never look back. We will find another way. I don't want to see you in pain." Lyra turned her head and looked over her shoulder at Wyatt and I. I wasn't sure why but Wyatt nodded, clearly having caught on before I had. Before I could figure it out, she turned back to Dom.

"But if you want to, we can stay here and help these people," she told him.

Dom lifted his head and looked into her eyes like he was searching for something.

"Stone has it covered. We have enough to work on, but ... maybe after everything is done, we could look into it more," Dom sounded unsure as he asked.

It was almost like he didn't want to burden us and that was when I realised. He had never brought this to us because he thought it was his problem, his responsibility. He didn't want to burden us. He was being ridiculous.

"We are a pack," Wyatt told him firmly. "We are family. Your problems are our problems. Once Lyra has established her final bond, we will get Stone out of here."

Dom just nodded, but he didn't look convinced. I couldn't even imagine what he was going through. How it must feel to have a brother that was out of your reach and potentially in danger.

"Do you think your father was telling the truth? That they knew what the witches were doing?" I asked him, needing to know the answer before I could decide just how much I was willing to help these people.

"Before I would have said no, but now, I don't know. If what Stone is saying is right, maybe. But it's also just as likely they came looking for information and my father just put it together after the fact," Dom looked thoughtful for a moment before he just shook his head and shrugged.

There was no way for us to know right now. I could understand why he might have kept this from us, but it still stung. I thought we had more trust between us than that.

CHAPTER 36

LYRA

C aleb had been quiet ever since Stone had left us last night. Dom had gone down to the main library floor this morning and we hadn't seen him since. It was well past lunchtime now and I was starting to worry. There was something about this place which was just creepy. Maybe it's because everyone lived over a library, but it was so quiet. There weren't even any sounds of children playing. It was just silent.

We raided the fridge in the small kitchenette an hour or so ago, but Dom hadn't come back for lunch. He said that he would be a while, but I was still worried.

Caleb was napping in the bedroom. The guys had been insistent last night that one of them was going to stay awake and keep watch. Something about what Stone had told us last night had put them on edge and they were convinced we needed to leave the library as soon as possible.

I could tell that Wyatt was unsettled because he couldn't seem to sit still. He seemed to be on a circuit of the living room and the kitchenette and I was becoming fascinated watching him, trying to guess just where he was going to move to next. It had gotten to the point where I was just holding the book in front of me as a decoy, so I could keep covertly watching him.

He had just been sitting opposite me, sitting back in the armchair with his right knee bouncing in agitation. His next move was to then start pacing behind the little sofa, three steps then turn and back again. After, he moved to the kitchenette and started opening random cupboards, before opening the fridge and just staring into it. My money was on the front door next, it was the next logical part of his loop and I was intrigued to see what he was going to do when he got there.

With a sigh, Wyatt slammed the door shut and then turned around and leant against it. This was it, this was the next move. I almost felt giddy to see what was going to happen next. With a huff, Wyatt suddenly straightened and took two steps forward out of the kitchen.

"Why are you looking at me like that?" he asked, squinting in suspicion at me.

"What? Me? I'm not, I'm just reading," I said, sinking a bit behind the book I had in my hand. I just hoped that he didn't ask what it was about because I had absolutely no idea.

A playful smirk ticked across his mouth, "Really, you're just reading?" he laughed, striding into the sitting room area.

Damn! I'd distracted him off course.

Wyatt sat down on the sofa, throwing an arm behind me and pulled me against him so that he could look at the book I was holding.

"And are the mating rituals of lowland unicorns a particularly fascinating subject for you?" Wyatt asked seriously, peering at the page in the front.

"What?" I blushed, quickly scanning the page in front of me, which actually detailed a ritual for invoking a wind spirit. "Hey! That's not funny!"

"It was a little funny," he laughed, pulling the book out of my hand and laying it on the arm of the sofa.

Wyatt ran his index finger from my collar bone up my neck, before hooking it under my chin and tipping my face up to him. He gently ran his tongue along my bottom lip, but when I tried to lean in to kiss him, he drew back with a smirk.

"Stay still little angel and you'll get your reward," he told me, his voice dropping low.

His head dipped back down and his lips slowly worked down my neck as he pushed me backwards onto the sofa, following me down. When his lips reached my shoulder, he reached up for the straps of my cami top and hooked one finger under each. Slowly running them down my shoulders, he gently pulled the straps off my shoulders, pulling the whole thing down my body, slowly revealing it to himself. With the silky cami gathered around my waist, I'm left lying on the sofa in my black lacey bra and I knew that my hard nipples were trying to push their way through the lace. He quickly stripped it from me, giving him an unobstructed view of my breasts.

Wyatt trailed his fingers down my body, goosebumps pebbled my skin as he traced his path down to the waistband of my jeans.

"Do you want to play a game?" he asked, his eyes flicking to mine in amusement as he started to unbutton my jeans.

I just nodded, words completely failing me. Wyatt leant back and stripped me of my jeans and panties in one pull, he even managed to pull the cami over my hips and took that with him. I'm left completely bare laying back on the sofa with him looking down at me. The hunger in his eyes as he stared down at me made me writhe in delight. I'm definitely going to enjoy whatever game it is that he wanted to play.

Standing up, Wyatt stripped off his clothes until he stood gloriously naked in front of me. My mouth ran dry just looking up at him. He really was the perfect example of what a man should be. Reaching down, he picked me up off the sofa and set me on my feet in front of him. Spinning me around, he leant into my back, trailing his fingers down my cleavage and across my stomach. I leant into him, hungry for his touch. I could feel his hard cock pushed against my back and it made me tremble with need. I felt like it had been too long since I had one of my mates, since we came together, wrapping ourselves tightly into our bond. I'm not stupid. The chances of us finding my fourth mate were small, so I wanted to spend every second I could in the meantime enjoying the life I had, the life that was always supposed to be mine. The life that was stolen from me.

"On your knees my love," he whispered into my ear and I dropped down to the ground without any hesitation at all.

Wyatt chuckled, but I knew he wasn't making fun of me. It's a laugh of satisfaction, a promise of what's to come.

I felt Wyatt kneel down behind me, as he placed a soft kiss on my neck, his lips trailed down my shoulder. His fingers trail down my arms until he links hands with me.

"Do you think you could do what you're told, little angel?" Wyatt whispered into my ear. "If I told you not to move, do you think you would be able to hold still?"

"Honestly? Probably not," I admitted, because right now, being able to feel his naked body pressed against mine, all that I can think about is everything I wanted to do to him and everything I wanted in return.

"How about you try?" he asked.

"Now that I can do."

Pulling my hands behind me, he wrapped my hands around the back of my thighs and then sat me back on my haunches, trapping my hands between my thighs and my calves. Reaching around, he put a hand on each of my knees and pulled them apart, spreading my legs.

His fingertips trailed up my legs and body until he's cupping my breasts and pulling me tightly back against him.

"You're absolutely perfect, Lyra. Every single inch of you is a picture of perfection. I'm never going to let you go, not without a fight."

I could hear a touch of sadness in his voice and I knew that he's worried about what's going to happen if we couldn't find the fourth in time.

"I'm not going to leave you," I told him leaning back against him. "I just got you back, I'm not going to give you up that easily."

He gripped me tightly against him and there was nothing but safety in his arms, a promise that this was forever and we would never be apart.

"I love you Lyra, it's always been you. I loved you the moment that I saw you and for every second that followed. Loving you was the only thing that got me through the years that we were apart. Loving you is the only thing I want to do for the rest of my life."

My eyes well at his declaration, but they're not tears of sadness, they're tears of joy.

"I love you Wyatt. I think I loved you before I even knew you. I never knew what it was that drew me down into this realm, that drew me to that stream. But it was you, I was always supposed to find you, it was always supposed to be us. I know we went through a lot to get here and I know that we still haven't finished walking this path, but we will do it, we will get through this together."

One of Wyatt's hands came up to brace around the front of my neck. He held me tightly against him, but he wasn't cutting off my air, he's just making me aware that he was in control as his alpha nature shone through him. His other hand trailed down between my legs and he delved between my thighs, two fingers pushing straight inside of me.

"I'm never going to let you go," he whispered into my ear as his thumb came up to work my clit.

I ground against him and he pulled his hand away.

"You're supposed to be staying still, you know," he smiled against my neck as he gently bit down on his mark.

Shivers rushed down my spine and the first moan slipped from my mouth. His hand is back between my thighs before I even came back to my senses and I tried my hardest not to writhe against his talented fingers.

"I want to hear you come for me sweet girl," he whispered into my ear, his thumb circling around my clit again. "I want Caleb to be able to hear our mate taking her pleasure from his alpha."

My head fell back onto his shoulder as he worked me with his fingers. Surrendering myself to nothing but the feeling of his hands holding me in place, it's freeing. There was freedom in giving myself over to him.

His lips dropped kisses down my neck and across my shoulder, peppering them with bites and nibbles. His hard cock ground against my ass. All I could feel was the storm growing inside of me.

I'm so close, there would be no holding it back, not that I wanted to. I wanted what he was giving me more than I cared to admit. He's addicting and I'm a fucking lucky girl because this is one addiction I'll never have to give up.

As my pussy started to quiver and clench around his fingers, he pushed a third inside of me. The pinch of the stretch inside of me and his unrelenting thumb circling and flicking across my clit finally pushes me over the edge.

All thoughts of holding still flew from my mind as I pressed back into Wyatt riding the wave. Even if Caleb had been asleep, there was no way that he wouldn't hear the screams that were coming out of me.

Just as I'm coming back to myself, Wyatt gripped my hips

and lifted me up, pulling me tighter back against him, pushing me down on his length. Even though he stretched me with his fingers, it's nothing compared to what he fills me with now. My back arched and he slipped deeper inside me as we both groaned at the sensation.

"Oh, fuck yes!" Wyatt groaned as he pushed himself deeper still. "You feel so good, baby."

Still holding tight to my hips, Wyatt started to move inside of me and it's everything that I needed. Everything that I wanted. I can't stop myself from moving with him. Lifting myself up and slamming back down to meet his crashing hips.

The only sounds that filled the room were skin slapping against skin, accompanied by Wyatt and I groaning at the sensations of us coming together.

Wyatt's hand came back up to my throat. It's almost like he needs something to keep a hold of and he uses that hold well, pulling me back down against him harder and faster as we both chase our release.

"I'm going to come," I panted out as I felt that familiar sensation building inside of me.

"Damn fucking straight you are," Wyatt growled.

Slipping his other hand off my hip he suddenly pinched my clit between two fingers and the orgasm slammed into me. My back arched further as my head fell back onto his shoulder, Wyatt's pace picked up again and he slammed his hard cock into me, riding me through the wave as my pussy clenched and gripped at him. It's almost too much to take and as Wyatt comes with a roar, his hand at my throat grips me tighter and something about that sensation pushes me into a second orgasm as I opened my mouth in a silent scream.

Wyatt sat back on his heels, holding me tightly against him as we both pant in exhaustion. Part of me wanted to get up and find a bed for us both to curl up in, but the rest of me doesn't want to ever move, feeling completely satisfied just being held in my mate's arms.

Eventually, Wyatt reached behind him and pulled a blanket and the cushions off the sofa, making a nest around us on the floor. Lying back, still in his arms we spent the next few hours talking about our hopes and dreams for the future, pretending that the rest of the world and the problems waiting for us there, didn't exist. It's just me and my mate, waiting for my other mates to come and join us while we make our plans and just be.

CHAPTER 37

DOM

Fuck! I should have known it was too easy to just walk back in here and find what I needed. My father must have seriously low expectations of me if he for one moment thought I wasn't going to notice his spies all over the fucking library. I couldn't even get near the section I needed without him finding out what I'm looking for. I've just spent the last four hours walking around, picking up random books, in the hopes of throwing them off the scent. It was the only plan I could come up with, look at so much information that what we are actually trying to find gets lost amongst the chaos. The problem is, as soon as I start looking at fated mate bonds the reason why we are here would be glaringly obvious.

I sat down at the table I had commandeered, with stacks of books surrounding me. Unfortunately, if I was going to make this look convincing, I was actually going to have to look through them, to at least give off the impression that I was researching something. I've tried to stick to topics that would be obvious to anyone that knew of the troubles the pack have been going through. If I'm honest though most of this information I'm just pretending to absorb.

Stretching in my seat and cracking my neck as unsubtly as possible, I take stock of my surroundings. They aren't even pretending they're not watching me. Three mages are sat at various other tables in the room, just staring in my direction. I suppose you have to at least give them marks for honesty. I've been putting it off for as long as I can, I either need to make a move for the information I want, or I need to call it a day.

My rumbling stomach decides for me and I stand up gathering the books I've collected. The only option we really have now is going to be talking to Stone about this and getting his opinion, he knows the politics of what is going on better than I could having been away for so long. Depositing the books in the returns trolley, I grab my jacket and head for the door. I haven't even made it three steps when one of my father's spies collects the books off the trolley and takes them away, no doubt for my father to look through. I just don't see why he is so concerned about me right now.

Striding back up to the apartment I don't miss the mage tailing me all the way to my door. I'm going to need to be careful in how I meet with Stone, we're going to have to rely on him coming to us if my movements are being monitored so heavily.

Inside the apartment, the others are all lounging in the living room talking softly. As soon as I closed the door behind me, Lyra was up out of her seat and bounding towards me. I couldn't even express how grateful I was that she wasn't holding any kind of grudge over me for what I confessed yesterday. Caleb hadn't looked at me the same ever since and I knew that I'd deeply hurt his feelings. This was not the way I saw our relationship together starting out. I could only hope I hadn't ruined what we had begun together. I couldn't give him up and I definitely couldn't give Lyra up. I'm prepared to drop to my knees and beg for his forgiveness if that is what it's going to take. I'm not going to fuck this up. I couldn't afford to, I wouldn't survive on my own again, not when everything I'd ever wanted had been within my grasp.

Lyra snuggled into my arms and I couldn't stop myself from lying my cheek on the top of her head and the sigh of relief that came out of me just from having her there.

"Did you find anything out?" Wyatt asked, not content on waiting for me to speak.

With an arm around Lyra, I led us back over to the others and dropped down onto the sofa, pulling her into my lap.

"No," I admitted, "my father was less than inconspicuous with his spies. I was constantly watched and I didn't even want to pull the books, for fear of alerting him to our current situation."

"So, we're no closer to an answer and we have just potentially added more enemies to our radar," Wyatt sighed.

I could sense that he was pissed off, but he didn't seem to be taking it out on me at least. Anyway, I had been the one to tell them that coming here was a bad idea. I shouldn't have let them persuade me otherwise.

"That's not entirely true," Lyra added, before anyone could say anything. "We still have Stone, he said he would come and find you today. Perhaps he can help."

"Hmmm, are we really sure that we can trust him though," Wyatt grumbled. "There's something about him that I don't like."

Ah, so it was Stone that was going to face his ire in this situation. While a part of me felt the need to defend my brother, there was also a part of me that was more than willing to throw him under the bus if it meant an easier time for us all while we were here. Yep, decision made. Sorry, Stone!

"I'm shocked you're not immediately leaping to my defence, brother," Stone's voice came from the kitchenette and sure enough, there he was, rummaging through the refrigerator.

Pulling out another platter of sandwiches, he brought them over to the coffee table, before dropping to the floor and lounging against Caleb's chair, with one in his hand. Something about having him so close to Caleb while he was angry with me was setting me off though.

"Rather you than me, brother," I smirked at him, immediately hating myself for saying it.

Stone cocked his head to the side in thought and I couldn't tell what was running through his mind right now. We'd been apart too long and his time surviving this place alone had definitely changed him.

"Can you do that?" Lyra asked me, changing the subject and preventing Stone and I from descending into brotherly squabbles.

"No, portal magic is stronger for me. I'm not as advanced in apparition as Stone is," I told her. There was a time when I would have been embarrassed about this, but as I'd grown older, I'd found that my other strengths had offset any of that. Perhaps my lack of proximity to Stone had helped as well.

Portal magic was a bittersweet thought for me. I'd worked hard to advance in it as much as I could, but I couldn't help but wish I'd tried harder. When I think back to the day the academy fell and the retreat through the forest. I would have been able to save us, if maybe I had just tried harder. As it was, the portal that transported the four of us back from the Moon Side, was the biggest I had ever been able to cast and it wiped me out for far longer than I thought it would. I knew realistically that it would probably be another hundred years or so before my magic advanced to the level of transporting a group the size of the academy survivors, but it was still a bitter pill to swallow.

"Don't be so down on yourself, brother, at least you can take others with you," Stone said, seeming far less like his usual, playful self than normal.

The mood in the room was sour, to say the least, and I felt the urge to try and move matters forward.

"You were right, father is posing a bigger problem than I had anticipated," I told him, steering us back to the subject we really need to address.

"Hmmm, he has been different since you arrived. He's meeting with someone, but I don't know who. All I managed to gather was his obsession with her and whatever secret he thinks that you are hiding."

I looked to Wyatt, ultimately I felt like he was going to be the one that had the final say here. Just how much were we going to trust Stone with? He may not have declared the position, but Wyatt was clearly the Alpha of us all. Even I found myself strangely affected by it, which was something that when all of this died down, I would love to look into more.

"If you trust him, then he needs to know," Wyatt simply told me.

Stone looked almost giddy with excitement as he grabbed another sandwich, passed it behind him to Caleb and then took another for himself. The simple move set me on edge. My eyes flick to Caleb of their own accord and I realised that he'd at least drawn his concentrated gaze away from the fire. I could tell he hadn't forgiven me, nor should he, until we had the opportunity to at least talk about it, but he didn't seem to be holding on to his anger quite as tightly.

"Lyra is my mate," I blurted out, holding onto Caleb's gaze, needing the strength of knowing that he was still here with me. "She is mate to all of us."

Stone's face was almost comical in the journey it took from excitement to disappointment and then ending in confusion.

"No, she isn't," he finally settled with. "Mages don't have mates, least of all shifters."

"I'm not a shifter," Lyra smiled at him and before any of us can stop her, she added, "I'm an angel."

Wyatt threw his hands up in the air with a sigh of annoyance and she just stared him down.

"What? We said we were trusting him."

"Not with everything," Wyatt huffed in exasperation.

"Well, I didn't know that," she pouted, crossing her arms across her chest and glaring at Wyatt with the cutest stink eye I'd ever seen.

Caleb was grinning at the sight until he realised that I was also smiling at him. His face quickly shut down, but I could see the corner of his mouth twitching with the smile that he was holding back.

"You're an angel," Stone said, rolling his eyes in disbelief. When he realised that none of us are laughing or denying it, he suddenly added, "You're a fucking angel!" only much louder this time.

"Sshhhhhh!" we all hissed at once.

"Father's spies are always close by, can you tone it down a bit," I snapped, fighting the urge to throw something at him. Unfortunately, the only thing to hand was Lyra and I'd be damned before I let my brother get his hands on her. Just the thought of it had me holding her tightly against me.

Lyra to her credit just laughed and after wriggled on my lap to loosen my arms, leaning forward to grab two sandwiches. She stared down at them in confusion before asking, "How is this plate always full of sandwiches?"

"Magic," I shrugged. It's not really that big a deal considering where we are.

Lyra, however, looked impressed as she started to eat her first sandwich and settled back against me.

"Can we stop talking about fucking sandwich magic and get back to the issue at hand," Stone hissed. "How the fuck did you mate with an angel? And why would you bring her here?"

"It's not like I was walking down the road one day, tripped and suddenly found myself mated with an angel. She's my fated mate. This is what was always meant to be," I shrugged getting to the point where I'm just past the drama of that part now. Everything else just seemed to dwarf in comparison.

"We came here because we need help," Lyra told Stone gently, drawing his attention away from me. "I need help."

My arms flexed around her and I could almost see the concern radiating from Caleb and Wyatt.

"Lyra's story is long and not relevant right now. All you need to know is that she needs to complete all of her mate bonds and she has one more mate that we urgently need to find for her to be able to do it," I told Stone.

And just like that, I could see that he's hooked. Stone always loved a mystery, I'm convinced that's why he chose to stay here instead of leaving with me. He hated that feeling you got when you thought you'd missing something.

"How to trace a fated bond?" he murmured and I could see the wheels turning in his head already.

"I wanted to look at the soul magic books in the library, but father's spies were everywhere. I didn't even dare go near that section," I said, slumping down on the sofa and feeling like a failure.

"Why leap immediately to soul magic?" he asked, looking suspicious.

"Two birds with one stone," Caleb added, saying the first thing I've heard since I dropped yesterday's bombshell.

Stone doesn't even ask this time, but I can see the question dancing in his eyes.

"One of our friends is a Soul Whisperer and we said we would look for any information that we could on his magic as well," I filled in.

Now that has him sitting up straighter.

"Of course, if you could harness the power of a Soul Whisperer, you could use that to trace a fated bond."

He actually looked impressed as he thought about it more.

"You would need to look into similar types of magic, see what techniques would transfer across to work for your Soul Whisperer," Stone murmured, getting to his feet and starting to pace.

"That was what we were thinking, but at the moment we are limited in our options. We may have inadvertently pissed off a god or two and Valhalla and Asgard are not options for us," I admitted.

"You could try to trap a reaper, see if they would strike a bargain with you for information. Dangerous though, too dangerous," Stone said, dismissing the idea even as he had it.

"We were thinking about a necromancer," Caleb told him.

"What's that? You were thinking about suicide?" Stone scoffed sarcastically.

I had to give it to him, that was pretty funny.

"What's the big deal with necromancers anyway?" asked Lyra.

For some reason, when she asked the question, Stone seemed to soften his response to her, if it had been one of the others, he would have scoffed at them.

"Necromancers have corrupted their magic into a control over life. They not only control the dead, but they can extract the very life out of anything. Their whole power source is another living creature's essence. If you go near one, you risk becoming either one of their pawns or worse, one of their batteries," Stone warned her.

"Why would someone risk so much just to have control over dead things," Lyra asked, wrinkling her nose in distaste.

"Some believe that through necromancy, you could see with certainty everything that will happen in the future. That by piercing the veil between life and death, you can find all of the answers to every possible question," I explained to her.

"That and the immortality. I'm pretty sure the immortality is what sells it to most of them," Stone added.

We all sat there, silently trying to absorb everything that everyone had said.

"Can't we just ... I don't know, get a book about necromancy instead?" Caleb asked, wincing in anticipation of being told how stupid that idea was.

"They've all been removed from the library," Stone said casually, still lost in his thoughts. "As much as it pains me to suggest this, this might not be the best place to find the answers you need."

If we couldn't find the answers here, we were screwed. There was nowhere else. The Mage Library is the biggest depository of information in our realm. The only library that came anywhere close to it was the library at Alexandria in the human realm, but that got destroyed during the Dragon Wars hundreds of years ago.

Stone was watching me nervously and when I realised that he actually had a suggestion, I felt like I was going to throw up. How does everything just seem to go from bad to worse?

"You need to ask the witches," he cringed.

"No! Absolutely not!" Wyatt shouted, jumping up from the sofa.

I'm not sure what he's aiming for, but he at least doesn't seem to be going for Stone as he started to pace the floor in agitation. "I will not trust the witches with my mate," Wyatt spat out.

"Look, I have a connection in one of the covens who may be able to help you, she has been researching tracing spells. I don't know if it will work for your kind of connection, but it is the only thing I can suggest at the minute. Necromancy is never the answer. Ever! If your friend needs information on his magic, then he should wait until it is safe to speak with one of the other sources you've uncovered," Stone explained passionately.

He's right. Fuck! I don't want him to be, but he is right.

"How long will it take you to get in contact with this witch?" I asked Stone.

Wyatt turned on me, rage flaring in his eyes. "No, don't even think it, Dom, this is not an option. We will not go to them for help. They cannot be trusted. They will sell her back to him as soon as they would give us assistance. You know this as much as I do!"

Stone opened his mouth to say something, but then his eyes lost focus as his mind drifted to something else. When he suddenly seemed to focus back on us, he simply said, "I have to go. I will try and get back to you tonight, tomorrow morning at the latest. Stay out of the library and stay away from father," he warned and then he was gone, disappearing down through the floor. The annoying fuck.

Wyatt was still standing in the middle of the room with his fists clenched at his side. I could see the flash of his wolf pushing against him as he struggled to hold back the shift. I never thought that it would be me that he was fighting so hard to hold his wolf from and I'm not going to lie, it hurt. Being the only non-shifter out of the three of us it was hard enough seeing myself as pack. When your Alpha turned his rage against you, it was even harder.

"Wyatt!" Lyra snapped, "Get a hold of yourself and don't you dare look down on him like that."

Wyatt's top lip curled up in a snarl and Lyra was immediately on her feet facing down the Alpha wolf.

"He is your packmate and I am your mate. Control yourself," she snapped again.

Caleb shuffled to the edge of his seat and I could see that he was seconds away from springing between them. It would be foolish to step between an Alpha and what they perceived as a challenge, but Caleb and I would both do it to protect our mate.

In a move of astounding self-control, Wyatt tore his eyes from Lyra, spun on his heel and stormed into the bedroom, slamming the door behind him.

"What the fuck?" Lyra sighed quietly, dropping down into the vacant seat on the sofa.

"It wasn't anything personal. It wasn't about Dom or you, it's just that the witches are never going to be an easy subject when it comes to Wyatt," Caleb explained to her.

"I know. I know what they did, what they did to your pack. But you two aren't acting like that, you both have your-selves under control. If this is our only option, the only choice that we have, then we either take it, or we all go home and wait for me to die," she snapped. I could hear the anger in her voice before it dipped down to sorrow. "I'm not ready to die, I'm not ready to leave you," she told us quietly.

Caleb climbed out of his seat and dropped to his knees in front of Lyra, holding her hands clasped between his own. "It's harder for Wyatt," he explained. "When the demons attacked, I didn't see the pack as home anymore. I'd been away at the academy and my wolf was having trouble accepting Marcus as my Alpha. Dom was the only person that I saw as pack back then. When the demons attacked the packhouse it was a slaughter. So many died. No one knew how to protect themselves and Marcus sent out the untrained wolves for slaughter. He knew what he was doing. Wyatt couldn't make a move against him, because he was trying to protect you. He stood by and followed Marcus' word and had to watch nearly all of his pack brothers die. He chose to protect you and even though I know that he would make that choice a thousand times over, he still hates himself for it. He hates himself for a lot of things that he had to do back then."

Lyra's eyes filled with tears as she listened to Caleb explain. I knew they had talked about their feelings of guilt to each other, but I also knew for a fact that Wyatt had not told her about this side. About the things that Marcus made him do on the pretence of keeping her safe. The fact that it was all lies only made it worse for him to bear when he found out. But I think I was also starting to get to know Lyra now and whilst what Caleb had said to her was the truth, it was also the worst possible thing to tell her right now.

Taking hold of Lyra's chin between two of my fingers, I turned her face to me. "This is not your fault," I told her forcefully.

The tears that had been lingering on her eyelashes started to fall and I could see the complete devastation in her eyes at the torment she was imagining Wyatt had been through. I did not doubt that whatever he had gone through, it would have been infinitely worse than any of us could ever imagine, but that wasn't going to help Lyra right now.

"It is not your fault that Marcus put him through those things. He was truly evil. There was something depraved and twisted about him. None of us saw it in time to be able to do anything about it. You hold absolutely none of the blame for what Wyatt went through," I told her, making sure that she was definitely listening to what I was trying to say to her.

Lyra nodded her head slowly and I am not all that convinced she actually meant it, but her tears had at least stopped falling and she didn't look as devastated as she did moments before.

"I should go and talk to him," she said quietly, turning to look at the closed bedroom door.

"Give him some time to calm down first," Caleb suggested getting up and striding into the kitchenette. "Now what other food does this fridge of yours magic, because this wolf cannot live on sandwiches alone."

And with that, the mood was broken. Lyra chuckled to herself as Caleb opened the fridge searching inside. I knew he was not going to find anything in there because sandwiches are actually all that magically appears in there, but that's actually because the spell is on the platter and not the fridge itself. But he's right. It would do us all good to sit and share a proper meal tonight, one without my father's barbs. Lyra still needed to keep her energy up and it would help us fortify our now fragile pack bond to spend the time together. This pack was so new to all of us and it was bound to take time for us to build the bond that came with it. It was going to take time, time to work through our differences and time to become acclimated to thinking of ourselves as a group rather than individuals. Lyra had brought us all together. We were building something together, something that was precious and worth spending time building a strong foundation for.

CHAPTER 38

WYATT

L yra and the others crawled into bed a few hours ago. She's pushing herself again and I hated how hard she was on herself. But, I had to give it to her, she did seem to be improving. The naps that her body was forcing her to take when she reached the point of exhaustion seemed to be getting farther apart. Not by much, but it was a relief to see that she was improving rather than declining. Especially considering how fucked up this entire situation seemed to be. Everywhere we turned, all we found were more problems instead of answers.

I felt like sitting here in the living room while they were sleeping was punishing no one except myself. Not that I want to punish any of the others. This afternoon just got all kinds of fucked up. I didn't know how to explain myself. I didn't know how to work through all the shit that kept spiralling out of control in my head. I felt like all I kept doing was just fucking everything up more and more. I nearly lost control earlier. I nearly shifted in the living room like some fucking newbie pup! It wasn't Dom's fault, it wasn't even aimed at Dom. I felt like I was losing control of my wolf, that he was pushing away from me because I'm so consumed by my own guilt that he's starting to believe it too. I had never felt like I was so separate from him before.

Sitting on the sofa feeling angry and sorry for myself wasn't going to fix anything. For now, I needed to make sure that the others were safe while they slept, as soon as Stone was back with the information he had for us, we needed to get out of here. This whole place was creepy as fuck and I couldn't wait to leave.

Setting aside my own fuck up, my wolf was agitated. I could feel him pacing in my mind. I needed to shift and run, to work off some of this energy and connect with him again. The urge to mirror him and start to pace the room was strong, but I pushed myself further into the sofa, trying to ignore the restlessness inside.

I was so on edge that when Stone suddenly came hurtling through the living room wall, I nearly ripped his throat out before I realised who he was. Luckily, because I jumped out of my seat, ready to attack him, I was there to catch him as he started to collapse to the ground. Pulling him over to the sofa, I gently lowered him and took in the state that he was in. He was still wearing one of what I was assuming was his trademark suits, but his shirt was torn and stained with blood. His left eyebrow was split open and he had a black eye coming in already. It looked like he'd split his lip as well. He was clutching a bag to his chest like it was the most important thing in the world. Whatever had happened, it had clearly ended in violence.

Stone gripped my shirt in his fists, pulling me closer to him. He was obviously in pain and looked like he was on the edge of unconsciousness.

"Get out," he whispered, "you need to get them out now." His eyes rolled back into his head and he collapsed back onto the sofa unconscious.

I had a moment where the world just seemed to stop, holding its breath, waiting to see what was going to happen next, then I exploded into movement. Running to the bedroom door, I threw it open, rushing to the bed. The others were already stirring and Caleb seemed immediately awake, sitting bolt upright at my entrance.

"We have to leave, we have to leave now. Dom your brother ..." was all I got out before everyone started to move.

Dom was immediately up and moving out of the room, Caleb was pulling on his trousers and Lyra seemed to already be completely dressed and standing beside me before I had even taken note of her moving.

We all gathered back in the living room where Dom was kneeling beside his brother, checking over his injuries.

"All he said was that I had to get you out. We need to move now, I don't want to get caught up in whatever is coming for us," I told Dom, as he looked up at me in concern.

I moved to the sofa to Dom's side and grabbed one of Stone's arms, ready to haul him up.

"What are you doing?" Dom asked.

"We're taking him with us, he's obviously not safe here anymore," I told him.

Dom sighed in relief and taking Stone by the other arm, he helped me haul him up so that he was braced between the two of us. The bag which he had been holding onto fell to the ground, but Lyra quickly picked it up and put it over her shoulder.

"Caleb take point, we need to move out of the building as quickly as we can, Lyra I need you to stay directly behind Caleb, Dom and I will be right behind you," I told them as we moved to the apartment door. "Dom, can you open up a portal big enough for us when we get out the main door?"

All of the colour drained out of Dom's face as he took in what I was asking him. I knew how he was going to feel about this, the portal he had opened for us before had been the biggest he had ever achieved and now I was asking him to go even bigger. I could see exactly what he was thinking, no he couldn't. It didn't matter, the four of them were portaling out of here no matter what.

Caleb caught my eye and I could see the worry swimming in his gaze before he nodded firmly and started for the door.

"No matter what, we don't stop. Dom, don't use any magic if we need to fight our way out, Caleb and I will shift," I told them. "We move fast and we don't stop."

I had no idea what sort of defences they had here or even what the fuck we are running from, but there was no way that I was not going to get my pack out of this place.

Caleb took a deep breath and threw open the door of the apartment, judging by the shriek of surprise he was not expecting the elderly bundle of woman-shaped crazy that was standing outside and immediately threw her arms around him.

"What the fuck, Frannie?" he shrieked. "How are you even here right now?"

Frannie cracked out into hysterical laughter like he had said the best joke in the world and patted him on the shoulder.

"No time, no time," she suddenly muttered, slapping Caleb across the back of the head. "Come, come, Frannie knows a secret way."

She immediately started to skip down the corridor in the opposite direction from the way out. I had a brief moment of indecision, perhaps partly because, if I was being truly honest with myself, Frannie still freaked me out a bit. But, when it came down to it, Frannie had saved us more times than I even think we had realised. If we were getting out of this place, Frannie was going to be the one to make sure of it.

Caleb didn't even have to think about it and was immediately following Frannie to wherever she was leading us, Lyra dutifully following behind him. I could see her peering around him, trying to get a better look at Frannie. I couldn't blame her, she was a whirling whirlwind of craziness.

"Frannie, this isn't the way out," Dom huffed, dragging Stone along between us.

He was completely out of it and we physically had to drag him down the corridor.

It was quiet, like it always was. Apart from his family, a collection of spies and now Frannie, we hadn't seen anyone else while we had been here. We had been sitting in the apartment most of the time, but I still would have expected to see someone out here, some sign of the families that were apparently supposed to live here.

We kept jogging down the corridor, my wolf was practically salivating at the thought of someone feeling like they could come for our pack. He wanted them to come, he was ready for them and nothing and no-one was getting close to anyone we loved.

We rounded a corner and Frannie ran over to a set of double doors leading to a balcony. I hoped she wasn't expecting us to jump because we were four storeys up right now and there was just no way we were going to be able to climb down while Stone was unconscious.

"Open, open, open," Frannie sang, dancing and twirling in front of the windows.

Caleb looked back at me, seemingly unsure of if he should do as she was telling him. I was just about to nod to tell him to go ahead when the sound of running footsteps echoed down the corridor from the way we had come.

Without waiting for a response, Caleb tried the handles, but they didn't budge. Frannie rolled her eyes, unhappy with the assumption that she wouldn't have just done that herself. Looking at the doors in suspicion, Caleb took a step back and then threw himself at the windows. They bowed outwards but held firm.

"I can hold him," Dom said, pulling Stone closely to himself and hitching him higher up his shoulder.

I dropped Stone's arm as soon as I knew that Dom had him.

"On three ..." I told Caleb standing beside him as we both braced to charge the door down.

The footsteps grew louder behind us and we could hear them shouting now. Caleb's head whipped in the direction of the sound before he turned back to me and shouted "Three!" and we both charged at the door.

They bowed out, further than the last time, but still, they snapped back again, bouncing us off them.

Mother fucking magic!

Taking position with Caleb again, this time with Lyra beside him and Frannie shrieking in joy beside me, we all braced to charge together.

"Three!" Frannie cried in joy before the four of us charged again.

The doors bowed further out and just as I was convinced that they were going to push us back in again there was a snapping sound and we suddenly flew outside onto a narrow balcony. I managed to catch myself on the balustrade, wrapping an arm around Frannie to stop her from charging over the edge with her own momentum. Caleb wavered his weight at the edge and Lyra just calmly stepped up beside us. If I hadn't seen her charge just as hard as the rest of us, I would have assumed she had just stepped through the open door.

"Open, open," Frannie called urgently, grabbing Dom's arm and dragging him through the door as he hauled Stone's dead weight with him.

Caleb and I quickly took Stone from Dom as he looked around confused. He opened his mouth to say something, but then he scrunched up his brow in confusion.

"We're outside of the warding," he said, clearly confused.

Frannie stuck her head through the doors then ducked back outside with a shriek of alarm. Slapping Dom across the back of the head again she told him, "Open NOW!"

"Right, right," Dom said flustered. He started to mutter what I knew was the incantation for the portal spell and Frannie stepped up beside him, taking his hand and joining in the chant.

The portal seemed to suddenly slam into existence in front of us on the other side of the balustrade. There was no slow spread of it like usual.

The mages who were no doubt chasing us were close enough that they sounded like they would be rounding the corner any second. Grabbing Lyra around the waist, I picked her up and threw her over the balustrade and straight through the portal.

"You are so fucked when you get through to the other side," Caleb laughed, as he climbed onto the balustrade and jumped through after her.

He was right, but right now I did not give a single fuck, she was safe and that was all that mattered.

Frannie clambered up the balustrade and leapt off with a battle shriek echoingly familiar from the one I heard her yell when she stormed a demon horde.

Dom and I had the unfortunate job of hauling Stone up onto the balustrade and then with a shrug, we just pushed him over and into the portal. The man was fucking heavy!

I waited for Dom to jump and just as I leapt three mages sprinted through the doors after us.

Shifting mid portal probably wasn't something I should have done before I knew that it was safe, but instinct overrode any common sense I had and I landed on the opposite side of the portal on four paws. Spinning on the spot, I crouched low to the ground, a vicious growl tearing from my throat as I braced waiting to see if those mages had been stupid enough to follow us. This was our territory now and I would rip them apart before they got one single step closer to my pack.

I don't know how long it took, but eventually, the portal flickers closed and no one comes through after us. My fur has bristled and my teeth bared, it's not until I feel Lyra's hand gently stroke across my head that I start to relax. Casting my eyes around me, I realise that we had landed outside of the packhouse. Aria was standing at the top of the steps, guarding our back like always. She had a sword in each hand and almost looked disappointed that no one had followed us through. It was only when Dom asked Caleb to help him get Stone inside that everyone seemed to snap into movement and head towards the house.

CHAPTER 39

LYRA

We had all gathered into the library, Stone was laying across the same sofa we had put Dom on what felt like so long ago. The rest of us were gathered at the other end of the room when Kyle stormed into the library. He took one look at Stone before turning to the rest of us.

"What the actual fuck?" he muttered quietly.

"We ran into some trouble and had to make a quick exit," Dom told him, "Stone is my brother, he came to warn us to get out and we ran. Frannie got us out of the building."

Frannie was knelt on the floor in front of the fire, watching the flames dance around the fireplace. I had no idea who this woman was or how she got into the Mage Library, but I was under no illusion we would have made it out without her. Those mages had come from the direction of the exit and my gut was telling me they had been waiting for us there.

I crouched down beside her and gently placed my hand on her shoulder. She didn't turn her head or even acknowledge I was there beside her. She just continued staring into the flames.

"Thank you," I told her in earnest, "you saved us."

She cocked her head to the side, but stayed staring straight ahead.

"So much to do, busy, busy, busy, busy, busy," she whispered.

I turned around and looked at Wyatt, who was the closest to me. I was willing to bet he wouldn't stray far from my side for a few days given the sudden run we had just had to make. He reached out a hand and helped me to my feet, walking over to where the others had started to sit so that we could join them. I looked over at Frannie, sitting in front of the fire alone and immediately felt sad for her. She seemed so isolated even though she was sitting in a room full of people.

"Frannie is a kitsune," Wyatt said as he sat down beside me. "She is a seer. She can see all of the potential outcomes of every possible action. It is rare for a seer as powerful as she is to live as long as she has. Her abilities make it hard for her to know what is present time and what is a vision."

My heart broke as I watched the elderly woman, kneeling in front of the fire muttering to herself. What must it be like to know what is going to happen? To feel the responsibility of guiding the people you care about through every correct action.

"I thought she was at the Shifter Council headquarters with Madame Nines," Aria said looking to the woman with sympathy in her eyes.

"I think Frannie is wherever she needs to be and we were lucky she decided today was the day she needed to be at the Mage Library. I have no idea how she broke through the wards, let alone discovered the way out she showed us," Dom said, shaking his head.

"She saved us ... again," Caleb said quietly. There was

clearly a story there and I realised that if what everyone was saying was true then I might owe this woman more than I could ever repay.

Aria got up from her seat and sat with her legs crossed besides Frannie.

"Causing trouble again?" she asked her, staring into the fire beside her.

"Always!" laughed Frannie, throwing her hands up in the air.

They sat in silence with the rest of us watching them, every so often Frannie would just giggle to herself muttering "trouble, trouble, trouble," and Aria sat with her, keeping her company.

It was only when Stone groaned that we all dragged our attention away from them. Dom was immediately kneeling by his side as he started to come round.

"Ah god, fuck my life! Dom you shit, why'd you have to come strolling back into the library and fuck everything up?" he groaned as he tried to sit himself up.

Dom helped him get sat up and he leant back with a groan, wrapping one arm across his ribs.

"Mother fucking shit! Where's the bag?" he suddenly said, sitting up straighter and then groaning from the pain it must have caused. From the way that he was holding his chest, I would bet he had probably broken a few ribs.

"I have it here," I told him, passing Dom the bag so he could give it to him.

Stone locked eyes with me and I couldn't tell what emotion ran through them. It looked suspiciously like he was blaming me for everything that happened and when I took a moment to think about it, that was probably accurate. Dom would never have had to go back to the library if it hadn't been for me.

Stone opened the bag and peered inside before he sighed

in relief and slumped back down in his seat, his face pinching in pain.

"What happened, Stone?" Dom asked quietly.

No one else in the room said anything, not wanting to disturb them and needing to know the same thing. Braedon wasn't here yet, but when he did arrive, I didn't want to be the one to have to admit we had failed to find any answers for him. Not only that, but there was no way that Dom, and probably Stone, would be able to go back to the Mage Library again.

Stone groaned as he shuffled in his seat, trying to get comfortable.

"After we spoke, for some reason I decided it would be a good idea to look inside father's casting room," he explained. Dom inhaled a gasp of shock and even though I didn't know why, I gathered that was a pretty big deal.

"Fuck, Dom, it's worse than we thought. The things in there. He's ... I don't even know if I want to admit it. There was so much blood and ... something, something was in there," he finished on a whisper.

"What do you mean something?" Dom asked hesitantly.

"I don't know. There was a cage in the back and it was covered. I didn't go in far enough to see," Stone shuddered as he explained. "But the noises coming from it, it didn't sound right. I didn't have time to investigate any further, I heard someone coming. I grabbed this and I ran. Father was waiting outside. He just fucking laughed at me, then two mages attacked me from behind. I was able to apparate to get away and I came straight to you."

Stone's face had turned a deathly white as he explained. Whatever he had seen or heard in that room had obviously shaken him and I didn't think we were getting the full story from him. Perhaps it was something he wanted to speak with Dom about privately first.

Everyone stayed fairly quiet, me because I didn't want to

interrupt the two brothers, but I imagine the others were fairly confused about what was going on.

Kyle looked like he was just about to start asking questions when Dom sank to the floor with a sigh. He sat with his back against the sofa and his legs stretched out in front of him before he started to explain things to Kyle.

"You can't count the Mage Library as an ally. It would appear that they were aware of the witch's activities and didn't feel the need to tell anyone. There also seems to be some kind of internal power play occurring, or at least that is what we believe," Dom filled in.

Stone looked like he wanted to add something, but then at the last minute, he kept quiet.

Kyle sighed, rubbing his hands across his face. "I'm going to have to take this to the Shifter Council and they are not going to take it well."

The awkward silence stretched across the room before Frannie's voice quietly drifted across. "Problems, problems, so many problems, but this one does not belong to you," she sang before she got to her feet and skipped out of the room.

"I hate it when she does that," Kyle mumbled, looking around the room at us. "I need to go and deal with this, Wyatt can you get Dom's brother set up in a room?"

Wyatt nodded and Kyle, with a reluctant looking Aria, left us alone in the library.

"Father is practising necromancy?" Dom whispered once we were alone.

"It looked like it," Stone confirmed. "It should have been obvious, his declining sanity. The way he was acting."

"There's no way you could have come to that conclusion. It only seems obvious now because we were talking about it earlier today," Dom told him. "I know it's probably the wrong time to say this, but I'm glad I've finally got you away from that place."

For a split-second, anger seemed to flash across Stone's face, but then he seemed to relax. "I know, brother, I'm glad to be back with you too," he admitted.

"Come on," Dom said, climbing to his feet and helping Stone to stand, "let's get you somewhere you can rest. All of this we can deal with in the morning."

Dom looped one of Stone's arms around his shoulder and it was kind of sweet to see him looking after his brother. Wyatt followed them out of the room to show them where Stone could stay. I wouldn't be surprised if we didn't see Dom for the rest of the evening, but I couldn't blame him for wanting to spend time with his brother after they had been apart for so long. I also had a terrible feeling that there was more to their background, that the two men had survived something, or rather someone, that had bonded them as close as siblings could be.

Caleb came and sat down beside me, putting an arm around my shoulders so I could lean into him. We sat soaking up the comfort of just being in each other's presence.

"This is a crazy ride you've brought us on," Caleb suddenly said with a quiet laugh.

"I hope it's not a ride you're regretting," I told him self-consciously.

"Oh sweets, I'd take that ride to the ends of this realm and beyond, as long as you were right there beside me," he murmured gently, kissing the top of my head. "Come on, I know you must be exhausted, let's get to bed."

Caleb tiredly climbed to his feet and then held out a hand for me to take. The firelight glinted off his blue eyes and he smiled down at me. He was a truly beautiful man, all of my mates were. I almost felt like everything I went through, every challenge, every torment, was to earn my place at their side. I'm still not sure if I truly deserved them.

Reaching up for his hand, I let Caleb pull me to my feet.

My head swam as I stood and it felt like the room started to spin and dance around me. Caleb slipped an arm around my waist and caught me as my legs failed me and I started to drop.

"Woah there!" Caleb said, pulling me close to him. His other hand came up to cradle my cheek and I rested my head there while my eyes came back into focus.

When I felt like my legs were steadier under me, I managed to stand firm on my own two feet.

"Sorry about that," I mumbled embarrassed. "I must be a bit more tired than I thought."

Caleb squinted at me in suspicion and I didn't blame him, even I didn't believe that one. I felt strange, but I couldn't put my finger on it. Aurel's words came echoing through my mind "*the angel will start to fade ... eventually they succumb to death*". This wasn't good. We were running out of time and we still had absolutely no idea where my final mate was.

CHAPTER 40

CALEB

I hadn't been able to take my eyes off Lyra all night. She had tried to play off her weakness last night, but now that she was sitting in the morning light, I could see the dark shadows gathering beneath her eyes and the slight tremble that was starting in her left hand. She was starting to fade.

My wolf was already howling mournfully in my mind. It was almost as if he could sense her fading in front of him. Part of me felt like it was already too late, that we had already run out of time. I could hear Wyatt and Dom moving towards the bedroom, so I quickly slipped out of the door to intercept them before they reached us, not wanting Lyra to hear what I was about to say. I knew she would just try to play it off as not being serious, but if she was declining quickly, or had just now reached a stage where it had become visible, then we needed to move quicker. I couldn't cope with losing her. I wouldn't survive without her. None of us would.

"What's wrong?" asked Dom, as I came rushing towards them.

Stone was missing from the group, but judging from his

condition yesterday, I expected he was going to be laid up for a day or two at least.

"Lyra is weakening," I said, getting straight to the point. "We need to start making some progress and we need to get it done now. I can't lose her. We can't let her fade," I stuttered out, I could feel myself starting to freak out. It was almost like now that I was with the safety of my packmates, I was letting myself start to spiral. The problem was now I'd started, I didn't know if I was going to be able to stop.

"We might have something," Dom said, he wrapped one hand around the back of my head and drew me into him. "I have you, and all of us together will do this. We won't fail her," he whispered to me and I let myself have a moment to soak up his quiet confidence. When I stepped back, Wyatt gave me a firm nod and we all went back inside the bedroom.

Lyra was sitting up in bed, drinking a cup of tea. Even though she looked like she was starting to become ill, she was still beautiful. Her golden, blonde hair shone in the sunlight that was filtering in through the window and she almost seemed to glow. She was radiant in every sense of the word. She must have been truly magnificent when she had her wings and I was saddened that I had never gotten the chance to see them.

Dom went over to sit on the side of the bed. He picked up her right hand and I saw him subtly press his finger to her pulse point as he held her hand. Her left hand I had noticed the tremor in, was hidden beneath the covers. It wasn't a good sign if it had reached a point where she felt the need to hide it from us.

"How are you feeling?" Wyatt asked, sitting down on the bottom of the bed.

Lyra rolled her eyes, took Dom's hand and laid it properly against her pulse point for him. There wasn't much we could get past her.

"Strange," she answered honestly. "I can feel that the muscles in my body are growing stronger, but I feel weaker in myself. Less like I'm tired now, but more like the energy just isn't there. I'm not even sure if that makes sense," she said, shaking her head.

Wyatt reached out to squeeze her foot reassuringly. "We may have some good news."

"Stone was able to tell us about his witch contact last night when we got him to his room. He had already contacted them to request her assistance before he ran into trouble at the Mage Library. She is in the same coven that one of the Elites are currently sequestered to. Aria has sent Echo to meet with her with instructions to update her on Stone's position and request that she contact us urgently. We hope to hear back from her later today," Dom explained.

"That sounds good. That's good news right?" Lyra asked, looking to us all hopefully.

"Stone is convinced that she will be able to help with some form of spell or ritual. Kyle seems confident that she will assist, even if just to help garner some goodwill back from the pack."

Lyra nodded thoughtfully. "Does this expose the pack to any kind of risk?"

"No," Wyatt confirmed, "the only one risking exposure is you."

Lyra was truly showing her nature that she was worried about the pack over herself.

"Good," she said with a confident nod, "so what shall we do today to distract ourselves while we wait?"

The mood in the room immediately heated and Lyra's cheeks tinted with a delicate blush as she realised what she had inadvertently insinuated.

Wyatt let out a booming laugh. "I don't think you're quite up to anything like that."

"Oh, I wouldn't rule me out just yet, I'm suddenly finding

myself all kinds of energised," Lyra laughed, her voice dropping to a husky note.

Wyatt looked almost pained as he stood up, "As much as I want to see how accurate that is, I have a meeting with Kyle that I'm already late for."

As he stepped towards the bedroom door and away from Lyra on the bed, I could see the indecision in his eyes. I also knew however, that this particular meeting was about the house he had shown to Lyra and the work which the pack had already started while we were away. A team of carpenters had come across from the bear sleuth and they had just finished one of the other cabins, as the only other ones on the rota so far were empty, ours had been pushed to the next in line. Wyatt was supposed to be meeting with them all at the house to go through the work that needed doing.

Wyatt quickly stepped back to us, kissed Lyra on top of the head and then with a groan that had us all laughing at his expense and stormed out of the room, closing the door behind him.

There was a slightly awkward pause as we all just looked between ourselves and then suddenly we were all laughing. I crawled up onto the bed with Dom and Lyra and we just laid back and relaxed.

"We don't have to do anything. We can just hang out. Maybe we could drag a tv in here and watch a movie," I suggested with a wince at just how lame that sounded.

Lyra laughed and snuggled in next to us. "What's wrong, boys? Would you rather watch a movie?" she asked innocently.

Dom and I looked between each other. "Maybe this is the opportunity that we need to talk about something," Dom started.

"We already had that talk," Lyra said, cocking her head to the side in confusion.

"Yeah, we talked about the feelings," Dom started looking

to me for support, but I just shrugged, having no idea where he was going with this. I was just as confused as Lyra was.

Dom huffed in annoyance at us both and I couldn't help the answering grin that I gave him.

"We didn't talk about the practical implications," he said seriously.

Lyra and I looked at him in silence, before looking at each other and then we just exploded into laughter.

"Like what's going to go where?" she wheezed out between laughter.

Dom patiently waited for us both to stop cackling, but I could see that he was getting pissed off with us.

"I'm sorry, I'm sorry," I spluttered, finally pulling myself back under control. "You're right, we should talk about this," I said, clearing my throat to try and stop myself from laughing.

Lyra took a little longer with the giggles, and fuck me if it wasn't adorable watching her laying there giggling away without a care in the world right now. I couldn't wait until this was just life for us.

"Okay, okay, I'm okay," Lyra grinned and then pulled herself back under control. She literally shook her whole body, like she was trying to shake the giggles away, and then smiled. "I think this is really a conversation for you two to have though."

"I don't think we need to talk about it," I admitted. "Yes, this is all new for all of us, but I think we should just see what happens and where the moment takes us," I told them honestly. I didn't want to live my life on a script.

"Does anyone have any limits though," Dom asked and he was right, we should at least discuss that. "Is there anything you wouldn't be comfortable with Caleb and I doing to each other or to you?"

"No," she answered, sounding kind of breathless. Now I could get on board with wherever this was taking us.

"I don't want to put any limits on us either," I told him.

Dom smiled and leant across Lyra towards me, "No limits sounds like a good idea," he murmured as he closed the gap and kissed me.

I knew I should be conscious of the fact that Lyra was lying beneath us, but everything about the three of us just felt natural. Walking away from them when Dom was going to complete the bond with her, had been more difficult than I had thought, but I knew they needed that time together. Just like how there would probably be times in the future when we needed to be alone, but right now, the three of us here was everything that I wanted and needed it to be.

As Dom pulled away from the kiss, I looked down to see Lyra grinning up at us. There was no judgment in her eyes, there was nothing there but heat.

I couldn't stop myself even if I wanted to, as my head dipped down and I kissed her softly. Dom moved to her side and kissed her neck, running his tongue over our intersecting marks. Something about the way that his mark joined with mine just felt right.

When I pulled back, Lyra had a look on her face like there was something she wanted to do and I can't say that it didn't turn me on. Something about her had changed since we had completed the bonds. It was like a part of her had been freed and she was embracing the side of her where she just gave in to pleasure. After all of the time she had spent locked away she deserved to have that, she deserved to spend the next decade drowning in every drop of pleasure that we could wring out of her beautiful little body.

In one quick movement, Lyra slipped over the top of Dom so that he ended up in the middle and she looked up at me with a grin on her face. Dom just looked amused at the clear happiness that was radiated out of her.

"What are you up to?" I laughed.

"I decided," she said, dipping her head down and running her tongue along Dom's collar bone, "that I wanted a taste of Dom," she grinned.

"Oh, really?"

"Mmmm, I think he's going to be delicious," she said with a wicked grin.

She started kissing her way down Dom's chest and I could see exactly what she wanted to happen, but also appreciated that she was letting me decide just how much I wanted to join in.

Keeping my eyes locked with Lyra, I dipped down and ran my tongue down Dom's chest until I reached his nipple. Lyra reached Dom's other nipple at the same time and we both ran our tongues and nibbled at his stiffening peaks.

Dom had his fists clenched at his side and I could feel his chest rising in pants. This was definitely going to be torture for him but in the best kind of way.

Lyra started making her way down Dom's body and I followed the path of kisses that she was laying for me. Dom's abs quivered beneath us and almost like he couldn't hold himself back anymore, I felt his hand come up and his fingers run through the back of my hair.

I flicked my eyes up to his face to see him staring down, watching us both making our way down his body. His eyes were banked with heat and his lips parted as he panted in lust. He had never looked more beautiful than he did in that moment.

By the time that we reached the waistband of his boxers, I was actually pretty impressed that he was managing to stay still.

Lyra's fingers dipped into the waistband on one side, and not wanting to be left out, I took hold of the other side. Together we drew his boxers down and off his body, revealing his hard length to us.

Dom and I had only ever kissed. The feelings were there, we had been dancing around them for years not quite ready to acknowledge them. But we had never done anything sexual with each other beyond that kiss.

"Remember all anyone has to do is ask to stop if they start to feel uncomfortable," Lyra told us both gently, almost as if she could sense how we were feeling. There was absolutely nothing in the world that was going to make me stop right now.

I moved first and having both of them watch me as I reached out and ran my tongue around the head of Dom's cock, lapping at the bead of precum that was already there, was the most erotic thing I had ever done in my life. Lyra grinned and started to lick her way up the length of Dom's cock, slowly making her way up to my mouth.

"Fuck!" Dom groaned out and I felt his hand clench in the back of my hair.

My cock was straining against my boxers and I felt like a teenager about to blow in his pants as soon as Lyra's mouth met mine. Her tongue darted out to meet mine and we both tangled them around Dom's cock, trying to kiss each other with him between us.

I withdrew and started to work my way down his length as Lyra took him into her mouth, swallowing him down deeply.

"I can't," Dom gasped out, "if you keep doing that, I'm going to come and I don't want to come yet."

He sounded almost desperate and I couldn't stop myself from reaching out and gently cupping his balls as Lyra pulled off his cock with a pop.

Dom reached down for Lyra and while sitting up hauled her up into his lap, his lips hungrily falling onto hers as he devoured her mouth. Getting to my knees between his legs, I pressed against her back, my own lips running up her neck to the shell of her ear. Swiping my tongue out and sucking her lobe into my mouth before biting down.

Lyra groaned and ground down onto Dom, making him hiss. I couldn't help the laugh that burst out of me, he shouldn't have pulled the little minx into his lap if he couldn't take it.

His eyes flashed to mine and in an instant, his hand was tangled in my hair as he dragged my face over Lyra's shoulder and kissed me harshly. I loved this dominant side of Dom.

A rip wrenched through the air and Lyra suddenly gasped. Looking down I saw that Dom had torn both sides of Lyra's panties away and she leant up on her thighs as he ripped the material out from beneath her.

There was a wild look filling his eyes and I knew the feeling. The feeling that if he didn't get inside of her in the next few seconds, his heart might explode. The need, the want, rushing through your body and the only way to stop it is to push your cock into the wet heat that lived between her thighs.

Dom gripped hold of Lyra's hips and positioned her, hovering above his cock. She writhed and wriggled trying to push down onto him, but he held her steady, his tip teasing at her entrance.

"One day soon, you're going to take Caleb and I both at the same time. I want to feel his cock sliding into your ass, while I take your sweet pussy," he told her.

Just as Lyra opened her mouth with a breathy moan at his words, he slammed her down on his length and that moan became a scream.

Fucking hell, Dom was burning me up right now.

"Would you like that, baby?" I whispered into her ear.

Pressing flush against her back as she adjusted to the sudden presence of Dom's cock inside of her. Trailing my fingers up the back of her thigh, I found her pussy filled with Dom's cock and circle my fingers around her opening. Both of them moaned at the sensation and Lyra's forehead dropped down to Dom's as they clung to each other, taking in the pleasure as I trailed my fingers around where they joined. Once I was wet with her juices, I slid a finger up through the crack of her ass.

"Would you like it if I took this beautiful ass for you one day?" I asked her as I pressed down against her hole.

Lyra moaned and ground down against Dom and my finger. Her head fell back onto my shoulder and Dom took the opportunity to drop his mouth to the beautiful breasts that she now had on display for him.

"Yes, Caleb, yes, I want you," she panted.

"You're not ready for me yet, but soon," I told her. "Now I want you to ride Dom and I'm keeping this right here," I said, pushing my finger inside her as I spoke.

Dom swore and I knew her pussy would be gripping down on his cock like a vice. She started moving gently at first, no doubt getting used to having something filling both holes. I couldn't wait until I was slamming my cock inside of her ass, feeling Dom's cock rubbing against me through her thin walls.

As she started to relax more into the sensation, she picked up her speed, Dom's hands on her waist, helping her to keep her rhythm. I pushed my finger deeper inside her, so she was taking me to the second knuckle now. She groaned at the intrusion then ground deeper and harder against Dom. Pressing my finger into her walls, I could feel his cock sliding in and out of her.

"Holy fuck!" Dom burst out, no doubt feeling me rubbing against him.

Lyra's moans grew louder and I could feel her muscles starting to flutter inside of her as her orgasm crept closer. Her rhythm picked up again and I withdrew slightly from her hole before holding my hand steady beneath her so that as she crashed down onto Dom's cock she was fucking her ass on my finger as well.

She came with a scream. There was no gradual build-up, it was starting and then it was suddenly there. She shattered around Dom and watching her movements grow choppy as she tried to ride out the pleasure filling every part of her body, was the most beautiful thing I had ever seen.

I withdrew from her and she clung to Dom for a second as she came back down into herself.

"I think Caleb deserves a reward, don't you?" Dom asked her.

She nodded wordlessly and Dom lifted her off his still hard cock and turned her around to face me. How he hadn't just come when she did, I had no idea.

I backed away a little to give them both room to move and found myself kneeling on the end of the bed, not sure where Dom was going to go with this. As his hand came between her shoulder blades and he gently pushed her down, bending her over in front of him, a grin lit my face.

Lyra stared at the outline of my hard cock through my boxers in amusement.

"I think you're entirely overdressed for what Dom has in mind for you," she said, smiling up at me.

I don't think I have ever removed a pair of boxers so quickly in my life as I did in that moment, much to the amusement of the other two, but I didn't care in the slightest bit because when Lyra closed her mouth around my cock, I fell straight into heaven and there was no way I was ever coming back.

My head fell back as I basked in the feeling on my mate's mouth around my cock and her tongue swirling around my length. I knew the moment when Dom pushed his way inside of her as she gasped around me.

He started out slowly moving inside of her. I was trying to

keep my hips still, not wanting to overwhelm her, but it was so fucking hard. Especially when she started to moan from the sensation of Dom fucking her and the vibrations felt like they ran straight down my dick and into my balls.

Fucking hell, she looked like heaven kneeling between us. Her face flushed and her golden hair spilling out around her.

She brought one hand up to my ass cheek and started to move my hips in time with Dom. Grinning down at her, as she looked up at me through her eyelashes, I started to move in time with her movements, I could take a hint.

Her groan of approval echoing down my dick told me this was what she had wanted.

Dom's pace started to get rough and I could tell that he was about to come, to be honest, I'm impressed he's got this far. From the pants and moans that Lyra is giving out around my cock I can tell she's not far away either and I was already feeling the ache in my balls that said I wasn't far behind them.

Dom came first, gripping Lyra's hips and slamming into them with an urgency until he shouted her name and ground hard against her. It was almost like a ripple effect, watching his face as he slipped under the waves of sensation was enough to push me over the edge. I tried to pull out of Lyra's mouth, but she latched onto my hips and held me in place as she drank me down. It was so fucking hot. But Dom wasn't happy with leaving things there and he had already reached one hand down to her clit, just as I pulled out of her mouth she came like a freight train had slammed into her. Leaning back up on her knees, she leant back against Dom's chest and I followed her across the bed, sucking one of her nipples into my mouth and biting down, giving her a hint of pain to chase alongside the pleasure. She grasped the back of my hair and held me in place as she rode out the shockwaves and I was all too happy to give her exactly what she needed as I bit down, pinching her nipple between my teeth and then lathing the sting away with my tongue.

We arranged ourselves back in the bed so that Lyra was between us and we all haphazardly wrapped our arms around whoever we could reach. It had a distinct puppy pile vibe to it that was making my wolf very happy. We hadn't taken a pack room yet and I was finding the sleeping arrangement for our new pack hard to deal with.

"You seem different," Dom murmured and I looked up thinking that he was talking to me, but his gaze was firmly fixed on Lyra.

"What do you mean?"

"I don't know, you just don't look as tired," he shrugged, but I could see something that looked like curiosity in his eyes and I recognised his mage-like thirst for knowledge starting up.

"Well you guys did kind of tire me out," she laughed and I laughed along with her. "But I do feel a bit better, less worn down than I did this morning I suppose."

Lyra's face scrunched in concentration and she held her hands out in front of her as if they were going to hold all of the answers she sought in them. Pushing them back down I wrapped my arms around her tighter.

"Well, how about we all have a nap and then when we wake up, we can see if maybe you've recovered some more of that energy," I said, nuzzling my face into her neck.

Now that we'd started, I didn't ever want to stop and a power nap before spending the rest of the day in bed together sounded like the best idea in the world right now.

CHAPTER 41

LYRA

S omething about being with my mates seemed to make the fade slow down, even retreat a bit. Okay, let's just call it what it was, having sex with them seemed to energise me. When I had woken this morning, the symptoms were definitely noticeable, to them as well as me. But now, my vision was clear and the tremor in my hand had stopped. I hoped this witch was going to help us, and help us quickly, because if we were going to have to set out again to wherever this fourth mate was, I needed to do it before I lost too much of my strength. I mean, there was always the option of constant sex with my mates, you know purely just to keep me going, and I was definitely on board with that idea, especially after being with Dom and Caleb together. I'm not naïve and I had heard some of the older angels talking about doing similar things, but it always sounded like more of a chore than something to be enjoyed. Oh, how wrong I had been!

We spent the rest of the morning lying in bed, just enjoying being together, in every single way that we could. There was something beautiful about being able to see Caleb and Dom feel free enough to be together. To finally give in to what they truly wanted. It saddened me that they thought they would have to hide this from the rest of the pack, or that they wouldn't be accepted if they were open about their feelings for each other. Maybe I should have told them about Liam and Sykes. I don't see the problem in loving who you want. As long as it made you both happy and no one was getting hurt along the way, what did it really matter?

By the time lunchtime rolled around, I was starting to get suspicious about where exactly Wyatt had run off to.

"What's Wyatt doing?" I asked, trying to sound casual and failing miserably.

"You'd be a terrible spy," Caleb laughed. "Didn't they teach you spy techniques in your angel school?"

"No, the massive glowing wings always gave us away," I laughed.

He was right though, subtly was definitely not a skill of mine. Maybe I needed lessons or something. Not from Aria though, she was about as subtle as a brick after it had been smashed into your face at least twice. Maybe that was why I liked her so much?

"You didn't answer my question though," I pointed out after a minute or so of their silence.

"Didn't we?" Caleb asked, trailing his lips down my neck and across my collar.

Dom started to mirror him on the other side of my neck and I felt my eyes wanting to roll back with pleasure.

"I know you're trying to distract me," I managed to get out on a breathy sigh.

"We could always stop if you wanted us to," Dom said. I could hear the cocky tone in his voice and feel his smile, as his lips brushed against my skin.

As Caleb's lips closed around one of my nipples, if my

mind hadn't already been made up, it definitely would have been then.

"Absolutely not," I murmured, feeling even better than I had a few moments before and feeling more than ready to be distracted again.

CHAPTER 42

ARIA

"How long until you expect to hear back from Echo?" Kyle asked, striding into the kitchen where I was standing at the stove, cooking dinner for us all.

He wrapped his arms around my waist, kissing me gently on the neck, before resting his chin on my shoulder to watch what I was doing over my shoulder.

"Any time now," I told him, as I tossed the pan of chicken with fajita spices.

He huffed in annoyance, but I knew it was more to do with not liking that he had pack members at one of the covens more than anything else.

"My girls are more than qualified to deal with this," I told him gently, even if my overriding instinct was to slap him.

"I know, I just can't trust any witch until one of them has given me a good reason to."

"They can't give you that reason if you never give them the chance too," I told him gently.

I understood how he felt. After living through the same battles he had, I couldn't help that deep down I wanted to hate them all. But I had to believe that there were some that either didn't know what the others were doing, or just plain didn't agree, but had no way to stop. I couldn't condemn a whole race of people on the actions of a few. Assuming that it was the actions of the few.

"How are the Council talks going?" I asked, knowing that this wasn't going to be a topic which made Kyle any happier but still needing to know his answer.

"Trace is pushing for us to make a move against the covens in retaliation. He is refusing to allow any of their representatives to attend the Council grounds for negotiations," he sighed and I could hear the frustration in his voice.

"So, he's pushing for war," I snarked. I mean, let's call a spade a spade here.

"Yes, none of the other Council members are supporting him, but my worry is that the Felidae pack is massive, easily the largest pack now that we have suffered the losses we have. He could easily make a move on his own and then we are forced into a situation of whether we stand by him after he well and truly fucks us all."

"I won't commit the Valkyrie to this," I told him, "they suffered too many losses in the last fight and I won't risk more of them in an unnecessary fight."

It was harsh, but it also needed to be said. The problem was where I drew the line and if I really had any right to be drawing lines in the first place. I had always considered the Elites to be mine and I refused to risk them as well. But if Trace forced us into this fight, could I stand by and let the pack take on such an enormous risk without any form of back up? Trace had me between a rock and a hard place and if he wasn't careful, I was going to stab him for it.

"I can feel you getting angry," Kyle murmured.

"I don't like where this is inevitably heading."

"If you want, I can take you to the next Council meeting and you can find an excuse to stab him a bit," he offered.

"I knew you loved me," I said with an overly dramatic sigh.

"Always and forever," he said, kissing my neck.

"Urgh, yuck, it's like walking in on your parents doing it," I heard Aeryn say behind us.

Kyle laughed, stepping away from me while I abandoned the chicken on the stove and wrapped her in my arms. Aeryn left to return to her coven almost immediately after the Blood Moon battle. She had been in constant contact with us, it was the only condition I had for her going, but she was adamant that she was the best person to find out the position of the covens and how much danger they posed for us going forward. Having her back here, even if just temporarily, was at least settling a large portion of the nerves I'd had since she had left us.

"You're not going soft on me, are you?" she laughed, even though she was hugging me back just as hard.

"Am I not allowed to miss one of my favourite warriors?" I smiled, taking a step back so that I could run my eyes over her.

Aeryn gave an exaggerated eye roll, before spreading her arms out wide and slowly turning on the spot. "See, everything is accounted for. Not even one little bruise or scratch."

I knew she was taking the piss out of me, but I didn't even care. She was one of mine and if she had come back to me with so much as a scratch, I'd be going back to the coven with her to demonstrate my upset. That thought made me pause for a moment. Was I just as bad as Trace? Shaking my head, I filed that away to think about later. Fucking hell, if I started to find myself sympathising with him, I might need to find some kind of hospital to check myself in to.

"I feel like you're having an entire conversation in your head right now and not even filling us in on the details,"

Aeryn said, cocking her head to the side, as she just watched me sort through my thoughts.

I'd noticed myself doing this more and more recently. I knew I was being withdrawn from the pack and everyone else around me, but I was still struggling, even if my talk with Lyra had helped me to start dealing with my issues.

I waved her off, but I didn't miss the concerned look on Kyle's face. He didn't even try to speak with me in my mind to see if I was okay. They had all given up doing that a couple of weeks ago. I knew he could feel my guilt and sorrow radiating between our bond because I could feel his concern. But right now, I needed to be a bit selfish. I needed to work on me if I was going to come out the other side of this and I was lucky enough to have mates who understood that I needed some space, to sort through the mess of emotions in my head.

"Where is Echo?" I asked, taking a seat at the kitchen table.

Aeryn sat down across from me and Kyle strode over to the cooker and took over cooking dinner. See, there was a reason why I kept them all around.

"She decided to stay on at the coven," Aeryn told me, visibly wincing as she spoke.

She was expecting me to be pissed and deep down I was. But I also knew that if Echo had decided to stay, then either she or Aeryn had a good reason for her to. I trusted them enough to know they would come to me when they needed to. So, taking Aeryn by surprise, I just nodded.

"Did she fill you in on the problem we have?" I asked her.

We had told Echo to be as vague as possible. We still weren't in a position to know just how far we could trust this coven. They'd be like family to Aeryn and they may not have been present at the Blood Moon battle, but at the end of the day, we still didn't know just how much they were aware of the other covens' plots.

"She just told me that the pack needed assistance and that

you needed to be put in contact with Leona as quickly as possible."

I nodded again. This group of women was as loyal as it came. The fact that they would do whatever was asked, without question, warmed me inside. I felt exactly the same. If these girls needed something, I would be there, it wouldn't matter what their reasons were. These women were just as much my pack as everyone else here, regardless of what race they were, they were my clan, my tribe. Together no one could stand against us.

"What can you tell us about Leona?" Kyle asked, giving up all pretence of cooking and coming to join us at the table.

I rolled my eyes and got up to rescue our dinner, which he had just left on the stovetop, before joining them again.

"She is the High Priestess of the Coven of the White Tree. She is trustworthy. If you need her help, she will give it to you, I know she will," Aeryn said confidently.

"And what about the witches' plot against us, how much did she know or participate?" Kyle growled, getting straight to the point.

I was surprised by him. He was usually understanding and fair, but like every shifter around, he was having trouble holding on to that when it came to the witches.

"She took absolutely no part in that," Aeryn said, straightening in her seat and I could see that he had offended her. "None of my coven was involved, we would never condone anything like that. How could you even suggest that I would be involved in that?" she turned her face away from us and I knew that Kyle had gone too far.

"We all know that you would never be involved, Aeryn. You were there with us. You fought valiantly and you saved so many lives. I know what kind of person you are, Aeryn, and I would never believe something like about you. But I do not know Leona. I need to know that you have absolute faith in her before I can risk exposing the pack," Kyle reached across and laid a hand on Aeryn's arm.

She didn't pull away, but I could see that she still wasn't happy with him. I couldn't really blame her. It must be difficult to be here when everyone seems to blanket hate all witches at the moment.

"I would trust her with my life," Aeryn said firmly.

"Would you trust her with the life of Wyatt's mate?" Kyle asked her simply, pulling his hand away and sitting back in his seat, watching her reaction closely.

"Wyatt has retrieved his mate," she said, sitting up straighter, "that's amazing news!"

She looked so genuinely happy and I couldn't help but smile as well. It was good news. I had never met Wyatt before we came here, but even I could see the difference in him since he had found her again. Caleb and I had been close at the academy and I was glad that he had found his place in their pack.

"She is also mated to Caleb and Dom," Kyle said, still watching her.

I didn't like this crazy suspicious side of him.

"*Stop treating her like she is our enemy,*" I whispered into his mind.

Kyle physically reared back in his seat when he heard me. This was the first time since the Blood Moon battle that I had reached out to any of them to mind-speak. After the initial feeling of shock, I felt a flood of relief come through our bond.

"*I've missed you,*" he whispered into my mind.

"*I know, I'm sorry. I just needed time.*"

"*You never have to apologise for that.*"

"*You know we can trust her. She is one of my Elites, she would never betray us. If she trusts Leona, then I trust her as well,*" I told him.

"*And if Leona betrays us?*"

"*Then I will kill her and no one will dare to betray us again,*" I said coldly.

And I meant every word. Something about my very nature had changed over the last couple of months. I was done fucking around. These were my people and if they wanted to get to them, they were going to have to come through me first.

CHAPTER 43

WYATT

We were sitting in the kitchen eating dinner and everyone at the table was trying to monitor Lyra without her realising they were doing it constantly. She had, of course, realised in about five seconds what was going on though. Ordinarily, she would have called them out on it, but she seemed too lost in her own thoughts and the others didn't seem to have caught on why just yet. The tremor was back in her left hand and it was taking all of her concentration and effort to keep it from them.

"When does she get here?" Caleb asked for the fourth time.

"Anytime now," Aria replied, for the fourth time.

Even though it was annoying us all, no one was going to call him out on it, because we were all feeling exactly the same.

Lyra eyed the plate of bacon in the middle of the table with a sad look. I knew she wasn't going to reach out for some, no matter how much she wanted it because then she would have to move both hands across the table and everyone would know. She slumped back in her seat with a sad look on her face and even though my wolf was going crazy because he knew that she was deteriorating again, his need to make sure she was eating enough was even stronger. Sending a glare across the table I reached forward and dragged the whole platter across to her, leaving it in front of her plate before scooping up a stack of bacon and putting it on her plate. Kyle just smirked across at me. Fucker! He was going to be riding me about this for years. I'd like to see how he acted if Aria ever got sick.

Smiling softly, Lyra just picked up the bacon with her right hand and slowly started to eat. My wolf at least settled a little now that she's eating. Hopefully, after today we could get some answers and be one step closer to finding the last in our mate bond. The not knowing is the worst part. Watching her trying to smile, when deep down she's hurting just as much as we were, is the worst thing I had ever experienced in my life.

Everyone just sits and eats quietly. Caleb was practically vibrating in his seat and I'm impressed that he hadn't had to resort to pacing the room just yet.

Kyle suddenly sat up straighter and cocked his head to the side like he's listening. "She's here," he said, standing up and starting to move for the door.

I hated it when they do that mind speak thing, it's so freaky!

Not knowing what else to do, we all just trailed out after him and ended up standing huddled around the front door in front of a very confused looking witch and a slightly pissed off looking Aeryn. I was kind of seeing how this must look from her perspective and I could see why she was pissed.

"Well, I hadn't expected such a warm welcome," the new witch in front of us said, as she calmly took us all in.

She looked to be somewhere in her forties, but in our world, that didn't really mean much of anything. Her blonde hair was braided to the side and she looked so out of place standing there in her maroon pantsuit.

Aeryn clearly looked up to her, but she was her high

priestess. If it came down to it, I wondered who she would choose between, Leona or Aria. On any other day, I would have said Aria, but with the hostility that she faced from every shifter around, just because she was a witch, you couldn't blame her if she was starting to feel isolated from everyone else. And right now, she was looking more protective of Leona as she stood there and watched everyone she had previously considered to be on her side, standing against her people.

"Thank you for agreeing to come all of this way to help me," Lyra said, striding forward and breaking the tension.

"I haven't agreed to help anyone yet," Leona said smoothly, "but I am here to hear your terms. Perhaps you would like to invite me inside before you start asking me for favours."

Kyle immediately bristled. Letting an unknown witch onto our territory was whole new levels of stupid given our recent history. The fact that he was even letting us do this and going against his very nature meant the world to me. He had grown up to be a far better man than his father, than most men I had ever met. His shoulders stiffened, but he stepped back and indicated the door to the library.

"Please come inside," he said. Impressively, it would only have been obvious to those who knew him, just how much he had to force those words out.

We all awkwardly filed into the library, taking various seats around the room. Aeryn stood protectively at Leona's back and I saw the pain flash through Aria's eyes as she took in the sight of her friend taking a metaphorical step away from her.

"Thank you for coming all of this way to meet with us," Lyra said, trying to smooth over the awkwardness.

"I have to say I was intrigued to receive the request, especially considering the hostility my coven has been subjected to over the recent weeks. I would not have come at all had Aeryn not vouched for you," Leona said simply and I could tell that she was pissed.

Unfortunately, Kyle was also still pissed, even if it was understandably so, it was not going to help our situation.

"Hostility!" he seethed. "I think we faced more than enough hostility ourselves when the witches sent demons to the academy and massacred all of our friends! When they sent them here to my pack and murdered over fifty of my pack mates," Kyle roared, standing from his chair, his fist hitting his chest at the mention of the deaths in our pack.

Leona's face flushed with anger as she responded quietly, but still firmly, "And we had nothing to do with any of those attacks. We had members of our coven at the academy, not just Aeryn, they all died alongside their classmates. We have experienced losses too."

She was poised and calm as she spoke, but genuine emotion came through in her voice. We had never considered that they would have lost just the same as we did.

Kyle stayed standing, locking eyes with her. You had to give her some respect, not many could hold the stare of an alpha wolf, especially one as powerful as Kyle. But she didn't waver. She didn't break and she didn't grovel. She stayed firm and she won at least some respect from him for doing it. With a firm nod, Kyle returned to his seat and turned back to Lyra, indicating for her to continue.

Lyra looked a bit uncertain and who could blame her, this just got infinitely more awkward.

"Right, well, so I need some help tracing my last fated mate and we were told that you might be able to assist," she said, getting straight to the point.

Leona sat back in her chair and crossed her legs, steepling her hands in front of her lips. She tapped them absentmindedly while her forehead wrinkled in concentration. Everyone in the room seemed to hold their breath as they waited for her to answer. I thought that she was thinking about a possible solution, that maybe she had come here in good faith after all. But I was obviously wrong.

"Such a thing would come with a steep price," she finally said, grinning.

"And what would this price be?" I asked her coldly.

She had us between a shit place and an even shitter place and she knew it. She knew that we wouldn't have reached out to her unless we were desperate and because of that, she could ask us any price she wanted. It's not like we could refuse.

"The pack will bear whatever ridiculous cost you come up with," Kyle snorted. He really was not helping the situation now and I was fighting the urge to just get up and slap him.

"Oh, but this isn't just anything that you are asking for. You're asking for something extremely valuable and I think that the price should be something equally rare and valuable. Don't you, little angel?"

Caleb and I were on our feet as soon as she had uttered the word angel, blocking her view of Lyra with our bodies. Caleb's teeth were bared as he growled at her, even though he still stood before her in his human form. I could feel magic rippling at my back and I knew that Dom was ready as well.

Leona leaned forward, I could see from the look in her eyes the satisfaction she had for having us right where she wanted us. "I would have asked for some feathers, but you appear to have mislaid your wings." She actually had the audacity to laugh at that. "Did you think you would be able to hide your identity from me? You may be waning, but the light radiating in your blood still screams angel to anyone with enough magic to feel it."

Fuck! Who else had we mistakenly outed Lyra to in our haste and stupidity?

Aeryn, who was still standing behind Leona, shuffled uneasily. I could appreciate how difficult this must have been for her. Essentially, she was trapped in a room between two groups of people she had at one time called family. If Leona escalated this any further, Aeryn was going to have to choose a side, we just had to hope that she chose ours.

"Seeing as you are lacking in feathers at the moment, I would be more than happy to take payment in the form of blood." The grin that stretched across Leona's face mocked us.

For a moment, no one moved. It was almost as if we couldn't believe what we were hearing. I don't know what we had thought we would achieve by inviting her here. There was no way that we could allow her to take payment in the form of Lyra's blood. We had no idea of what she would be able to do with it. If there would be any form of repercussion, not just on Lyra, not just on the pack, but for shifters as a species in general. The woman sitting before us was not only part of a race that had tried to exterminate us, even if at the time those reasons had seemed sound, but she also now held a grudge because of the consequences of their actions. We were balancing on a very fine edge and war was starting to feel like an inevitability.

Leona suddenly stood, her mocking grin still firmly in place. "Well, it seems like you all have quite a lot to think about. I can do what you need me to and you know my price," she passed what looked like a small glass bottle to Lyra. "When you have your answer, break the bottle and I will know to return."

With that, she turned and left the room. Aeryn hesitated for a moment, then started to follow her out.

"Aeryn," Aria called out, standing from her seat. Her voice broke as she said her friend's name almost in question.

"I'm sorry Aria," was all Aeryn said as she walked away.

Aria dropped back down into her seat and I could see from the expression on her face just how crushed she was from her friend turning her back on her. Liam and Sykes bracketed her, kneeling beside her. She looked so lost. Looking between my packmates, we all seemed to come to the same conclusion. Lyra stood and joined us and we quietly left the room so that Aria's mates could comfort her. She had been doing so well recently in slowly coming back into herself after the crushing guilt and depression she had experienced following the Blood Moon battle. I just hoped that this wasn't going to set her back.

We climbed the stairs and returned to my old rooms. I couldn't wait to get the house set up. It was strange for our pack to separate out at night and not all share a room together. My wolf hated it. He needed our pack around us so that he could watch over them when they slept. He needed to protect them, it was his right and his privilege as an alpha. I hadn't stepped up and claimed the alpha position yet, in the beginning, it just didn't seem like I should. I didn't feel like I was worthy of it. I hadn't realised back then that it wasn't about being worthy of it, it was about proving to myself that I would always put them first. That they were always going to my top priority. The only way that I could do that was by taking the position I knew I had been born to take. Caleb had made no move to take on the alpha role. His wolf wasn't an alpha and I knew he had no desire to do so. Dom may have some alpha qualities about him, they shone through whenever he felt any kind of threat to any of us. But he wasn't a wolf and he didn't have that inherent need to step into the role. After everything that had happened at the library, I knew that he had no desire to take on a role like that any time soon anyway. That just left the mystery fourth mate. I'm not entirely sure if I care if he wants to lead the pack. These are my people and I will be the one to stand for them. There was nothing that I wouldn't do for them.

CHAPTER 44

LYRA

"Break the bottle," Wyatt said, sitting down on the edge of the bed.

"We need to talk about this first," I told him gently, looking to them all.

Looking around the room and seeing my mates, or at least the ones that I knew about, gathered around me, I realised just how lucky I was that I got this opportunity to spend this time with them. Would I have liked more time? Of course, I would. Was I going to put them in danger just to get it? No. I couldn't do that to them.

"What is there to talk about?" Dom asked, striding to the window and staring outside. "Do we like this? Of course not. But she was our last chance. The only option that we had left. We're out of time. We've seen you declining Lyra, no matter how much you try to hide it. There's no time left to try and find another solution."

He didn't turn around to look at any of us as he spoke. It's as if he couldn't even look us in the face as he says it.

"We have to talk about the risk of giving my blood to her," I sighed.

"*Fuck the risk!*" Dom shouted, spinning around from the window and took one stride closer to me before he stopped, fists clenched at his sides.

I looked across at Wyatt and Caleb at least expecting some support from them. It was after all their people that were at the most risk. Caleb was sat on the bed, his hand wrapped around the back of his head as he sat hunched over staring at the ground. Wyatt was leaning against the bedroom door with his arms crossed over his chest. If there was ever a picture of angry reluctance, Wyatt was it right now.

"I can't believe you don't even want to discuss this," I huffed. "Vampires took my blood and gained the ability to walk in the daylight. What do you think is going to happen when some witch has it? And then what do you think they will do with that? Who do you think they are going to point that kind of power at? Hmmm, now who do they have a problem with?" I added sarcastically, one finger tapping on my bottom lip.

"I don't give a fuck! They don't give a fuck! If they want to come at us, they can and we will deal with it then. You know why? Because you will still be standing there beside us Lyra," Dom walked towards me and dropped to his knees at my feet. "I am kneeling in front of you Lyra, down on my knees, begging you. Please do this. Do it for us. We can't survive without you."

Dom rested his head against my stomach and I felt my shirt grow damp from his tears. This was going to be one of the hardest things I ever had to do.

Dropping to my knees in front of him, I cradled his face in my hands and lifted his head so he would look at me. The tears streamed down his face and I felt my cheeks grow wet as my own broke free to join his.

"You will survive this. We can't risk potentially hundreds of people just to save my life. You know that I'm right."

Dom shook his head silently and continued to break down in front of me. Watching this strong man fall apart in front of me broke my heart. Because this man was also my mate, it felt like it was ripping out my soul and shredding it to pieces.

"Actually, we won't," Wyatt said quietly from behind me.

"What?" I span around and lock him with my gaze.

"We won't survive this. Or at least Caleb and I won't. Our wolves have mated with you. Once you die, they will lose their minds in grief and someone will have to put us down."

My head snapped back to Dom and he just silently nodded at me. How had I not known about this? I couldn't do this to them, but how could we potentially condemn the pack as well? I could feel my mind starting to spiral out of control. This wasn't fair. They had been through so much. Why would fate match us together, to only tear us apart like this? It was cruel. Hadn't they been through enough already?

While I was distracted, I must have missed the sound of the door opening because the next voice I heard was Kyle's behind me.

"You are pack Lyra, and we stand with our own," Kyle said.

I turned around at the sound of his voice and found him and Aria standing in front of the open door.

"Let them try and come," Aria smiled coldly. It didn't quite reach her eyes though. I had seen the look on her face when her friend had left. It hurt her and it was still hurting.

Aria held out her hand and I knew exactly what it was that she wanted. I looked down at the bottle in my hand. This didn't feel right, it felt selfish and immoral. How could I justify putting my needs above all of these people? Except it wasn't just my needs, it was Dom, Caleb and Wyatt as well. It was the lives of at least two of my mates. And that was the moment that I knew. Yes, I would. I would be selfish. I would do this thing for them. I would do anything for them.

Passing the bottle across to Aria, she simply tossed it over her shoulder and it smashed on the wall behind her. Wyatt tutted at the mess and Aria just laughed, striding out of the room.

"Come along then, back to the library," she disappeared around the corner, but I heard her voice trailing behind her. "We should probably knock together some lunch or something. I'm absolutely starving!"

Kyle smiled grimly. "I'm going to sort out some food, she gets cranky when she's hungry. And when she's cranky, she gets all stabby." He walked away, laughing.

It wasn't the first time that someone had said that to me about Aria.

It was not even an hour later when Leona strode back into the library and took a seat beside Liam, helping herself to the food laid out on the coffee table.

"I'm so glad that you got back to me so quickly," she smiled, biting into the sandwich that she had put together.

"Where is Aeryn?" Aria interrupted.

"She decided to go home," she shrugged. "She wanted to get back to her friend."

"Echo?"

"Yes, that was the one," Leona grinned.

"We haven't heard from her since she left to find Aeryn. Aeryn mentioned that she decided to stay with the coven," Kyle leapt in.

I could see Aria's face growing red and she looked pissed. Maybe I was finally going to see this stabby side of her that everyone kept talking about.

"I'll pass a message to her when I return and ask her to give you a call," Leona smiled. I somehow had the feeling that she had no intention of doing what she was saying. "Now shall we get back to business?"

Leona placed a dagger and a bowl on the table. I hadn't

even seen her reach for them and there was no way that she had that thing hidden away in the ridiculous clothes that she was wearing.

"Before we make an agreement, I need to know a few things first. Just how much blood is it that you want and what exactly are you intending on doing with it?" I asked her.

"I won't need much," Leona shrugged. "Enough for the spell that you need and one more. Does that sound fair?"

I nodded because it did, she could have asked for much more and we wouldn't have had any choice but to give it to her.

"You didn't answer my other question," I pointed out.

"No, I didn't," Leona smirked, placing her sandwich down and delicately wiping her fingers on a napkin. She looked across at me and cocked her head to the side, making it clear that she had no intention of telling me anything.

"Do you plan on hurting anyone with it?" I asked, needing to know that much at least.

Leona's eyes flicked back and forth as she searched my eyes. For a moment I thought that I saw her cocky façade crack, but it was back in place so quickly I wasn't sure I had seen it or if it was just wishful thinking. "I have no intention of harming your pack," she finally said. "I can give you my word on that."

A rush of breath puffed out of me in relief. I didn't know if I could trust her, my gut told me that I couldn't. But she had at least told me what I wanted to hear and eased my guilt, even if only for a little bit.

I picked up the dagger and with one quick and sure movement, sliced through the palm of my right hand. Holding it out over the bowl, I clenched my fist, squeezing it tight to help the blood flow. Leona sets a greedy eye on the bowl. She looked like she was practically salivating at its contents. It was a look I had seen before during my time with the clan and I really hoped she wasn't going to do what I thought she was.

After a few minutes, she nodded and Caleb quickly pulled my hand back, wrapping it in a napkin and putting pressure on my wound. Dipping his head forward, he pressed his forehead against mine. His calm, reassuring presence washed over me and I sighed. Kyle was right, no matter what it took, we had to protect each other. I'd do anything to save this man beside me.

Leona pulled the bowl across the table until it was in front of her. "I'm going to need a map," she said, looking at everyone sitting around the room.

Kyle cocked his head to the side and then nodded. "Liam is bringing us one."

Leona smiled gleefully. "I had heard that magic was returning to the shifters. Aeryn told me about your increased abilities, but it seemed so unbelievable."

No one answered her. Clearly, no one wanted to engage in any form of conversation with her, but it was just starting to get awkward now. Leona stared down into the bowl, obsessing over its contents. This didn't bode well for me. I was almost certain what she was going to do with it and one hit was never going to be enough. When all of this was over with, I was going to have to watch my back, because she was definitely going to be coming back.

Liam eventually walked into the room carrying a massive picture frame holding a map inside. The table was cleared of food and the map laid out on top of it. Leona had been standing in the corner of the room, hunched over a small side table. She kept pulling little pouches and tins out of all of her pockets and sprinkling them into another one of the glass bottles.

Wyatt was glaring across the room at her. If I wasn't confident of the type of person that I knew him to be, I would have worried that he was planning something. He wouldn't risk my safety, but as soon as that spell was performed, I was pretty sure that Leona was going to want to get out of here as quickly as she could.

"Done," she finally said, tipping a small amount of my blood into the bottle, before sealing it and giving it a shake.

"That's it," scoffed Kyle, snatching the bottle from her.

"Of course," she snorted. "It's not exactly hard to trace a fated bond."

Leona rolled her eyes and then put the last of her herbs away. Straightening her jacket, she picked up the bowl containing my blood and then started to walk towards the door.

"All of this time, you've known how to do this all of this time," Liam muttered in shock as he stared at the small bottle. "Why wouldn't you have ever said anything?"

He looked just as shocked as the rest of us, but Leona just grinned and opened the door up to leave.

"You never had anything I wanted before," she simply said and then left.

It took a while before any of us looked. They were all staring at the door in shock. Bomb officially dropped.

"Just pour it on the map," we heard her shout before the sound of the front door closing.

"What do you think she is going to do with the rest of the blood?" Liam asked.

"She's going to drink it," I said, turning back towards the map and peering down at it. It looked like the entire realm, but it wasn't very detailed. It was almost like they didn't know all of the details to fill it in.

"Sorry, it sounded like you said she was going to drink it," Liam laughed as everyone came over to join me.

Kyle passed me the bottle and I pulled the top off. "Do

you think I just pour it in one place or like spread it around a bit?" I asked, looking up at them.

Everyone was just staring at me.

"Did someone else want to do it?" I asked unsurely. "What?"

"You did just say that she was going to drink it, right?" Liam asked again.

"Yeah, I've seen that look before. Hunger. She's going to drink it and see what it will do for her," I shrugged. "Or at least that's what I'm guessing."

"Okay," Liam said, turning back to the map with his eyebrows raised and a look of shock on his face.

"Go ahead sweetheart," Wyatt said, pushing my hand back over the map.

It almost felt like I should be saying something. That this was some poignant moment we would look back on, and I should be saying something that we would remember, preferably something wise and witty. Instead, I just turned the bottle over and emptied the now sludgy contents into the middle. No one had said to spread it out, so I was just going to take a chance. Nothing seemed to happen for a moment, but then the mixture began to hiss and bubble, evaporating away. A fine mist started to gather over the map until it had a blanket of mist completely obscuring the map beneath.

"So, they're not in this realm?" Caleb asked, sounding about as confused as I expected we all felt.

Just as he spoke, the mist shimmered and then dropped with a splash back down onto the map, completely covering it in a thin watery layer of blood. That is, all except for one small area. Dom pulled a marker pen out, from who the hell knew where, and drew a circle around the blank area. Then with the left-over napkins from lunch, we wiped the glass clean, revealing the map beneath.

"Oh, for fuck's sake!" Wyatt sighed, looking down at the map.

Caleb just looked down at the map for a second and then threw his head back and laughed. "The fucking Moon Side! You have got to be shitting me!" he laughed.

"I'll start getting the bags together," Dom sighed, turning and leaving the room with Liam at his side.

"Is this where you found me before?" I asked, staring down at the map. Without there being many markings on there, it was hard to tell where we had been before, or where the little abandoned house was that we had taken shelter in.

"I think it was more around here, it's hard to tell without any landmarks," Wyatt told me pointing to a part of the map that didn't look too far from where it was saying my fourth mate was located. "This is maybe half a day or so away."

"How long will it take you to reach here?" Kyle asked, staring down at the map.

"If we portal into the same place, it's about a day's hike to the edge of the Moon Side. Dom couldn't get us any closer because of the interference of whatever spell has been cast over the area to keep it dark. From the border, it's probably another day or two hike to wherever this place is," Wyatt trailed off.

I knew exactly what he was thinking. It would take us a couple of days to locate my mate, then it's not like we were just going to form a bond immediately, that was going to take a while as well. We didn't know how much longer I had left.

"I can't believe we're going back into that place, it's creepy as fuck," Caleb sighed.

"I think we should rest tonight and set out first thing in the morning," Wyatt said, his eyes still locked on the map. "That way we can get to the border by nightfall again, camp on our side and then set out to whatever is here," he said nodding at the map.

"There is one small problem," Aria murmured, we all looked up and saw the frown on her face. "You're saying that it's going to take you three or four days to get to this location. What if he moves on?"

"Then we're fucked," Wyatt told her simply.

CHAPTER 45

WYATT

We all piled into my room that night, none of us wanted to be far from Lyra. She was weakening and we were all desperate to bring this to an end. We just needed to find our fourth. They had to form the bond with her. In my mind, I couldn't even think of a reason why they would refuse to do it. If they didn't want her that would be fine, they go on with the rest of their lives doing whatever they wanted, as long as they bonded with her first. Just because they were bonded didn't mean that they had to stay together. I'd fucking beg if I had to. I couldn't lose her. I could feel my wolf starting to spiral out of control just at the thought of it. As I stared down at the beautiful woman laying in my arms, her golden hair spilt out across the pillow as she slept peacefully, I knew that I would do absolutely anything for her. I wouldn't be separated from her again.

We just had to hope that our fourth would see in her what we all did. That they would welcome the chance to come into the fold with us. We would welcome them with open arms, they were our brother, fate had already promised them to us just as much as to her. They were pack.

Dom and Caleb were already awake. We all had been for at least an hour at this stage, we just didn't want to wake Lyra. She was going to need all of the energy that she could get.

"I've been thinking about something," Dom murmured from the other side of the bed and I leant up to look at him over the top of Lyra. "Have you noticed that Lyra is different after she's been ... intimate with us?"

I had no idea what he was talking about and Caleb looked equally confused, for about all of two minutes, before he seemed to find some form of clarity.

"After we were all together," he cleared his throat uneasily and I smirked at both of their uneasiness to talk about sex with me, especially since I knew for a fact that the thing they were talking about was a threesome. "Lyra seemed better afterwards, her hand wasn't shaking anymore and she said that she didn't feel as worn down."

"What so you're trying to insinuate that you have some kind of magic sperm," I laughed and I heard Lyra giggle beneath me.

Looking down, I was met with her beautiful brown eyes staring back at me.

"Is this seriously what you all talk about when I'm asleep," she smirked.

Fuck, she was beautiful, and for a moment I was rendered speechless just staring down at her in my arms.

"No, what I'm trying to say is that I think when we are all intimate together with Lyra that she is somehow obtaining energy through our bond with her," Dom said looking ever so slightly annoyed with me. Note to self, the mage did not like being made fun of.

Everyone seemed to stop as we thought it through. It was true that Lyra did seem better after we had been together, but I had always just assumed it was hormones or something. But he was right, she didn't immediately deteriorate, if anything she seemed better for at least a day or so afterwards. I looked down at her again, my eyes flittering across her face and taking note of the shadows under her eyes, even though she had just slept for several hours.

"How are you feeling?" I asked her quietly, concern coating my voice.

Lyra shifted in the bed next to me and her eyes started to darken in heat. It would seem that her mind was going to the exact same place that mine did a minute before.

"Because I think you look like you could do with a bit of a top-up," I smirked and I felt Caleb shift closer to her other side.

"Yeah, she looks a bit tired still," Caleb murmured, as he started to drop kisses down her neck, pulling the strap of her top off her shoulder when it got in the way.

"Dom," I said, looking up at the man himself. "Your mate needs you."

He grinned as he slipped over Caleb and settled between Lyra's legs, pushing up her top, he started to gently kiss and lick across her stomach and down to her hip bone. I leaned back into Lyra's lips, "How about we put Dom's theory to the test?" I whispered, before sealing her lips with my own.

She tasted like the sweetest treat and I knew I was the luckiest man in the realm, because I would be able to keep kissing her for the rest of my life. She groaned against my lips and when I pulled away and looked down, I saw Dom feasting between her legs and Caleb playing with her breasts.

Dropping kisses to her mouth, I pulled back so I could watch every emotion and every sensation flow through her face. The way that her eyelids flutter as she writhed on the bed. How her soft lips parted as she gasped, as she rode the wave of bliss that her mates were giving her.

I ran my thumb across her lips, pulling her bottom lip

down as I went, before dipping back down to taste her again. Slipping my tongue inside her mouth to twirl with hers, I swallowed down every moan that slipped from her lips.

My wolf is basking in watching the pleasure our pack brothers are giving her. Watching the way that she groaned and writhed beneath their attention. This is what our pack was made for. To worship her.

Her back arched and her breasts heaved as she started to pant, glancing down I could see that Caleb had moved down to join Dom between her legs. They both had one of her legs hooked over their shoulders. Dom was working her clit with his tongue and Caleb was pushing two fingers inside her.

I could tell that she was about to come, her cheeks were flushed and her eyes were filled with lust. Her moans were getting louder. Dom was holding her hips, refusing to let up and taking her right to that edge.

I watched her face for every moment. I watched her fall apart, as she called out our names. My cock had never felt as hard as it did in that moment, my wolf was howling in joy and I had never needed her more than I did right then.

"Tell us what you want?" I asked, staring down into her eyes as I watched her come back into herself. "What do you need, baby?"

I could tell that she was uncertain, that she didn't know if she could ask for what she truly wanted. She'd spent so long with her freedom taken away from her, without being able to do whatever she wants or needs. It was time for her to finally be free.

"Anything you want," Dom said, kissing the inside of her thigh, "anything at all."

She looked between the three of us and I hoped that she saw the amount of love that was shining back at her.

"I want you all," she said slowly.

"You have us all," I told her, kissing her.

I could see that she was struggling to ask for what she wanted and now isn't a time to push her.

"Dominic, I think our mate needs to feel you inside her," I told him, letting her off the hook of having to voice her own needs, just this once.

Caleb moved out of his way and suddenly Dom grabbed Lyra hoisting her up into his lap, making her giggle.

"Is that right?" he asked, nuzzling into her neck as she straddled his lap. "Do you need me, my mate?" he said, biting down gently onto her shoulder.

"Yes," she gasped.

Lifting herself up and slowly lowering herself down his length, it's the closest she's come to telling us what she wants. Wrapping her arms around his shoulders, she started to move, slowly at first with Dom.

"Caleb, get behind her," I told him, my eyes fixed on Lyra and Dom.

A growl from my wolf slips through me. He liked this, he liked this a lot.

Caleb knelt behind Lyra so she could lean back against his chest, her head on his shoulder. His hands came up to brace her breasts as he rolled her nipples between his fingers. Dom lifted up onto his knees, lifting Lyra with him, giving him the room he needed to quicken his pace. Caleb leant down and captured her mouth with his and she reached back to wrap her hands around the back of his head and draw him closer.

They were all beautiful to watch, not just her. All of them together, this was where we were meant to be. Lyra suspended between the two of them, her mouth falling open in ecstasy. I never realised how much I would enjoy watching my pack with Lyra, I had always thought that any intimate time between us would be something we would do alone, but right now, watching them with her, I'm discovering things about myself that I never knew.

Dom must be growing close to his release because it's like he can't hold himself back. His hips pick up to a furious pace as he slammed himself inside her. His teeth are clenched and I could see his grip around her hips tighten. Lyra was writhing in pleasure where she lay between them, being held up off the bed by both of her mates, completely at their mercy. Caleb is too busy worshipping Lyra with his lips, peppering kisses up and down her neck before tilting her lips to his own, to pay too much attention to Dom. But every so often, his gaze slid up as he watched his pack brother work.

Suddenly Dom pulled out from Lyra and hoisted her up in his arms. Swinging himself around, he sat down on the edge of the bed and placed Lyra in his lap. Pulling her back flush to his chest, he slid her back down his length, hissing at the sensation of filling her pussy again.

"Caleb, on your knees in front of her," he growled as he pulled Lyra's legs to the outside of his own.

I'd never seen the mage act so dominant before. Caleb immediately obeyed him, dropping to the ground in front of them. Lounging back on the bed, I decided that I was content to watch them before taking Lyra for myself. I'm happy for us all to be together, but my only interest in this scenario was Lyra, and I'm not entirely ready to be so close to my pack brothers just yet.

Dom opened his legs, pulling Lyra's legs open with his own. She was spread out before Caleb, her sweet pussy on display with Dom's cock filled her to the brim. Caleb licked his lips in anticipation, it seemed that he was already on board with what Dom had planned and it was only Lyra who didn't seem to quite understand what was happening.

Caleb crawled forward on his knees before he dipped his

head down and ran his tongue around Lyra's clit. Her head immediately fell back onto Dom's shoulder as her back arched and she moaned her approval. No matter my previous reluctance, seeing her like this, between them, I'm filled with the need to feel her. Moving to Dom's side, I took one of Lyra's nipples between my teeth and ran my tongue across the pinched tip. The sounds coming out of her were exquisite, as she pants and writhes. Her movement caused Dom to hiss out a sound of his own approval.

I watched as Caleb's hands slipped beneath her ass and he started to lift her, letting her drop back down over Dom's length, as he helped her ride Dom's cock. His tongue was moving from her clit to sweep down and circle Dom's cock every time he slid her up and revealed it to himself.

My own cock was painfully hard and I was surprised by just how much I wouldn't mind being in Dom's position right now. I could imagine the sensation of Lyra riding my cock as Caleb's tongue worked my length and if I wasn't confused before, I definitely am now. I'm fairly certain that I didn't have any feelings for Caleb and it was just the thought of the experience that was turning me on. I just didn't know that something like that would be a turn on for me. Deciding that now wasn't really the time for me to be examining my own sexuality, I returned my attention to Lyra's breasts and reached up to tease her other nipple with my fingers while I worked over her already stiffened peak with my tongue.

Dom held out for longer than I thought he would, but he inevitably came hard as Lyra screamed out in orgasm, riding him hard. He fell back onto the bed, accompanied by Lyra's husky chuckles.

Caleb looked up at me in question and it was the first time that he had regarded me as an alpha. My wolf was practically brimming with pride at the look of question in his eyes and I knew that a smirk had stretched across my face. I knew exactly what I wanted and I knew that he was going to enjoy it just as much as I would.

"Where do you want me, alpha," Lyra purred at me, drawing my attention back to her.

"On your knees on the bed," I told her as I shuffled myself back into the middle of the bed with her.

Dom had rolled to the side and was lounging on his side, with his head propped up on his hand, watching as Lyra crawled into the middle of the bed. I couldn't blame him, she was mesmerising like this.

I quickly pulled off my boxers before I knelt behind her, running my hands over her ass. It was absolutely perfect and one day soon I was going to take it. Not today though, I knew that she was going to need to work up to it.

I took my time to tease the entrance of her pussy with the head of my cock. Caleb moved in front of her and Lyra didn't need any prompting to take him into her mouth. His head fell back on a sigh and she moaned her approval as his hips snapped forward, no doubt pushing himself into the back of her throat.

I waited until he withdrew and then started to move forward again before I sank inside her in one swift motion, keeping a grip of her hips so as not to push her further onto Caleb. The wet heat of her pussy wrapping around my cock is nothing short of bliss. She's still so tight, but I can already feel the flutter in her muscles as she started to climb towards orgasm again.

I kept myself sheathed to the hilt as I spread her ass cheeks before me. Running my thumb around her hole she moaned in encouragement and before I could think any further, Dom was passing me a tube of lube from the bedside table, which I sure as hell didn't put there. I can't say I'm not grateful that he thought ahead though.

I grinned at him as I took it and he lounged back on the bed, watching Caleb slowly fuck Lyra's mouth.

Coating my thumb in lube I slowly ran it around Lyra's hole, making sure that she was ready for what I intended. Her pussy clamped down hard around my cock in anticipation and I slowly started to pull myself out of her. The whimpers and moans coming from her mouth spurred me on, as my hips snapped forward and I started the process of the slow withdrawal again. I wanted her completely focused on the two cocks working inside of her before I started to push my way into her ass. I wanted her completely relaxed and surrendering to the pleasure of the moment to make this as easy as I could for her.

I slowly started to pick up my pace and Caleb mirrored my own movements as we fucked Lyra from both ends in tandem. I could feel that she was close, I knew that she was going to come any moment so I gently pushed one finger into her ass as she started the climb back up towards her release.

She groaned in approval as my finger breached her ass and I started to work her in tandem with my cock. I'm close to coming myself and I know that I don't have much time. As soon as she had relaxed and was taking one finger with enthusiasm, pushing herself back against me, I knew that she's ready for more and I slowly worked a second finger into her ass.

As soon as both fingers were slowly fucking her ass, I picked up the rhythm with my cock again, unable to hold back any longer.

Caleb lost his pace as he came down her throat, his eyes fixed on the way my fingers were breaching her ass. It would seem I'm not the only one that wants it.

Lyra hungrily swallowed him down and as soon as Caleb fell back onto the bed and into Dom's waiting arms the dam inside me broke and the last bit of restraint that I had snapped. Gripping onto Lyra's hip with one hand, I slammed my cock into her pussy as hard as I could and she shouted out her encouragement. I couldn't hold back as I fucked her as hard as I could, her greedy pussy clamped down hard around me trying to keep me inside. She didn't need to worry though, I'm not finished with her just yet.

Lyra started to rock back to meet me just as hard as I'm pushing forwards into her. The lube that Dom passed me is making easy work for my fingers to slide in and out of her ass with just as much enthusiasm. I may have underestimated just how ready our little angel was and I slipped a third finger inside as I started to feel my balls tightening and I knew I was about to lose myself inside her.

The sensation of having her ass and her pussy stretched and filled at the same time was too much for Lyra to take and she clamped down around me. It was all that it took for me to lose myself and I came so hard it almost hurts. Lyra was already screaming out her release, so I pulled my fingers free of her ass, gripping her hip asI slammed inside her one last time.

We both fell back down to the bed, exhausted and sated. This woman was absolutely perfect and the next time that I got her into bed, I already knew exactly what I'm going to do.

We pulled the covers up over us and everyone settled back into the bed. Last night was the first night that we'd slept as a pack and now as we laid here basking in the afterglow, I'd never felt my wolf as relaxed as he was right now. He was happy to finally have our pack together and safe, at least for the time being anyway.

"I've been thinking …" Lyra started.

"Wow, I thought we did a pretty good job back there but if you had time to think …" Caleb joked.

Lyra flushed the most adorable shade of pink and I wrapped her tighter in my arms. "Go on," I urged her.

She propped herself up on one elbow and looked across at

Dom. "You should try drinking some of my blood," she suddenly blurted out.

I'm not sure what I had been expecting her to say, but it definitely wasn't that. From the look on Dom and Caleb's faces as well I'd guess they were as shocked as I was. Dom's mouth just dropped open, like he was about to say something, but his words just suddenly abandoned him in the process.

"Just think about it," Lyra started to explain. "We need to get to the point on the map as quickly as possible. Leona clearly thinks that my blood is going to have some form of effect on her or she wouldn't have asked for it. We should use that to our advantage."

She's making sense, but equally, I'm not sure that it's my decision to make. Dom would be the one that would have to drink the blood, any side effects would be his to bear. It needed to be his decision. Looking over at him, I could see that he was weighing up the decision in his mind. Lyra was right, we needed every advantage that we could get. It was hard to forget that we were in a race against time here and the worst part was we had no idea when it was going to run out.

Dom slowly started to nod his head. "You're right," he said slowly. "But we need to consider the potential for side effects and the worst case scenario."

"What do you mean?" Caleb asked with a frown. This was going to be infinitely worse for him because he didn't just love Lyra, he had the exact same feelings for Dom as well. How was he going to feel potentially putting Dom at risk to save Lyra's life.

"We don't know what will happen to me when I drink it. I may not even be able to open the portal, or I may get it open and not be able to come with you," Dom explained.

"What do you mean that you might not be able to come with us," Caleb asked and I could see the panic starting in his eyes as he sat up in bed.

"If we are talking about trying to punch through the spell surrounding the Moon Side and portaling further into that side of the realm, the amount of energy that would be needed ... I may be drained, assuming that it's even possible in the first place," Dom told him softly, trying to calm him down.

"What about Frannie?" Caleb asked, "She helped back at the Mage Library, maybe she can help again?"

Dom started to nod until I interrupted.

"Frannie's gone, she disappeared shortly after we got back. No one knows where she is."

Caleb visibly deflated and I could see how worried he was.

"Maybe it's a bad idea," Lyra said. "We should just stick with the original plan."

"No, you're right. We'd be foolish not to try. If it can give us the advantage we're hoping for, it could cut days off the journey," Dom reasoned.

I could tell that Caleb wanted to disagree. That he didn't want to risk Dom.

"What about Stone?" I asked, my mind searching for any way to make this safer for Dom. "Could he do what Frannie did?"

"Theoretically ..." Dom said, drifting off as he thought it through.

We all stayed silent, waiting for him to fill us in with whatever he was planning.

"I need to speak with Stone," Dom suddenly said, jumping out of the bed and quickly dressing. We didn't even have a chance to ask him what he wanted to talk to him about before he was out of the door leaving the rest of us behind.

"I suppose we're getting up then," Caleb said, almost reluctantly as he just snuggled in closer to Lyra.

"Maybe two more minutes," I agreed, mirroring him on her other side.

Lyra just laughed but made no move to get out of bed. The three of us laid there just enjoying each other's company.

"You know, Wyatt, we should really let Lyra have a shower before we set off," Caleb said, feigning innocence.

"You're just full of good ideas this morning," I laughed before suddenly scooping Lyra up in my arms, accompanied by her squeal. "To the shower!"

CHAPTER 46

DOM

As we stand outside of the packhouse with all of our bags packed, saying our goodbyes, I couldn't help but look around at the people surrounding us. Lyra looked healthier than she had for a long time. She's even got these adorable little pink flushes to her cheeks, I'm not sure if it's because she's feeling better or if she's thinking about this morning. Just the thought had my cock hardening in response. We definitely needed to keep doing that. Seeing her laid out on the bed with my pack brothers feasting on her was nearly enough for me to suggest that we delay leaving for a few hours, or maybe days.

"I know what you're thinking about," Caleb murmured from beside me. His hand gently touched my lower back and then traced down the curve of my ass before it fell away. Fuck! The fucking tease.

"Only because it's the exact same thing you're thinking about," I groaned.

It must be obvious to everyone around us what is going on, but I just don't care anymore.

Aria and her mates were busy talking amongst themselves

and weren't paying all that much attention to us. But my brother, who had been chatting with Lyra, had got one eye on us and a frown on his face. I should probably fill him in on what was happening with me, seems as he's my brother and he's going to be around more now. I hoped he would accept it. I knew that it wasn't completely unheard of in the mage community. We didn't have women living in the library unless they were there to provide a mage with a child. Once the child was born and the mother was no longer needed, she left, usually returning to her own coven. Unless that child was a girl and then she left after the birth, taking the child with her. Mages got lonely and with an abundance of men and not many easily accessible women, well let's just say that arrangements are sometimes known to be made. They are never public arrangements though and there are still some who frowned on such activities. It was nearly unheard of amongst the ruling families anyway, because they had enough power and influence to have an easily accessible mistress if they wanted one. I could remember a time when my father used to disappear most nights and I was convinced that was where he was going. Now wasn't the time to have this conversation with Stone though, even if I did want to delay our departure. Although Stone had been fairly out of it yesterday and maybe a delay wouldn't be a bad idea. He was insisting that he was fine, but I was worried if my brother's system was going to be able to handle this.

Lyra came over with Stone, smiling at Caleb and I, and I felt the wolf beside me swoon at the sight of her smile. I'd make fun of him for it, if I wasn't feeling the exact same thing.

"You lot are just ridiculous," Stone laughed, looking between us all.

"Just you wait, brother, once you have your mate with you, I'll be reminding you of this," I told him.

Stone sobered immediately. "I'm a mage Dom, I don't get to have a mate."

"Obviously that can't be true," Lyra laughed, "Dom is a mage and he has me."

The look on Stone's face would have been funny if it wasn't also a little bit sad. He looked so shocked, but there was a glimmer of hope there as well. We had been raised the same as every other mage, being told that fated mates never happened for our race. I couldn't help but wonder now if that information had been purposefully withheld from us, or if they actually believed it. Knowing my father and the other ruling families as I did, it was more likely that they were just withholding it for some reason. I couldn't for the life of me figure out why though.

"It's time," Wyatt said, striding over to us.

That was all it took for the nerves to start. I didn't want to do this. No part of me wanted to do this.

"Are you sure about this?" Stone asked, looking just as worried as I was.

"As sure as I'll ever be," Lyra said, pulling two bottles out of her pocket and passing one to each of us. I looked at it in confusion for a second wondering where it had come from. "Aria helped me out this morning, I thought this might make it a bit easier for you," she said, smiling sheepishly.

"Don't take this the wrong way," Stone said, looking at the bottle grimly, "but this is really gross, babe."

Wyatt growled and I almost laughed at the look on his face.

"Probably best not to call her that in front of her mates, brother, me included," I told him, feeling a simmer of annoyance as well.

"Noted," he said with a grin.

Pulling the top off the bottle, I held it in front of me,

peering suspiciously at the contents. I look at Stone who was watching me, the sealed bottle still in his hand.

"As if I'm going to go first," he laughed when I raised an eyebrow in question at him.

"Fuck it," I sighed, knocking the bottle back.

I shuddered as Lyra's blood slipped down my throat. Argh god, that was kind of gross! It was the consistency. Thicker than water but not quite syrupy. I could feel myself wanting to gag, but holding onto my idea of manliness, I managed to suppress the urge. What I couldn't suppress though was the full-body shudder and the look of disgust as I smacked my lips trying to get the taste out of my mouth.

"You're not really selling it to me, brother," Stone laughed, watching me shudder once more.

I think it was worse because I knew that it was Lyra's blood. Urgh! How did vampires do this all the time? Oh god, don't think about it! It was making me want to gag again.

As my brain ran away with me, I suddenly felt something stirring inside of me. I paused for a moment as a warm sensation started to build in the centre of my chest. Raising my hand to press against the strange feeling was just a natural reaction, but before I could reach it, I felt like I had been punched in the chest. All of the breath rushed out of me and I doubled over trying to suck in air. Dropping to my knees, I clutched at my chest, trying to fight the building panic of not being able to draw in enough air. My eyes flicked up and I saw Lyra in Caleb's arms, trying to reach for me, but he was holding her back. I was confused why he would keep her away from me, but then a flash of white flickered past my eyes and as I managed to calm my mind I realised that my magic was circling my body, out of control. Stone was looking at me with panic in his eyes, which was understandable considering that he now clutched an empty bottle in his own hand. The strange thing though, now that I had caught my breath, this out of control magic wasn't an unpleasant sensation. It was almost like when I was just on the verge of sleep, holding Lyra in my arms. That sense of complete calm at knowing I held her close to me. And that was it, that was why, this magic, it wasn't mine. This was Lyra's magic. This was the smallest piece of Lyra's magic that had been held in the mouthful of blood she had given me. I looked up at her in awe. She was the most powerful being I had ever been near. How did she contain this amount of magical potential within her tiny body? More importantly, if she was this magically charged, how could it be possible she no longer had access to it? Where the fuck was it all going?

I took a deep breath and centred myself in the moment. I felt the swirling magic caressing against my skin and drew it deep inside of me. It was a good job I was about to expend a massive amount of it, or I don't know what I was going to do. I couldn't help but wonder if Leona was aware of the effects and if she was, just what she was planning on doing with it.

Just as soon as I had myself centred, I opened my eyes and saw that Stone was on his knees opposite me. The magic swirling around him was incredible. Is this what it had looked like with me? There was a thick grey and white opacity to it, almost making it look like clouds, light flashed through it like lightning in a storm. Which made sense, considering they had called Lyra the Stormchild.

Stone seemed to be struggling to try to find his centre and the magic continued to swirl around him. Suddenly, I found myself being held back, but by Wyatt instead.

"Give him a moment, he's got this," he murmured.

I could see Stone mumbling something under his breath. The clouds around him seemed to thin, until suddenly he threw his head back on a gasp and they rushed into his body.

We all just stood and gaped at him, even the others had stopped talking nearby to watch it all unfold.

"That was different," Lyra said, looking at Stone in concern.

"Fucking hell," he gasped, clutching his chest. "It was like it was fighting me, like it knew it didn't belong. How did you get it under control so quickly?" he asked me, frowning.

"It didn't feel like that to me, it felt like ... Lyra." Fucking hell, I could feel myself blushing now.

"Well whatever it is, it's fucking powerful. Damn girl! Where are you keeping all of this inside of you?" Stone said, struggling to get back up to his feet.

Caleb strode over and helped him up, supporting his arm, until he was steady on his feet. I wasn't entirely sure how I felt about that, but I tried to shove that petty emotion deep, deep down.

"That's the question isn't it," I mumbled, as I straightened myself out.

Taking a deep breath, I could feel Lyra's magic rushing through me. It was incredible. What worried me was how addictive it felt like it could be.

"Let's get this show on the road, shall we?" Kyle said, striding over to the group, but looking more than a little wary of us all now. "How far do you think you can take the four of you?"

Liam brought the map out that we had used before and laid it out on the ground in front of us. Crouching down to examine it, I found the spot where we had roughly landed before and then took stock of my centre and the new magic rushing through me. The only difference this time was going to be that I had another person to take along as well.

"I think I can breach the barrier this time," I murmured, looking up at Stone for confirmation of how he was feeling. He looked surprised, but then he nodded. He must be feeling the rush as well. I hoped he would be able to burn most of it off with this spell or he was going to need to find some other way of expelling that magic while we were gone.

"Okay, let's do this," Stone said, cracking his neck and stretching out his shoulders. "You start the chant and begin opening the portal, then I'll funnel everything I've got across to you."

I nodded and turned to the open space behind me. Here goes nothing!

Planting my feet shoulder-width apart, I took a deep breath. Bringing the image of the map into the forefront of my mind, I concentrated on the area we needed to be, before starting the chant. I could feel the power of Lyra's magic, filling my words in a way that mine never had before. It almost felt like they took on physical form, floating in the air around me. Magic crackled in the space in front of me and I could feel the push back of the Moon Side's barrier spell, but when Stone's hand landed on my shoulder and he started to filter his own power into me, it almost seemed to pop, as the full force of Lyra's magic combined with my own punched through. This was why we had never been able to punch through the spell before. We never had enough force to do it. Mage magic was nothing compared to what she had inside of her. She was a raging stormy ocean, compared to the gentle stream we had harnessed. This amount of power in the wrong hands could be truly devastating, and we had just handed it over to Leona with the barest of questions.

The portal slammed into being in front of us. There was no gentle growth, no quiet expansion. It roared into existence and everyone took a step back in surprise.

"Incredible," Stone whispered.

The chant complete, I took a step closer to Lyra, but as I stepped away from Stone, he seemed to waver on his feet. Catching him around the middle, I made sure that he was steady on his feet before letting him go.

"Don't worry about me, I'm just a little worn out. Go and save your girl. When you come back, we need to talk," he told me with a sad smile.

He was right. It had been too long since we had seen each other and there was too much left unsaid between us. Not to mention, I knew that he had made headway on what was happening at the Mage Library and, now more than ever, I believed it was something we needed to keep an eye on.

Kyle, Aria and the rest of her mates stood quietly by. There were no words of farewell, or wishing of luck. There was no option but for us to succeed and return home. To fail in this was unimaginable.

Wyatt stepped through the portal first, ever the protective alpha. He was so close to stepping up and claiming the position and I was so proud of how much he was working on himself. He seemed to finally be coming out of the crushing guilt he had been tormenting himself with all of this time. I wasn't sure how the whole alpha thing was going to work for me initially, I wasn't a shifter, but it did weirdly seem so natural. Despite my previous positions and the roles of authority I had held, I was more than happy to turn to Wyatt and seek his advice and guidance when it came to our family, our pack.

Caleb and Lyra headed through the portal next and with a slap on the back from a wobbly Stone, I followed them through, closing the portal behind me.

It was strange stepping from bright morning daylight into the dusky gloom that was the Moon Side, or at least their version of day anyway. Looking around and getting my bearings, I realised that whilst we had indeed managed to punch through the barrier spell and portal here, we hadn't made it too far from the barrier itself. I could see where the sun was just managing to still reach the ground, far on the horizon. It wasn't as far as I had wanted to get us, but I wouldn't have been able to push much further through without draining myself to the point of unconsciousness again. As it was, I was feeling pretty guilty for how much Stone had pushed through to me.

"Nicely done," Caleb said with a grin, looking around him. "What have we saved? About a day and a half maybe?" he asked, squinting at the horizon.

"I'd say maybe more," Wyatt replied. Turning his back on the daylight and taking in the gloom in front of us. "We've got about a day's journey to the region we need to be searching," he said before suddenly tensing up and leaning forward, inspecting the sight in front of him.

The portal had opened up on this side in one of the plains type areas of the Moon Side. It wasn't a surprise, from our hike through last time, we had found that this part of the realm was covered in them. Probably because nothing could really live here with the lack of sunlight. Whilst that meant we had good clear sightlines around us, it also meant we had absolutely no cover if we needed it. That was probably why the figure in the distance, that was now making its way closer to us, had put Wyatt on high alert. There was no way they would have missed us portaling in here or the fact that we were now standing here with absolutely nowhere to go. The only thing really in our favour here was that they were completely alone. The benefit of being in the middle of this plain was that there was no way that they, or anyone that was travelling with them, would be able to hide. We easily outnumbered them. That being said, they were still poten- tially a threat for Lyra and what we hadn't considered before this moment, was how much of a trigger that was going to be for Wyatt.

Wyatt suddenly exploded into his wolf, and he was a wolf out of control. Snarling and snapping his teeth, he took off towards the approaching figure. We didn't even know who this was, but Wyatt's wolf clearly wasn't going to take any chances.

"Wyatt!" Lyra screamed after him.

He didn't even slow down. The figure had come to a stop. They didn't even try to run away, they didn't pull a weapon, they just stood calmly with their hands at the side, waiting for the inevitable.

Lyra was beside herself with panic and took off at a run after Wyatt. It was something that she couldn't afford to be doing, she might be feeling better now, but we didn't know how long it was going to last, or how quickly it could drain if she exerted herself.

"Lyra, stop!" Caleb shouted, taking off after her.

When he caught up to her, Caleb wrapped his arms around her, holding her tight. I could see her struggling in his grip as he held her close to his chest and whispered into her ear. She calmed quickly, but I could see how distressed she was.

There was no stopping Wyatt, he was lost to his wolf and none of us were going to be able to take on a rabid alpha wolf intent on defending his mate.

"Please, please stop him," Lyra begged as I reached them.

There was nothing that we could really do, he was almost upon whoever it was that happened to be here and there would be no way to reach him in time, even if we did have the strength to hold him back. But then, almost as if it had heard her plea, I felt the last remaining remnants of Lyra's magic stir inside me. Without a second thought, I sent it out, praying I had enough left for this to hold, and formed a barrier around the lone figure, standing there waiting for Wyatt's rabid wolf to reach them.

It was mere seconds later that Wyatt collided with the barrier. Bouncing off, his wolf paused, shaking his head and then launched himself at the barrier again. The person inside didn't even flinch, they just waited. It was almost as if they were praying the barrier would break, that they were waiting for death to come for them from the jaws of this rabid wolf.

Wyatt kept slamming himself into the barrier, I felt every impact deep within my chest. As soon as Lyra realised what was happening, she went running for Wyatt again, but Caleb held her back.

"You need to conserve your energy," he told her as he held her hand and we jogged towards the scene in front of us, rather than sprinting like we all wanted to.

Lyra was nearly beside herself, especially when she saw who it was contained within the barrier.

"Damon," she murmured, trying to pull herself free from Caleb again, only for him to keep her moving at the pace we were all comfortable with.

It didn't take long for us to reach the barrier and whilst I want to keep Lyra safely behind me, I knew deep down that Wyatt's wolf wouldn't hurt her, no matter how crazed and rabid he might seem right now.

"Wyatt!" Lyra snapped.

It made absolutely no difference to Wyatt's behaviour as he continued to slam into the barrier, it did, however, get the attention of the man inside.

"Ly! What ... what the fuck?" he looked confused, but I was betting that all of us looked pretty fucking confused right now. "You were supposed to run, you were supposed to get out of the Moon Side."

He sounded so broken as he said it and I realised that this was a man who had just about given up. It was the only possible explanation for why he would have stood and waited for the wolf running towards him to reach him. He was clearly a vampire, but what was confusing me was the appearance of him. His skin was sallow and clammy, he almost looked like he was sick, but vampires didn't get sick.

"I did get out, but I came back again," she explained.

I mean that was true, but without the reasoning for why we had returned, it did seem pretty stupid, which was apparently the same conclusion that Damon had reached.

"Tell me you're joking," he sighed, tipping his head back and staring at the sky. "You know that Cassius is going out of his mind trying to find you, right? This is the least safe place for you to be. The only reason why I'm here now is because he told me that if I found you, he would let me keep you for myself," he scoffed.

That was definitely the wrong thing to say, because Wyatt, who was starting to calm down, renewed his efforts to get through the barrier. Not just that, but I could also see Caleb was struggling to keep his own wolf reined in. It was impressive he had managed for this long really, especially with his alpha so out of control nearby.

"This isn't because you promised to come and save me, is it? I told you not to," Damon asked, looking confused.

"Erm ... no. Sorry, it should be, but I'm kind of not done saving myself yet," Lyra admitted. "Why are you out here in the middle of nowhere anyway?"

It was kind of adorable how they were just chatting away and ignoring the rabid wolf next to them.

Damon's eyes flicked between Lyra's for a moment and he hesitated. I reached out and took hold of Lyra's hand because I knew she wasn't going to like what she was about to hear.

"I thought he would kill me. I was prepared to go out like that, doing one final good thing. I hate that place. I hate what they were trying to turn me into. If I could get you out, if I could make sure that you were free, then I knew I would have done enough to pass on peacefully. But he didn't kill me when he found out Ly, he tossed me into a cell so that he could watch me starve to death and it hurt. It really fucking hurt. The hunger, the thirst, the need for the one thing that makes me feel sick to be what I am. I didn't know I could hate myself any more than I already did, but I was so very wrong."

Tears silently streamed down Lyra's face as she listened to his confession. She squeezed my hand tightly and listened as he continued.

"Then Edwin came back without you and suddenly I was being dragged out of my cell and thrown at his feet. Cassius started telling me how he understood why I would do what I did, that he knew you were beautiful and he couldn't blame me for falling in love with you. I didn't bother telling him anything different, he wouldn't have understood anyway. He told me that he would let me have you, that all I had to do was find you and bring you back. That it would be different this time, we would protect you. Everyone was telling me that it was for the best. That Cassius would never stop looking for you, that it was the only way to protect you. He gave me a week and sent me out to find you and bring you back," he looked down at his feet as he spoke.

I could see the shame radiating from him, but Caleb had gotten the completely wrong impression.

"What? So, you just thought you would come out here and persuade her to go back to that hell hole with you?" Caleb sneered.

"No!" Damon shouted. "I would never do that to her, I thought she had left the Moon Side."

"Well the fact that you seem to have found yourself here, exactly where she is, seems to say otherwise," Caleb shouted back at him.

"I didn't come here for her," Damon said, his voice trailing off as his eyes locked into the distance behind us. Then he finally admitted. "I just wanted to see it one last time, I just wanted to ..."

He couldn't even finish his sentence, but I knew it was important for the others to fully understand what was happening here. Especially if we were ever going to calm Wyatt's wolf down enough for him to shift back.

"You just wanted to walk out into the sun one last time," I finished for him.

Damon looked away in shame and my heart broke for this man. He had been ripped from his home and turned into what he considered to be a monster. He had probably seen and done terrible things. His last redeeming act had been to save Lyra and now he wanted to go out on his own terms. We had all seen a vampire exposed to sunlight and it is not something I would ever care to experience again. I don't know if he knew just what was in store for him, but I think that he had reached a point where he just didn't care anymore.

"You were going to walk into the sun?" Wyatt's voice came from beside us and a wave of relief washed over me, knowing that he had managed to come back into himself. "You would have done that to protect our mate?"

"I will do that," Damon corrected, still not meeting our eyes, his gaze firmly fixed on the ground. "I can't go back to that cell and I can't stay here with you. Cassius can find me anywhere through his sire bond. It's too dangerous for her to be near me."

"Dom, drop the barrier," Lyra told me quietly.

I let go of the magic and Lyra stepped forward to Damon. None of us stopped her, it felt like we were intruding if I was completely honest. This man had given up so much for Lyra to be able to escape the clan house and now he was willing to make the ultimate sacrifice as well. It felt wrong to stand and watch this moment between them, which was probably why it was so surprising that when Lyra reached him, she raised her hand and slapped him across the face with enough force to make him stagger a step to the side.

Damon raised his hand and rubbed his very red cheek, a look of complete shock on his face.

"How dare you!" Lyra said, raising her voice, "How dare you have so little faith in me that you would decide to end your life rather than trust me to protect you."

Lyra's face was flushed red and her voice hitched in the middle. She was pissed, but she was also upset. I wouldn't want to be in Damon's place right now.

"You cannot protect yourself from him, let alone anyone else," Damon scoffed, rubbing at his cheek. "Some people would be fucking touched," he finally mumbled. "Find it fucking noble or something."

"Don't make me slap you again," Lyra threatened. "For fuck's sake, fucking walking into the sun, fucking idiot."

Spinning round, she levelled her glare at the rest of us. I wasn't quite sure what we had done to deserve her wrath at the moment, but that fierce angel we had glimpsed in her before was starting to shine through again.

"How much further? We need to get this done quickly before this idiot finds some other way to try and kill himself."

"Hey!" Damon muttered in outrage.

"About a day in that direction takes us to the general area and then hopefully, when we see it, we'll have some kind of idea about where we go from there," Wyatt said, barely holding back the smirk.

"Right, you," Lyra said, turning her glare back to Damon, "follow us. Let's just get this done."

"Lyra, what part of Cassius being about to find me did you not understand?" Damon scoffs incredulously.

"He gave you a week to find me, yes?"

"Well, yes ..."

"And how long ago was this?" Lyra interrupted.

"Two days," Damon told her, frowning in confusion.

"Well, he isn't going to be following you around waiting for you to find me. Cassius is a self-entitled egotistical twat! He'll actually believe you are going to do what he's told you to. He won't come looking for you until your seven days are up, which means we have five days to get this done, get back to the pack and prepare for the attack."

Damon looks taken aback by what she is saying. "I can't go back to the pack with you."

"Why not?" she asked, looking confused.

"Because I'm a fucking vampire, Ly!" he said, throwing his hands up in the air.

"Can we discuss this while we're walking?" she asked, "Because we're got a lot to do and we're kind of on a timetable."

"I'm liking this sassy version of her," Caleb murmured next to me as Lyra and Damon continued to bicker and started walking in the direction that we needed to head.

"It's different," Wyatt confirmed watching them closely. "It's almost as if she is feeling better," he pointed out.

I took a moment to look at her before answering. Caleb seemed to be doing the same. She was definitely more energised, but I couldn't decide if that was because she was so pissed at Damon, or if it could be that she was starting to feel less drained. Could it be because she was moving closer to her fated mate? That seems too much to even hope for and as she stumbled over a rock in front of her and Damon caught her, I decided it was just wishful thinking. Lyra didn't even stop her ranting as Damon set her back straight on her feet and just kept telling him off as they walked a few steps ahead of us.

"Aren't you going to go and protect her from him?" Caleb asked Wyatt with a smirk.

"I'm not getting in the middle of that," Wyatt laughed.

Unfortunately, Lyra heard that one and her glare was suddenly turned back towards us. Hanging our heads like naughty children, we continued on, even if we did start sniggering at this strange but ultimately fortunate turn of events.

CHAPTER 47

LYRA

Pretty much every single muscle in my body felt like it was on fire. The extra energy I had been able to absorb through our bond this morning had definitely gone, and so was the buzz of adrenaline I had got from finding Damon. Now, as we continued to walk towards we didn't even know what, I felt like every footstep reverberated back to me, like the sound of a ticking clock, and the only thing that it was telling me, was that I was running out of time.

I didn't even see it in front of me until Wyatt pulled me to a halt and behind a tree on the edge of the treeline. We had been walking in silence at a steady pace for the last hour. Only stopping once through the day for a break to eat. The tension between us was strange. The guys were wanting to push forward and get this done because they were worried about me. No one was talking about if it was going to be weird just bringing someone else into the group. Damon was hovering on the side-lines, probably wishing that he wasn't here, because when he found out what we were doing, he looked shocked, to say the least. When Wyatt filled him in on my deteriorating condition though, he started to look just as determined as the rest of them. We had better find this fourth soon because I couldn't cope with them all ganging up on me for much longer.

The building that now loomed in front of us just seemed to pop up out of nowhere. We had been walking all day and not seen a single sign of life and now there was this massive building just standing in the middle of nowhere. In fact, building wasn't even the right word. It was more of a compound. High wire fencing ran around the edge, every so often guards were walking the line, keeping watch. Inside there was one massive building, it looked similar to how I would have imagined the packhouse would have looked if someone had built it a hundred years ago and then just left it to ruin. Some of the windows were broken, a section of the roof looked caved in and dark stains crept down its once white exterior. In the grounds of the house there looked to be about six low-level bungalows, similar to barracks, dotted about. Apart from the guards, there didn't seem to be anyone moving around, but from the lights shining in all of the buildings, it seemed fairly safe to bet that more people were inside.

"What is this place?" Dom asked, quietly watching the scene in front of us for any clues.

I had absolutely no idea and by the silence of the others around me, I was guessing that they were as equally mystified as I was.

"He's going to be in there, isn't he?" Caleb sighed. "Of course he is because it would be just our luck that the one person you need to mate with to save your life is somehow locked inside a heavily armed building."

I grinned at him and he rolled his eyes at me, shaking his head like I was a crazy person. I mean, it was pretty funny! What would be even funnier, in maybe more of a sad and not actually funny way, would be if we got all the way in there and he actually wasn't there. Man, my life!

"So, we're all pretty convinced our next move is going to be getting inside there?" Wyatt whispered.

"It looks like a prison," Damon muttered, his eyes firmly fixed on the guards patrolling the fence. "No, that's not it ... it looks like a concentration camp." His face blanches white, but I had no idea what he's talking about.

"I don't know what that is," I clarified and I could see that the others were looking just as confused.

"It's something that happened in the human realm ... it happens in the human realm. There was a war, nearly the entire realm ended up at war with each other. One side, they had this thing against certain groups of people, hated them just for being who they were. They rounded them all up and they put them in these camps. It was terrible, thousands died. Some from starvation, some from the conditions, some were ... they were herded into gas chambers and killed," Damon explained.

Everyone was stunned into silence.

"What ... how ..." is all that Caleb managed to get out.

"This still happens?" I asked, confused. "They still do these things?"

"They give them a different name, but yeah it still happens. Some countries try and stop it, others turn a blind eye to it, it never stops though, does it? The hate," Damon sounded truly broken as he whispered his last words.

I looked at the compound in front of me with fresh eyes. The guards patrolling the fences were watching the inside, they weren't watching for any threats approaching from the outside. The searchlights were pointing at the grounds around the bungalows, not the outside of the fence. They're definitely keeping something in and not something out.

"So how do we get in?" Dom asked.

"I'm not sure getting in is going to be the problem, it looks more like getting out is going to be the hard part. I don't know about you, but I don't want to spend the rest of my life somewhere like that," I told them, shuddering at the thought.

"Those guards are vamps," Damon muttered, "so you need to keep your voices down."

"How do you know that?" I screamed at him and he looked at me like the insane crazy person that I am.

"Because I can hear their lack of heartbeat," he looked nervously back at the fence line. "You do realise they're coming right?"

"Mission accomplished!" I said smugly.

"Yeah, well done babe, probably could have done with thinking out the escape plan first though," Caleb chuckled.

'Babe?', I'm not entirely sure I like the sound of that, but before I have time to complain, Dom quickly asks, "Should we be running or something, you know, to at least make it look convincing?"

"No," Wyatt told us quickly. "Lyra is going to play the damsel and faint and the rest of us are going to put up a weak fight, be overpowered and taken inside. If it looks like they will go for the kill, rather than capture, then we take these four out and come up with another plan," he murmured quietly to keep the quickly approaching guards from hearing him.

"I absolutely will not," I scoffed, outraged at even the implication I would faint at the first sign of trouble.

Wyatt grabbed my arm and hauled me close to his chest. "Just this once Lyra, do this thing for me. We know you are not weak, but it works best for us if they underestimate us from the beginning."

I could see the fear and the determination blazing through his eyes. I didn't know why I was worried before about us getting out of that place. There was no way that Wyatt would allow them to keep his pack restrained. We were always going to be safe while we had him by our side.

I nodded once, not trusting myself to speak without

starting to argue my side again. At the end of the day we needed to get inside and it wasn't really important how we went about doing that, even if my pride was arguing, very loudly, that it was.

It didn't take long for them to reach us, now that I thought about it, there was probably no way they hadn't heard us talking about letting them capture us. Oh well. As long as they didn't try to kill us, we should hopefully get what we want anyway.

The guys rushed to meet them head-on, Damon pushed me aside and I fake hit a tree and dropped. How humiliating! I could hear the scuffle of the fight around me and the need to open my eyes and look is nearly overwhelming. When it all eventually quietened down, I felt someone grab hold of me by the back of my jacket and lift my body off the ground.

"Fucking idiot," someone sneers, before blinding pain smashes into the back of my head and everything faded to darkness for real this time. Huh! I guess they did hear us.

———

I woke up in a dark room and the first thought that flashed through my mind was that I was back in the cage, back at the clan house, that everything had been a beautiful taunting dream. My head pounded and raising my fingers, I felt a wet patch of hair at the back of my head. I heard the faint shuffle of movement and froze. There was someone else in the cage with me, I wasn't alone. I could feel my heart starting to pound. I was supposed to be alone. I was always alone. The bars kept me in, but they kept them out as well. Images of Edwin and his seeking fingers flashed through my head, had he finally come for me, was this it?

Sudden movement sounded next to me and before I could utter a sound, or move, a pair of muscled arms were wrapping around me and a hand was placed firmly over my mouth. I felt myself pulled back against someone's chest as they wrapped themselves around me. I struggled, but my every movement made my vision swim and white flashes of light burst in front of my eyes.

"Ly, Ly, it's Damon," a voice hissed from a face pressed against my cheek. "You are not in the cage. You are not in the cage," he repeated over and over, gently rocking me back and forth with him until I was able to bring my panic back down.

"Where are we?" I asked him once I've got my head in the right place and myself back under control. "Where are the others?"

"I was a bit out of it when they brought us in, the good news is that we made it inside. The bad news is that they separated us into different holding cells. I think they're right next door to us though," Damon explained.

I could feel myself starting to spiral again, so I closed my eyes and breathed deeply to keep myself centred. Maybe the cage life had left more of a mark on me than I had thought.

"Okay, I'm okay," I said, moving out of Damon's arms and climbing to my feet.

He had managed to talk me down, but it didn't feel right sitting there with his arms around me. Damon was my friend. He had helped to save my life, I had no doubt about that, but he was never going to be anything more than a friend and I didn't think he even wanted to be. Damon had been my confidant, my friend, and he always would be.

"We've been in here about half an hour, so not long. I heard them talking about reporting it in," Damon explained, standing up and going over to where the door stood firmly locked closed.

While he pressed his head to the door, listening for anything outside, I checked out the room we were in. It was completely bare, the floor was cement and there was a drain in the middle which didn't bode too well for us. Apart from the door, there was only one tiny window at the top of one of the walls, which none of us were going to fit through. The only way in and out was through the door. Not that we could escape just yet, we hadn't done what we had come here to do yet.

CHAPTER 48

WYATT

They dragged Dom, Caleb and I into the cell next door to where they had dropped Lyra and Damon. My wolf was out of control and it was taking everything I had to keep him contained. It was a good job that I was only semi-conscious when they brought us in because I would not have been able to control him when they separated us.

Caleb had already come to and Dom was starting to stir on the ground where I had propped him up in the corner.

"Where's Lyra?" Dom said, suddenly coming to consciousness.

"She's in the cell next to us with Damon," Caleb told him, crouching down beside him to check on him. "She's fine, they threw us all in here and then left. Damon will look after her, he's done it before."

That sets my wolf on edge. He shouldn't have to look after her, she should be here with us, where we could do it. I fucking hated having to rely on someone outside of our bond to care for our mate.

Footsteps sounded off from down the hallway outside of our locked door and we all moved a few steps away from the door. When it swung open, six guards entered, all armed with swords and daggers. It seemed like these vampires didn't expect us to cause trouble though, because none of them are drawn. Four more appeared in the hallway outside of the door, holding Lyra and Damon between them.

"Come with us, our Captain is waiting for you. Cause any trouble and the woman dies first," he sneered.

That's why they don't expect us to cause any trouble because they thought they had us by the balls. I looked over his shoulder and met Lyra's gaze, she gave me a small shake of her head and a soft smile. Looked like we were going for a walk then. I supposed it made sense. We could hardly start a fight now when we aren't anywhere near close to finishing what we started. We came here for a reason and I'd be fucked if we left before we were done. Lyra's very life was riding on it.

I looked back at the guard who had spoken and was still smirking at me and just nodded in agreement. He turned around, without even bothering to say anything else and we just followed him out of the room, the other guards closing in around us.

What was this place? It was insane, they had nearly as many guards as we had for the entire pack before they were slaughtered by the demons. It just didn't make sense. Why build something like this in the middle of nowhere? And how did no one know that it was here? I know this is the Moon Side, but surely someone would have come across a heavily guarded facility and word would have got out somehow. This was one hell of a secret to be able to keep.

We didn't walk for long. We headed down the hallway, which was filled with doors. I had no doubt they led to the same type of rooms as the one we had just left. The guards surrounding us had managed to keep Lyra separated from us, but at least with her walking in front of me, I could see her. If they even made one move in her direction, I would tear them all to pieces, consequences be damned.

At the end of the hallway, we headed up a flight of stairs and came out in what must have once been a grand entryway. The floor was cracked and chipped, but it looked like it was once marble. The remnants of a broken chandelier hung crookedly above and a staircase spirals around the walls heading up to the other levels. We must be in the big derelict house we saw in the centre of the compound.

Over to the side, light shone out of a set of double doors and muffled voices floated out towards us. The guards didn't stop their pace and we walked inside where a man sat behind a large desk with a map rolled out in front of him. Another vampire stood next to him deep in discussion. They both stopped as soon as they saw us.

We were marched directly into the middle of the room and a swift blow to the back of our legs dropped us all to our knees in front of the desk.

"Welcome to The Farm," he gloated, spreading his arms wide as he stood and moved around the desk so he could stand over us. "My men tell me that you foolishly wanted to become guests here."

No one moved and no one said a thing. I'm not sure if he's waiting for a response from us, or what. Lyra and Damon looked confused, neither knew about Marcus and his seedy little journal. Caleb and Dom seemed to be schooling their expressions quite well. In fact, out of all of us, I'm probably the one that is going to give the game away. The fucking farm. We saw so many references to this place in the journal, but couldn't work out anything of its true purpose.

"Nothing to say? Such a shame. Well, The Farm is always in need of some fresh meat, so I am happy to welcome you here for your foreseeable future. As long or as short as that may be. There are very few rules here. Firstly, you will meet your quota. The other residents will fill you in on what that requires. Secondly, if you try to escape, I will choose one other resident at random and have them tortured and killed in front of you. Should you make a second attempt, then I shall select two, and so on."

He practically looked like he was ready to jump up and down, clapping in glee, the twisted fuck. My stomach dropped at the sound of the quota and what that could entail. It's also not too happy about what was going to happen when we escaped. Could we really sentence six other people to death once we're ready to get out of this place?

He turned to the guard who escorted us all here and informed him to allocate us to a bungalow and then sat back down at his desk effectively dismissing us. Is that it? Everyone clambered back up to their feet and we were escorted out of the office, through the front door and down the steps into the cold night air. They didn't seem to be paying all that much attention to us now and we formed a protective circle around Lyra as they led us to the nearest bungalow that still had lights on inside.

They don't bother to knock and just throw the door open. The people inside don't even seem surprised, just turned to look blankly at the door.

"Inside," the lead guard sneered, pushing Dom who was the closest towards the door.

We all filed inside, confused as all hell. I didn't turn my back on the guards, so I saw them leaving as the last one slammed the door closed.

Inside the bungalow it was silent and when I turned around about twenty people were standing staring at us. While everyone was shocked into silence, I took the chance to take stock of our situation. The bungalow looked like it had been set up like a dormitory of some kind, beds lined both sides of the walls and there looked to be a small rough dining area at the end, there were only a few chairs, definitely not enough to fit everyone here. The beds were old metal-framed, rusty in places. The mattresses look so thin that they seemed almost useless and there was only one sheet sitting crumpled on most of them. It was just one room, so wherever the bathroom was, it wasn't here. The bungalow itself looked to be made from rough-hewn wooden planks. It was barely held together and you could see through the walls in places. It must leak when it rains. How do they live like this? This place looked like it had been in operation for years judging by the state of it, how were they even surviving?

Looking at the people in front of us, I realised that they weren't. They're clearly suffering from the effects of starvation. Their bones stuck out through their skin, dark circles gathered under their eyes and they looked like they already had one foot in the grave. But even through all that they still looked fierce, suspicious of the strangers now standing in their midst.

"You're all fae," Dom breathed out in awe, taking a step closer to them. "How is this possible?"

The group in front of us seemed to brace, ready to fight, but I had no idea what was going on here. They silently stared at us as the tension in the room seemed to thicken. I'm pretty sure this was about to end in a fight rather than a discussion. Caleb subtly moved Lyra behind him. She's not looking good, she should have healed from where she took the blow that knocked her out, but I could still smell her blood on the air. We needed to get her to someplace safe so that we could check her over. If she wasn't healing, then she was fading quicker than we thought.

I braced, ready for whoever was going to come for us first, the wolf in me was itching to establish our dominance here, even if it was an impossible group of fae we were facing off against and not a pack of shifters.

A commotion started towards the back of the group and a male fae pushed through to the front. He looked far too thin and tired, just like the rest of them, but he seemed to still hold some strength in his body as he moved them all aside with a sense of urgency.

Gritting my teeth, I prepared for him to reach us, if I put him down quick and hard, perhaps the others would back off and realise they didn't stand a chance against us. They may outnumber us, but some of them barely looked like they could stand, let alone fight.

As he broke through the crowd, I could see the wild fury burning in his eyes.

"Back away from my mate," his voice boomed through the bungalow.

Caleb relaxed a little, a smile taking over his face, "Well, that was easier than we thought it would be," he grinned.

CHAPTER 49

LYRA

As I watched him push his way through the crowd in front of us, I immediately knew who he was. I'd felt this three times now and the feeling was as familiar to me as breathing now. This was my mate, my fourth. As I took in his condition and this place where he had been held, a wave of anger started to boil deep down inside of me. Who had dared to treat my mate like this? Who had done this to all of these people?

As he broke through the crowd of people, I peered around Caleb to take him in. He's wearing simple cotton trousers and a shirt. They look worn in places, but everyone else seems to be wearing something similar. He's too thin. I could tell that this was not his natural build. Whilst he'd retained some of his muscle mass, you could tell from around his face and his neck that he's suffering from starvation of some kind. His dark skin seemed like it was duller than it was supposed to be and even though his deep gold eyes glisten with fury, they seemed to lack the shine of life in them you normally saw in a person. But there was something about those gold eyes, about the way that he took me in. I wanted to go to him. I wanted to feel his arms around me. I could feel the connection between us, almost like it was a physical thing. Like it had a mind of its own. There was a faint stirring of my magic deep, deep down inside of me. It knew that the last connection is close, it knew that I was close to healing that broken bond left behind by the loss of my wings.

As he growled "back away from my mate," at my other mates, the overriding feeling washing over me is a giddy form of lust at his growly booming voice. I felt like I should be annoyed he was talking to my other mates like that, but at this very moment, I just didn't have it in me.

Caleb muttered something and then stepped away from in front of me and suddenly he's here standing right in front of me. I didn't even have to think twice as I walked into his arms and he dropped his head down, pressing his cheek firmly against the top of my head.

All of the people in the room seemed to burst into conversation, but a bubble of calm surrounded me and my new mate as we found solace in each other's arms. Wyatt, Caleb, Dom and even Damon all slowly moved around us, almost as if they thought they needed to guard us from the others in the room.

"You're bleeding," I heard his voice rumble, even though he didn't pull away.

"I was knocked out when we were brought here and my wound isn't healing," I mumbled, snuggling against his chest.

"What?" he suddenly shouted, pulling me away from his chest and looking for the injury on my head. This came with a lot of poking, which actually hurt, so I ended up batting his hands away from me with a hiss. It comes out more angry kitten than pissed off angel, which just made him laugh, but then try to find it again anyway.

CHAPTER 50

KIERAN

I couldn't believe it! My mate was here. I never wanted this life for her, but now that I had her in my arms, I couldn't ever imagine letting her go. It's clear from their protectiveness that these other men with her are her mates as well, but I could live with that. It's not unusual. I'm just lucky she found her way to me.

"Why isn't this healing?" I murmured, once I found the deep cut on the back of her head that was still oozing blood.

The way that she is hissing and fussing about it is just plain adorable. She's definitely a firecracker, that's for sure.

"That's part of the reason why we came to find you," the angry looking one said. "Is there somewhere we can go to talk?"

Looking around, I realised that everyone was still standing around us with varying looks of shock on their faces. We didn't get new people here. It had only happened once in the eighty-nine years since we came here and I'm not sure that counted anyway. It was hard not to be suspicious when they just walked in here out of the blue.

"There's an empty bungalow down the way that we can

use," I told them. "It's not in very good condition, but it will do for some privacy for now."

I made our excuses and herd the newcomers out of the bungalow, leading them down to the empty one. I didn't even know her name, but I couldn't seem to stop touching her. She didn't seem to mind though and seemed quite happy to snuggle up against my side. I didn't think I'd been this happy in a very long time, maybe even at all.

When we reached the abandoned bungalow, I lit a few lanterns and we pulled some chairs into a group in the middle. This had just turned into a storeroom for broken and unused furniture since it is no longer needed, but at least it gave us a space to talk.

Once we're all sat, an awkward silence seems to descend over us. My mate just looked around the group of us with wide eyes from her place on my lap where I put her. I was glad she hadn't tried to move away from me yet and the others seemed quite accepting over my need to keep her close.

She turned back to me and with a soft smile, and just said, "Hi."

She's got such a soft, beautiful voice and her blue eyes are sparkling in amusement, no doubt at how strange this situation really is.

"Hi, I'm Kieran," I said, for the purely selfish reason that I desperately wanted to know her name.

"Lyra," she told me and I could feel myself wanting to sigh in bliss at the sound of it.

The others chuckled while they watched us.

"Were we like that?" one of them asked no one in particular and I could see the grumpy one shoot him a scowl.

With a sigh one of them starts, "How about we get the introductions out of the way and then we can maybe start trying to explain a few things?" he suggested. "My name is

Dom and this is Wyatt and Caleb. I'm a mage while Caleb and Wyatt are both wolves."

It didn't escape my notice that he hadn't mentioned Lyra's species, but before I could ask her or any of them, he followed it up with a question I hadn't expected.

"I'm sorry, I'm still struggling with this part, how are all of you here? How did we not know about this many fae residing in the realm still?"

"We came here to pay the tithe," I explained, confused. Surely this should be well known with the realm. Our sacrifice should be written in history, or had the outside world really gotten that bad.

They all looked around themselves, seemingly confused.

"Forgive us, but we don't know what you mean? Perhaps if you could explain it, assume that we know nothing and start from the beginning," Dom suggested.

Okay, this seemed strange, but I supposed I can do this for them.

"The fae as a people had been fighting the Demon Wars for many years, with the assistance of the angels. I was part of an advance unit moving to the fields of Galvinae to obtain reconnaissance. We wanted a better picture of the layout of the land because we had plans for an all-out attack, a final push to win the war. We had three recon teams of twenty-eight moving in to support each other because of reports of demon activity in the area. One further team of eighteen of our elite fighters were providing backup. Once we reached the battle-field, there were no signs of any demons, but we found a contingency of angelic warriors. They told us they had infor-mation about a massive invasion force moving into the realm. They were pulling out their soldiers because the odds were impossible. King Haryk was discussing a withdrawal with them, but he was concerned about where the Fae would be safe."

I could see the looks of confusion on their faces, but I continued on with our history.

"The King was able to enter into negotiations through the angels for the Gods to open up a new realm for our people to seek safe harbour. It was a hard decision because we didn't want to abandon the rest of the inhabitants in the realm, but they explained they would do what they could do to assist them as well. The amount of magic needed to open and sustain the new realm was more than they had access to, so a tithe was needed. Those of us on the battlefield agreed to come here, to The Farm, to satisfy the tithe. Some died during the first week, the strain was too much for their bodies. But those of us remaining here have continued with the tithe to keep our people safe."

"That would mean that over a hundred fae came here," Caleb said in shock. "How many of you are still here?"

"Our numbers have reduced to seventy-nine. It has been hard to make up the tithe for the missing fae, but we have managed up until now."

They looked shocked, but I'm proud of what myself and my people had been able to accomplish here. It had been a great sacrifice, but knowing that we had kept our kin safe had made it all worthwhile. A lot of us left family behind and knowing that they were able to get somewhere safe was enough for us to weather any hardship that had come our way here.

"Who were the angels that conducted these negotiations for you?" Lyra asked with a frown.

I'm not sure what had upset her about my story. Perhaps she didn't understand just how much of an honour it was for us all to be here.

"I do not know their names, but I believe they were from the Archangel Council." This just seemed to concern her more. Perhaps the angels did not survive the war and that is why she is sad. "Tell me, what is it like in the outside realm? Did the other races survive the invasion force?"

Lyra looked to the other three and I would swear that the only emotion on her face was distress. I wrapped my arms tighter around her. Seeing those emotions on my mate's face was harder than I could imagine.

Dom's mouth had dropped open in shock. I could see him trying to form words and say something, but he seemed to be at a loss.

Eventually, Lyra turned back to me. "I'm so sorry to have to tell you this," she told me quietly. "but what you've just told us … that isn't what happened."

I laughed at first because I was there, and whilst the past nearly ninety years had been hard, I haven't exactly lost my mind. But when I looked around and saw that they all looked deadly serious, the only emotion that seemed to take hold of me was fear, but I had no reason why.

"The Battle of Galvinae did take place eighty-nine years ago," Dom started slowly. "The fae rode out into battle against the demon army that advanced into the realm. The angels didn't come in support and … they were nearly wiped out."

Lyra took hold of my hand and squeezed it, but I'm frozen in my seat and barely felt it. I didn't understand what they were trying to say to me.

"No, no … the battle didn't go ahead, we saved our people," I stuttered.

Lyra snuggled in closer to me and I squeezed her tightly to me. How was this happening?

"I don't understand … King Haryk was there … why would they do this to us?" My mind started to spin and I knew panic was starting to set in. "They're all gone," I whispered.

"No," Lyra said firmly, she took my face in both hands and turned me so that I'm looking her in the eye. "Some survived.

After the battle, they did leave the realm and went to Galvinae. Some are even back in this realm now. I met one, he's mated with our friend, part of our pack."

"How many are left?" I asked, needing to know, but also dreading the answer.

"I don't know," Dom said, looking at the others who just shrugged. "When we get back to the pack, we will find out together. We will find answers."

"This is so much to take in," I said, shaking my head. I could feel the tears collecting in my eyes, thinking of all of the people we left behind. Some here left their mates, their families. "How are we going to tell everyone this?"

We all sat silently, I clung to Lyra like the lifeline she was. How had my entire world just fallen apart in a matter of moments?

"We can tell them for you," Lyra offered quietly.

"You didn't tell me why you came here?" I realised.

Lyra looked nervously across at the others and this time Wyatt filled me in. "Lyra needs to establish all of her mate bonds. She's fading and the only thing that can stop it is by completing all of her bonds," he said sadly.

"That's why your head isn't healing," I realised, panic flaring through me again.

Lyra nodded and then winced from the movement. "I lost the connection with my magic and I was told that finalising my bonds was the only way to reconnect it."

"Lost ... how? Are you a mage ... I mean witch?" This was so confusing.

"I ... well I lost it when my wings were taken from me." Her face fell and as I started to put the pieces together, I felt the blood drain from my face. "I'm an angel," she whispered, confirming my very worst fears at that moment.

I leapt out of my seat and Lyra tumbled from my lap onto the floor. Caleb was there immediately, pulling her into his arms, as I scrambled away from her. Hadn't they taken enough from us? This was all just another trick.

I watched as the tears poured down her face at my rejection and even though every part of me wanted to go to her, to comfort her, I couldn't. How could I trust her? How were we ever supposed to trust an angel? Why would fate play this cruel trick on me?

Dom started to move towards me, holding his hands out in front of him like he was trying to calm a wild animal. Maybe he was, I felt pretty out of control right now.

"It's not what it sounds like. Lyra is only in her twenties, she wasn't alive back then. We didn't know anything about what happened to you until you just told us about it. She lost her wings because the angels physically tore them from her back. She isn't with them," he explained, trying to calm me down.

"Why would they do that?" I asked suspiciously.

"Because she met me," Wyatt said and I could hear his guilt shining through in his voice.

"No, wait, that isn't the entire truth and I want to be completely truthful with you, I don't want there to be any chance at a misunderstanding," Lyra said, from where she was safely held in Caleb's arms.

It didn't escape my notice that the other two had moved in front of them, putting themselves between me and her. To protect her? They thought that they needed to protect her from me. And that was the slap in the face that I needed. They thought I was going to hurt her. She was my mate. I could feel that deep down in my very soul. Did it matter that she was an angel? It did at first, but looking at her now, with the tears streaming down her cheeks from my rejection, it seemed like the least important thing in the world.

"Let me explain," she said quickly, no doubt mistaking my silence for further rejection. "Wyatt is right that once they learnt my mate was a wolf, I would have had to fall to be with him. If they even allowed it. Before I had the chance to make any decision, an angel from another flight reported me for visiting the realm. It was forbidden, and the archangel council took it as evidence that I was corrupted. If they determined that I was corrupted, they would have wiped out my entire flight for fear that corruption had spread. To keep it contained. I chose to fall to save them. I would have done it eventually anyway. It was an inevitability. I just hadn't had the time to make any plans with Wyatt before it happened."

"Finding you like that ... Lyra I don't know if I would have ever been able to agree with you going through that," Wyatt's eyes glistened and she was immediately there to comfort him.

"It's done now, if Aurel and Samuel hadn't stepped forward and done what they did, it could have been much worse. Some angels do not survive the process," she murmured to him.

"You're telling me that cocky fuck did that to you," Wyatt fumed, straightening up with fury burning in his eyes. "When I see him again ..."

"Now, now, as the lady said, I did her a favour," came a voice from the corner of the bungalow making us all spin around to see who had been able to listen in without us realising they were there.

Suddenly in Wyatt's place there stood a golden snarling wolf who leapt at the owner of the voice as he stepped out of the shadows. An angel, and given the previous discussion, I was guessing either Aurel or Samuel.

Just as Wyatt's wolf seemed about to make contact with the angel, he just batted him out of the air. Wyatt sailed across the bungalow and slammed into the wall. There was a crack that I was praying for his sake was just splintering wood and he dropped to the floor, unconscious.

"Now before any of the rest of you get any ideas, I am just

here to talk," he sighed. "I always seem to find you in the most interesting of places, dear Lyra," he laughed, before walking over and arranging himself in one of the seats with his wings draping over the sides.

Lyra looked over at Wyatt in concern, but Caleb was holding her so tightly that she couldn't go to him. Dom and the quiet vampire seemed to be standing between the two angels ready to face off with their new one and that only left me. I rushed over to Wyatt, confused about why I feel so concerned about him, but just going with it. Tonight has been a night of far too many revelations and I felt like we hadn't reached the end of them yet.

Wyatt shifted back to human as I reached him and I could see that he was starting to come around, kneeling beside him, I ran my hands across his head, checking for injuries, but he didn't seem to be bleeding. When I finished checking him over, he had come round enough that I found him staring up at me from the ground.

"How are you feeling?" I asked him, realising that maybe me running my hands all over him may not exactly be what he wanted to wake up to.

"Fine," he said quietly. Sitting up, he winced a bit, "Okay, maybe I've been better," he laughed.

His eyes found Aurel sitting with the others and a low growl started in his chest.

"I think we need to hear him out," I told him quietly. "I need answers before I have to tell my people ... everything."

Wyatt's eyes locked with mine and I felt like he could see inside me with his determined gaze. Suddenly he just nodded and was then climbing to his feet, with a little of my assistance. We joined the others over by the chairs and Wyatt sat down slowly, growling softly. All his display of aggression did was make the other angel smirk at him. I had a feeling this situation could very easily escalate and from the smirk on this angel's face and what I had just learnt he had done to Lyra, I'm not sure if it was going to be Wyatt, or me that was going to snap first.

"You have found your fourth then," Aurel said, addressing Lyra.

"Yes, why are you here?" she asked, getting straight to the point.

"We had information that the Council was hiding something here and Samuel sent me here to find out. Imagine my surprise when I saw them escorting you inside."

"Do you know what this place is?" she asked him through gritted teeth.

I was quickly reassessing the situation, perhaps it would be Lyra that snapped first.

"Yes, do you?" An emotion flicked through his eyes that I couldn't quite place. It almost seemed like fear, but I had no idea what it was he could possibly be afraid of.

"They call it The Farm, but we haven't exactly got around to discussing it's exact purpose yet."

"Hmmm, that is quite an apt name, I suppose," Aurel said, looking at me like I was some kind of specimen to be examined. "They collect a tithe from you, yes? Have you explained that part to them yet?"

I shook my head and the others looked at me curiously.

"What is a tithe?" Caleb asked, his face scrunching up in confusion.

"Historically it was an offering to the gods, people would give them a tenth of their income or produce," Dom said, cocking his head to the side. "But I don't see how that equates to this situation. They call this The Farm, but you don't seem to farm anything, or at least that we could see."

Aurel threw his head back in laughter at the confusion on the others' faces.

"They aren't the farmers," he said, suddenly sobering. "They are the cattle."

Lyra turned to me with a look of absolute horror, the others didn't look much different. Strangely, the most overwhelming emotion that I felt was shame. We had all been so proud of the sacrifice we were making, of what we were doing for our people, for our families. But it was all a lie.

"How do you pay the tithe?" Lyra asked quietly.

"Blood. They collect our blood and harvest our magic from it."

"But ... why?" Lyra asked, turning back to Aurel.

He just shrugged. "I don't know. I can tell you what they're not doing with it," he said grimly. "Saving your people. There is no requirement for magic to sustain the realm that the fae are in. It isn't even an individual realm, it's part of the world tree. It was always there."

Wyatt had watched me in concern throughout this, not moving his eyes away once. "We can get into this more once we get everyone out of here," Wyatt said, finally moving his eyes away from me and glaring across at Aurel. "Can we count on you for any kind of help at all?" he sneered.

The angel just grinned, he clearly didn't find this wolf intimidating at all.

"I can maybe arrange you a portal that will get you all out of here, which is more than your mage here can do," he said slowly.

"But?" Lyra asked him and even I could hear the annoyance in her voice.

"Nothing in life comes for free, Lyra," he smirked at her. "You know what I want."

Is this fucker trying to blackmail my mate?

"We don't need him, we can get out without him," I blurted out, even though I had no idea why I said it. I had absolutely no idea how we would get over eighty people out of here and then to somewhere safe. Most of the fae here were too weak to fight.

"Don't listen to him, he's clearly delirious," Aurel laughed. "We are your people, Lyra, and we need you," he whispered, suddenly sounding completely broken, his cocky exterior finally breaking.

Then I heard the last sound I needed to hear right now. Fucking hell! Why do bad situations seem to just go from bad to worse?

The faint cackling laughter seemed to run through the room and surprisingly, the only person who seemed surprised by it was Aurel, as his head whipped around to see who was also in here.

In the blink of an eye, she dashed across the room and with a flying leap, landed sitting in Aurel's lap, with her arms around his neck.

"Silly angel," she laughed, pulling out a ladle and hitting him on top of the head with it.

"Ow, fuck ... what ..." Aurel stuttered, staring at the old woman currently sitting in his lap.

"Frannie, come here, sweetheart, he's not someone that you want to mess around with," I said, trying to coax her over to me.

"Frannie?" Wyatt said, looking shocked, "How in the hell did you get here?"

"Wait, do you know Frannie?" I asked, looking around the group of people in front of me with renewed suspicion.

"Of course, we know Frannie, she's part of our pack," Wyatt grumbled. "Has a tendency to wander off and cause havoc everywhere she goes," he said under his breath.

Frannie cackled in glee and smacked a big sloppy kiss on Aurel's cheek, much to his disgust. The rest of us were just trying to hold in the laughter at this massive angel suddenly finding himself pinned under a tiny old lady and not knowing what to do about it.

"How do you know Frannie?" Lyra asked with a smile on her face, it was kind of hard to not smile when Frannie was around. She had a way of making any situation seem lighter than it was.

"She just turns up every so often. I think the first time we saw her was about five years ago, a sickness ran through the camp and she just showed up and made a massive batch of some kind of herbal tea that cured everyone. Now she just seems to show up every now and then, almost like she's checking in on us. Sometimes she brings food or medicine for us," I explained, smiling at Frannie who has turned her attention to me.

Some of the fae didn't like being around her. She's clearly as mad as a badger in a box and no one knew quite how she got that way. But there was something about her that I found strangely calming. We all owe her our lives, at least once over. She'd done so much for us over the years.

"You didn't think to tell us about a massive camp of fae that needed our help, Frannie?" Wyatt asked her, more than a little annoyed.

Frannie jumped up out of Aurel's lap, much to his relief and walked over to Wyatt, smacking him on the head with the ladle. "Not the time yet," she muttered, before turning around and presenting me with the ladle with a flourish. Ours actually broke last week and this was obviously the latest in her long line of gifts.

"Okay," Dom said, shaking his head as if in confusion. "Okay, let's just address getting out of here for now and we can deal with everything else back at the packhouse."

"Frannie," Dom said, lowering his tone to a more gentle level and catching her attention, "do you know how to get us out of here?" he asked her.

Frannie just nodded her head and started skipping around the group, before she dropped down onto the lap of the vampire who had stayed quiet up to now. "New friend," she said, stroking the side of his face. To give him his due he just grinned in amusement at her and I realised that he was maybe not all that bad. There was something about him though. I didn't feel like there was a sense of kinship there, but he clearly seemed to care for Lyra a lot.

"Frannie," Dom snapped a little and she slowly turned her head to look at him, rolling her eyes. "How do we get out of here?" Dom asked her a little more patiently this time, but I could see how much it was costing him.

"Grumpy angel," she said like it was obvious and was annoyed that we would even be asking her again.

Aurel sat back in his chair and smirked. Fucker knows that he's our only option and he knows that Lyra isn't going to have a choice, but to agree to his terms.

"You heard the lady, I'm your ticket out of here and you know what I need you to do in exchange."

Frannie leapt out of Damon's laps and threw her hands in the air with a huff of exasperation. Stomping over to me, she held out one hand, wiggling her fingers in a gimme gesture. With a shrug, I just passed her back the ladle with a smirk of my own, but it was obvious what was about to come. Storming back over to Aurel, Frannie set in on him.

"Bad angel, bad angel," she grumbled, reinforcing each word with a smack of her ladle.

The rest of us in the room just laughed, because watching this little old lady take a ladle to Aurel is possibly the funniest thing I think I had ever seen and everyone else seemed to agree.

"Enough!" Aurel roared, grabbing hold of Frannie's arms and holding her still on the spot. "If you hit me one more time with that fucking ladle I'll …" but then his words trailed off as he locked eyes with her and they both stood frozen, staring into each other's eyes.

Everyone looked around in confusion, Wyatt was frozen halfway out of his seat, having jumped up as Aurel grabbed hold of her.

"My apologies Madame Kitsune," Aurel said, after a few moments, gently letting go of Frannie and sitting back in his seat, "I did not realise who you were."

We all just sat and watched Frannie stare him down. It's the most cognizant I've seen her. Eventually, she just nodded and turned away, she passed me back the ladle and then slipped out the door of the cabin without a word.

"I will take my leave too. I should have arrangements for the portal within the next few hours. You're going to need to spread the word around the other fae and gather them somewhere, here preferably," he stepped back into the shadows and then he was just gone.

Lyra stood up and opened her mouth to speak, but suddenly her eyes rolled back in her head and she collapsed. We all moved as one to catch her, but Caleb reached her first, taking her into his arms and gently lowered her to the ground. Dom was immediately at their side checking her over.

"What's wrong with her?" I asked, watching Dom carefully examine her.

My need to pull her into my arms was strong, I couldn't believe I pushed her away earlier, that it even crossed my mind that this wasn't right. She's my mate. My other half.

"She's fading faster," Dom murmured, almost to himself. "her head is still bleeding, it's not healing at all."

"We need to get her out of here and back to the pack-house," Caleb said, clinging tighter to her. "They need to bond."

I looked around the group of them in shock. Yes, I needed to bond with my mate, but not like this. She was ill, it shouldn't be like this. We should have the time to get to know each other, to cherish each other. Bonding was a beautiful sacred thing. This didn't feel right, it felt like I was going to be taking advantage of her.

"I can see what you're thinking," Wyatt said gently, as he braced a hand on my shoulder. I tore my gaze away from my mate and met his eyes and I could see the same sorrow and desperation there that I was feeling myself. "She's dying, Kieran, and you are the only one who can save her. I know that this isn't the way you saw yourself bonding with your mate, but you have a lifetime together to make up for that."

I nodded because what else could I really do? I couldn't let her fade away and die. I couldn't lose her, not now that she was here with me. Not now that I know, she's meant for me.

CHAPTER 51

WYATT

Lyra was still out cold in Caleb's arms by the time that Kieran had spread the news through the fae in the camp. Some of them had been reluctant to believe a word of what we were saying, the rest I think had been here so long they would believe anything if it meant that they could leave.

Eighty-nine years! How any of them had retained their sanity for that long was a complete miracle. When had this world turned into such a shit show of manipulators and liars? Virion was not going to take this well. Finding out that your father had conspired with the angels, at the very least, and let them do this to so many of his people. And why the fuck he let them all ride into that fight afterwards? I couldn't figure it out. What did he have to gain from nearly wiping out his entire people? This was insanity.

The plan was simple, so it was obviously going to go wrong. When did anything seem to go right for us nowadays? At least we had found Kieran. That much at least had gone right. Now we just needed Lyra to wake up and for them to make the final bond. Then at least we could stop worrying about the speed of her fading. We would only have to deal with those that were trying to take her from us afterwards.

Damon, Dom and Kieran had moved out to the three inhabited bungalows. The plan was that we would be bringing the three groups to the portal, under the pretence of everyone going to breakfast. The guards were apparently quite hands-off apart from guarding the outer fence. Unless it was tithe collection day and guess what day it was today?

Caleb and I were waiting in the empty bungalow, guarding Lyra, while we waited for Aurel to come back. We had to get this going before the guards came in, but we were missing one fucking dick of an angel and the portal that he promised us. If he didn't come through on this, I was going to kick his ass. I was going to rip him apart piece by piece and my wolf was going to ...

"What's got your knickers in a twist?" the angel in question asked as he strolled out of the darkened corner. The fact that he could do that was starting to piss me off as well. "What happened?" he suddenly asked when he caught sight of Lyra. For a second, I could have sworn that panic flashed through his eyes.

"She needs to complete the final bond, the wound on her head isn't healing and we need to get her back to the pack-house now to treat it," I snapped at him.

I could maybe accept the fact that my mate was unconscious in my packmate's arms might be making me a bit irritable right now. Did I care? Absolutely not.

Aurel waved his arm and a portal roared into existence behind him. "Take her through now, take her first."

We didn't need to be told twice. Caleb gathered Lyra up in his arms and with a nod from me, he was sprinting through the portal. I sighed in relief, but I had already seen the immediate problem that we had. The portal was massive, we should have known that it would be. It had so much magic pumping through it, that it roared its presence into the world. Why hadn't we considered this? There was no way they wouldn't know this was here. There would be no sneaking the fae through this portal as we tried to make some kind of faux breakfast. They needed to evacuate and they needed to do it now. This was no longer about stealth, it was a race.

I locked eyes with Aurel, who gave me his signature smirk, "They should probably move a bit faster, don't you think?"

What I wanted to do was find out what it would feel like to pulverise his nose with my fist. What I actually did, was turn and sprint out of the bungalow as fast as I could. I needed to get the fae moving and I needed to buy them enough time to get through the portal.

As I stepped outside into the gloom that was morning on the Moon Side, I was hit with the relieving sight of the fae already starting to pour out of the bungalows and flood towards the portal. The problem was they weren't moving fast enough. The guard had already realised something was happening and the race was on to intercept them. Some of the fae were obviously suffering, they were malnourished, some of them looked ill, they were too weak to make it. And the vampires knew it. They weren't going to make it. We weren't going to be able to save them all.

I shifted as I ran. We needed to delay the vampires as long as we could, to give the fae at least a chance. Damon swerved off his path to join me and Dom came to a halt, pulling his magic and preparing to fight. Kieran tried to join us, but Dom screamed at him to get the others through the portal and he reluctantly started herding them faster towards it. We had twelve guards racing towards us and three of us facing them down. The odds were definitely not in our favour.

One particular group of fae had fallen behind and I could hear Kieran arguing with them, but I couldn't make out the words because I'm solely focused on the three vampires closing in on me. They've obviously been trained and have spread themselves across the field, engaging each of us in groups. They don't need to take us one on one, they outnumber us enough to be able to swarm the three of us standing against them.

I darted forward, as fast as my paws could take me. I knew the only way to survive this was to even the odds as quickly as possible. That meant going in quick and coming out bloody. I ran straight at the vampire in the middle of the three. I saw his eyes flash in excitement and I knew they were entering into a feeding frenzy. They were part demon and part beast and their prey, the fae, ran from them. If they managed to contain them in The Farm, it wouldn't be without cost.

At the last second, I darted to the side and leapt at the vampire on the left who thought he was going to circle around to where my back was exposed. He didn't even have time to scream as my jaws clamped around his throat and the meaty sound of a rip filled the air. His cold blood filled my mouth and as much as I wanted to gag on it, I knew I didn't have time. I didn't ride his body down to the ground, I knew that he was dead even if his brain was taking a moment to realise it. Bracing my paws on his chest, I used him as a springboard and leapt at the vampire who had been in the middle. Unfortunately, he had enough time to bring his arm up in defence and I missed my mark on his throat and locked my jaws around his forearm instead. The other vampire, who was trying to circle in the opposite direction, wrapped his arms around me, but I had just enough time to lock my jaw before he tore me away, taking most of my current victim's forearm with me. He let out an almighty screech, dropping to the ground, cradling his arm against his chest as he tried to crawl backwards away from me and the vampire that was trying to wrestle me to the ground. I had to give him his due, he's locked his arms around me and he isn't letting go. He's kind of got himself in a bit of a bind really, as soon as he lets go, I'm going to tear his throat out, but he couldn't do anything without loosening his arms first. It's a rookie mistake. He should have thrown me clear, rather than following me down to the ground. Maybe these guards aren't as well trained as we all thought they were.

I quickly glanced around to see how the others were faring. Dom seemed to have one down and three circling him. Damon unfortunately still had five guards circling him, but he was either holding his own, or they are playing with him.

The vampire that was trying to pin me finally loosened his grip to try and get a better hold and I managed to roll onto my back. Bringing up my back legs, I raked my claws straight through his abdomen and felt his flesh yield above me. It was enough for him to loosen his grip more in reflex and that was all I needed to clamp my jaws around his throat and tear it out. I'm doing him a favour really; his guts are already spilling out of him and it's better to go this way than the slow bleed out he had on the horizon as he tried to hold his insides in the right place.

I scrambled back up to my paws intending to help Damon. Dom looked like he was about to take another down and Damon is fighting worse odds. It's actually pretty impressive that he'd got this far considering. As I staggered towards him, I saw the group of older fae that Kieran was arguing with approaching us. They could barely stay on their feet; they'd be slaughtered if they got involved in this.

Kieran was hanging back and once I got a look at his face, I knew something terrible was about to happen. Then everything just seemed to happen in slow motion. One of the older fae locked his eyes with me and shouted for me to run for the portal. I'm confused with why he's telling me to run, until he smiled softly at me and I saw the glint of the blade in his hand. He roughly swiped the blade across his chest and the thin shirt that he was wearing quickly saturated with blood. The other four mirrored his movements, slashing into their own bodies quickly and fiercely and then I realised what was about to happen. Damon was suddenly beside me, screaming for me to run and Dom was sprinting towards us. I couldn't take my eyes away from the fae man as he turned his face towards the crowd of remaining vampires still left alive.

They swarmed over the fae, tearing into their bodies. It was a feeding frenzy and they weren't gentle about it. Chunks of flesh were torn free as they all tried to sink their fangs into the nearest bleeding fae. It took a moment, but they inevitably surrendered to the pain and the screaming began.

Dom and Damon were forcing me to move, pushing me towards the bungalow, but no part of me wanted to leave these people behind. Logically, I knew they were gone. I knew that they'd sacrificed themselves to give the rest of us the chance to get away. That they'd given their lives willingly to save us, but I still didn't want to leave them to die here alone. They didn't deserve to die in this fucking shithole.

"Get a hold of yourself," Dom screamed at me, as he grabbed me by the scruff of the neck and hauled me through the door to the bungalow.

The last few fae were slipping through the portal and Aurel was standing there with the same fucking smirk on his face.

"You look like you've been busy," he laughed as he stepped through the portal.

The screaming had finally stopped outside and it was only a matter of time before the vampires came back to their senses and came to find us. Kieran followed us inside and slammed the door shut. We all took a moment to just stop, before we moved through the portal and left the Moon Side, hopefully for the last time, behind us.

As my paws hit the soft grass outside of the packhouse, my gaze zeroed in on Aurel. I'm just about to launch myself at him when the fucker just laughed and flew away. I really fucking hate that guy. It was only when the screams started coming from Damon that I was pulled out of my anger filled haze. Fuck! The sun shone brightly down on us, as we stood on the grass outside of the packhouse. Damon had dropped to his knees, screeching in agony, as his skin started to smoke. Before any of us even had a chance to flinch, let alone run to his aid, Aria was there, wings stretched wide, swooping down from the sky. She barreled into him at top speed and hurled him into the shade of the house where the sun couldn't reach him. Dom was by his side immediately, but none of us knew how to treat this. He stopped screaming, but he was lying so still on the ground that it had the fae around us whimpering in distress. This was one of the men that helped save them and now he'd been taken down so easily by something as simple as the sun.

Lyra stumbled out of the house with Caleb at her side and we could see just how much it was taking out of her to do it. I caught her in my arms as she moved towards us, she was exhausted and she was weak, but she was determined to reach Damon.

"He needs my blood," she whispered weakly.

I reared back like she had slapped me. Not only did I not want any fucker sinking his teeth into her, but she was too weak to be able to do this. She must see the look in my eyes because she runs her hand across my cheek and smiled.

"I need to do this, Wyatt. He saved me, now it's my turn. My blood will let him walk in the sun. We'll set up a better system for next time, but we have to do this now and he can't afford to wait," she told me.

I knew that she was right, I knew exactly how much I owed him because I'm holding her in my arms right now. That didn't mean that I liked this though.

"I know," I told her, letting her go.

Kyle and the rest of Aria's mates had all run out of the house and Virion was looking around the fae in shock.

Resting one hand on my shoulder Kyle came up beside me. "I've got you if you need me," he told me and I nodded, because I knew I'm definitely going to need him for this.

Sykes came to my other side and I could feel Caleb at my back.

My wolf was pacing in my mind, he knew what was coming and he was not fucking happy about it. Taking a deep breath, I closed my eyes and tried to centre myself, reaching out to my wolf with my mind to try and gently calm him, without letting him force his way through to trigger my shift. The fact that he couldn't see Lyra right now was pissing him off even more, but I knew that I wouldn't be able to contain him if he saw Damon bite into Lyra. I didn't want to be the rabid wolf that needed Kyle to hold him back.

When Kyle's hand gripped me tighter, I knew that it's happening and the low growl coming from Caleb behind me is all the confirmation that my wolf needs as he starts to slam into the edges of my mind, demanding to be released. He doesn't understand the necessity of this. He just runs on pure instinct and his only instinct right now is to protect his mate and he thinks that I am failing in that.

I didn't even realise that a single tear had tracked its way down my cheek until I felt Lyra's soft hand brush it away. Her sweet scent fills my mind as I breathe her in deep.

"It's all over now," she told me softly, leaning into my body as she does.

As I wrapped her in my arms, the others let me go, leaving me to seek my solace in my mate. I almost daren't open my eyes for fear of what I was going to see. My wolf calmed instantly at her touch and I didn't feel like I was at risk of shifting again. It's embarrassing to have such little control, but his half rabid nature from the loss of her is going to take time to resolve.

"What happened?" Kyle asked, finally pulling me back to reality.

Virion is standing in front of us with awe and confusion on his face. I couldn't blame him, we just pulled over seventy fae out of nowhere and dropped them into his lap. The information bomb that Kieran dropped on us back at The Farm replays through my mind. I did not want to be the one that told them about this.

"We found him, we found the fourth," I said, spinning around, the sudden panic of Kieran being missing hit me. I'm jumpy as fuck right now and I'm not proud of it. When I finally found him reassuring a group of fae, my mind settled. "We found him at The Farm."

I knew I wasn't making any sense right now, but if I'm honest, I just didn't know if I'd got the balls to be the one to explain it all. I clutched Lyra tightly in my arms and she wrapped her own around my waist. I could see Dom getting ready to explain for me, but I am the Alpha in our pack and it's time for me to step up and take on that responsibility. None of them should have to take on the responsibility of doing this. None of them should have to tell Virion exactly what his father did to betray his own people. Kieran must see that something is happening with us and he comes over to join us. He must be starting to feel the pack bond between us and it must be confusing for him because it's not something that the fae normally experience.

"Let's take this inside, the pack will take care of them. We should discuss this privately," Kyle said, turning to Virion and wrapping an arm around his shoulders.

He pulled him in close and whispered into his ear. I couldn't get past the shocked look on Virion's face. He knew it was coming. He knew just from my hesitation that this wasn't something he wanted to hear. Kyle pulled his head down so that his forehead rested against his own and I watched as Virion's eyes fluttered closed. Whatever Kyle was telling him worked, because a moment later he nodded and we all headed into the house. Several of the pack were already moving between the fae, giving out blankets and making sure that no one was injured. How are we ever going to get to the bottom of all of this mess?

We go to follow them into the house before I stop. "Damon?" I suddenly remembered.

"Aria and Sykes have taken him inside to rest, the

y're going to meet us in the library," Kyle told me as he strode away with the others.We've settled in around the library and Lyra has cuddled up in Kieran's lap much to his initial shock. She is trying to stay awake, but the way that he's stroking her hair and holding her close is a losing battle for her.

By the time that Aria and Sykes make it down to the library to join us, Virion looks like he's about to either pass out or throw up. I know how he feels, because before Aria even has the opportunity to sit down, I just blurt it out, unable to hold it in any more.

"The Farm was a prison camp for fae, they've held them there for eighty-nine years, collecting their blood and harvesting their magic."

Virion's mouth dropped open in shock and I could see the questions forming in his eyes.

"Your father made a deal with the angels, before the final fight," I blurted out again. It's like I'd got the verbal shits, I just couldn't hold it inside. But now that it was out, I felt a massive weight lifting off my chest.

"What do you mean he made a deal?" Virion asked and I could see the denial forming in his eyes.

Thankfully Kieran jumped in with an explanation. "The angels told him that if we went to The Farm and continued to satisfy the tithe, they would be able to arrange for a safe realm for the fae to take harbour in before the demons sent an invasion force."

"That is how he arranged for Galvinae to be made?" Virion asked, with a look ranging between panic and confusion.

"No, that was the lie he told to your people when he traded them in to have the magic drained from their blood and then lead the rest of them to their slaughter on the battlefield, even though he knew that no one was going to ride in and help them," I spat out and instantly regretted it. "I'm sorry, I'm sorry. It's just ... if you had seen that place ..."

"I understand Wyatt," Virion said stiffly, before turning to Kieran. "I just find it hard to believe that he would have led my mother, his mate, into a battle that he knew they couldn't possibly win. That he knew would lead to nothing but death." Hello denial, my name is Virion.

"He didn't," Kieran said, looking confused. When he saw us all staring at him in question, he answered slowly with a look on his face that I'm sure I had only moments ago. "She was with us," he said slowly.

Virion's face broke into shining hope, but I could see how uncomfortable Kieran looked and I didn't need him to say anything to know what it is he's dreading to say.

"No," I said firmly to Virion, to draw his attention, to save my new packmate from having to do this himself. "She wasn't there anymore. She's gone, Virion, she didn't make it."

His face cracked and his pain was there for all to see. I felt like the worst person in the world, to have given him that glimmer of hope and then to tear it away from him again. Aria was immediately by his side, pulling him into her arms. He didn't cry or speak, he just leant into her, seeking whatever comfort he could get. No one spoke, no one wanted to interrupt. This wasn't a time for us to intercede, we shouldn't even be here, we shouldn't be intruding on this moment.

Kyle dropped to his knees in front of Virion and wrapped an arm around his shoulders, pulling both Aria and Virion into his arms. Something had changed between them. Something was definitely different. I could hear him murmuring words of comfort to him and it just got really fucking uncomfortable in here.

Turning to Lyra, to at least try and give them the illusion of privacy, I saw that she had finally fallen asleep in Kieran's arms. He looked all kinds of torn up and I know he wished that she was awake right now. She needed sleep though. This was the worst I'd seen her. He's staring down at her like she's the most precious thing in the world and he'd be right. Some days I still couldn't believe that she was actually real, so I knew exactly how he felt.

"She's weakening," he murmured to me, trying not to wake her.

"I know."

"It doesn't feel right to bond with her when she is like this, it feels like I'm taking advantage or something."

"I know."

He looked at me with such pain in his eyes, I know how he felt because I felt exactly the same.

"But if you don't do this, then she dies," I told him simply.

He just nodded and turned back to stare at her.

When I gathered up enough balls to look back at Virion, he pulled himself back together. Aria was sitting on his lap and Kyle had taken the seat she was sitting in before, one arm draped along the back of the sofa behind him.

"Right, let's just get a few things straight before we start heaping more piles of shit on this situation, shall we?" Kyle sighed.

I feel for him right now. This was really not the time to have to take on an alpha role.

"The Farm was set up to harvest magic directly from the fae?" I'm not exactly sure who he is asking the question to, so I just nodded in agreement.

"Virion's father traded his people in exchange for Galvinae being built?"

"No," Dom interrupted. "We have learnt that isn't the case. The realm already existed, or so Aurel said."

"Safe passage then?" he asked.

"Maybe, I don't think we can ever really know without asking him," I said, glancing at Virion who was just staring blankly into space at this point. I couldn't blame him. I think my mind would have checked out for a bit if I was him as well.

"But why still go to the battle then? If he already bargained for Galvinae and he knew that the angels weren't going to turn up, why go when he knew they would just be slaughtered?" Kyle asked, frowning.

Virion flinched at the question and Kyle's hand gripped his shoulder in support.

"Again, we have no way of knowing without asking him," I shrugged.

All we had here were questions. We didn't have any answers.

"Can you tell me what happened to my mother?" Virion whispered, but he might as well have screamed it for how quiet the library fell after.

Kieran's face filled with a sad kind of respect and he nodded. "It was the third winter that we had been there. A sickness ran through the camp. We think that it was a side effect of the magic drain. We'd already lost about ten fae the night before. Everyone was ill, we couldn't keep up with it. As soon as one person seemed to be coming through it, three more looked like they were knocking at death's door. The tithe came up due and everyone was so weak. We didn't know that she was going to do it, she didn't tell anyone," Kieran's head fell and he couldn't look Virion in the eye. "They drained her dry, she gave them everything and they still came knocking, because it wasn't enough to satisfy the tithe. But she saved so many lives, so many were spared from the tithe that week and had the chance to regain some strength. We lost five more to the sickness, but I know it would have been so many more if it hadn't been for her sacrifice."

Tears poured down Virion's face as he learned about the death of his mother. About the quiet sacrifice, she made to save her people. She was a far better person than her husband, a far better person than most people in the world. It wasn't fair that she left him and he was left with only his traitorous father. Even if there was a reason for whatever deal he made, it could never be good enough to sacrifice all of those people. The fae were nearly wiped out. It made no sense at all.

"We need to discuss what happens next," Dom said awkwardly. "We've pissed off the vampires by taking Lyra and now we've liberated The Farm as well. They are going to be coming for us and now we have some of the last remaining fae sheltering here. We need a plan."

"How much time do you think we have?" Kyle asked, suddenly all business.

"I think we can safely assume they don't have any of Lyra's blood stockpiled from her description of her time there, but we can check with Damon when he is conscious to make sure. Tonight, probably more like tomorrow night, if you factor in getting word back to the clan house and mobilising everyone. That's assuming they have the capability to portal travel and do it directly from the Moon Side."

Sometimes I forgot how smart Dom is.

"We've got ten hours until sunset. You need to rest up and we'll start making plans. We'll fill you in later," Kyle said and I can't say I'm feeling bad about being dismissed right now. "How is Lyra doing?" he asked gently, his eyes fixed on her.

"Not good," I whispered, looking at her peaceful, sleeping face.

"She's going to get better now though, right?" Liam asked and I'm surprised when I tear my gaze away from her and see that everyone in the room is looking anxious right now.

I didn't want to say anything, we all knew that Lyra needed to bond with Kieran if she was going to get any better, or at least that is what we assumed was going to happen. But I didn't want to put any pressure on Kieran. I couldn't imagine how he must be feeling about all of this right now. Finding and bonding with your mate was supposed to be the most memorable experience of your life and I felt like we were taking something precious from him right now.

"Let's go up to bed and get some rest. Nothing is going to happen but sleep for a while," I said to everyone, but more to Kieran. I may have only just met him, but my wolf and I knew that he was pack. He was ours now, and it's our duty to care for him as well.

CHAPTER 52

LYRA

I woke with a start, my brain was still trying to push images into my head of Damon lying dying on the ground, screaming in agony, as the sun burned away his flesh. I realised it was a dream, but my heart was pounding and I could feel the adrenaline surging through my body.

Fingers started running through my hair and I relaxed back down into the bed against whoever it was that was spooning me from behind.

"It's just a dream," I heard Kieran murmur behind me.

A small part of my brain wondered why I wasn't finding it strange waking up in bed with a practical stranger, but I already knew why. Kieran was not a stranger to me. It didn't matter that we only just met, that we didn't know anything about each other. He was my mate and I could already feel him inside my heart.

"I never dreamt I would be able to have this," he whispered quietly, as his arms wrapped tightly around me.

I knew how he felt. I knew what it was like to be imprisoned, even if at the time he didn't realise completely what was happening.

I pulled one of his hands away from me so that I could watch myself link my fingers through his. He gripped me tightly, almost like he's afraid I'm just going to slip away.

"I know what it is like to live in a cage, to have your freedom taken away from you, how it feels to suddenly be free, but terrified that it's going to be ripped away from you. No one is taking this from you, you are here with us and no one will ever take you away from us," I reassured him.

His arms wrapped tighter around me and I felt him bury his face into my hair. His arms were shaking and his chest stuttered behind me and I knew he was crying. He's got eighty-nine years of betrayal to let out of him and I clung to him as best as I could while he worked his way through it. I couldn't even imagine how he felt about what his king had done. They must have had loved ones, a family that they left behind believing that they would be safe. Most of them would be gone now. Hardly any of the fae survived. It's only then that I realised that Kieran may be grieving more than just the loss of his own freedom.

We stayed like that for as long as he needed, clinging to each other, not daring to let go. As his grip loosened on me, I turned in his arms, so I was facing him. Running one hand down his cheek, I wiped his tears away with my thumb and he pressed his face against my palm. I could feel the bond between us, it was just a shadow of what it would be when it was finally completed, but it was there and it was insistent on what it needed from us.

Kieran's lips met mine in fierce desperation. I met him with the same enthusiasm. We became a clash of teeth and tongues as our hands roamed over each other, desperate to just feel something, anything that wasn't pain or sorrow.

I pulled frustratingly at Kieran's clothes which foiling my plans to get to more of his skin and I felt him smile against my lips. Instead of pulling off the clothes that I'd decided were greatly offending me, he rolled me onto my back and his lips started to trail across my jaw and down my neck.

"We don't have to do this now if you don't want to," I said, because I'd started to feel a little like I was taking advantage of him.

"Oh, we are definitely doing this," he said, before biting down gently on my shoulder. My hips bucked and a moan slipped out of my mouth before I realised I was even doing it. "But you're going to lie here and let me worship you the way you should be."

I mean, clearly I'm not going to say no to that and I couldn't help the smile that flickered across my lips in response. Everything about this felt right; everything about him felt right.

Kieran's hand dropped to my waist and he gently started to draw my top up. I leant up so that he could pull it straight off and his hands dropped to the waistband of my shorts as he pulled them away, baring me before him completely.

Kieran pulled his shirt off over his head and I couldn't help but stop as I took in his bare chest over the top of me. He had no body hair and he was completely smooth, but it didn't detract from him, if anything all of his smooth gleaming skin on display just seemed to highlight every dip and curve of the muscles sculpting his chest and stomach.

He smirked when my breath hitched at the sight of him and I could see the self-satisfaction radiating from him at my reaction to his body. I couldn't exactly hold it against him, all I could think about was how much I wanted to run my tongue over him.

Keeping his gaze locked with mine, Kieran slowly dipped his head down as he lowered down to my breast. His tongue came out and he lapped at my nipple all the while keeping his eyes on me. I couldn't look away, watching his mouth descending to me was one of the hottest things I'd seen and I knew he could tell exactly what he was doing to me.

I arched against him, desperate to feel his lips close around me, needing something more. He knew exactly what effect he was having on me, but he didn't give me what I wanted, with a smirk he just drifted across to my other breast, trailing his tongue along the swell of my breasts as he went. He was driving me mad when he repeated the same motion on my other nipple. His breath across my wet skin made me pebble in delight, as he curved his tongue around my rock hard nipple.

"Kieran, please, I need ... I need more," I begged, squirming where I lay.

He grinned up at me. "You're going to get everything you could ever want sweetheart ... eventually."

I groaned, part in frustration and part in delight, because this was exactly what I needed to take my mind off everything that had been happening recently.

Kieran still kept his eyes locked with mine as he started to glide lower down my body. His tongue darted out as he tasted and kissed his way down. When he reached my belly button, he gently ran his tongue around the edge, before he licked a slow lazy path down to where the heat was building between my legs. My hips twitched upwards on their own, as I was desperate for those gentle touches to turn into more.

He paused just above where I wanted him and I felt his hand run down my thigh before he hooked it under my knee and drew my leg up and over his shoulder. Still, with his eyes locked on mine, he bypassed where I wanted him the most and started to trail his lips down the inside of my thigh instead.

The breaths were panting out of me as I squirmed on the spot. I needed so much more and this teasing was driving me insane.

Suddenly Kieran's lips sealed on the inside of my thigh and he sucked hard and deep on my soft skin. I arched my

back as the pain blended in with the sudden shock of pleasure
of finally getting something more.

Kieran just grinned and leant back before gripping hold of
my hips and quickly spinning me so that I was face down on
the bed. My hands came up to brace me and I giggled in
surprise at the sudden movement.

I could feel Kieran shuffle behind me and then when he
leant forward, pressing himself along the length of my body, I
could feel his hard cock nestled against my ass. He must have
taken this chance to lose the last of his clothes. Fuck, he feels
amazing!

Kieran ran his tongue along the shell of my ear, while he
threaded his fingers through mine, pressing my hands down
into the mattress. I squirmed in place, needing some kind of
friction and his hard cock was so close to where I needed it. It
would be easy for him to just push himself inside of my aching
heat and I was ready to beg him for exactly what I needed.

I tried to grind back into him, but just as I shifted my hips
back, he pulled away and started to trail his lips down the back
of my neck and follow the path of my spine as he worked his
way lower. I could feel that body starting to tremble from all
of his gentle teasing touches.

Just as his lips reached the very crest of my ass, I felt his
knee come between my legs and spread my legs apart so that he
could kneel between my legs. His hands grabbed hold of my
hips and he lifted me from the bed so I had my ass in the air
and my chest pressed to the mattress. I could feel his breath
against the wetness pooling between my legs.

"Are you ready, little angel?" he asked, his voice pitching
low.

I didn't have it in me to form words any more and I whimpered in response, causing him to laugh. He'd got one of those
male, self-satisfied laughs and all it did was make me wetter.

He trailed one finger through my wetness and it felt

incredible. Being starved of anything but gentle touches all this time, had made me hypersensitive and needy and he knew it.

His lips closed around my clit as he tipped my hips and I felt him push his thumb inside me. I was already there, I was so close and he'd barely had to touch me. His tongue circled my clit and I could feel his thumb moving in and out as he spread my wetness around.

I can feel the orgasm growing in the pit of my stomach and my hands clenched at the covers beneath me. As he sucked my clit into his mouth, I felt like the orgasm detonated inside me. My face was pressed into the pillow beneath me, but there was no covering the moans and scream that he dragged out of me as he kept working my clit, riding me right through one orgasm and straight into a second one when he pushed his thumb into my ass.

Before I could even catch my breath, his mouth moved away from me and I didn't even feel him lining up to me before his cock slammed inside. I was so wet and so turned on, that he didn't need to take any time trying to work his way in and from the feel of him I definitely would have needed him to. I could feel the delicious stretch and even though I still hadn't seen what it is he was packing, I could tell from the way he seemed to fill me up that he was definitely large.

His hands came to my hips and he slowly dragged his cock nearly entirely out of me, before he slammed back into me again. It was a delicious combination of slow and hard.

"Fuck! I have dreamt of this moment for years and you feel better than anything I could ever have imagined," Kieran gasped out.

His hips picked up his rhythm and his arms wrapped around me, lifting me up so that my back leant flush against his chest. His hands came up to cradle my breasts and he trailed his lips down my neck as he hammered into me.

I could feel another orgasm building inside of me and I

knew exactly what I needed. Kieran seemed to falter and I knew it would be from the confusion he must be feeling about what he wanted to do right now. I tipped my head back onto his shoulder and pulled his mouth back towards my neck.

"It's okay," I panted, "it's because of our pack."

I didn't really have it in me to be able to explain at any greater lengths. Thankfully he didn't need any further explanation and he gave in to what he needed. I felt his teeth close in around my shoulder as he bit deep, placing his mark on my body. It triggered the orgasm in me that was being teased into existence and he groaned as my pussy clamped down on his cock. With a shout, he came and I dragged his arm in front of me so that I could leave my own mark, sinking my teeth into his bicep.

Kieran gently guided me back down to the mattress, following me down so that he was spooned behind me, his cock still inside of me. He pulled the covers up over us and held me tightly against him.

"My beautiful mate," he murmured into my neck as he kissed me softly.

I snuggled into his arms, suddenly feeling exhausted.

"How do you feel?" Kieran asked, and I knew what he was referring to.

I took a moment before I responded, taking time to think and take stock of my body. "Tired and ... I'm not sure." I frowned.

And I'm not. I could feel a strange sensation in my chest. Almost like my magic was unsettled, like it was rolling around in my chest trying to get comfortable.

"In a bad way?" he asked, leaning up on one elbow so that he could look at me.

"In a ... it feels weird and I don't know what's happening kind of way," I responded completely unhelpfully.

I was born with my magic, it had always been there. When

I lost it, it was like losing a piece of me, but considering I'd just had the wings torn from my back, it wasn't something I was completely concentrating on at the time, given the whole agonising pain thing I had going on. Once I'd dealt with the pain, there was nothing but this empty void inside me. Now it felt like my magic was swirling inside that void, trying to remember where it fit.

"Did it work, though?" he whispered.

"Kieran, this wasn't about magic, this was about us as mates, coming together and completing our bond," I told him. I didn't want him to feel like I'd just used him. This magic wasn't all it was about between us.

"I know," he told me, but I couldn't tell by the tone of his voice if he truly means it. His head dipped down and he leaned his forehead against mine. "It's always going to be about you, but I just need to know, I need to know that you're not going to leave me."

I twisted around in his arms and snuggled close, draping one leg over his hip so that I could squeeze in as close as I could get.

"I can feel my magic, it's unsettled and confused, but it is there," I told him and he smiled.

It's a blinding smile filled with joy and relief and it's impossible not to return.

We laid in each other's arms just talking and trailing our fingers over all of the bare skin still on display, not having bothered to get dressed again. I found myself telling Kieran about my time in the education camps and the things I had to do in my training. I didn't know why, but I felt like if I laid out all of the worst parts of myself now, then at least he would understand me. He would know how they tried to turn me into a monster and hopefully how dangerous the other angels were. I'd not forgotten about what Aurel is pushing for me to do and I knew he was not just going to let it drop because

Frannie started smacking him with her ladle. Kieran just let me talk. He didn't interrupt or ask any questions. When I faltered, he just reassured me. At first, I was worried this would taint his view of me, but I could tell it didn't. I needed this more than I realised. A way to purge my soul before we started out on something new together.

After I'd finished what I wanted to say, at least for now, we laid in each other's arms.

"What does it feel like?" he asked me.

"What does what feel like?"

"Your magic."

"Oh, it feels like what it is. It feels like a storm rolling through me, like destruction and power. It feels like vengeance, begging to be released," I muttered.

Before we could discuss anything further, a gentle knock came on the bedroom door and Wyatt slipped inside. I could tell by the heated look in his eye that he wasn't jealous by finding us lying here in bed in each other's arms, in fact, it seemed more like he wished he could join us. Just the thought sent a flash of lust through my body and I'm certain that my two mates knew exactly what I'm thinking, or at least judging my Kieran's hardening cock, I'm sure he had a pretty good idea.

"I'm sorry to disturb you both, but we're going to meet downstairs to go over the plans for tonight. I thought you might want to be there," Wyatt told us, clearing his throat.

I looked at Kieran and he just shrugged, leaving it up to me. I knew he wouldn't want to miss this and I appreciated that he was giving me an out and supporting me in it, if that's what I wanted. But this was my fight just as much as it was theirs, in fact, probably more so. I wouldn't be standing on the side-lines. If I could just get my magic under control, there wouldn't be a need for a fight at all.

CHAPTER 53

KIERAN

Everything about Lyra was amazing. As we followed Wyatt down into the basement of the house, she slipped her hand into mine and I felt myself sigh like some lovestruck fool. Wyatt turned around and grinned at me, no doubt knowing exactly how I felt.

It wasn't unusual for fae females to have more than one mate, so I knew that if I was ever lucky enough to find a mate, I would gain brothers as well. But this mating circle was strange and against everything we had ever thought true. We had always been told that fae only mated with fae. The sting of Haryk's betrayal was still fresh. There was no way I would be calling him King ever again. What other lies had he dished out to us all? He had ruled over the fae for nearly 500 years. How could he have done this to us? What could anyone have possibly offered for him to agree to this?

While my mind was running away with questions, I missed where we were actually going until we came to a stop inside a room which was literally covered in weapons. Everyone else was here and Kyle and Aria were bent over a table examining a map together. Wyatt came to stand beside me, resting one hand on my shoulder. There was something about him that seemed to settle the raging emotions in me and when I looked at him in question, he squeezed my shoulder tight. He's obviously the alpha in this pack that we had and it surprised me that I could sense that.

"How many vampires does Cassius have in his clan?" Kyle asked Lyra, looking up from the maps.

"A lot," she shrugged. "I don't know the exact numbers, but I'd say over a hundred."

No one seems to be worried about that, but personally, I thought I was going to throw up.

"Will he call on any of the other clans to assist him?" Kyle said with a frown.

"Definitely not. Cassius wants to and is in the process of, wiping out the other clans. He won't turn to them for help, it will seem too much like a weakness and I doubt they would agree anyway."

"That's good news at least," Kyle muttered, turning back to the map.

"I don't think he will bring the whole clan with him," Lyra said. Kyle frowned in confusion, but before he could say anything, she explained. "Edwin was his strongest enforcer and he does have others, but a lot of the clan are not fighters. He won't risk drastically reducing his numbers, because that's the reason why he has been able to gain so much power, so quickly. The other clans fear him for how quickly he has been able to expand his clan and maintain it at that size. A drastic reduction in numbers would be a sign of weakness and most likely prompt an attack on the clan house. He will hold back the weaker members of his clan, those that aren't trained to fight, to keep up appearances on the Moon Side."

It made sense, but I didn't understand how she could possibly know that. She must have seen the question on my face though because she added, "I heard a lot while I was there, they just treated me like food. Once they had what they wanted, I might as well not have even been there."

My heart broke for her. She'd told me about how she had been held at the clan house, but she hadn't gone into much detail. Wyatt looked across at her in concern and I could see the worry on his face. He gripped my shoulder tighter, but this time it was because he needed the reassurance. When his eyes met mine, I nodded, we didn't need words, he knew what I meant. She was with us now. We wouldn't let anything happen to her again. Wyatt shuffled a little closer to me so that his side pressed against mine and I leant into him a fraction so that he could feel me there. This alpha wolf was more vulnerable than he let anyone else know.

"Okay, so we're preparing for an unknown number, but we know that it's more than what we have," Kyle grimaced. "The fae are in no fit state to fight, we have the pack enforcers that Aria has been working with. How many Elites can you get back here before tonight?" he asked, looking at Aria.

"Aeryn is refusing to side with us and Echo is out of contact and possibly missing," Aria gulped, her voice breaking, "Britt can't leave Valhalla. Mae, Harmony and Nix are with the Felidae Pack and we can't pull them out. Trent and his guys are back, so we just have four."

"Four is better than none and we have our own magic," Kyle said, sliding an arm around her.

"Plus, we've got you, kitten," Liam grinned at her across the table.

"Yeah babe, you've been dying to stab someone for weeks, this is your big chance," Sykes laughed.

Aria and her mates were definitely a strange bunch, but it seemed like we were going to need their brand of crazy if we were going to make it through this.

We spent the next hour looking over the plans, going over how many fighters we had—not enough—and weapons.

"What about Damon?" Caleb asked. "He might be able to give us an idea on numbers, weaknesses, what to expect."

Kyle was already shaking his head before he even finished. "We checked on him earlier, he's still unconscious. He's healing slowly, but I doubt he's going to be waking up any time soon."

"We need to make sure he has blood to feed on when he wakes up," Lyra said, looking worried. I couldn't figure out the relationship she had with this vampire, but she clearly cared for him, and the others didn't seem concerned by his presence.

"We will put something in place, he's not going to need it for now because I doubt he's going to be waking up anytime soon," Kyle told her reassuringly and he radiated confidence from him. It was hard not to trust him. This was my first time around shifters and they were definitely an interesting bunch.

Virion and Braedon walked in when we were just about finished. "I'll fill you both in on the plan," Kyle told them as we were turning to leave to prepare.

Braedon went straight to the map and Aria's side but Virion hesitated at the door.

"Can we talk?" he asked me.

He looked nervous, but I didn't for the life of me know why. I nodded and he indicated the door with a nod of his head. Following him out, he led me up to a kitchen where he set about silently making tea for us. Not knowing what else to do, I sat down at the table and waited until he was ready to talk. The others hadn't followed us, apparently deciding that whatever Virion wanted to talk about, he wanted to do it in private.

Placing the cups down on the table, he finally sat and spoke, "I spoke with the other fae and they told me everything you've done to protect them," he said quietly. "Thank you."

"They are my people," I said slowly, not sure what I was even trying to say, "You would have done the same."

"This is all happening because of my father." I could hear the shame radiating from his voice. "Our people ... everything that you went through, is because of my family. They did this to you."

"No," I said firmly, "your mother gave her life for us, she saved us. She walked out of the door one night, not telling anyone where she was going and she made the ultimate sacrifice for us. She didn't do it for thanks or praise, she didn't want anyone to feel like they owed anything to her. She just walked quietly into the night and she saved us all. She was the best of us and she was your family too. Do not tarnish her name by speaking ill of her." I had never felt anything more strongly than I did right now. I wouldn't let anyone disrespect her name, ever.

"I can hardly remember her anymore," he admitted quietly.

I couldn't imagine what he must be going through right now, but the look on his face was giving me a damn good idea.

"She would be proud of you," I told him and the look he's giving me is nothing but disbelief. "You're clearly a good man, you've taken in these people, caring for them. You're a lot like her."

Tears collected in his eyes. "How can I face them? How can I ever make up for what he did?"

"Love them, just like she did. Show them that you are her son and not his. Do the right thing," I whispered.

He nodded resolutely. What else was there really to say? We're about to walk into a fight that we might not be walking away from.

"I've sent word to my brother to come to the packhouse. I haven't said anything about what is happening yet. I don't want my father to find out. If anything happens tonight,

Aubron is a good man." He winced at that and I couldn't help but laugh. "My little brother can be misguided at times, but he has a good heart. He will help them."

I knew exactly what he's saying. If he didn't make it through tonight, then his brother would be here for them. But what I'm worried about was if he didn't intend to see the end of the night and how he's going to go about doing that. We fae were a proud and noble people, some fae had fallen on their swords for less.

Virion walked away leaving me sitting at the table with our untouched drinks.

"You okay?" I heard Wyatt ask from behind me.

"I think he's going to do something," I started. How do you tell someone that you think one of their friends is going to run into a fight with every intention of not coming out of it alive?

"Yeah, I got that too. I'll speak with Kyle," he sighed. "Come on, let's go get you some fighting leather and weapons then try and talk Lyra out of joining the fight." He grinned at me and I couldn't help but smile back.

I'd love to see him try and talk her out of this.

"I think I'll stand on the side-lines for that conversation and you will too, if you know what's good for you," I grinned, as we headed back to the basement room.

"Probably, come on, let's go find you something sharp and shiny to play with," he laughed, walking away and I couldn't help but follow. If anything, I was looking forward to seeing Lyra put him in his place. I had a feeling she was probably the only one the alpha let do that and judging from the look on his face, I also had the feeling he absolutely loved it.

By the time we made it back into the strange room downstairs, Aria had equipped almost everyone with swords and various other blades. She looked me up and down and then pulled a sword off the rack and passed it to me.

"This should suit you fine," she said, nodding. Turning back to the rack, she pulled off some daggers, which she passed to Dom and his brother.

The sword she'd given me was definitely beautiful. It was lighter than I was used to, but then I didn't have the muscle tone that I used to, either. I used to carry my father's sword, but I didn't know where it was now. We had to give up all of our weapons when we went to The Farm. There was no one left in my family that it would have gone to, not that they would probably still be around even if I had. It seemed impossible that everything was gone, everyone is gone.

"You doing okay there?" Wyatt asked, cutting into my thoughts.

"Yeah, just ... you know ..." I shrugged.

"I know," he sighed, patting me on the back. "Let's just get through tonight and then we can concentrate on everything else. They're safe now. We won't let anything else get to them."

Looking in his eyes, I could see how sincere he was. How much he meant what he was saying.

Dom was busy with Stone in the corner, explaining to Braedon the theory behind his magic. Caleb was talking to Aria, with Liam going over the last final details of the attack. Even with all of these people in the room, it felt like it was just me and him. He radiated comfort and companionship. I could see now how shifters became so loyal to their alphas. It was because they knew they would do anything for them, always protect them and in turn, they wanted to protect them too. This feeling of pack was enough to fill all of the dark places inside of you. I think it might even be enough to fix some of the broken parts.

CHAPTER 54

LYRA

We were all standing on the steps of the packhouse, watching the sun go down. There was something in the air. It seemed impossible that it wasn't going to go down. Everyone was brimming with nervous energy. Braedon probably more than most. Dom and Stone had spent the last few hours talking theoretical magic with him. No one had any practical experience of what he could do and yet they seemed to think he could do the impossible: control the vampires.

The fae were taking shelter on the top floors of the packhouse. They'd had to set them up barracks-style in some of the rooms and put up some temporary beds, but the conditions here were much better than what they were used to. It was only temporary anyway, as soon as we had this situation dealt with, we would look for a more permanent solution.

Seven pack enforcers and some of the pack that Aria referred to as her Elites were covering the back of the packhouse. The rest of us were here, standing at the front. I knew Cassius. I knew how he thought. He wasn't going to creep up to us and try and surprise us. He would walk right up to the front door, so he could give his big, bad guy speech because that was exactly how much of a dick he was.

Aria looked positively giddy about what was coming up and her mates stood solidly at her back. I wasn't feeling quite as confident as the rest of them. My magic still felt like it couldn't settle inside of me and no matter how much I'd tried over the last couple of hours, I couldn't connect with it. No one had mentioned anything or asked about it, I think they could tell from the look on my face that it wasn't something I wanted to talk about. I should have known that Aurel was holding something back and that it wouldn't be as easy as just completing my bonds. But the thing is, I could live without my magic, over the years I hadn't exactly gotten used to not having it around, it had still felt like there was something missing inside of me, but now that I had my mates beside me, it didn't seem like that big a deal.

Wyatt stood by my side and Caleb was on my other side. Both of them gripped my hands tightly. Dom and Kieran were standing behind us, waiting patiently. Stone stood uneasily beside his brother.

It didn't take long for him to come. As soon as the last rays of the sun had disappeared, I heard his laughter echoing through the trees in front of us.

"Look at you, little bird, making friends already," Cassius laughed as he emerged through the trees.

His clan followed at his back. Not his entire clan, unless he was hiding them somewhere, but he still had at least sixty vampires behind him. It was a lot more than the twenty-two fighters we had. They had us outnumbered.

"You see, the problem I have, little bird, is that your friends here have taken something that belongs to me. Well, a lot of somethings. Not only that, but they seem to be playing with my favourite toy," he growled. "And I don't like to share my toys! I can forgive the execution of my enforcer. He was on your land and a threat to your pack, but right now, you're going to return my property to me, or the truce that we have between the vampires and the packs is going to be well and truly broken."

Everyone around me looked as confused as I am. I didn't think anyone was aware of any truce.

No one made a move, Kyle was staring down Cassius and the anger radiating from him seemed to be enough to shake the ground. In fact, if I wasn't mistaken, I think there was a slight tremble starting to happen.

Cassius started to look confused and almost a little nervous, but before he could say anything, it was Aria's turn to start laughing.

"Silly little vampire trying to make big boy demands. Here's what's going to happen. You gave your evil speech 'they belong to me' and then we say 'no they absolutely fucking do not', Lyra is pack and the fae are free. You're going to stamp your feet a little bit and have a bit of a temper tantrum and then I'm going to kill every last one you." Aria smiled across at him, her wings bursting from her back and the faint glow of flames flickers around them. They're breathtaking and a small part of me hurt at the sight of them.

"She belongs to me!" Cassius roared across the space between us.

"Temper tantrum. Totally called it," Aria faux whispered across at Kyle who stood next to her.

"You definitely did, babe. Have I told you how hot you look when you get your wings out like that?" Kyle said, pulling her close and kissing her like we weren't just about to all fight for our lives. It was sweet.

Cassius was past the point of even being able to speak now that he'd basically being talked down to and annoyed. He just roared out his displeasure, which set a couple of Aria's mates off with the giggles. It was actually getting pretty funny now. I used to be so scared of Cassius, but standing here now I saw him for what he really was, nothing. He was just a self-inflated, little man with ideas of himself that were far bigger than what he could ever achieve.

As he finished his roar, there's a brief second of silence and then they charged. Cassius didn't even bother to move. He just stood there with a look of smug satisfaction.

Kyle immediately moved into action and walls of earth shot up out of the ground, separating off the vampires into smaller groups and herding them where we wanted them. Aria gave out a hoot of glee and soared into the first rush. Pulling out two swords, she set about cutting down any that came near her.

Wyatt and Caleb both shifted and charged into the vampires who were coming towards us. It was brutal and it was bloody as they leapt into the fray, tearing into anyone that came near them. Dom was busy throwing up shields where he could to protect their backs and push the vampires where we wanted them. Stone was at his side trying to help, but I could see that even now he was starting to falter.

Without any magic on their side, the vamps only had their fangs and claws to fight with, but we apparently had more magic than I was even aware we had on our side.

Virion, Sykes and Liam were all wielding magic, crafting one of the elements into whips that they used to slash out at any vamps that approached them. Braedon was hacking into any that came too close with the sword he held in his hands. He hadn't attempted to use his magic and I knew that he lacked the confidence to do it.

Despite the efforts of everyone around us, there was still a pack of vamps approaching the steps of the packhouse where Kieran and I stood. We were the final guard for the fae inside. No one could make it past us. I wouldn't say that we were losing at this point, we were just overwhelmed by their numbers, but judging from the way that Aria was moving across the now battlefield, the numbers wouldn't be in their favour for much longer.

Kieran darted around me to take the advancing vamps on by himself, trying to shelter me behind his back almost as if he thought that I needed to be protected. He's adorable! As a vamp rushed him from the side and ducked under his sword, the vamp behind it was already distracting Kieran enough to leave his side wide open. I darted forward and with the sword that Aria handed to me earlier, hacked off the head of the vamp that was attempting to touch my mate. I dove under Kieran's sword arm and followed an upper swing of my sword through another vamp's neck. Spinning on the spot, I came back to Kieran's other side and engaged two vamps there, so that he could deal with another which was approaching from the front.

They seemed to have got the idea that we weren't going down easy and the three of them backed off until they were just out of reach. The only way for us to go on the attack now would be to separate, but there was no way we were prepared to do that. It almost put us in a stalemate. I say almost because they had all the time in the world to wait for more vampires to come and back them up, before attempting to swarm us again. Whilst the fighters on our side were still doing well, we hadn't taken down enough vampires for any of them to be able to come to our assistance any time soon.

I could see that Dom was starting to tire. This was the plan though, he would use his magic until he couldn't push it any further and then he would back up Wyatt and Caleb with his sword. But he seemed to have not realised his limit and as he drew his sword, I could see he was already unsteady on his feet. Stone was down and out for the count behind him, he was already shaky before we had even started. We tried to make him take shelter with the fae, but he wouldn't hear of it. Now because of his stubbornness, Dom was stuck trying to stand guard over his passed-out brother instead of backing up my other two mates.

Aria and her mates had gotten separated from us and that meant that Wyatt and Caleb were getting dangerously close to being isolated from the rest of us. Caleb seemed to be struggling to keep up with Wyatt, who I feared may have finally lost control of his wolf. He tore into any vampire that came near him, but he wasn't putting any of them down permanently. Quite a few pissed off vampires were surrounding them with fairly large chunks missing from them, but, if anything, all it was doing was pushing them further and further into a blood-lust. Wyatt just looked like he was playing with them rather than making any thought out moves, he looked like he was on the verge of turning feral.

Cassius stood at the back by the tree line, laughing glee-fully at the sight in front of him. He hadn't once stepped forward to help his people. I wasn't surprised, he wasn't one to get his hands dirty. He much preferred letting others do that for him.

A vampire seemed to try and take advantage of what it assumed was my distraction and as my eyes locked with Cassius', my sword hand darted out as I leant back to avoid the incoming fangs at my neck. Unfortunately for the vampire that they belonged to though, my aim was true. My sword sliced across his abdomen, and with a shriek, he fell back trying to keep his insides where they were supposed to be, with his two now bloody hands.

The other vampires surrounding us all collectively took one more step back and in turn, Kieran shuffled infinitesimally closer to me. He really did draw the short straw out of all of them, being the sole mate left to guard me.

It was hard not to watch Aria and my eyes kept flicking over to where she stood. Any vampire that came near her got cut down and she was glorious in the way that she dominated the battlefield. Unfortunately, the vampires around her hadn't surrendered themselves to a feeding frenzy and had retained enough of their wits about them to try to stay out of her reach or at least only dart in and out to keep her attention. Judging by the growls coming from her, it was starting to piss her off. Her mates were wielding their elemental whips like they had been using them since toddlers and were driving the vampires towards her, but they always ducked away at the last minute. Every time she failed to make a killing blow, Cassius laughed and it was winding her up more and more.

It wouldn't be long until someone made a mistake and when that happened, it was going to be fatal for the rest of us fighting together, because if one of us fell, I had no doubt that the rest of their packmates would lose their minds.

We needed to somehow turn the tide in our favour. We'd taken down more than a few vampires, but they still outnumbered us. The fuckers didn't even seem to be getting tired and we had one mage down and another looking a bit shaky on his feet. Dom was looking far too vulnerable for me to be comfortable right now and if we weren't covering the door to protect the fae, I would try to make my way to him.

I couldn't afford to close my eyes right now, but I did what I could to try and centre myself and felt down into that cavern that once used to be filled with my magic. It was no use. I could feel my magic there, but it was rolling around almost like it didn't fit where it once used to be. I couldn't grasp it hard enough to draw it out and the frustration of not being able to wield what I knew would be enough to bring this to an end, was nearly enough to distract me from the fight.

Footsteps sounded in the house behind me and my first thought was that they'd somehow found their way inside and had flanked us. I immediately spun and went back to back with Kieran, raising my sword, ready to take down whatever was storming our way.

I needn't have worried though, because it was Trent and his packmates who appeared in the doorway and not someone out for our blood.

"The pack enforcers are holding the rear. You were right, their full force came to the front and we've only had a few try to sneak through. We thought we would be better coming to see if you need help at the front," he quickly explained.

He looked around the battlefield, which was now behind me, with a visible wince.

"Can you hold this door?" I asked him and he just looked at me like I'd insulted him. "Fair enough, we're going to back up Dom, shout if you need any help," I told him and even though he nodded, I didn't believe he had any intention of following through.

I turned back around to see that the vampires we had previously been holding off were clearly getting ready to rush us again. I was surprised that the appearance of the others hadn't made them any warier.

"On two we charge," Kieran murmured to me. "Our best chance is to punch straight through to Dom, then take a stance surrounding Stone."

I nodded in agreement because it was exactly what I had been about to suggest. Apart from the group of five vampires that we had crowding us, there were only three more between us and Dom and they were currently facing off with him, with their backs to us.

I looked to Dom and he subtly nodded to me. I could see the relief in his eyes in knowing that someone was coming to help. He didn't look steady on his feet at all, but he was steadfastly holding his position to protect his brother.

Kieran gave the count and we charged at the same time as the vamps did. Thankfully Trent and his pack were there to help and as Kieran shouldered one out of the way to clear the path for us, Trent was there closing the gap behind us to prevent them from following through. From there it was pretty easy to run through two of the vamps with their backs to us, as we charged to Dom's side.

I felt like maybe I should feel worse for cutting down these vampires without considering that they were at least still people. Damon was a prime example that they were not all bad. The problem was there were so many faces here that I recognised, faces that had sunk their fangs into my flesh before and I found that part of my heart hardening as I looked at them. I truly didn't care if they found themselves on the wrong end of my sword, in fact, there were a few of them I would relish the opportunity to gut and then behead. Shaking my head, I tried to clear my thoughts. This was the monster that the education centre tried to turn me into, it wasn't the person I was now. I wouldn't let them win. I wouldn't become that person again.

Some of the vampires surrounding Aria and her mates seemed to realise that we had evened out the numbers and started to move towards our group. Dom was barely able to stand at this point and the one vampire that we hadn't managed to take down seemed to be a much better fighter than the others we had encountered so far. He'd successfully kept Kieran busy as Dom dropped to his knees beside me.

"Fuck! Thank god you came, I don't think I can keep this up," Dom said as he dropped to his knees in front of me. "Stone didn't have anything left to give and I couldn't cover him and the others at the same time. I've used too much."

I could hear his words starting to slur as he spoke and I knew that he was fighting the urge to pass out as well. I started to panic about how we were all going to get out of this. I tried again to grab hold of my slippery magic, but it almost felt like it flipped me off and then skipped away laughing. I had never felt this helpless in a fight before.

"Having some trouble?" I heard Aurel ask from behind me.

I knew he was a dick, but right now I had never been more relieved to hear his voice. Spinning around, I saw him striding towards us, but the most surprising thing that I couldn't tear my eyes off was what he was holding in his hand. Vampires were surrounding us and I was standing there like an idiot gapping at the angel striding before me because he held the flaming sword of Michael in his hand.

"How did you get that?" I asked in awe. I had never laid eyes on the fabled sword before. It was supposed to be one of our most guarded treasures. If he had been able to remove it from the Counsel Building, then things in Angelus must be worse than I had realised.

"I just borrowed it for a bit," he smirked. "You look like you need some help ... you know what I need from you," he hurried out and I realised right then that there was every chance that I may kill this angel in front of me.

Before I could open my mouth to tell him to fuck off back to Angelus, Samuel set down behind him.

"Aurel! We discussed this, the decision is to be hers and she has said no, there are other ways ..."

I didn't have time to listen to them bicker about their own problems when I was in the middle of a fight which they apparently had absolutely no intention of helping with. Movement out of the corner of my eye had me spinning away from them. Three of the vampires were trying their luck and I darted forward, spinning around Kieran, I took the head off one and then ran, dropping low, to take the legs from a second at the same time that Kieran removed its head. We made quite a good team.

Spinning back to the other side of him to keep my eyes on

the fight, I felt an explosion of pain ram into my back. My arms threw wide and my head fell back from the force of it, it almost felt like someone had punched their fist through my back. The pain was overwhelming. All of the air was forced from my lungs and I could feel them spasm in my chest as I desperately tried to draw in some kind of breath.

I knew there was no one behind me but Aurel and Samuel, and they wouldn't have allowed a vampire to sneak up on us even if they were intending on staying out of the fight. Looking down in confusion, tears blurring my vision, I almost didn't understand what I saw at first, but the point of the Michael sword stuck out of my chest and my blood flowed freely from the wound. I could feel my life pouring down my front as it followed the path of my blood as it flowed.

Aurel's hand on my shoulder was the only indication that he was still standing behind me, as he leant in close and whispered into my ear. "It didn't have to be this way, Lyra, you brought this on yourself."

I could hear Kieran and Dom both screaming my name, as my vision started to fade and narrow down to nothing but black. The excruciating pain of the sword being ripped back out of my body was the last thing I felt, before everything went black and I fell, never feeling myself hit the ground before the darkness swallowed me whole.

Chapter 55

Caleb

Wyatt had lost his fucking mind and it was taking everything I had just to keep up with watching his back. He was so reckless that he was verging on feral. When he took me aside this morning and told me he was worried he would lose control of his wolf when the vampires turned up, I agreed to stand beside him no matter what. Of course I did. Not only was he my alpha, but he was my pack brother. There was nothing that I wouldn't do for him. I didn't realise it was going to be like this though. How had we not known how bad Wyatt was and how much it must be taking for him to keep control of his wolf on a daily basis? I'm a little ashamed of myself right now for not seeing just how much pain he must be in.

The fight was an absolute bloodbath and that was not just because Wyatt had turned feral. He was tearing chunks from vamps as soon as they got close to him. He'd taken a few bites himself and I could see the slow ooze of his blood from some of his wounds. They didn't look to be too bad though, which was more than I could say for the vamps around us. Wyatt was indiscriminate in his rage. Any part of them that came near him fell foul of his jaws, he didn't even seem to care what danger it put him in, to be able to sink his teeth into them. There was a fucking arm lying on the ground next to us for god's sake!

For all of his feral rage, we'd only managed to kill three vamps, the others were circling us, trying to seek out a weakness. It was obvious they had fallen into a feeding frenzy, their eyes were completely bloodshot and some of them were drooling in anticipation. What I hadn't realised was that it could be vampire blood that affected them, just as much as our own. Don't get me wrong, they weren't in danger of feeding on each other, they solely had their sights set on us for that, but every time Wyatt managed to tear another piece off one of them, their blood coated the ground and the others enjoyed it more than any sane person ever should.

A flurry of movement behind us distracted me for a second and I sighed in relief as I saw Lyra and Kieran making their way to Dom. The two of them moved fluidly around each other, watching them fight together was spectacular, almost like they had trained all their lives to move that way.

I could see the relief on Dom's face when they reached him, Stone was already down and I didn't know why. Hopefully, he wasn't hurt badly because I didn't know if Dom would be able to take losing his brother so soon after getting him back.

Unfortunately, my distraction with Dom cost me dearly and I felt the talons rake across my shoulder as fangs found my throat. I had a brief moment where my heart dropped, as I realised that I didn't want this all to end yet, I hadn't had enough time to be with Lyra. Wyatt ripped the vamp away from me and I heard the crunch of bone as his jaws clamped down and severed the leg that he had a hold of them by. I whimpered as my front leg gave way underneath me and collapsed to the ground, the pain in my shoulder was taking my breath away and I had no way to try and slow the bleeding in this form. I could feel myself weakening and I knew that this was it. I couldn't fight any more and Wyatt wasn't in enough of his right mind to protect me now that I was down. I tried desperately to climb back up to my paws, I wasn't ready to go yet. I wasn't ready to leave when I finally had everything that I wanted. My front legs just collapsed underneath me, unable to take my weight.

Wyatt was tearing apart the vamp that touched me in front of me. He was already dead, but that didn't seem to be stopping Wyatt. He was tearing into his flesh like it personally offended him that he tried to be something resembling a person. Blood and tissue flew all around us and the rest of the vamps had made the sensible decision to take a step back. They watched on in horror as Wyatt's front claws crunch down into the dead vamp's chest and he tore at his throat so savagely that he nearly decapitated the body in one go.

I could feel myself weakening and sagged further to the ground as Wyatt finally lifted his head. His golden hair was nothing but red and he looked like he'd just walked out of a horror movie. His wild eyes were filled with rage, but then his eyes fixed on something behind us and I saw the panic flare just as I saw something break in him. I whipped my head around just in time to see Aurel drive a sword through Lyra's back. Her arms threw wide and her head fell back onto his shoulder as he leaned in and whispered something in her ear.

I felt the bond inside me tremble, twist and pull tight. It hurt more than anything I'd ever experienced, it felt like a piece of my soul caught on fire and then I realised that was because it did.

Aurel pulled the sword out of Lyra and as she started to fall to the ground, I felt our bond pull tight and then shatter. The pain was indescribable, but it was nothing compared to the grief and despair that I felt as my mate fell to the ground dead.

Lying my head on the ground I just stopped, I stopped fighting to live, I wished I could just stop breathing. It would come in time though, I could still feel the blood trickling from my neck wound. If it didn't take me soon, one of the vampires would. Closing my eyes, I embraced the pain and the despair, I wrapped it around me and held it close. It was all that I had now.

Don't go far, my beautiful mate, I'm coming.

CHAPTER 56

WYATT

All I could feel was rage and I loved it. I couldn't get enough of the taste of their blood in my mouth, of the sounds of their screams as I tore into them. They came here for my mate and even though a part of me knew there was no coming back from the feral rage that had taken over me, I didn't care. If this was what it took to keep her safe, then I gave it willingly.

The vampire that injured Caleb was dead at my feet and all I could smell was the intoxicating scent of the fear pumping out of the ones still surrounding us. The scent of Caleb's blood faintly lingered in the background and it did nothing but fuel my rage higher, as I looked around desperately seeking my next victim.

I almost felt like I'd completely lost myself, but it was not until I watched my mate get run through by one of her own and drop dead to the ground, that I felt the true agony of our bond shattering and fully sunk into my feral rage.

Throwing my head back, I howled out my grief for the world to hear. This was my song now. One that spoke of desperate pain and broken hearts. It was the opening note to what would be my bloody suicide note to the world. She was gone. The only thing in this world which kept me anchored to my sanity, was gone. What was the point anymore?

I turned back to the vampires that surrounded me and the fear that I smelt from them before was nothing compared to what I could smell now. I inhaled deeply, ratcheting up my need for violence to indescribable levels. Then I fixed my gaze on my prey. I watched the shiver that passed over them as they realised that they were never the predator here, that we'd just been playing all this time and then I made my move. It was going to be bloody, it was going to be glorious.

I'll be with you again soon, my love.

CHAPTER 57

DOM

I was already on my knees, so it didn't take too much of the reserves of my energy to drag myself over to Lyra. Even though I felt the agony of the bond twisting and breaking inside of me, I was still holding on to some naïve hope that maybe she still lived. But she was so still and there was so much blood.

I could hear the screams of Kieran's rage behind me as I dragged her limp body across my lap and into my arms. I knew that he was taking his rage out on the vampires behind me, but I couldn't find it in me to care anymore.

Running my hand across her soft cheek, I lifted her to give her one last kiss. How could she be gone? How was this happening?

The gaping hole in her chest where her heart used to be made my shirt sticky with her blood. It wouldn't be long before the vampires would descend into a feeding frenzy. It would all be over soon.

Aurel just stood smirking down at us, still clutching the flaming sword at his side. I should get up, I should tear him apart. I just didn't seem to be able to let her go.

The other angel who arrived with him grabbed hold of him and punched him square in the face. "We agreed she would have a choice!" he screamed at Aurel, who was still smirking past the blood that was now pouring from his broken nose. "It wasn't supposed to be this way. She deserved to have a choice."

He sounded almost defeated and I couldn't wrap my head around what he was saying. Why would Lyra ever agree to do this? She didn't want any part in their civil war.

"Choice!" Aurel screamed, spitting a mouthful of blood onto the ground. "Why should she get a fucking choice when the rest of us have none? What makes her so fucking special, Samuel?"

"She has already given up more than you would ever consider."

"And look at what she got in return. A few moments of pain and now she has four bonded mates," Aurel screamed, throwing his hand out at Lyra. "Why should she get to live a life filled with happiness and love, when the rest of us are condemned to an eternity of misery?"

"A few moments of pain ... are you out of your fucking mind? You were there Aurel, I know you were because your hands were just as bloody as mine. It took six hours for us to remove her wings by hand. Six hours of agony, while we tore them from her piece by piece. Then you let her rot in that fucking cage for nine years instead of telling us where the fuck she was!" Samuel roared.

"She was supposed to be punished," he scoffed.

"For what? For finding love?"

"For choosing them over us!" Aurel's chest heaved as he glanced around manically. "Look at them! Brawling in the filth over blood and magic. What makes them better than us? Why would she choose them over us?"

"Us? Is that really what's bothering you, Aurel?" Pure hate flashed across Samuel's face. "I know what you did."

Aurel blanched, but Samuel pressed on.

"I know it was you that reported her for coming down here. I chalked it up to naïve, misguided loyalties. When you started talking of rebellion, of change, I thought you were repenting for what you did. But that's not what this is, is it?"

Both angels fell quiet, all of the battlefield seemed to have fallen quiet. Everyone's attention was on them as the truth finally came out.

"She should have been mine," Aurel seethed. "She would have been mine in the next breeding allocation. Do you know what I went through to ensure that happened? Then I find her sneaking down here to be with that mutt."

No one spoke. He had her cast out because he was jealous?

"Then she goes and makes the ultimate sacrifice for us and I knew, I knew that she was meant to be mine after all. That it was just a test. It needed to be done to get us here. Together we will all spark the rebellion and when we take our rightful places on the Council, I will finally take her as my mate."

Samuel's mouth was just flapping about like a fish at the moment and I couldn't blame him. I wouldn't know what to say either.

"Then why would you kill her?" Kieran screamed from behind me before he dropped to his knees next to me.

"She isn't dead," Aurel scoffed. "She's an angel, she's fucking immortal, you idiot."

I looked down at my mate lying in my arms, there was a gaping hole in her chest, her heart wasn't beating and she wasn't breathing. But hope still flickered inside me.

I looked to Samuel because there was no way that I could trust Aurel right now. He simply nodded at me and I felt all of the breath leave my body in a single whoosh. It was only then I looked up and took in the true devastation that surrounded me.

The vast majority of the vampires were dead and Aria was panting, coated in blood behind me. Her mates had all taken positions surrounding her, but they looked just as exhausted as she did.

What remained of the vampires had regrouped behind Cassius who was still standing in his original place except for this time he had Wyatt's limp body lying at his feet. Looking around in desperation, my eyes finally find Caleb. He was laying so still, I couldn't fucking take this. I felt like my heart was in pieces already, but the fact that he wasn't looking at us, that his head laid limply on the ground, told me all that I needed to know. I wouldn't survive losing both of them, I didn't know if I could survive losing just one of them.

"Here's the deal," Cassius barked from behind us, "return to me what is mine and I'll give you back this wolf." He kicks Wyatt in the side and I hear his weak groan drift across to me. "You're going to need to make a decision quickly though, he doesn't have much left in him." Then he had the fucking audacity to laugh.

Kyle turned to look at me, apparently, this was going to be my decision. The thing was I knew Wyatt and I knew what he would want me to do. This vampire was fucking stupid if he thought he was going to walk out of here with Lyra while any of us were still left standing.

I gently set Lyra down on the ground and clambered to my feet with the assistance of Kieran. Loosely gripping my sword at my side, I braced myself for what was bound to be the second wave of their attack.

"Have you always been this stupid?" Aria snarked across the silence.

Cassius reeled back like she'd slapped him. "Do you care nothing for this wolf?"

"I mean he's alright ..." she started and one of her mates, Sykes if I had to guess, snorted in amusement.

The wind picked up around us and even though night has descended, the clouds started to roll across the sky. Cassius looked shocked into silence by Aria's flippant dismissal of Wyatt and didn't seem to know what his next move should be.

The wind rushed through the trees and the creak of boughs breaking filled the air.

Samuel and Aurel stepped up beside me, taking in the scene around them. Aurel's gaze was fixed on the sky, watching the storm clouds move in before he turned back to Cassius and just started laughing.

"Ah man, you are so fucked!"

Even Samuel seemed to smile a bit at that.

A blinding flash filled the sky as a bolt of lightning hit the ground next to Cassius. He shrieked and jumped away as he looked around wildly at the rest of us to try and see who was responsible.

The wind was blowing so fiercely now that some of the vampires were having trouble standing, a couple having dropped to their knees. It was strong where we were, but didn't seem at all as bad as they were faring. Stones and debris were whipping up from the ground and one of them went down with a cry as something slammed into the back of his head.

"Release my mate!" Lyra screamed as she flew into the sky behind us.

The sight was enough to floor me. The fact that she was even breathing was enough, but her wings were truly magnificent. Gleaming gold wings stretched to her sides as she hovered in the air and the rage that filled her eyes made me instantly hard. She's alive.

"Little bird, back in all your shining glory. You had us worried about you for a bit, so worried in fact that one of your mates just laid down and died," he cackled like it was the best joke in the world.

"Release my mate," she repeated, quieter this time, but filled with so much fury.

Cassius continued to laugh, he was clearly deranged if he didn't see the danger he was in right now.

"I don't think you understand, little bird, surrender yourself to me and I will let the wolf walk free, but act quick ..." he didn't get a chance to finish his ridiculous ultimatum before the wind picked up again and he was just plucked off the ground and into the air until he was writhing in mid-air in front of her.

"Foolish little vampire," she said and it almost sounded like she felt sorry for him. "You know I recently saw what happens to a vampire when he gets exposed to the sun, it was a truly terrible sight."

"I hate to tell you this, but it's as dark as night can be," Cassius sneered back at her before he attempted to struggle free from the wind which held him in place.

"Whatever makes you think I would need the sun?" she asked, and he finally fell still.

It was the first moment where he had enough common sense to actually look terrified. He should be.

The vampires who had collected at his back fled. They knew what was good for them and they probably also knew there wasn't going to be enough of Cassius left after this to make them regret running to save their own lives.

Aria and Liam rushed to Wyatt and helped him to his feet. He looked unsteady, but he didn't look half as bad as Cassius was making out. I had no idea how he got him to shift back to his human form though.

All three of them made their way over to Caleb and while my heart and soul were pleading with me to go with them, I couldn't make my feet move. I didn't know if I could survive seeing his broken and bloody body on the ground. Not yet. I just couldn't do it yet.

A bolt of lightning flashed across the sky and hit Cassius in his left arm. He shrieked in agony as the blackened appendage dropped uselessly to his side. Panting through the pain, he glared at Lyra flying before him. She looked like a vengeful goddess with her golden wings on full display at her back.

"Is that the best you've got?" He half laughed and half grimaced at her.

With a sweet smile, she just said, "No," and then bolt after bolt streaked across the sky, colliding with his twitching, pulsating body. Cassius screamed with every single one and there were too many to count. The smell of charred flesh filled the air as Lyra's storm dispensed her wrath down on him.

Even as his screams fell silent the lightning still continued, bright and constant, burning into our eyes and leaving white streaks across our vision.

When they finally stopped colliding down on the object of her hatred, and the wind finally slowed, all that fluttered back down to the ground were a few charred lumps of what was once Cassius and a sprinkling of ash.

Lyra landed at my side just as Wyatt carried Caleb over to us. He lay limp in his arms and I already knew that he was gone. We wasted so much time. We could have been together. We could have been happy while we were waiting for Lyra to take her place at our side.

I dropped to my knees and Wyatt placed Caleb across my lap, he knew what we meant to each other. He knew just how much it was hurting me to have lost him, my other mate.

I'm surprised at first when Lyra doesn't take her place on the ground beside me, when she doesn't cry or show any grief at the loss of one of her mates. I didn't understand how she could be standing, ignoring the body of this wonderful man who lay in my lap. I held him to my chest, grasping onto the last part of him that I had. I'd never be ready to let him go. I couldn't even imagine a life without him in it. My bond with Lyra still laid broken in my chest, shattered by her own death and I had never felt more alone. My entire world right now just boiled down into nothing but the pain of loss.

"You did this," Lyra growled out and when I looked up, I saw that her rage had now turned to Aurel.

Aurel just smiled. He didn't care. There was no way that Lyra could know what he had done, just how thoroughly he had betrayed her or the reasons for why he would do it.

"I can bring him back for you," Aurel said, with that same smug smirk on his face. "I'm the only one that can and you know it."

I reached out and grasped hold of Lyra's hand. If this was possible, if he truly meant what he was saying, I would do anything. She squeezed my hand slightly, but gave no impression to anyone else that she was paying any attention to us. It was confusing, but I understood. She wasn't showing her hand.

"Do it," she hissed at Aurel.

"You know what I need in return," he smirked.

The rage entered her eyes again and if I wasn't mistaken, Aurel might just be ever so slightly terrified of her.

"Let's just stop fucking about shall we, and just put it all out there on the table. You will resurrect my mate and you will do it now, if you don't or if you don't do it properly ..." she took a menacing step towards him and grasped his shirt, hauling him towards her, "I will flay the skin from your body until you are nothing but meat without a sack to contain you."

Aurel actually looked turned on and if it wasn't for the fact that I was holding Caleb right now, I would start making Lyra's threat a reality. As it was, Kyle is having a hard time holding Wyatt back, even if he did look like he would collapse if Kyle let him go.

Samuel took a step closer and it was clear that he was backing Lyra in this. I didn't know what to make of this angel. He didn't seem to know what Aurel had planned, but I'm still not sure if we could entirely trust him.

"Fine," Aurel huffed, rolling his eyes as he took a step back from Lyra straightening his shirt back down. "This isn't the last time we will be talking though Lyra, have fun reforming those bonds of yours." And with that, he took off into the air and left.

I'm aghast with shock and I didn't think I'd hated anyone more than I did him right then, which was saying a lot considering everything we had been through in such a short amount of time.

"I will keep an eye on him," Samuel told Lyra and she nodded in acknowledgement. "I didn't ..."

"I know, Samuel," she interrupted.

"Will it be alright if I return to speak with you, once we have a few things straightened out in Angelus?"

Lyra nodded and Samuel took his leave as well, leaving us all standing here confused.

"Lyra," I whispered, tears collected in my eyes because Caleb still laid in my arms and no one had fucking done anything that they were supposed to do.

She crouched down beside me and ran her hand down my cheek, before leaning her forehead against mine. I was so confused, but I couldn't help but soak up the reassurance that she was giving me.

Caleb suddenly gasped and convulsed in my lap, curling in on himself and groaning in pain. Lyra was immediately there at his side.

"Breathe through it, just breathe," she soothed him.

The relief that engulfed me was overwhelming and I

didn't even feel the tears until one of them dripped down onto my hand. Reaching out, I pulled Lyra towards us and she collapsed against me as I clutched the two of them to me. The tears fell fast and seemed unstoppable. Lyra wept gently as well and Caleb slowly lifted his arms and wrapped them around us both.

I heard the shuffle of people leaving and I knew that Aria and her mates were letting us have some privacy. Two bodies fell to their knees beside us and it didn't take long for both Wyatt and Kieran to wrap their arms around us as well.

We stayed like that for as long as it took for everyone's tears to dry. Clinging to each other, to our pack, as we realised just how easy it was for us to lose this, to lose each other and everything we had ever known to be important in the world. It didn't matter how long we had been together, it didn't matter who met whom first. What mattered was that we had each other here and now, that we had all survived and that we were still together. Cassius was gone and the threat against Lyra was at least over. There may be some of his clan left, but I doubted they would dare to return after Lyra's display of her magic. The angels could be a problem for the future, but right now, I couldn't bring myself to care. Samuel seemed like a potential ally and we had so many friends who were now like family, I knew that we could stand against anything.

The pack as a whole still faced many challenges, but our little pack right here had definitely earnt the right to have a break from them. It was time for us to reform our bonds and just be together. To be a family. To start a family. It was time to just live.

EPILOGUE

LYRA

Yesterday still seemed to linger in my mind, like the remnants of a bad dream. Aria and her mates had essentially herded us back inside so they could deal with the aftermath of the battle. They knew there would be no separating us for some time, and I appreciated them more than I could say right now. I couldn't seem to stop myself from touching Caleb. He had died and I'd come so close to losing him forever.

Aurel was a problem that was going to need to be dealt with. When Samuel eventually turned up again, I was going to have to gauge how much allegiance he had to the other angel, because there was no way I was going to allow him to walk away from this.

All of that was a problem for another day now, though. Right now, it was about our pack. About healing.

We had all showered and fallen into bed last night, sleeping in one tangled mess. I had known it would make the two wolves amongst us feel better, but it was more than that. Now with the bonds broken, I needed the closeness to them to remind myself that they were there. I felt like I had a gaping hole in my chest for a whole new reason. I didn't feel complete without them. But last night, we had all been exhausted. None of us were up to re-establishing the bonds then. There was even a part of me that wondered if we should wait. Instead of rushing to complete the bonds this time, we had a fresh start. We could get to know each other better. We could do things the way they were meant to be done. There was no pressure on us to do anything right away this time. Maybe I should be giving them the chance to do things the way they always imagined it would be done. To do it properly. I could do that for them if that was what they wanted. They had all done so much for me already, and I could give them this one thing. Even if it was probably going to be one of the hardest experiences of my life. I huffed out a breath in defeat—I could do this.

Opening my eyes, I was hit with the realisation that I was alone in the bed. Sitting bolt upright, I was surprised to find that the rest of the bed was empty. My first thought was that something had happened. Had we been attacked again? But there was no way that I could have slept through something like that. Or at least I didn't think I could, I had been pretty exhausted. My wings fluffed out on either side of me, and I couldn't help but trail my fingers over the tip of one of my wings. If there was one bit of evidence that yesterday hadn't been some kind of mass induced hallucination it was these. I couldn't believe they were back. Flying had come to me like second nature. As soon as I woke up yesterday, taking to the air was instinctual. Trying to get situated in bed last night? Not so much. It had taken a lot of tired manoeuvres to fit myself, four mates and my massive wings into bed last night. In my defence, I had never tried to share a bed with anyone the last time I had wings. We were definitely going to need a bigger bed though. I was feeling some wing envy right about now, knowing that Aria could shift her wings when she needed to. That was a trick I definitely wished I could do.

Whilst I was distracted considering my wings, the bedroom door quietly opened and Wyatt slipped inside the room.

"We didn't think you would be awake yet," he said, slipping into the bed beside me.

"You all left," I said quietly, not realising how much that actually hurt until I said it.

"We were finishing off a surprise for you," Wyatt smiled. "Get dressed. The others are waiting to show it to you."

My eyes fluttered across his face as I considered what he was saying. My mind seemed to be sticking on the worst possible point of the situation—they left me. Slowly I spun my legs to the side and got out of bed, walking silently over to the wardrobe. I didn't know how I felt right now. Logically, I knew the loss of our bonds was probably making me think irrationally, but it was like my mind was just stuck on one thought—they left me.

I found a halter neck, vest top in the wardrobe that I could make work with my wings. I would need to find some more wing friendly clothes today. Pulling out a pair of leggings to add to my outfit, I quickly got dressed. When I turned around, I found Wyatt standing quietly behind me with a look of concern on his face.

"Hey, are you okay, sweetheart?" he asked, gently pulling me into his arms like he wasn't sure if it was a place I wanted to be.

"Of course," I murmured and even I'm not convinced by it. Thankfully Wyatt just frowned and let it go. "Let's go and see this surprise, shall we?" I said, giving him the best smile that I could manage in my confused state.

"Sure."

Wyatt took me by the hand and led me down the stairs and

out of the front door of the packhouse. He didn't say much of anything, but his grip on my hand was comfortingly tight. If I had any doubts about whether he still wanted to be my mate, they would have been erased by the way that he didn't seem to want to let me go.

I quickly realised where we were heading and after a while the silence between us didn't even feel awkward. It's more of a companionable silence and I found myself drifting closer to Wyatt until he dropped my hand and wrapped his arm around my waist instead. My closest wing gently brushed against his side as it wrapped around him, and he gently smiled at the sensation.

"Are you sure that everything is okay?" Wyatt asked me quietly as we started to approach the house he had taken me to, what seems like months ago now.

"I just ... wasn't expecting to wake up alone this morning," I told him, feeling a little silly now that I'd said it out loud.

Wyatt came to a stop, and his arm around my waist stopped me in my tracks as well. He spun me around to face him and wrapped his arms around me.

"I'm sorry, sweetheart. We didn't think. We didn't expect you to wake up so early, and we thought we would be back before you woke up." I could see he was being genuine from the look on his face.

I could never doubt Wyatt. It was always him for me. I hadn't known the others for as long, and I didn't know them as well, but Wyatt, I felt like he'd been at my side for years, even though we had been separated for all that time.

"What if they don't want to be my mate now that the bond is broken? Now that they have a second chance and there's no pressure for them to complete the bond ..."

Wyatt silenced my rambling with a quick kiss. "Come on. I think when you see your surprise, you're going to realise just how much we all want this," he reassured me as he started to walk again, pulling me along beside him.

When we broke out of the trees and the house came into view, I saw all of my mates gathered in front of the house talking and laughing with each other. A smile stretched across my face as I watched them. It was like they'd always been together like they'd always known each other. Even though their bond to me was broken, the bond they had between each other still held strong.

"Lyra!" Kieran cheered when he caught sight of me.

All of them turned towards me and the happiness that was on each of their faces completely erased any doubts that I may have had. Grinning back at them, I walked over to where they were gathered in front of the house and straight into Dom's waiting arms. Caleb dropped a quick peck on my cheek, and Kieran squeezed my hand.

"Come on," Wyatt said with a grin, striding past us and into the front door.

The rest of the guys hadn't been out to the house yet, as far as I was aware, so I'm assuming that we're here to show them what it's like inside. I actually felt a bit bad now that Wyatt and I decided to go ahead and ask Kyle if we could have the house without consulting them. Kieran wasn't around then, but Caleb and Dom were, and it was probably something we should have consulted them on. I didn't think they would mind, but it wasn't the way we should be starting out our lives together.

"If you don't like it, I'm sure we could look for something else," I said as we all moved to the front door, following behind Wyatt.

"Do you like it?" Kieran asked.

"Of course!"

"Then that's all that matters," he told me with a grin.

As we passed through the door, I noticed that it was

different from the last time we had been here. In fact, it looked brand new and had been painted a deep red colour. Stepping into the house, my breath caught in my chest as I took in the rest of the changes.

The downstairs was still open plan, but someone had been through and cleaned the entire place. A brand-new kitchen had been fitted, and the stairs and walls had received a coat of fresh paint.

"When did this happen?" I asked, spinning around in awe.

The flooring had been stripped back down to the wood, and it gleamed in the sunlight coming through the windows.

Over by the fireplace, the ground was covered with blankets and pillows. Someone had laid out a picnic breakfast, and I grinned at the sight of it.

"You did this for me?" I realised.

Wyatt pulled me into his arms, and the others gathered around us. "Everything that we do is for you," he whispered, dropping a gentle kiss to my lips.

Pulling back, Wyatt grabbed my hand and led me over to the kitchen area. "The carpenters got the new kitchen in for us, and the pack helped clean and painted it over the last few days," he said, showing me the beautiful kitchen, which was now in place. "The bathrooms have been updated, but we don't have any furniture yet. The carpenters have got started on a bed for the master bedroom, but we thought you might want to help pick out the other bits."

I stood in complete awe, staring at the gleaming appliances and the smooth worksurfaces. This was far better than cage life!

"It's beautiful," I whispered, feeling some treacherous tears starting to build in my eyes.

"They said we could add a deck to the front and wrap it around the side if we wanted," Caleb added, practically vibrating on the spot with excitement.

I looked around at all of my mates, each of them filled with the same happiness that I felt and realised that this was it. This was what we had been fighting for. The chance to have a life together, and it was all going to happen here.

"Let's eat and we can talk about what we want to do with the house," Dom said, guiding us all over to the area which had been laid out for the picnic.

We settled down amongst the blankets and the pillows and I munched away on a bacon sandwich in happiness. I had my eye on some of the pastries next. There was enough food here to feed us ten times over!

"Do you all like it?" I asked them. "I know that Wyatt and I kind of chose this house without consulting any of you."

"It's beautiful Lyra, but as long as you like it, then I'm happy," Caleb smiled, leaning into Dom who was sitting beside him.

"I would live anywhere as long as it was with you," Kieran added softly.

Dang! These guys were the best! I found myself grinning a bit slap-happy and not caring in the least. It was a beautiful house. My mind turned to what we could fill the three empty rooms upstairs with and I realised that, for the first time in a long time, I finally felt at peace. Yes, there were still things that needed to be dealt with, but none of them were urgent. Right now, all I wanted to do was just take the time to live—a life free of cages and death threats, one just filled with happiness and love.

"So how big a tv are we talking about?" Caleb questioned with a grin.

The guys entered into a debate on the best size and type of tv while Kieran watched on in amusement. Like me, he probably had no idea what they were talking about. As the others bickered away, he slid closer to me, dropping a kiss down on his mark on my shoulder. My head immediately fell to the side to give him better access and a breathy sigh left my mouth.

"You know there is something else that we all need to decide first," he said, gently biting down over his mark.

"What would that be?" I asked, my voice dropping low, coated with lust.

He nuzzled against my neck before adding, "Exactly how long you plan on making us wait before we get these bonds back in place?"

"Me make you wait?" I laughed, "I thought you guys would want to wait so that you got the chance to do it properly this time, the way you'd always wanted to do it."

Kieran leant back to look at me and I realised that my other three mates had all moved closer to us while I was distracted. Caleb was the first to start laughing and it quickly rippled through the room as we all joined in. I wasn't even sure what I was laughing at, but it was definitely needed to break the tension in the room.

"Sweetheart," Wyatt growled as he prowled closer to me, "I feel like a shadow of the person I was without our bond. The sooner we get it back in place, the better. There is no right or wrong way to do this. The others may want to wait, and that's up to them if they do, but I want you, I want us and I don't want to wait a minute longer."

Wyatt continued prowling forward until I had to lay back while he crawled over the top of my body, looking down at me as hovered above. Wyatt dipped his head down and as soon as his lips reached mine, I wrapped my arms around him and drew him closer to me. I didn't want to wait. I didn't want to wait a second longer.

I felt movement beside me and when Wyatt drew back, I found the others had closed in around us, being careful not to kneel on my wings. They were definitely going to take some getting used to in these types of situations.

"We don't want to wait, Lyra. I don't want to be without our bond for a second longer than I have to," Dom told me as he sealed his lips to my own.

I felt Caleb move closer and kiss down my neck as someone else hooked their fingers into the waistband of my leggings and pulled them off, together with my underwear.

Everyone became a flurry of movement as we all started to strip, clothes scattered everywhere in our haste. When I was finally naked, I had Dom and Caleb on either side of me, Kieran and Wyatt kneeling in front of us.

Dom was trailing his fingers across my stomach and Caleb was slowly working his lips across my shoulder. Even though they were both very distracting, I couldn't take my eyes off Wyatt and Kieran in front of me. Wyatt's hand gently cradled Kieran's shoulder and he was looking at him in question. I had seen a few side glances from them both, and the confusion coming from Wyatt especially, and I was starting to wonder if our bond worked in other ways. Kieran's hand slowly moved to Wyatt's cheek as he stared deep into his eyes.

"I don't know why I'm doing this," he muttered as his thumb gently brushed across Wyatt's cheek.

"It's not something I've ever done before either," Wyatt told him.

Dom and Caleb briefly glanced over at them, before returning their attention to me. I couldn't draw my eyes away from them though. There was something about seeing my mates together that made me run hotter. They were taking their first steps towards whatever was growing between them and it was a beautiful thing to see.

Wyatt moved first, leaning into Kieran and gently brushing his lips across the other man's. They both seemed unsure, but the gentle kiss soon turned heated as Kieran opened his mouth to Wyatt and clung to him. I could see the battle of their tongues as the dam of emotions broke open between them, both of them pulling the other closer.

They didn't draw apart. When the kiss was finished, they stayed in each other's arms, panting slightly and leaning their foreheads against each other.

"Wow," Kieran simply said, a smile brushing across his lips.

"We definitely need to explore that further and soon," Wyatt grinned.

I was happy for them both. We had a beautiful thing building between the five of us and I for one was very excited about seeing what it was going to grow into.

"You're far too distracted," Caleb murmured to me, just before he sucked one of my nipples into his mouth and bit down to bring my attention back to him.

At the same time, Dom seemed to have grown tired of his tickling, teasing touches across my stomach and with one hand wrapped around my thigh, he lifted my leg to the side, spreading me wide.

Wyatt and Kieran took no prompting as they both dropped down between my legs, both of them feasting on my pussy which was already wet from the show they had given. It was hard to tell who was doing what, but the sensation of both of their tongues tangling around each other as they worked my clit was intoxicating. One of them pushed a finger inside me, and I felt like I was going to come already.

Dom moved to the opposite breast from Caleb and both of them started to lick and tease at my nipples.

Feeling all four of their mouths on me at once was almost too much, and if it wasn't for their hands holding me down, I knew that I wouldn't be able to hold still.

The first orgasm exploded out of me, but none of them stopped and I was starting to grow too sensitive from their attention. Trying to squirm free, I felt all of their grips on me tighten.

"One more time, baby," Wyatt growled from between my legs and it was enough for the need to bank higher inside of me.

Someone's hand slipped lower, and I felt a finger start to circle around my ass. Ass play was definitely new to me. I had no experience outside of what I had done with my mates, but I found that it was something I surprisingly enjoyed. As soon as I felt that finger start to push inside me, that second orgasm was brewing and I was greedy for their touch once more.

"Oh, fuck, yes!" I groaned and from Kieran's chuckle between my legs, I was guessing that he was the one that was currently giving me what I was greatly enjoying.

From my position pinned between my mates, I needed something more. I needed a way to move. Somewhere to work through all of the energy that was building inside of me and I knew the perfect way. Reaching out to my sides, I took Caleb and Dom's cocks in each of my hands and started to stroke them. They both groaned in unison and Caleb bit down hard on my nipple that he currently had between his teeth. It made my grip tighten and his moaning intensified.

It was hard at first to coordinate myself with both hands at the same time, especially with all four of them doing their very best to distract me.

Kieran was working another finger into my ass and Wyatt had joined in, plunging two of his fingers inside my pussy.

Dom's hand came up to my face and he tilted my head so that he could press his lips against mine. His hips were starting to move as he began to fuck my hand, while his tongue tangled with mine.

They didn't need any warning of my impending orgasm, because I couldn't have stopped myself from moaning even if there was a reason I wanted to. Dom pulled away from my lips just as I reached the peak and screamed out my release, watching my face as I cried out in ecstasy.

They all moved away from me and as I sat up, Wyatt guided me onto Kieran's lap. As I straddled Kieran's lap, his hard cock brushing against me, Wyatt leant into my back, between my wings, and whispered into my ear.

"Are you ready to take us both at the same time, sweet mate?"

If it had been possible, I think I would have come just from his words alone because the answer was yes, I absolutely was!

Kieran slowly guided me down his length, and my head fell back onto Wyatt's shoulder in bliss. The feeling of him filling me was incredible, but the anticipation of feeling Wyatt as well was riding me hard. Kieran laid back against the blankets, and I felt Wyatt's hand behind my wings pushing me down with him, my sensitive nipples were grazing against his chest as I lowered myself down. Kieran gently moved inside me as if he couldn't hold himself still even though he was trying to.

I felt Wyatt's fingers graze against my ass as he spread a cool liquid over it. I'm not sure that we really needed the lube, I felt more than ready.

Kieran slowed to a stop as I felt Wyatt move closer behind me, the tip of his cock gently grazing my ass.

"If you want to stop you just have to say," Wyatt told me.

Having Kieran holding still inside me and the anticipation of Wyatt knelt behind me was nearly more than I could take. I'd already come twice, but I was feeling needy and restless already.

"Don't ever stop," I said on a breathy sigh as Kieran pulled me all the way down to lie against his chest and sealed his lips over my own.

Wyatt's hard cock pushed against my ass and I had a brief

moment of pain as he started to gently push himself inside. Kieran wasn't exactly small and with the added addition of Wyatt pushing inside me, it almost felt like more than I could take. I desperately needed Kieran to start moving. I needed something, anything because I felt like I was about to go insane from the lust alone.

I looked up and saw Caleb and Dom kneeling next to us. Caleb had Dom's cock in his hand as he lazily stroked him while they both watched the scene in front of them. When Caleb saw me looking at them, he grinned and bent down, running his tongue around the head of Dom's cock. Dom groaned at the sensation and ran his fingers through Caleb's hair as he swallowed him down. Kieran turned his head to see what I was looking at and grinned at the sight. I supposed this would be the first time he had ever really seen the two of them together and I briefly wondered if he had been aware of their feelings for each other, before I became distracted again by what Wyatt was doing. He had finally pushed his full length inside of me and both he and Kieran were paused, hilt deep in me.

Wyatt's hand stroked up my spine and between my wings before returning to my hips.

"It's important that you try to stay still, sweetheart. Let us do all of the work," Wyatt told me before he started to drag his length out of me again.

It was almost more than I could take, the slight pain of him pushing inside was completely gone now that I'd adjusted to his size and all that was left was the heady feeling of having two of my mates inside me at once.

As Wyatt started to push back into me, Kieran started his slow withdrawal out. I didn't know how they were timing it, but they both alternated strokes inside me, and it was a constant, intoxicating sensation as they both worked my body together.

I struggled to keep my eyes open as I held as still as I could, totally surrendering to the sensations they were pulling out of my body. They started to pick up the pace and then I was spiralling out of control as the waves of orgasm flowed through me. Kieran grunted and slammed himself inside me as he came, his teeth dug deep into the side of my shoulder as I bit down into his in tandem. I didn't have time to bask in the sensation as I felt Wyatt pull me up against his chest and his own teeth bit down over the mark he had made before that now intersected with Kieran's. Not being able to reach his shoulder this time, I pulled his arm around me and sank my teeth into his bicep. The tang of blood filled my mouth, but it wasn't unpleasant. It was Wyatt.

Both bonds flared back to life between us, and I felt my magic caress against them. It was so different from the last time. The reformed bonds felt stronger, almost like they could take on physical form if they wanted to. I could feel both Wyatt and Kieran inside my chest, I could feel how content they felt with the bond back in place and their satisfaction from our time together. I could feel love radiating down the bond from both of them.

"That's different," Wyatt mumbled, as he and Kieran slowly pulled out of my body.

He turned me around in his arms and kissed me gently before I moved away from him. They might be satisfied, but I had two other mates and my body was already craving them.

I set my sights on Caleb and Dom who were still next to us and crawled over to them.

"You don't have to do this now, if you don't want to," Dom said, looking at me with the slightest bit of concern.

I didn't say anything, the need for him was riding me too hard right now and there was only one thing that I could think about. It was almost like now that two of the bonds had been reformed, my magic was demanding that the rest be joined to them as well.

I crawled straight to Dom, pushing him down onto his back on the blankets and without a word took his beautiful, hard cock into my mouth. So far, I had been denied this and I needed it more than anything else in this moment. Dom groaned at the sensation as I took him deep, swallowing down his length when it reached the back of my throat. I wanted to feel him come in my mouth, it was all that I could think about, the need flooded my mind and I couldn't move past it.

"I don't think she wants to wait," Caleb chuckled as he moved up behind me. "Is this okay?" he asked as he moved behind me, between my kneeling legs.

I wiggled my hips at him in response, not wanting to take Dom from my mouth for long enough to answer him properly. It was all the response that Caleb needed though, as he pushed inside me in one fluid movement. My pussy was already trembling around his hard length just from the sensation of feeling him inside me. That combined with Dom's delicious cock inside my mouth was just about all I needed.

Caleb slammed himself inside of me, his need ratcheting up with my own as he chased his own release.

"Fuck baby, you look so beautiful, bent over and taking Dom like that with your wings fluttering around you," Caleb moaned as he slammed himself inside me.

His grip on my hips tightened as he took what he needed, giving me just what I wanted in return. The sounds of my pleasure, muffled by Dom's cock as I swallowed him down again.

"I'm not going to last like this," Dom groaned as he looked up and watched Caleb fuck me.

I could see the desperation in his eyes when I glanced up. As much as I wanted him to come in my mouth, we couldn't complete the bond this way and my magic was insistent as I could feel it gliding along with the faint beginnings of the bond forming between us.

"Let's not tease Dom too much, baby," Caleb murmured as he pulled me up off Dom's cock and flush along his chest. His hips kept snapping forward as he drove himself inside of me and his hands came up to cradle my breasts, his thumb and index finger rolling my nipples between them.

I groaned my approval at the sensation and when I caught the look on Dom's face as he watched us, I knew that he had thought of something he wanted as well.

Moving himself around, Dom came back to join us, lounging at our side, where he had the best angle to access my pussy. His lips closed around my clit and he sucked it into his mouth, his tongue lashing against me as Caleb continued to pound away inside me. I felt Dom's mouth grin against me as he started to lathe his tongue along my pussy and judging by the groan of approval that came from Caleb, I was guessing I wasn't the only one that was benefiting from Dom's tongue right now.

It was more than I could take for now though. The next orgasm slammed into me without any warning, and I felt my pussy clamp down hard on Caleb's cock as he slammed himself inside me. Dom's tongue kept working my clit as I screamed out my release as I leant back and bit down into Caleb's neck over my old mark. Caleb lost his pace as he started to come, moving my head to the side, he sunk his teeth into my neck, leaving his mark again.

I was still riding the sensation of my orgasm when Caleb pulled out of me and Dom pulled me into his lap and straight down onto his waiting cock. It was enough to throw me straight into the next orgasm, and my teeth found his shoulder immediately as I clamped down onto him.

Dom swore at the sensation and grasping my hips worked me up and down his length as he hammered into me. I knew he was close, between Caleb and myself we had been constantly teasing him. He had never taken me as hard as he was doing now, as we crashed against each other. I felt like I was going to come again already and I was starting to worry whether I had it in me. I'd lost count of how many orgasms I'd already had and it felt a bit like another would finally shatter me into a million pieces.

"One more time, baby," Dom growled. "Give me one more," he said as he leant up on his knees to get a better angle.

Not satisfied with that, he pushed me back down onto the blankets, my wings spread out to either side of me as he pulled one of my legs over his shoulder as he seemed to slip even deeper inside me. With a different angle, Dom finally seemed satisfied, as he picked up his pace again and we were crashing together once more. One of his hands dropped to my clit and he pinched it between two fingers, detonating one final orgasm from me. I screamed as I came, my entire body shaking from the overload of sensations that Dom demanded from me. He lost his rhythm and he finally grunted out his own release before he fell forwards and bit down over my heart, leaving his final mark.

The bond between us flared into existence and my magic roared in satisfaction as it flooded out of me and through the now completed bonds. All of my mates groaned in bliss at the sensation of my magic flooding into their systems and I was filled with feelings of lust and love.

Once we all came back into ourselves, we crawled into a pile on the blankets which we then pulled up around us as we caught our breath. Life was going to be much more fun if that was going to be a regular occurrence.

Part of me was worn out, and yet another part of my mind was already starting to think about what I wanted to do next.

"How are you still horny?" Caleb laughed.

"Can you feel that?" I asked him, even though I knew that he could because I could feel it radiating back from him.

"We can all feel it," Wyatt laughed from beside me.

"How about we nap, eat something and then there's something else that I really want to try?" Caleb said with a grin.

"Is that why you brought so much food?" Dom asked, looking around the remnants of our picnic, which had got pushed to one side.

"I like to be prepared!" Caleb said.

I grinned along with the others because frankly, it was the best idea I'd heard in a long time.

Settling down with my head on Wyatt's chest and feeling Kieran snuggle up behind me, I closed my eyes with a sigh. This was where we were all supposed to be. Starting out this new life together. We had so much to make up for, and probably still a few problems that needed to be dealt with, but for now, we deserved this. We earned this time to be ourselves and build the life we had all been denied. A life filled with freedom, love and loyalty. Things we had all been denied in our journeys to find one another.

ACKNOWLEDGMENTS

If it takes a village to raise a child, then it definitely takes a tribe to get a book to this point.

Firstly, massive thanks go to my alpha reader Kris. Thank you for adding the two million commas that I missed out and correcting my terrible punctuation and grammar. You have the patience of a saint and an uncanny ability to talk me down off a ledge.

Secondly, Em, my beta lovely, thank you for all of the support and the laughs and generally just being you.

Finally, Michaella, thank you for everything. For catching my inability to use question marks and everything else, the rest of us were blind to see.

Without you ladies, this book would have been a shadow of what it currently is. I truly cannot thank any of you enough for all of the help that you've given me.

It really helps me if you write a review for the book, so that I can make sure that you all like what I'm writing. Constructive criticism is just that, constructive. It helps me to get better at what I do. Just try not to be too mean because I totally will cry if you are 😊 Also, on a purely selfish note, the more reviews you kindly write for me, the further the books can reach. It also helps motivate me in the middle of the night when I'm on my millionth edit and close to pulling out my own eyes.

About the Author

Thank you for reading my book! If you'd like to stay up to date with the news about upcoming releases and other events, check out my website. www.catejcooke.com

Newsletter exclusive content is also available to subscribers featuring extra scenes for some of the books.

Printed in Great Britain
by Amazon